Married.

The fact unnerved her, even though the impromptu arrangement would end upon arrival in New York. Until she could obtain a legal dissolution, she remained chained to a captivating man who conducted business with a pirate along with those dubious snakes Mulworthy and Uncle Percy. Perhaps she might uncover evidence to prove him a spy. Then what? After his selfless act of kindness, could she expose him as a traitor?

Her brain pounded with a myriad of disjointed thoughts. To clear her mind, she gave a shake to her head, and dislodged the loose pins in her hair.

Griffin, resplendent and glorious, smiled. "Ready?"

Ready? No doubt he meant the game, yet she imagined his words held some greater importance. Was she ready for this sham union of husband and wife? In a matter of seconds, she had made a life-altering decision—a decision she hoped wouldn't torment her the rest of her days. Now, seated an arm's length away from a man who roused unfamiliar urges, her brain addled by wine, she feared she had made a terrible mistake. Yet what choice did she have?

Griffin studied the game pieces while he slipped the leather tie away from his hair. The chestnut brown hair fell to his shoulders, the curled ends so enticing she could scarcely draw her gaze away.

"You have the first move." He dipped a strong chin at the game board.

"Yes, of course." It required every ounce of concentration to ignore him.

Praise for Joyce Proell

AMARYLLIS is the Heart Through History
RWA 2015 Romance through the Ages winner
of A Man for All Reasons

Amaryllis

by

Joyce Proell

Amaryllis

Cover Art by *RJ Morris*

The Wild Rose Press, Inc.
PO Box 708
Adams Basin, NY 14410-0708
Visit us at www.thewildrosepress.com

Publishing History
First American Rose Edition, 2019
Print ISBN 978-1-5092-2425-8
Digital ISBN 978-1-5092-2426-5

Published in the United States of America

Dedication

For my husband, Ken, and daughter, Kate,
Always

Acknowledgements

My thanks to all the people at Wild Rose Press, who work so hard to publish great books.

In particular, I'd like to thank my editor, Kinan Werdski, for her kindness, wisdom, and diligent oversight of those dangling modifiers; also, many thanks to RJ Morris for the spectacular cover art.

And most of all, I'd like to thank my dear writing friends Brenda Whiteside, Jody Vitek, and Mary Schenten, who showed continued interest and support of *Amaryllis* through its many iterations.

Chapter One

England, 1777

After a weary night of travel, Griffin Faraday stopped and let his horse drink from the stream beside the road. He dragged a hand across the grit and stubble on his cheek and squinted against the early morning sun, relieved his business in England was at an end. All he needed was one more day without mishap. Then it was on to New York with the English no wiser as to his deception. Surely, he could manage such a tricky feat.

Beneath him, his horse shifted. The head jerked up and its ears cocked at the growing rumble in the distance. The urgent drum of horse hooves signaled trouble. Had the English discovered his covert activities? Had they learned about the guns for General Washington? If so, countless lives would be lost, and his most certainly, if he were captured.

His breathing quickened. A powerful charge shot into his limbs. He had to flee, but his tired horse would never outrun a cavalry. Nor would the thin copse of trees alongside the brook offer concealment. "Damn."

The pulsation rumbled louder and echoed the anxious beat in his ears. His muscles coiled and he patted the ready knife handle sheathed to his hip.

A rider exploded from a far-off wood, almost flying over the crest, and plunged down the grassy slope. "A woman," he said, shocked at her perilous speed. She cast a frightened look over her shoulder just as another rider breached the mound and gave chase.

A relieved breath whooshed from his lungs. He wasn't the target.

The two riders tore across the open field, kicking up clods of dirt and raced past a lone crofter's cottage trellised with ivy. The woman hurtled recklessly forward. Her loose ebony hair fluttered as if flags whipped in a gale. She'd kill herself in a tumble if her pursuer didn't murder her first.

Griffin's fingers tensed around the reins. A voice in his head urged him to remain uninvolved, to ride off and forget what he'd seen. But he couldn't. What sort of man turned his back on a woman who needed help? He swung his horse toward her and galloped full-on. His thighs clasped around the animal's girth tight as a manacle. The rising thunder of horses clamored in his head. The woman sped across his path, her face clenched with alarm.

"Whoa! You there," he shouted at her pursuer. "Stop!"

Head bent low over the stallion's neck, the attacker advanced at a dangerous pace. Griffin swore and angled into his path. His heart banged against his ribs. The oncoming horse wheeled in fright. The whites of its eyes appeared to stretch and enlarge. The animal snorted and flung back its head. Its hooves dug into the earth and it jolted to a stop. The force pitched the rider into the air. Arms cartwheeled and his legs spun in space before he slammed into the ground with a sickening grunt.

Griffin winced as he imagined the man's pain

judder along his thighs and into his spine. He jerked the reins and swept from his mount. The smell of dust and sweet grass flooded his nose as he strode to toward the poor fellow.

The assailant, on hands and knees, swayed erratically. Auburn hair curled in a mess over his forehead. Anger radiated from his flushed face. "What in blazes do you think you're doing?"

Any hope Griffin might remain levelheaded evaporated at the man's surly tone. "I might ask the same of you." He offered a hand only to have it slapped away. "Conceited ass," he muttered under his breath. "I meant to aid to the lady. From what I observed, your objective was far from noble."

The woman had doubled back. She watched with a distressed frown as the fallen man pushed to his feet and whisked dirt from his coat sleeves. Though why she cared when he so clearly intended her harm made no sense to Griffin.

"Are you hurt?" she asked.

"Not enough to need a nursemaid," the surly rogue snapped.

Griffin's hands fisted. He wanted to clout the ass for his rudeness.

She made no reply, but her striking violet eyes narrowed with a rise of temper. At her show of spirit, Griffin felt a rush of blood, excited by her wild, untamed air. Unruly hair, black as pitch, tumbled at her shoulders. Dressed in a peacock blue riding costume and rosy cheeked, she exuded an undeniable vitality. As he savored the exotic sight, a fist slammed into his jaw.

Pain exploded and ripped into his bone. Grunting, he stumbled and ducked as another jab sailed past his cheek. With a grimace, he snatched his attacker's forearm and whipped him around. A knee thrust and the man dropped to the ground, with Griffin after him. They thrashed in the dirt and grass. Crude fury drove his assailant, but his wild, inexperienced jabs proved unsuccessful. Within seconds, Griffin straddled him and pinned his shoulders to the ground.

"Stop it," the woman shrieked. "Stop it this instant!"

"Can you be civilized?"

Griffin hissed and the man jeered, "Get off me."

"Gladly." As he eased his grip, the maniac bucked and tossed Griffin to the side but not before a blow clipped his chin. They leapt to their feet. Faster of the two, he snagged a wrist and twisted a limb behind the fellow's back. The hothead squealed.

"Stop it," she cried, frantic as she slid from her horse. "You'll break his arm."

Griffin frowned. Why should she care when he'd just saved her?

"Let him go. Please. He means you no harm."

No harm? Her fretful entreaty on behalf of the fool pricked at him. Was this his appreciation for his good deed? An abhorrent comprehension dawned. There'd been no danger. He groaned, irritated with his faulty judgment. When she graced her youthful pursuer with a sympathetic glance, he couldn't help but scowl in regret for his hasty involvement.

Stomach curdling, he shoved away the firebrand. He wouldn't risk jail for this unfortunate mistake. Nor would he miss his departure for New York. Washington had placed his faith in him, and by God, he would not disappoint.

The male stranger sniffed disagreeably with his nose high in the air. He gave a taut yank to his well-tailored, expensive lapels. "You must be mad to charge at me."

"The lady appeared in danger."

"You thought *I* meant to harm Miss Fitzhugh?" He chortled with snooty contempt. "It appears you're a bigger idiot than you look."

A muscle jumped in Griffin's jaw. He would gladly pummel the ass again were it not for his sworn duty.

"The lady was not in danger. This was nothing more than a spirited race."

Griffin sought her confirmation. "Well?"

A stiff nod signaled her agreement.

Embarrassment heated his cheeks. Clearly, he was more tired than he realized to misjudge a vigorous race as something more sinister. What a fool he was to chase after a damsel who didn't need rescue. An apology was in order, yet words of contrition stuck in his throat. He blamed her for sprinting about like a lunatic. "Do you always ride like a crazed woman?"

Feet set wide apart, she planted her hands on her hips. At her bold stare and the sheer strength of her presence, his breath snagged in his throat. Lord, she had pluck.

"There's no harm in a good race."

Who was he to argue with such confidence?

"I'm an excellent rider though I regret the misunderstanding."

A memory fluttered, a long-ago image of a similar wide-legged stance and the resolute set of shoulders and spine. The coal-black hair. The proud demeanor. His chest swelled with lightness. Could it really be his old tutor's bossy daughter? What was her name? Ivy? Rose? Lily! He caught himself before he blurted the name aloud. Better to keep quiet and be on his way.

"Lily," whined the young whelp. "Don't indulge the man. From the smell of him, he's spent the night in some hellish dive."

Griffin eyed the pissant, irritation heating inside, and remained silent.

"Give the man credit for coming to my defense," she cajoled. The offensive brat didn't deserve her sweet smile. "If I'd been in danger, you'd want someone to help me, wouldn't you?"

The man stammered as if uncertain whether to kill him or lie at her feet like a whipped dog. Griffin didn't think the fellow was the sort to forgive. Knocked off his horse and thoroughly trounced, he wouldn't forget his humiliation or the idiot who handed it to him.

Fed up and weary of the harangue, he retrieved his hat from the ground and swept into the saddle, prepared to take his leave.

"Thank you for coming to my rescue, Mister…?"

Sadly, it served no purpose to reveal his name or prolong this unfortunate incident. He wouldn't risk the unwanted attention. "My pleasure, madam."

He held her gaze, disappointed no light of recognition stirred in her astonishing eyes. If only the circumstances of their chance meeting were different. In another time and place, after the war was over, maybe their paths would cross again. He would like that.

"Lily." Her foul-tempered companion stood impatiently beside her horse, hands clasped together, offering a hands-up mount. "Let the hero go sleep off his drink." To Griffin, he said, "Pray we never meet again."

Griffin gave a curt nod and wished he were already standing on the boat and watching as the shoreline of England faded away. Only twenty-four hours more. Surely, he could go another day without the misfortune of seeing the odious prick again.

Chapter Two

"Something dreadful has happened to Papa," Lily said, chewing a thumbnail. Brow taut with worry, she stared at her uncle seated at his gilt ornamented desk. Amid the richness of his library where leather-bound books filled the glossy wooden shelves, she sank deeper into the plush brocade cushions of the settee. Her shoulders slumped.

Lord Percy Coventry regarded her with a bland, unconcerned air. "You worry too much." He stroked the silk stock at his neck. The late afternoon sun glinted off the garnet ring on his index finger.

"No, Uncle, you must take this seriously. Papa is in prison. Mr. Fletcher says so in his letter." For effect, she waved the recent missive from the New York attorney in the air.

In his usual fashion, Percy crimped his lips with annoyance and provoked an ongoing disappointment. Just once, she wished they could agree without an argument. Ever since she'd come to live with him seven years ago, communication posed a continual challenge. Since the death of her aunt, the situation had worsened. Constant loggerheads summed up their relationship.

"Mr. Fletcher says Papa was jailed for his public outcry about the British officers quartered at his house." My house, too, she recalled as a familiar ache, heavy as a stone, lodged in her chest. How she longed to go home. She wanted to have the pleasure of assisting Papa with his work and to enjoy the pretty flowers in the garden. And to sleep in her own bed.

Percy shook his head, as if he pitied Papa for a fool. "Once your father gets sick of jail and his ridiculous protest, he'll post bail. Fletcher can handle the details. Life will go on as usual when Henry accepts the British are in New York for good. Most likely he's at home as we speak."

"So why hasn't he written?" She slipped the attorney's letter into her dress pocket, too obstinate to accept Percy's glib explanation.

"You know how absent-minded he becomes when he works on a new invention. Besides, even without a war, the mail is unreliable. With our ships commandeered by American privateers, it's a wonder we see any news from the Colonies."

Stung by his words, she glowered and rushed to her father's defense. "Papa's never been too busy to write. And Mr. Fletcher's letter got through." No one would argue Henry Fitzhugh was thickheaded and lost to his work. Still, six months was a long time to forgo writing, even for him. The lack of contact, along with news of his imprisonment, fueled her apprehension and knotted her stomach.

Without thinking, she scrunched the pressed silk of her fashionable gown in her closed fist. Percy cringed, but before he could launch into another lecture about caring for her costly clothes, she spread her fingers and released the wrinkled fabric. She knew how he hated the expense to pretty her up, to make her a shining reflection of his well-dressed, glorious self. Image mattered to him, but not to her. Doubtless, the vainglorious man was calculating costs as they spoke.

She waited for him to utter a hopeful word about her dilemma.

"Lord Warwick wishes to marry you."

"What?" she blurted and sat forward upon the settee. *Marry me?*

"It seems surprising, does it not?" He simpered and dabbed his nostrils with a lacy hanky. "One might have expected him to choose someone more…" Glancing at the patterned swirls on the ornamented ceiling, he rotated his hand as though he might scoop the proper word from the air.

"Someone from a titled family," said Lily, astonished and flattered David wanted her for a bride. A special bond had been forged between them when she'd come to London after the death of her mother. Two lonely, awkward children, they'd become each other's support. She was forever grateful for his friendship.

"More traditional and refined," he added.

She bristled at his less than subtle reminder of her shortcomings. "David does as he pleases. Perhaps he recognizes my uniqueness." Criticized for being too bookish, she cut a jagged path between her outspoken manner and her odd interest in machines and mathematics, subjects avoided by a proper lady. David didn't seem to mind. Not many people were as accepting.

"A diamond in the rough, eh?"

"A challenge," she countered.

Two unwanted souls, together they'd struggled to make their way in a cruel and difficult world. Nevertheless, with David in London and Papa in New York, she felt her loyalties divided.

"I should think Warwick is inspired by your father's money. Henry has done well by his inventions and investments."

"You would make this into a mockery." As the third son, David was not likely to inherit his family's sizable fortune, but it didn't matter. Not to her. Hard as it was for Percy to accept, there were those who liked her. As for love, he held no such emotion in his heart. From the day she'd stepped off the boat, a frightened twelve-year-old girl, he'd made no secret of his dislike of children. He agreed to take her solely for Aunt Charlotte's sake. For his trouble, Papa saw him well compensated.

"Should he propose, Niece, I expect you to accept graciously. You may never see another opportunity."

Heat bled into her cheeks.

"Warwick asked my permission. I granted my approval this afternoon."

Astounded, she reared back against the padded sofa. "You? It's a duty reserved for Papa."

"It would be, if he were here." He huffed, as though blowing away an objectionable odor. "In the meantime, I have his permission to act on his behalf in all matters concerning your welfare. Very thoughtful of him, don't you think?"

At his smirk, every muscle in her body tightened. It took considerable effort not to shriek at the unfairness of him to make such an important decision. This was her life. Shouldn't she have some say in the matter? With a deep breath, she laid her palms one to each thigh, and forced herself to relax.

"So, you'll marry Lord Warwick." The comment wasn't a question but a statement of fact.

She answered without haste. "At present, there are more important concerns on my mind. Papa must be in prison or he'd have written. Perhaps he's sick or…" She faltered at the image of him shrunken and withering away with illness. An ache tore into her chest. "He may be dying."

For a moment, her uncle remained quiet. Wrapped in a luxurious satin jacket with an embroidered waistcoat, his bony shoulders drooped with a weary sigh. "Don't exaggerate your worries. I loathe hysterics."

"I need to go to him."

"To New York?" he choked. "What of the cost? And Lord Warwick?"

"I'm his only child. There's no one else." Only she, the loving daughter, could see to his care. It was her right.

Face pinched, he shifted his thin frame in the leather chair. "Your loyalty is misplaced for a father who, in all these years, has never found the time to visit."

The hurtful words scorched her skin and prickled her spirit. In shame, she dropped her gaze. Her hands trembled as she clasped them over her lap, her nails sharp against her skin. "As you said, Papa is a busy man." The words tumbled out, thick with emotion.

Over the years, she'd made excuses for Papa's absence. His scientific work consumed his time. Furthermore, losing a beloved wife sickened him with despair. In spite of the justifications, an ugly fear gnawed at her peace. Perhaps another reason beyond his prolonged melancholy better explained his decision to send her to England. Perhaps he didn't love her.

Stop.

Foolish thoughts would do no good. Shoulders pinched together, she sat up straighter, spine like forged steel, and forced a confidence shaky at best. "Had it not been for the hostilities in the Colonies, Papa would have sent for me." Whatever the truth, she would cling to the best of explanations.

He ignored her as if she didn't matter and shuffled the papers on his fancy desk with the gold inlays. Steam rose in her head. How she loathed his selfishness and petty cruelty. "I must go to him, without delay. He needs me."

And I need him.

"No, Niece. It's out of the question."

"I will go!" She stamped a foot.

"See here, young lady."

In the adjacent parlor, someone plucked a sour violin note and her uncle flinched. A rumble of voices in the corridor marked the arrival of early guests for the birthday celebration of Percy's new wife. Wearily, he rubbed a point on his temple, his cheeks gaunt to the point of cadaverous. She felt a rise of sympathy, aware she was a constant irritant to him, like a pebble in his shoe. A knock at the library brought him to attention. "Enter."

A liveried servant in blue and cream materialized in the doorway. He whisked across the thick carpet and proffered a silver tray to her uncle. Percy scooped up the card from its center. Brows wrinkled, he scanned the note. "Bring him to me at once."

"But Uncle." Lily's troubled voice pealed as the servant retreated. "We haven't finished."

"Oh? I do believe we have." Wigged head tilted, he

13

observed her with all the appeal of dirt-smudged onions. "You'll want time to primp before the party."

She slammed a fist against her knee and spewed an unladylike harrumph. "I'm as ready as I could possibly be. Will you not accept I must go to him?"

"You are not going to New York. Think of Warwick and your future."

She sprang to her feet. Every extremity tingled. "I must and I will." At the loss of her composure, she recoiled. Acting like a spoiled child would not gain his cooperation. When his bloodless lips twitched in satisfaction, all hope sank like a stone in water. She tamped back tears of frustration. For once, why couldn't he support her wishes? Before she could get her tongue around a word, there was another knock.

"Enter," he snapped.

"Uncle, please." In spite of her urgent plea, he directed his attention at his visitor. Curious, she turned to the door and gasped. Her early morning rescuer stood in the doorway. Seeing her near the settee, his jaw dropped.

"Oh, do come in, man," complained Percy. "You aren't the first bloke to gape at my niece."

"It's you," she declared.

The stranger blinked rapidly, as though doused with cold water. "Your niece?" he said, continuing to stare.

"Miss Amaryllis Fitzhugh in the flesh," Percy added wryly.

She marveled at the difference in the man's clothing and status. This morning he appeared no more than a common laborer, tired, dusty and fierce. Half a day later, garbed in elegant clothes, he emerged at her uncle's lavish home a figure of…well, quite a spectacular man.

"Miss Fitzhugh." He executed a polished bow.

Too confused to utter a word, she gave a quick nod. His broad, lean shoulders seemed to span the width of the doorway. Composed and steady after his initial shock, he regarded her with the warmest congeniality and set off a popping sound in her head. He grinned and the flash of perfect teeth in his handsome face sent blood racing up her neck. She couldn't recall a similar smile when he'd charged at David—when he'd been her bold protector. Short on air, she raised her hand to her tight throat. What was he doing here?

"Are you familiar with Mr. Faraday?" Percy asked. A battle waged to reclaim her voice. Before she could speak, he'd rapped his knuckles once upon his desk. "Well?"

"He came to my—"

Impatient, he flapped his lace hanky, waving the visitor further inside.

"We met while I was riding this morning."

At her uncle's insistence, the impressive man claimed a seat while Percy shooed her away with a glare of disapproval. "Be off, girl."

The rude directive thrust her back to their current argument. How dare he? Angry heat ran riot over her skin. She tensed, ready to stand and fight. Spine straight as an iron rod, she stomped to the door and twirled with a swish of satin. "I'll leave you to your guest." Her nostrils flared. "But I reserve the right to discuss this later. I mean to get my way."

Chapter Three

Lily stormed from her uncle's library with her fingers in a clenched ball. The news David wished to marry her could not have come at a worse time. More so, she doubted he would support a trip to New York. Yet go to Papa she must. Marriage could wait. Papa couldn't.

In the parlor, a quartet played a Haydn piece. Attracted to the lovely music, she swept across the marbled foyer and entered the party. A dozen early arrivals, elegantly clad aristocrats, pomaded and bewigged, milled about buffet tables covered with ivory linen. Extravagant silver centerpieces overflowed with flowers and greens, and stood among platters of sliced tenderloin, roasted grouse, partridges and delicate artichoke hearts. Too preoccupied to care, she paid the savory puddings and pastries little mind.

It would be cruel to accept a marriage proposal when her future was so uncertain. For the first time ever, she was pleased not to see David among the guests. If he held true to form, he wouldn't arrive until much later, at which point she'd be nursing a feigned headache in her bedchamber.

Twisting a dress bow with tense fingers, she floated among her uncle's guests, past the potted palms and cherrywood chairs set against a wall papered with a pastoral scene. She made a concerted effort to smile.

Beneath the mask, she stewed and planned. When the idea struck, she came to an abrupt stop.

Yes. That's it!

She would sneak away to New York on the first available ship. It was the only way, and Percy wouldn't discover her absence until it was too late and she was long gone. Giddy, she charged around the perimeter of the pale green room again, past the tall windows dressed with silvery blue drapes. Deep in concentration and lost in the details, she plowed into a solid wall of muscle. Crying out, she bounced backward. Her heart leapt into her throat when she recognized the barrier. "Oh, forgive me, Mr. Faraday."

With embellished surprise, he flattened a palm to his chest and pretended their collision knocked the wind from his lungs. "Must be very important." His mellow voice thrummed agreeably in her ears. "You were miles away."

New York, to be exact. "Yes, yes, I was," she admitted, embarrassed he touched upon her private thoughts.

She found herself drawn to his sensitive mouth and the contours of his strong-boned face. A queue at the nape of his neck tamed any curls in his dark, glossy hair. Without doubt, he was a tasty treat to behold. He far surpassed any delicacy ever created in Uncle Percy's vast kitchen.

In return, shrewd, bluish-green eyes studied her with a hint of amusement. It caused a stinging blush across her neck she hoped he didn't notice.

"I trust your business with my uncle went well." His association with the nasty man intrigued her immensely. She couldn't help but stare at him, expecting to see something despicable, a hint of a tainted character. Try as she might, she found no fault in his pleasing countenance. When he smiled, as he did just then, radiant like the sun on a cold winter's morn, she warmed instantly.

"A bit of trade and news from the Colonies," he replied in answer to her question. The gold silk buttons against his dark blue topcoat brought to mind stars in a midnight sky. "My only regret," he said, interrupting her perusal, "is that I ended your discussion with your uncle."

"Oh, that." She swallowed her disappointment, determined to see a positive outcome to her dilemma. "My matter will be completed, one way or another." She would get to Papa somehow.

On a wave of optimism, she asked, "Tell me you weren't harmed in your tussle with Lord Warwick this morning. David can be so argumentative at times."

"A hothead, indeed."

A servant with a tray of refreshments approached. He helped himself to champagne and stepped closer, bringing with him the scent of something pleasant and a little exotic, like nutmeg. "Would you care for one?"

She shook her head and watched, perhaps too closely for polite behavior, as he sipped the bubbly liquid.

"Miss Fitzhugh, are you familiar with a New Yorker named Henry Fitzhugh, a scholar and inventor of some renown?"

All at once, something awakened and fluttered, like tiny wings in her chest. "He's my father."

"That answers a few questions."

"Questions?"

"About an imp who sniggered when I erred in my math calculations?"

She tipped her head in confusion.

"You once boasted you would travel to Egypt." His mouth lifted at a corner. "You planned to explore the pyramids, on a camel, no less."

The sudden recollection exploded in her head, forceful as a sledgehammer. "Of course," she cried with excitement. "You're Griffin Faraday, one of the boys Papa used to tutor."

"Yes, my brother, Elliot, and I."

His expansive smile stirred an image of a lanky lad with shaggy hair who dawdled amid her Papa's messy, book-filled study. "You're so…" *Handsome*, she almost blurted and cleared her throat, trying to normalize her voice. "You're different. I'm sorry I didn't recognize you."

"It's been a long time."

The memories came fast, inciting an unexpected joyfulness not experienced in ages. "You set Papa's laboratory on fire."

"An accident, I assure you." He chuckled, seeming embarrassed.

"Fortunately, the flame was easily doused." All of a sudden, her mood was as effervescent as the bubbly champagne in his fluted glass. "I remember you had a pet snake which escaped from its container."

"Afraid so." At the admission, he colored slightly, but he smiled with humor.

"The snake gave birth and baby snakes slithered all over Papa's library." For effect, she shuddered theatrically and when he laughed, she joined in.

"I worried your father would toss me out on my

ear."

"He almost did."

She tried to reconcile the compelling face of this tall, elegant man to that of the boy's once youthful blush and dreamy-eyed manner. How she loved to hear the tales of his favorite knights and heroic battles. "Imagine," she mused and tapped her lip. "Griffin Faraday all grown up, and such a dandy, too."

"Hardly."

He glanced at a nearby table laden with Cornish hens and shrimp. By his swiftly hidden smile, she knew the comment pleased him.

A million questions danced in her head.

"Do you live in London? No, you couldn't," she answered. "I would have seen you and perhaps made your acquaintance."

"New York. I come to London on business."

Had he dropped a string of luxurious pearls in her hand, she couldn't have been more thrilled. "You live in New York City?"

"I do."

The hope of further good news quickened her pulse. "Have you, by chance, seen my father?" She held her breath.

"Regrettably, not in years."

"Oh." Her shoulders drooped. "Naturally, I had hoped."

His handsome face gentled with concern. "How long since you last saw him?"

"Seven years. Since I came to England."

"Ah." He reached out a hand, as though he might comfort her with a touch. However, in the next moment, the hand was behind his back and rested low on his spine. "I'm sorry. It's a hardship when families are separated." The kind words plucked a soothing note in her worried mind. "Perhaps one day, one of you will make the tiresome voyage."

"Mr. Faraday—"

"Call me Griffin. We're old friends. No reason for formality."

"If you prefer." His openness encouraged her. "Since you travel frequently, you must be familiar with crossing schedules. Are you aware of any ships bound for New York soon?"

"The *Phoenix* is set to leave in a week."

A shake of her head cast the notion aside. "Not soon enough."

"The *Providence* sails tomorrow. I've booked passage on her."

Her heart soared with possibilities. "You did?"

"Is there a message you wish me to give your father?"

Their gazes locked. Her foot tapped a nervous beat. "I want you to take me to New York."

Not a hair or breath flickered. Her palms grew damp and her throat dry as she watched him. Then he blinked. "Excuse me?"

"Forgive me." She clasped her hands, kneading her tense fingers. "I must go to my father as soon as possible. I fear something dreadful has happened." She disliked babbling but his pointed stare unnerved her. "He'd have written otherwise. He might be ill. As his daughter, I should be there." A pitiful image of a thin and sick Papa constricted her throat. "He might be dying." *Or dead.* She grimaced and tried to banish her fear.

21

When he spoke, his voice held steady. "Perhaps it's not so bad. Perhaps his letter went awry."

"I don't mean take me as your guest. Just help me book passage." Surely, she could scrape together enough baubles to pay the fare. She touched his arm, aware of the firm muscles beneath the fine cloth of his coat.

"Miss Fitzhugh—"

"Lily," she offered with a congenial smile. "Remember? Old friends." Perhaps an acknowledgment of their friendship might tug at his conscience and activate his loyalty. "If it were your brother or father in trouble, you'd want to go home as soon as possible."

Any likelihood charm or guilt might sway him dashed when he turned grim and humorless. His fingers drummed against his thigh. "Lily."

To hear her name spoken with such exacting firmness chilled her with foreboding.

"I understand your dilemma, but I'm not in a position to act as your guardian."

The curls fashioned on top of her head wobbled with a vigorous headshake. "I don't need a guardian. I simply want your help to get on that ship." The ill-mannered, desperate pleading should have embarrassed her, but she was too far gone to care. "Afterwards, you can go about your business. You can pretend not to know me."

"That's not possible." Utter conviction firmed his words. It was the sort of solid comment a battering ram couldn't penetrate. "I could no more ignore you than—" His eyes widened. His head snapped to the right as if he dared not look at her. He dragged a long-fingered hand over his bound hair, his handsome face gripped with distress. Several tense seconds later, his agitated spirit stilled. Whatever troubled him lay submerged behind a chilly, composed mask. "Not on the *Providence*. It's not the sort of ship to carry passengers."

"But you're a passenger."

"It's different." Straightening his shoulders, he appeared to grow taller and broader, and became a solid, impassable wall between her and Papa.

"I don't see how."

"The captain won't allow female passengers. He thinks a woman is bad luck."

She almost laughed. "How ridiculous."

"Be that as it may…" He tapped his chin, thinking and drawing attention to the thumbprint indentation in his strong jaw. "Besides, given the hostilities between England and the Colonies, it's a dangerous time to travel."

"Yet you travel by sea." Aware of the obstinate firmness in his face, she doubted the statement gained her any advantage. It was her life, so why should he care? She squeezed his forearm. "Please. It isn't so much to ask. With parents and siblings of your own, you can understand the familial bond. You can appreciate my great need to go to him."

His lips pressed tighter.

She waited and prayed. Each second stretched and slowed into the next.

"I can't help you." The absolute finality of his words clanged in her head—words no one ever wanted to hear. He raised a finger. "However, I promise to see your father. As soon as I reach New York, I'll go to him."

Visit Papa in a prison? "It isn't good enough."

His earnest expression caved in misery. She felt guilty for pressuring him, but what else could she do?

"I'm sorry. I can't help you."

"You mean you won't." The unfairness of it clawed at her insides. The fates had made a terrible mistake. Tonight, she'd been gifted an old friend, a cherished treasure, only to lose him moments later. Disappointing enough, any hope she might bond with her father and recreate a family lost long ago disappeared in a flash. Head held high, she gave him one final appraisal and a chance to change his mind.

He said nothing.

Anger seared her lungs. The letdown tasted bitter. Yet one thing remained firm. She would find another way.

"Do look in on my father, won't you?"

****

Griffin swore under his breath, frustrated and miserable as he watched her cross the room. One black ringlet dropped from the coil on her head and bounced against her stiff back. The deep wine color of her gown glowed like blood against her ivory skin.

She must think him a selfish coward. His gut tightened with rancor. Under normal circumstances, he would have reveled in the chance to offer his help. Yet these were not normal times and his activities were less than customary.

What right did he have to promise her safe passage when, at any moment, he might be arrested and charged with crimes against the King? His activities for the colonial army must remain secret. If all went according to plan, the *Providence* would take on a cargo of stolen

British guns. The weapons had the capacity for more accuracy than any musket available and would aid the outcome of the war. To bring an innocent civilian into the fray would be unconscionable and foolhardy. His first loyalty must be the completion of his mission. Under no circumstances would Lily Fitzhugh become a deterrent.

The idea of being with her aboard ship for weeks, with her laughter and honeyed voice and her fierce temperament aglow with challenge and raising his fires—well, it would be impossible. He flushed. War was no time for romantic fantasies or the sweet allure of reviving an old friendship, even if the girl was a beautiful woman.

Annoyed, and with no further need to mingle, he headed out the door. When he reached New York, he would go to her father. It was the best he could do.

Chapter Four

Amid the noisy gaiety of partiers, Lily hurried through the French doors into a balmy May night. A fat moon and tallow lanterns cast a silvery light across the rear terrace of the spacious house. Propelled by an angry disappointment, she hurried to a low rock wall skirted by a sloped manicured lawn below. Two flowerpots, brimming with colorful pansies, pink geraniums and trailing ivy, flanked the gateway. "Bah," she muttered.

The laughter of Percy's guests and a cheery mazurka spilled from the parlor windows, and added to the burden of her disillusionment. How did Griffin transform from a boy fixated on magical fantasies to an elegant gentleman who conducted business with her vile uncle? She considered it a wonder how people changed, and often not for the better. It also made no sense how being on a ship with her could be such a problem. He was so unreasonable. If the tables were turned and he needed her help, she would have given it, gladly. You helped one another. It's what people did.

As to the captain's superstition about women, a generous fare would surely ease his fear. But would she have enough coins and baubles to appease him?

She stamped a foot, vexed to be almost free from Percy's heavy thumb only to be thwarted. Had the stubborn New Yorker helped, she'd soon be on her way.

Still, no matter what occurred, no matter how difficult the quest, she would get to Papa—and soon. Jaw set, toes tapping, she focused on a way, but even the glorious scent of late blooming lilacs couldn't dispel her impatient mood. One plan after another hatched and crumbled to nothing but broken shards.

While the musicians played the last notes and fell silent, she knew further discussion with Percy would yield another dismal stalemate. They would argue, and she would receive no delight in agitating him. How she hated the continual acrimony, and released a shuddery breath.

"Such a sad sigh, Miss Fitzhugh."

With a gasp, she twirled around. Cecil Jones, legal counsel to her uncle, stood with his back to the double doors. "You startled me, sir." Her hand pressed against the fast tick of her heart.

He bowed slightly from the waist. "Forgive me, madam."

"What brings you to the terrace?" Years of experience with this slippery ferret taught her to take a guarded yet offensive position.

"Perhaps the same reason as you. To escape."

She hated being so transparent. With trepidation, she watched him cross the terrace, his inscrutable smile in place. What did he want? "Are you not amused by the party, Mr. Jones?"

He didn't bother to answer. "I see you are familiar with our American."

"*Our* American? Surely not mine." From now on, Griffin would never be anything except a well-forgotten memory.

He stepped closer, and her curiosity and discomfort rose in equal measure. No doubt, a matter more important than the need for fresh air propelled his visit to the terrace. "I couldn't help but overhear a bit of your conversation."

The smell of onion on his breath offended her as much as his admission of eavesdropping.

He lifted his chin and stared at the glowing night sky. "If your friend were of a mind, he would have found room for you on the *Providence*."

Clearly, he had something important on his mind. Whether she intended to stick around to hear the ferret out remained an unanswered question.

"You should go to New York. It's an important pursuit."

The statement jolted her, as if someone had shaken her by the shoulders. "Have you heard news of my father?" She assessed him warily, sensing the wheels turning in his devious mind.

"Nothing specific."

"Tell me." Chilled, despite the mild evening, she crossed her arms and gripped her elbows.

"Illness can overtake a man with such stealth, especially someone of your father's age."

Goose bumps pimpled her skin. Illness loomed large in her worries. If Papa died, her dreams of a family filled with love and acceptance died, too. With a shake of the head, she chased away the fear.

"Times are unsettled." He ground a fist into the palm of his hand, as if the two were pestle and mortar. "The line is muddied and unclear. A person must take a stand—one way or the other."

Her forehead scrunched in confusion. "What are

you talking about? I fail to see what taking a stand has to do with a man's health."

Treating her like a child, he flashed an indulgent, tolerant smile. "Politics, Miss Fitzhugh. One either stands behind the King or not." His clasped hands stilled. "Tell me, on which side does your father stand?"

The question was bold and worrisome given the current political tenor with the colonies. "My father is not a political man." At least he wasn't until recently. "In any event, Mr. Jones, it's no concern of yours."

A mirthless chuckle tolled. It dashed any hopes he might cease with his questions. "Good answer. Do I dare inquire as to your political leanings, Miss Fitzhugh?"

These cat-and-mouse queries fueled her caution. What mattered most was a home with Papa. "I don't concern myself with politics, but I stand behind the King and always will."

"Well spoken, young lady." His sharp gaze swept over the deserted veranda, as though he feared an eavesdropper lurked in a nearby bush. "About New York…"

Her pulse quickened.

"Perhaps I can be of assistance."

Hope shot in the air like a cannonball and plummeted a second later. Cecil would want something in exchange for his help. Tit for tat and miserly, he never did a favor without expecting one in return. She might not be willing to pay his price. Countless games of chess with the man had proved his cunning. She shifted on her feet, cautious yet curious enough to play along. "It would be exceptionally kind, sir, but why go out of your way to help me?"

"You may not be politically inclined Miss Fitzhugh, but these are political times." He spoke in a low voice, meant only for her ears. "We may not like the current state of affairs, or even care, yet sides have been drawn. Everyone will land in one camp or the other, whether one involves himself or not."

She waited, aware of the noisy thud-thud in her ears, afraid to hear more.

"I fear Mr. Faraday plays at both sides."

For a moment, her heart stopped. Then it kicked in, drumming louder than normal.

"The young man expresses his eloquent and rather voluble support of the King. Yet it's rumored…" A shift of his crafty gaze sent a chill along her neck. "He has deep ties to New York."

The ludicrous implication prompted a swell of hearty outrage. "The connection doesn't make him a traitor," she pronounced irritably and huffed at the ridiculous suggestion. "Don't forget, I lived in New York too, at least for a few years. I support king and country and don't wish to sever ties." For some reason, she wanted to strike out, to fight, and she couldn't say why. "Many New Yorkers support English rule. How dare you suggest—"

"Yes, yes." He fluttered his hands so she'd lower her voice. "You may be correct, but Mr. Faraday isn't just anyone."

Well, neither was she. Anxious to hear what sort of man Griffin had become, she angled her head closer.

"He ingratiates himself into the highest of circles, English venues where the most important decisions regarding the colonies are only whispered."

Every breath, every pulse beat, fell silent. "The highest circles?"

"Should his sympathies lie with his native home…"

Here he gave a dramatic pause. Any simpleton could deduce he believed Griffin was a spy. With a brittle stare, she debated whether to argue the point. For once, the lawyer had his information wrong. "You're suggesting Mr. Faraday is a danger to England?" She almost laughed. If she wanted, she could tell him a few things about Griffin Faraday. He was a dreamer and a jokester, a prattling charmer and regrettably, a selfish toad. Goodness. The man conducted business with her uncle. Birds of a feather…She shuddered in distaste.

As if he sensed her doubt, Jones gave a stiff, dismissive tug to his coat sleeve. "The young dandy is wealthy and well connected both in London and in the Colonies. The father is even wealthier and holds vast acreages essential to England's interests. We cannot afford to lose these resources. The elder rails about…" He lowered his voice forcing her to strain her ears. "He speaks ill of the King's directives."

This was all too much to swallow. "Are you suggesting the son is but a puppet for the father?"

Cecil answered with a sour face. "There are those who think he works on behalf of the King. In addition, there are those who believe he is a rebel agent. I need to know on which side he stands." He leveled her with such ominous consideration she rocked back on her heels. "I believe you can help me find the answer."

The stone slab beneath her feet seemed to shift. She struggled to breathe. This would be her repayment for Cecil's help—spying on Griffin. What a sordid, ugly affair. Against her soundest wishes, he meant to yank her into this conflict. She'd be pitted against her countrymen and used for political gain. Sadly, what choice did she have if she hoped to get to New York? She couldn't laugh and walk away now. Her father needed her. And she needed him.

She took a deep swallow, clenching and unclenching her hands. "They hang spies, don't they?"

Chapter Five

Griffin slid the quill into the inkstand and eased back in the desk chair, his shoulders and neck stiff from the work of deciphering. An arduous task, yet he took satisfaction in the skill he'd acquired over the past year in breaking code. Already he'd uncovered the names of three men, prominent supporters of independence, who secretly sold military information to the Crown.

He took a moment to rest and massaged his neck, delighted by the thin, wispy clouds outside the ship's window. He prayed the temperate weather would hold. Nothing could botch the rendezvous with the pirate and the French military officer. The colonial army needed those guns, and he aimed to deliver. Completion of his assignment mattered not just to himself but also to thousands who staked their lives for freedom.

The salty tang of ocean air whispered through the window. The first day of the voyage and already his mind wandered. Glancing out at the flat horizon, he imagined the fertile shore of New York on the horizon. It would be some weeks, and only with the grace of God, before he touched *terra firma*. He longed to see his parents and siblings.

Nursing regret, he supposed he would never meet Lily Fitzhugh again. Even though his motives were well intentioned, his refusal to help her left him feeling no better than a scurrilous rat. Her laughter had stirred a familiarity and comfort—a sense of pleasanter times, when they were young and life was free of worries and strife. Their shared recollections proved most enjoyable. Regrettably, further friendship with her was unwise. For the sake of his work and simplifying his life, he would keep a wide berth from all women—at least until the end of the war.

A knock at the door made him lurch forward in his seat. He flipped over his coded papers and swiftly covered them with a book. "Who is it?"

"Captain Mulworthy."

Enoch Mulworthy here? The unexpected visit caused a ripple of unease to flutter at his scalp. On previous jaunts aboard the *Providence*, the Captain summoned Griffin to his quarters when he wished his counsel. Why the change?

"Come in," he said puzzling the question.

The cabin door flew open. The swinging force startled him, and he sat up straighter, on alert.

The portly captain filled the doorway. Mulworthy advanced into the room like a storm cloud—thunderous and leaden with threat. Behind him, a slender-legged boy in a wide-brimmed hat, about thirteen or fourteen years of age, followed with a leather satchel clutched in his tight fist. However, despite these astounding first guests the colorful parade was far from over. Two raw-smelling sailors with stoic faces shiny with sweat hefted a mid-sized steamer trunk through the doorway. Their muscles flexed and glimmered in the thin light of the cabin. In one coordinated effort, they lowered the bulky case to the floor with a thunk. Mission accomplished and silent, they ambled from the cabin. The door closed with a snick.

Griffin hardly knew what to think. Baffled, he watched Mulworthy stomp over to the table in the center of the tiny room, his jowls vibrating with each pounding step. He dropped heavily into a chair.

The boy took up position near the door and dropped his chin to his chest. The slouch hat obscured his face. Dressed in satin breeches, a cutaway coat, fabric covered buttons and a frilly neck cloth, the lad looked as out of place as a rooster on a gilded throne.

"Seems Lord Coventry wishes ye tae be cosseted on yer tiring journey," Mulworthy complained with a growl.

"I beg your pardon?"

"Coventry sent ye an errand boy." Forehead creased with irritation, Mulworthy flapped a thick hand at the boy. "That is the whole of the story, is it not, boy?"

The lad kept his head down, his bag battened to his chest like a mail of armor.

"Speak up!"

The boy flinched.

"Why did ye hide in dry storage?" Flimsy strands of pewter-colored hair escaped his queue and hung slack at the side of his fleshy cheek.

Struggling to make sense of this, Griffin leaned forward, hands curled around the chair arms. "Captain, tell me what's going on."

Mulworthy ignored him and kept his probing gaze fixed on his captive. "You'll git no free ride. I'll see ye tossed overboard first, ye measly stowaway."

The boy's head shot up. "I am *not* a stowaway."

Griffin recognized the challenging stance, the stubborn jut of chin, and his heart lurched. Wild-eyed, he shot from the chair like a startled pheasant from a field of corn stalks. His breath came fast and shallow. A plethora of questions whirred in his head and left him tongue-tied.

"There's money enough for my passage," Lily Fitzhugh spat.

The corner of Mulworthy's mouth lifted slowly revealing his greed along with several tobacco stained incisors. A chubby hand pushed out, palm up. "Give it here."

Her tongue darted out, wetting her lips. "It's…" She set her bag on the floor and wiped her hand on her leg. "I'm certain he meant to give it to you. Perhaps he hasn't had the opportunity yet."

"Aye. Ye may have the right of it," Mulworthy said, though any simpleton could see he didn't mean it. "Who took the money from ye?"

Even from six feet away, Griffin could see her tremble. "Let me talk to the bloke alone." It required great effort to keep his voice calm. "You can see he's scared."

"Ohhh, scared," the captain mocked and appeared to derive cruel amusement from her discomfort. "The little dobber will talk, or I'll throw him in the hold."

This couldn't be real. All along, he'd worried British ships or bad weather would muck up his plans, but never this. Griffin scrubbed a hand through his hair, a swear word on his breath. "He'll have to go back. We must take him back."

"No! I won't go."

Mulworthy swiveled his head Griffin's way. Disbelief etched his strained features. "Are ye daft? Ye can't mean tae turn the ship around. Not a day can be lost. Of all people, ye should know…"

Griffin pointed a shaky finger at the intruder. "He can't stay here. I don't need a cabin boy."

"'Tis no difference tae me who takes the wee lap dog. Surgeon Mead or Mr. Flint might have use of him." His squinted appraisal of Lily soured Griffin's stomach. "For all that he's a pest, he's a pretty enough lad, ain't he?"

Griffin pressed both hands over the pressure mounting in his head. "God no. Strip the notion from your mind. The lad won't do for Mead or anybody else."

Head tilted like a furry dog, Mulworthy studied him with a hardy dose of suspicion. "Are ye familiar with this shite?"

Griffin bit down hard, uncertain what to say. Should he remain quiet and play along with her ruse? Or should he expose her to Mulworthy, who believed a woman on board was bad luck. "He's no boy." Anger tinged his words. "Tell him who you are."

Her gaze narrowed. She glared with such malevolence something inside bucked. "My name is Amaryllis Fitzhugh. I am niece to Lord Coventry."

Enthroned at the table, Mulworthy swore. "Salt of the dog!" Sausage-sized fingers dragged a path along his scruffy beard as he considered this quagmire. "Tell me yer uncle approves of this folly."

Shoulders drawn back, head held high, Lily stared at the man as if she were a queen and he a two-headed monkey. "Of course not. Had I his approval, there'd be no reason for this disguise." She gestured toward her servant's garb. "It was a simple means to get me on board."

"We're dead." Mulworthy groaned and dropped his forehead in his hand. "It'll be the firing squad at dawn once we're caught."

The man had a point.

Griffin stepped closer and inspected her get-up, appalled and astonished she'd accomplished the subterfuge in such short time. The ship set sail at seven in the morning. He'd seen her last night at seven o'clock. If she could perform the outrageous feat in twelve hours, what would she do in twenty-four? A week? His heart sank. "How *did* you get on board?"

With a big gulp, she wiped her hands on her thighs. The sudden attention to her shapely legs stirred his blood. Lord, he didn't need this attraction. Fury and alarm raced through his blood. This would never do.

"I…I'd rather not say." She shot a fearful glance at Mulworthy, who worked his jaw back and forth as if he might tear her apart with his teeth.

"Clearly," Griffin hissed, so vexed he feared he might pop, "you had help. You must have paid someone." His taut arms quivered with an urge to throw her overboard and let her float away in a launch. "Who?"

"I don't wish to get anyone into trouble."

"Trouble?" He grunted. "I grant you'll see worse before we land in New York." He wondered if her desperation to travel on this particular ship signaled more than a woman worried for her father. Was her plea last night at her uncle's soiree merely a trick to gain passage on this particular ship? Did she have a secret agenda? His blood chilled as he feared she might be an agent sent by the Crown to snoop into his activities.

"What time did ye come aboard? And don't lie." Finger pointing, Mulworthy glowered at her with equal doses of mistrust and fury, one eye in a squint.

Her gaze jumped around to avoid contact with her interrogator. "Around three o'clock."

"Tubbs," Mulworthy snapped. Face riddled with disgust, he pretended to spit on the floor with the most obnoxious of sounds. "He had the watch till four. The goon has yer passage money, does he?"

She blanched and nodded. Her fingers kneaded a button on her coat, appearing so defenseless it wrenched at him. He could have kicked himself for caring.

"I have a little money in my bag." She gestured to the leather satchel at her feet. "Perhaps it would be enough."

No. No. The idea of her being under his feet for the next month made his throat close. A daily dose of feminine wiles would be a torturous mix of Heaven and Hell. Images of shared meals, lively conversation and laughter caused a cold sweat across his brow. Icy pinpricks shot through his body. "We must take her back. We must!" In a panic, he circled around the table, about the only space to walk in the small cabin.

"Och, man. Be reasonable. "It's no possible to return the eejit and still make…" Griffin caught the unspoken words about the all-important rendezvous. They must keep their appointment. Mulworthy dragged a hand wearily across his stubbly chin. "Dinna be afraid, lad. She's only a bitty woman."

A woman, Griffin feared, who could rip his life to shreds. Arms stiff with tension, he chopped a hand in the air, as if it might sever this debate. "No! She's bad luck."

"'Tis true. But bad luck is here, and we must deal with it."

"Captain, please." As if in prayer, she knitted her fingers together, enacting a supreme game of manipulation with her beseeching manner.

"Don't say another word," Griffin ordered and glared at her accusingly.

It didn't require perfect vision or logic to see her fury. "What an insensitive prick you are!"

Air rushed from his lungs. *Insensitive prick?* He drew himself up, disregarding the subtle quake of his anger. "You, woman, have no idea the sorts of calamities which might befall you on your ill-advised journey. Pirates, kidnapping, slave trade and hurricanes." He didn't bother to mention British military vessels. With the navy's approval, they could seize the ship, press men from the crew and steal her should they desire. "And what about being the only woman on a ship full of needy men?"

A flush brightened her neck, but she held his stare, even as a spark of fear danced in her eyes.

Good Lord. Concerns for her safety would consume his journey. Bursting with frustration, he pumped a fist against his thigh. "Damn!" How would he hide the real purpose of this crossing? How would he hide the guns from her? In the hope he might cancel the sight of her from his mind, he closed his eyes. A slow, long breath steadied his nerves.

"Captain." Her voice was so earnest and pleading his lips curled with scorn. "My father needs me. He's in trouble."

Griffin knew she would gain no favors pleading to

the stubborn, hard-hearted Scot who mistrusted women and despised the English even more.

"It's dangerous to allow her to stay." His tone controlled, he waged another argument. "We can't risk it. She's the niece of Lord Coventry. Half the naval forces will be searching for her. It will put us in good stead if we return her to him willingly."

"Ha!" she cried boldly. "Uncle Percy is probably drinking a toast to my departure as we speak."

The older man raised a silencing hand. "What's done is done. We've no choice but to continue on."

Sworn to duty, Griffin knew all too well his first objective was to adhere to the schedule and the mission. "She'll cause all sorts of mayhem."

"I'll do no such thing. I don't understand why you're being so uncivil."

In disbelief, Griffin shook his head. If only he could reveal his assignment, but as a girl who'd spent the last years in Lord Coventry's home, she was British for all he could see. It would be nigh to impossible to live with her on this cramped ship, particularly if he couldn't trust her. More important, the question remained. Was she on board to spy on him?

The captain fingered an earlobe while he mulled things over. "If we meet another ship en route, I aim to pawn her off and good riddance tae ye."

Lily shrank against the door while Griffin choked back the argument forming on his lips. It sickened him to think what horrific things might befall her, without protection, on another vessel.

The captain drummed thick, blunt fingers on the table. "The question is, what do we do with her now?"

"Why can't I be treated like any ordinary

passenger? I'll stay hidden in my cabin if it would help."

"Cabin? Aye, as if I have a spare room. We're full up." He tilted his wooly head, assessing her with the battle-aged canniness of a man given to plans and getting his way. "If it's a cabin boy ye intended, so ye shall be."

"You can't expect me—"

Mulworthy's murderous glare cut her off. With the chair squeaking, he swung his bulk toward Griffin. "Lord Coventry sent ye a boy. For the remainder of the trip, she'll play yer cabin boy. I'll not be responsible for her." He swung back to Lily. "I'll leave ye in the care of Mr. Faraday."

"No!" Lily and Griffin clamored as one.

"I'll sleep in the…" Griffin choked on the next word. To sleep away from his cabin while his servant occupied his bed would only raise suspicion among the men.

She blinked rapidly, clenching her fingers. "Captain, I can't share a cabin—"

"Ye can and will share a cabin. Or ye can bunk in the bow with the crew. Yer choice." Mulworthy rose from the chair, his girth twice as wide as her gangly form. His dangerous expression brooked no argument. "I suggest ye keep tae yer master. If ye give me any more trouble, I'll throw ye tae the sharks. Lord Coventry be damned."

"Captain." He was determined to give it one last, reasonable chance. "This is a ship of men. We can't take an unmarried woman all the way to New York. Her reputation will be ruined."

"If ye care so much for her reputation, marry her."

Griffin quailed.

"And now, lassie." Mulworthy stuck out his beefy hand. "About that fare."

Chapter Six

"What a mad, foolish scheme," Griffin declared moments after the brute captain vacated the tiny cabin.

Shoulders braced, Lily steeled herself against more of his outrage. How on earth would they co-exist in this cramped space of furniture and trunks? She could scarcely blink without calling attention to herself. She'd have no peace. Escape from him was impossible.

"How could you do this?" Glowering, he stood between the narrow bed on his left and the desk at his right. The window behind him threw his face in shadow.

"I do apologize," she offered, perplexed that in spite of hostile circumstances she found the loose, curling hair at his shoulders enticing. "I had no idea my company would cause such a fracas. I assumed once the ship was out to sea, I could show myself and the matter of my presence would be…well, at least tolerated."

He grunted.

Even in the midst of a churlish temper, he looked attractive.

"What an optimist."

His sarcasm irked her, but she didn't blame him for being angry, although she considered his reaction, along with the nasty captain's, overdone. *Throw her overboard*? How preposterous. She wasn't a scoundrel or a murderer in need of punishment. She deserved better. "I had to do this. There was no other choice."

Hands jammed on his slender hips, he paced several steps over to the table and stopped. "You most certainly did have other choices. You could have booked passage on another ship."

"In a week's time? By then Papa could be dead." The image of sweet Papa in a fetid jail, riddled with disease and his belly empty, caused a sharp prick of tears. She steeled herself against crying, afraid that in her exhaustion she wouldn't be able to stop.

Griffin rubbed the back of his neck and heaved a massive sigh. The motion emphasized again the spectacular breath of his shoulders. He frowned. "If only you'd waited and booked passage on another ship, you could have taken along a companion. Done it proper."

The observation didn't make her feel better. Under normal circumstances, she would have agreed. A proper lady would never place herself in such unseemly circumstances. Nor would she wear a servant boy's clothes. To flaunt the conventions of society came with great risks. She knew the dangers and wasn't an idiot. Just desperate.

"Tell me, Lily…" A softer tone, almost kind, registered in his voice. "Did you at least leave a note, some word as to your absence?"

"I'm not so cruel as to disappear without explanation. I left a letter where my uncle was certain to discover it."

"You hope."

Even as his sarcastic words chipped away at her confidence, she met his stern, unwavering stare. Uncle Percy's glowered oppositions paled alongside Griffin's unyielding scowl. How would she cope with him? Weak with fatigue and hunger, she longed for sleep. If she had to argue, let it occur later, after a much-needed rest restored her energy. What she didn't need was an ongoing battle with another obstinate male—especially a man who eroded her poise with his handsome appearance and the jut of his strong jaw.

"Why does Captain Mulworthy distrust women?"

"Ask him, not me."

The dismissive words chilled like a blustery March wind. In her estimation, the captain outranked her uncle for his loathsome qualities. To be fair, she hadn't escaped Percy's acrimonious snake pit only to wind up in another tense and rancorous situation. If she could make the time on this voyage more agreeable, even if it meant being pleasant to Griffin or the Captain, she'd do everything within reason to achieve this peace. Seeing her chance, she swept a leather tie from the floor where it had fallen from his hair. "You dropped this."

He stared at her hand with an unreadable expression. Seconds passed while her uncertainty arose along with the heat in the stuffy room. She considered removing her coat, but not while he watched. It was somehow too personal; her body too exposed in the boy's shirt. Sweat broke across her brow as she waited. What was wrong with him? Why didn't he accept her offering?

At last, he reached forward and grasped the hair tie. When his fingertips grazed her palm, a strange, thrilling charge skittered up her arm. She snatched her hand away and his lips twitched with amusement. As her skin seared, she spun toward the door, imagining she heard him laugh. With nowhere to run, she faced him knowing there was no other choice but to deal with him.

He sat on the bed with a bemused air. Resigned to her current fate and unsure about what to say, she removed her hat and set it aside. She watched him as a mouse watches a cat. With graceful fingers, he smoothed and tied his thick hair. After shoving a pillow behind his back, he relaxed and fixed his gaze on her again. "You cut your hair."

She patted the queue at the nape of her neck. "It's the same length as yours."

"You had such…" He raised his hand as if he might touch his hair, then let it drop. "It's nothing."

"It'll grow back." The speed of her answer and the hope she might please him astonished her. Why should his opinion matter?

Short on sleep, her tired legs trembled. "I wonder if I might sit down." Not waiting for an answer, she dropped into a chair at the table relieved for the rest.

Another long, uncomfortable silence ensued. For the first time in her life, she was alone with a man in his bedchamber. Her palms sweated. Rather than stare at his long-limbed physique stretched casually across the bed, she glanced anywhere but at him. Two shelves with books hung on the wall. Beneath it, on the desk, his papers lay in a disorganized mess. His clothes hung on hooks by the door. At the washstand lay his shaving cup and a straight-edge razor. His personal possessions marked his intimate space. She was a trespasser. "I'm glad you don't wear a periwig," she blurted and licked her dry lips. She would fill the awkward air between them with idle chatter. "Even if they are the height of fashion."

"Nor do I powder my hair. None of that bears any significance. What am I to call you? Do you have a made-up name?"

"I hadn't..." She considered a moment. "Adam. Adam Marks would do nicely."

"Biblical. I like it." As if praying, he focused on the whitewashed ceiling as though it were Heaven. "God created man, called him Adam and set him in the Garden of Eden."

"This is hardly Eden." Instead of lush greenery and fruit trees, dull wooden walls surrounded her, the drabness broken only by a touch of red in the curtains.

"Don't be too certain. I'm sure there's a serpent or two around here."

He flashed a wolfish grin, but she took no humor in his teasing. Tired and out of sorts, she found him much too comfortable sprawled upon the bed for her peace of mind. One ankle rested over the other, arms crossed over his chest. He had an easy charm and was confident of his powers. In a sweat, she held his steady gaze. "I hope you're wrong about those serpents, Mr. Faraday."

"Oh, call me Griffin." His speech was as unhurried as his languid sprawl. "We're old friends, remember?"

She eyed him warily. What, precisely, was she to make of this creature before her?

Fingers intertwined, he tucked them behind his neck. His chest rose and fell on easy breaths. Beneath his penetrating stare, she might have been a toad, split and exposed for dissection. Ignoring a trickle of perspiration at her ear, she tapped a foot and waited for him to say something.

"When we're outside this cabin, anywhere else on this ship, you will refer to me as Mr. Faraday."

She drew back with alarm. "You can't expect me to sustain this charade. I never intended it to last the length of the voyage. It was only a means to board. A servant boy would not have been turned away, but a woman? You can see the dilemma."

He shook his head in disagreement. "If you have a problem with your status on this ship, I suggest you take it to Mulworthy. He will not countenance a sashaying woman. If his mother were alive and on ship, he'd be sorely tempted to throw her in the brig. Furthermore, it won't displease him to keep you locked up for the remainder of the trip if doing so makes the day run smoother."

"Do you intend to refer me to Captain Mulworthy every time I have a question or complaint?" The angry words rushed out.

He snapped his fingers with exaggerated surprise. "I forgot. As your master, you must answer to me in all things."

Slimy cur. She ground her molars to avoid growling like a dog. When not outright angry, he reveled in sarcasm and seemed to take perverse pleasure in her strained circumstances. Releasing a measured breath, she counted numbers in her head to cool her ire. "You seem to find this state of affairs amusing."

"In a time like this, humor is a lifeline. I leave tragedies for the playwrights."

"This predicament needn't be a tragedy if you'd have faith—"

"Faith," he scoffed as he sat forward. He rested his elbows on his open thighs. "I can assure you I will pray to the good Lord for a safe and quick journey."

"You needn't get angry." Goodness, his moods turned faster than a spinning wheel.

The linens on the bed crinkled when he shifted and dropped his stocking-clad feet to the floor. He leaned forward, and his fingers gripped the edge of the mattress. With rising apprehension, she sensed another shift in his mood. Then it came.

"If the circumstances had been different, if there wasn't a war, I would have gladly helped you..." He paused with a forlorn expression. A wave of a hand dismissed whatever he'd intended to reveal. He stood, and back to her, stared out the window. "As the captain said, what's done is done."

Remorse knotted her stomach. She never meant to cause trouble. If only he could accept her decision. Passage on the *Providence* was her only option. If she had it to do again, she would.

"You must be proud of your quick work," he said with an ironic note in his voice. He pushed away from the window and dropped into the chair across from her at the table. "Who else did you inconvenience to see your crazy scheme successful?"

Her chest squeezed. She hated to lie, but she could never reveal she worked for Cecil Jones. "My maid secured these servant clothes. When everyone was asleep, I managed to hire a carriage in the street."

"I see."

Discouraged by his cynical tone, she remained silent, uncertain what more she could say to make things better. She wiped her damp palms on her breeches. She wished she could trust him, but if Cecil was correct, Griffin was a spy. While her mind raced to redirect their conversation, her stomach grumbled.

Blushing, she clutched her belly.

"Hungry?"

"A little." In truth, she was ravenous. She'd eaten only a piece of cheese and a bit of bread since Uncle Percy's party. Her throat was parched. "I could use something to drink."

A pitcher and an earthenware glass sat on the table. He poured and slid the glass toward her. She drank it to the last drop. The room-temperature barley water tasted refreshing.

"I suppose you didn't get any sleep last night?" His elbows planted on the table, he continued his study of her. "You look exhausted."

"The rats were boisterous." She shuddered. The living nightmare had required all her strength not to rush shrieking from the storage room. A seemingly endless and vile experience, it ranked alongside her first ocean voyage for sheer unpleasantness. On her first trip, she'd been scared, lonely and confused about why Papa had sent her away. In spite of last night's adventure, she managed a few hours of sleep reclined on a sack of wheat. Even now, the smell of bilge water and mildew clung in her nostrils. How she longed to rid herself of her smelly clothes and wash her body.

"Which do you prefer first, food or sleep?"

Sleep? Her frantic gaze jumped to the rumpled bed covers.

"Not with me." His brusque tone suggested he'd been insulted. "I'm not a brute although we must agree on reasonable sleeping arrangements. I meant, would you care to rest, *alone,* or would you care for something to eat?"

"Oh." She swallowed her mortification. This tiring

escapade had unnerved her more than she'd anticipated and caused her to act like an idiot. "Food would be wonderful."

"Excellent."

"I wouldn't want to trouble you, though."

Chortling, he stood and stepped toward her. Alarmed, she swung away then realized her foolishness. Any notions she might be in danger were baseless. He'd always been a polite, nice boy. However, people change. This adult Griffin was a completely new beast. She didn't know what to expect.

He thrust her hat at her. "Put this on and keep it pulled down."

"Why?" She tried to read his face, saw the corners of his eyes crinkle.

"Since you signed on as my cabin boy, you may go to the galley and procure food. While you're there, get us ale, too."

Her jaw dropped. All her life she lived with servants. Being cast in the role of *his* servant left her stunned. "Why, I never."

"Come along." His voice cheery, he tugged her to her feet.

No, she wouldn't go, nor would she play this charade. Feet pressed to the floor, she tried to stand her ground but was no match against his strength. "I'm not hungry. I'll wait until…until supper."

One hand flung open the door. His other hand jostled her along. "You've been on a ship before."

"Not in seven years." She hated how feeble and afraid she sounded.

"Things haven't changed much." Smiling affably, he pointed toward the bow. "Make sure you tell Cook it's for me and don't dawdle. Once you get the food, it will be best to come straight back here."

Hand at her back, he nudged her over the threshold. With an outraged bellow, she twirled around just in time to hear the door close in her face. "Bastard." She resisted a blazing urge to kick the door.

A short while later, in a snit, she stomped back to his cabin. A tray of food in one hand and the other poised to knock on the door, she paused. Why should she do as he commanded? Who was he to order her about? If he wanted food he could damn well get it himself.

Chapter Seven

Griffin nudged Lily out the door and hurried to his desk, grateful for the sudden opportunity to hide the ciphering materials in his trunk. Once he'd locked the material among his clothes in the chest, he stretched out on the bed. He relaxed in the persistent pitch and sway of the boat and expelled a contented sigh.

He couldn't help but smile at the picture of Lily in the form-fitting breeches and a jacket with sleeves so long they touched her knuckles. And the silly hat! No servant's garb could hide the proud stance. The woman could no more act the obedient servant than the queen herself. Mulworthy was correct. She was the prettiest boy he'd ever seen.

On a more serious note, he wondered how they could carry out this charade. How could he, in good conscience, spend the night, much less a whole month with her in this cabin? As to any hope he might sleep when her every movement, her every sigh would be a whisper calling to him—well, it would be impossible.

Clearly, the woman was desperate, even a bit mad to go haring across the ocean dressed as a boy, and all for a father who hadn't the time to call her home after seven years. Whatever she hoped to gain from this familial reunion, he prayed it lived up to her expectation. It pained him to think she might be on a fool's errand.

He adjusted the pillows behind his neck and shoulders, unable to shake the notion her presence suggested a more sinister motivation. Ignorant of her political inclinations and coming from a British household, he had no reason to trust her in spite of her beguiling nature and devotion to her father. A rap at the door jerked him from his reverie. "Come in," he called, oddly excited as he sat up.

Samuel Church, first officer to the captain, popped his head inside. "Captain wanted you to study these maps, sir."

"Put them on the table, if you would."

Church, with hair black as night, crossed the short distance. His heels knocked against the planked floor and he set the items on the table.

"Did you, perchance, see Mr. Marks?" Griffin asked.

"Would that be the boy found earlier in dry storage?"

"The very same." No news remained secret for long on a ship. Griffin wondered when someone would guess the truth about the silly pretense of master and cabin boy. Then what? An uneasy chill flittered over his neck. Perhaps it made more sense to abandon the whole charade. After all, what could Mulworthy do? He imagined Lily locked in the hold. The picture of her asleep in a filthy hammock, surrounded by the salty crew and the lack of privacy raised his hackles.

He leaned forward and massaged his temple. "I sent Mr. Marks to fetch food and drink."

"Saw him head topside, sir."

Topside?

And so the trouble begins, he concluded. "Thank

you, Mr. Church."

Brow tight, Griffin donned his coat and followed Church through the doorway. Worry chipped away at him. Peck. Peck. Peck. As he climbed the ladder to the upper deck, his mind churned with all manner of unpleasant scenarios. When he didn't find her at the stern, he headed toward the bow. Just beyond the foresail, he caught sight of her sky-blue costume and the glint of a metal tray placed at her feet. What was she doing? Curious, he slowed his pace.

Nearby, the big fellow called Tubbs, along with three other sailors, worked a piece of cordage. Another sailor, wrinkled and weathered from the sea and sun, stitched a rip in a sail. Typical day topside.

"Eh, you. Boy." The breeze riffled Tubbs' sandy hair.

Lily turned to the man. In her hand, she clasped a chubby chicken leg. The broad rim of her floppy hat shadowed her face yet didn't disguise her wary expression.

"You can't stand there." Growling, Tubbs stomped forward where she stood at the railing. She stiffened. He towered over her like Goliath to the tinier David. "We got work to do here." With a beefy arm, he gestured to the uncluttered area of the wooden deck. "Ain't you never been on a ship before?" A derisive snicker brought a halt to the work of his shipmates. Their hungry gazes fixed on the game of cat tormenting mouse with amused expressions. Reveling in his power, he jutted his chin at the tray of victuals.

"Chicken?" he sneered. "Food's too fancy for a cabin boy." With gleeful menace, he thrust his face in hers. She jumped back, and her shoulders smacked the rail. At her painful grimace, the nasty man laughed coarsely and drew a few sniggers from his cohorts. "Go below, *boy,* and tend to your master."

"Leave off, Mr. Tubbs." Griffin spoke with quiet authority. He forced an easy gait and strolled closer. At his side, he stretched fingers that itched to curl and pound the lout. "Mr. Marks is not familiar with ship protocol."

"And you." He pointed at Lily. A quick appraisal revealed glistening chicken grease on her full lips. "Come with me."

As her jaw dropped, he spun about and marched off, his steps brusque as they slapped the deck. Before he headed below to his quarters, he glanced over his shoulder, appeased to see the dutiful servant follow in his wake. A blend of emotions clouded her face. Humility was not among the mix.

Inside the cabin, he spoke with uncustomary gruffness. "Close the door." He crossed to the desk on the far side of the room, half expecting the door to slam behind him. Instead, it closed with a soft click. Debating how to handle the situation, and annoyed he should even have to, he dropped like a boulder into his desk chair, swiveled around and pierced her with his stare.

Shoulders pinned to the door, she clutched the brass knob as if she might bolt. Where she might seek comfort or safety on this ship, he couldn't say. Even as she scowled with brows like jagged black paint strokes against a white canvas, he found her beautiful. As to her ferocity... He admired it, as well.

"Put the food on the table," he directed.

Whether in defiance or remorse, she remained

fused to the door, the pewter tray balanced on one arm.

"Put it on the table!"

At his bark, she startled and paled.

Immediately, he regretted his outburst. He wasn't the sort of man to frighten women. However, fear might make her do as told and keep her safe. Yet he found her sudden wariness of him, a man who only wanted to help her, offensive.

"I'm no saint, Lily. But I won't treat you cruelly."

A tense moment passed. At last she unpeeled herself from the door and crossed to the table with a stilted gait. She set down the tray.

"Please." He softened his tone. "Sit."

She slid into a chair, bowed her head and clasped her hands like a penitent.

He drew in a slow, steady breath aware he didn't want her in his cabin, didn't want her on this ship and didn't want her in his life. With a sigh, he released his frustration and resolved to accept the circumstances at hand.

The slouch hat hid her face. One sock hung loose at her calf. Her shoulders caved inward and she appeared both comical and pathetic.

"Please. Allow me." He came around the table. When he lifted her hat, she drew in a noisy breath. "I prefer to see your face." What a lovely face she had, with its high, rounded forehead and delicate chin. Full lips hinted at seductive, sweet mysteries.

"Would you care for a drink?" He tossed her silly hat on the bed. A sniff of the flask she'd brought from the kitchen made him glower. "This isn't ale," he complained. Once again he realized the challenge of their living arrangement. Heavy with foreboding, he sat and poured the weak wine into his mottled tumbler.

"I don't care for ale," she said in an even tone.

"I see. Not only did you fail to procure what I requested, you didn't return to the cabin." He tried to smile. The muscles in his face felt frozen. "As my servant, you need to follow directions."

A gust of chilly wind, almost as cold as her expression, blew through the open window. It fluttered the curtains and crackled the air with a volatile charge. With calculated slowness, she leaned forward and palms flat against the tabletop disarmed him with her pointed stare. "This bears saying once and not again." Spoken just loud enough for him to hear, her frosty tone sent a shiver over his skin as effective as any winter breeze. "I am *not* your boy." Each word snapped like a symphonic staccato and raised the fine hair on his arms.

Oh ho!

A thrilling quiver shot though his body, the kind experienced before a battle. What better fun than a good fight with a worthy opponent? In an effort to cage his exhilaration, he broke off a corner of bread, popped it in his mouth, and chewed with deliberation.

Chin elevated, shoulders thrown back, she sat as proud and prickly as a rose bush. With effort, he managed a placid expression. To laugh seemed unwise.

He poured wine into a cup and slid it across the table. Their gazes locked. He read the challenge daring him. She raised the cup to her lips and drank. The ripple of her creamy throat as she swallowed captivated him. Finished, she set the cup on the table and with a fingertip, dabbed a corner of her luscious mouth.

"Please, eat something." He slid the tray of food forward. "I promise not to confuse you for a piece of cheese and bite."

She growled low in her throat. "You were always such an amusing boy." Well-manicured fingers broke off a piece of the coarse-grained bread. Rather than devour it completely, she picked at the knob of bread and nibbled like a bunny.

Except for the creaks, thumps, and bumps of the ship, they sat in silence. In spite of the strained circumstances, he experienced a peculiar pleasure, almost as if he were at home bantering playfully with his siblings. Only Lily was far from family and his attraction to her in no way brotherly.

"Since death by starvation is no longer imminent, why don't you explain why I shouldn't treat you as my ship boy?"

"Bah! You mean to annoy me. You aren't so dim-witted as to think I'll accept Mulworthy's plan."

"Such lashing remarks will win you no support or friendship on this ship." To his dismay, those stunning eyes filled with moisture. Oh, no. He hated tears. "Forgive me," he stammered. "I meant—"

A raised palm halted further explanation. "I understand what you meant. It's I who should beg forgiveness. I have a sharp tongue, or so I've been told often enough. It's one of my many faults." A raw, vulnerable quality rasped in her voice

"Many faults?" How could this be? He crossed his arms and studied her, intrigued by the contrast between her reckless, confident demeanor and her personal condemnation. Anyone would agree she was lovely and an accomplished lady, as evidenced by her comportment and manner of dress last evening. What had happened in her life to cause such a harsh self-appraisal? Where did this loathing come from? He wondered if she'd been happy in London. Suddenly, against all wisdom, he wanted to know everything about her. "Tell me about your life in London."

She expelled a weary sigh. Gone was the fire of a few moments ago. Spine curled forward, her chin dipped valiantly as she batted away at her distress. As his brain scrambled to think of a sensitive remark to salvage the moment, she raised her head. "Do you intend to punish me for the rest of the trip because I resorted to this ruse?"

Punishment seemed a just reward for her imbecilic actions, yet such spiteful behavior was beneath him. It would also drive her away. Until he learned her true intentions and whether she could be trusted, he would hold her close.

Scooping a shiny apple from a wooden bowl, he tossed it in the air and caught it easily in one hand. "You think I'm the sort of man to make sport of a desperate woman?"

Her spine straightened. One inky brow arched in her milky smooth forehead. "I prefer the word persistent to desperate. I'm dogged when I want something."

"A regular terrier," he grumbled and replaced the apple to the bowl.

"As to *your* character…" The intensity of her fixed stare, as though she saw to his innermost core, unnerved him. "I'm in the dark. You heroically come to my rescue in the morning, and in the evening you meet with my uncle on mysterious business."

"Mysterious business?" he scoffed. "Not the case, I assure you. Your uncle is curious about a possible investment in the Colonies. Do you expect him to share his affairs with a niece?"

She drew back. "It's *you* who didn't wish to speak of the details last night. Do you have any idea what Uncle Percy is like?"

Defiant one moment, on the verge of tears the next and now full of challenge again. How could he tolerate the next weeks with her and come away from the experience whole and sane? "Pray. Tell me."

Expecting she might charge ahead with scandalous details, she simply stared at her lap.

He waited.

"Well, he's…He's not very nice."

A sudden urge to laugh tickled his throat. "I am familiar with countless men. Half could be described as *not very nice*."

"Be amused, if you must, but uncle has less than a stellar reputation when it comes to money and commerce."

"Are you worried about me, or do you think I swim in the same slime?"

She angled her chin, defiant and smug. "I leave the answer up to you."

This time he did laugh and quickly sobered. "Tell me. How was life with Uncle Percy? Did you get along?"

She reacted as if he pricked a hole through her skin and released all her strength. Once again, she deflated and curled inward. Her expression a gash of misery, she glanced away.

"Ah." He regretted asking.

"It hardly bears discussion."

A voice in his head urged him to keep his gob shut,

but he'd never been good at following his own counsel, so he asked, "Will you return to England, once you've seen your father?"

"I hope to persuade Papa to join me in London." Picking at the rim of the bowl, she shrugged a shoulder. "I don't know what the future holds."

"What of Warwick?" Remorse stung him the instant he asked. The less he knew of her personal life, the less chance he might come to care about her. As to the pompous ass, why should he care?

"David won't be happy." An index finger traced a thin crack in the grain of the wooden table. "I left him a letter. If I mean anything to him, he'll understand and wait until things with Papa are sorted."

"A kind-hearted and generous bloke." The sarcasm earned him her reproachful glare.

"Does my friendship to David matter to you?"

"Not at all." *Liar* said the voice in his head.

"I see."

Was it his imagination or did her soft-spoken response register disappointment? As their conversation stalled, she rose from her seat and meandered about the tiny room. At his desk, a wicker basket overflowed with the cast-off writings of a political essay. *Damn.* In all the excitement, he'd forgotten to burn the discarded remnants. Before he could stop her, she scooped up a crushed ball of paper from the floor.

His heart shot into his throat. "Allow me." Somehow, he managed to keep his voice steady and his actions smooth. Deft fingers relieved her of the incendiary note which he dropped casually in the basket and nudged the trash closer to his feet.

A charged, vibrant current licked between them.

Her quizzical expression left him unsettled. "I'm messy when I write letters."

"I didn't mean to insult you."

"None taken." He flashed his most charming smile, the one guaranteed to win the attentions of women.

Seeming impervious to his allure, her gaze alighted on his desk. "Your cabin has the look of an academic's study with books and papers. Papa could get lost in a book. Sometimes it seemed he preferred…" Her sad voice fell away.

"Preferred what?"

"Books more than people."

Lips downturned, she slipped into a seat at the table. The weight of dejection rounded her spine. "How's your brother?" She had the decency to inquire of his family when all he wanted was to pry out her secrets. Was she a spy?

"Elliot? He's married." Married to the woman Griffin once loved, he almost added. Best to forget the gloomy tale of love gained and lost. "He prospers and practices law in New York."

"Law?" Her face brightened. "I'm not surprised. Even as a boy, his intelligence sparkled."

What was he—a simpleton?

"Tell me about the rest of your family."

"When last I heard, they were all well." His feisty younger sister flashed in his head and touched off a smile. "Rebecca manages to beat away any suitors."

She leaned forward, all eagerness. "Has she concerns about marriage?"

"It's the permanence and the fear of making the wrong choice."

"And you? Are you married?"

"Me?" He reared back, shaking his head and waving a hand as if shoving away something distasteful. "No. Marriage is out of the question—for the present time. Too much travel, I'm afraid." War and the military had a most quelling effect on matrimony.

Watching him, she tapped a finger to her bottom lip. "What is your line of work?"

"Trade." The genuine commercial endeavor served to mask his military objectives.

"What sorts of things do you trade?"

Growing relaxed, he crossed a leg, ready to handle her questions. "Any item which makes life in the Colonies more comfortable."

"I see." She got up and at the desk, inspected the gold embossed book titles. "Shakespeare, Pope, Defoe." She paused, a finger on a book spine. "You like *Robinson Crusoe*?"

"I read it as a boy and hope to read it again on this trip."

She turned and studied him as one might a puzzle. "Do you read works with a political bent?"

Taken aback by her question, he carefully considered his answer. "I'm entertained by the occasional satirical essay. As to political commentary, there is enough in the broadsheets. It grows weary."

"Hmmm." She brushed aside the curtain and stared out the window, as if thinking. "It's hard to believe we are at war against our own countrymen."

His guard rose at the unsafe nature of the conversation. He wished he could read her mind. "An atrocity."

She swirled about, her manner unusually bright. "You support the King?"

"You act surprised." On purpose, he slouched in the chair, affecting a relaxed manner though her obvious and clumsy questions had him troubled. "It's best the nation stay united." Two could play at this game. "What are your beliefs?"

From her lips came a puffing, dismissive noise. "I'm not political. Uncle Percy forbade any discussion of politics. He considered such talk unattractive in women."

Yet she'd broached the topic. "You may find when you reach New York it is prudent not to make inquiries about a person's political beliefs. Lives hang in the balance depending upon the answer."

"Is it so bad?" Her bottom leaned against his desk and offered a momentary but pleasant distraction.

"You'll see." Pushing to his feet, he cast aside the image of her slender hips parked next to his dear books. "I suspect you'll want to rest."

With the toe of his boot, he drew open a storage drawer from beneath the bed. "In case you wondered…" She glanced at the covered chamber pot, blushed and gave a quick nod of her head. "There's fresh water in the ewer."

Wicker basket clutched in his hand, he went to the door wondering about the tempest in his midst. "I'll leave you to sleep. I won't trouble you."

Chapter Eight

Lily awoke to the sharp, echoing clang of a bell. Early morning light filtered through the curtains. The breeze through the open windows infused the cabin in a briny smell. Two plain wooden chairs and a table stood out distinctly in the grayish light. Stacked books sat on a desk jammed in a corner. Griffin's books.

Her pulse jumped. Rising up, she leaned on her elbows. Tangled bed sheets wrapped around her satin breeches and frilly shirt from yesterday. No strapping body of a male stretched out in the bed or anywhere in the cabin. With great relief, she wondered where the attractive fellow had gone.

Over the back of a chair lay her coat. Black lumps on the floor indicated her shoes, discarded shortly after he departed...sometime late yesterday afternoon. It stunned her to think she'd slept so long.

If Griffin had slept next to her, she would've noticed. Such a narrow bed wouldn't easily accommodate two people, particularly such a tall man. Nevertheless, a flutter of anxiety winged in her stomach. Where had he slept? She tossed aside the bed covers along with her worries and slipped from the bed, anxious to rid herself of the stale clothes she'd worn so long. As she stretched arms overhead and worked out the kinks, a devilish idea sprang to mind.

Excited, she yanked open her trunk which stood

alongside Griffin's. Honeycomb, her stuffed animal from childhood, lay tucked among the folds of her gowns. She loved the worn horse with the ragged mane. As childish as it might seem, he never failed to raise pleasant memories and make her smile. She patted the dear friend on the head and set him aside. When she located the perfect gown, she tugged it out and shook out the wrinkles as best she could. Neither Griffin nor the captain would bully her today. No doubt the ogre would have a snit when he saw her, but what could he do? Throw her to the sharks? Toss her in the hold? He'd said those things to frighten her into submission, but she'd show him. Superstitions aside, he would have to grow accustomed to a lady aboard his ship.

Hah! Her, a lady? Wouldn't Percy chuckle?

Later, dressed and her hair pinned back from her face, Lily paused in her reading of an essay written by Montaigne she found among Griffin's books. "Where is he?"

In his absence, she'd searched the room and found nothing to prove him a spy. If he had anything to hide, it would be in his locked trunk. When possible, she'd sneak the key from him.

Her stomach grumbled. The apple she'd eaten earlier hadn't quelled her hunger. Yesterday's stale, leftover bread crunched between her teeth when she took a bite. She washed it away with the last of the watered-down wine.

Her fingers drummed restlessly against the tabletop. As promised when he'd made a hasty retreat, Griffin hadn't returned to trouble her. For this, she could be grateful. Yet many nights remained of their journey. How could she spend the next weeks with him when his charm and his changeable moods left her so unsettled?

"All right," she announced with determination. "Enough of waiting. I shall simply have to venture out on my own."

Not until she emerged on the upper deck did she see another soul, though she heard the bump and clatter of men busy at their chores. Chickens clucked in their caged pens. She wrinkled her nose at the foul smell of hogs. When the weathered sailor noticed her, he stopped with his freckled hand on the rigging, and made a quick sign of the cross over his chest.

Goodness. Was a woman such a demon it spurred a man to prayer?

"Where does one go to dine?" She tried to ignore his rude stare and the wisps of oily hair flattened to his shiny pate.

"The captain's cabin, I reckon." He spat a glob of nasty sputum into a bucket and pointed to a door.

"Ah." She suspected this might be his answer given the door's special embellishments which defined its higher status. If the fellow detected her pained expression, he gave no notice. "Thank you, sir."

Facing the bulkhead, she studied the scrollwork above the doorway. In her mind, she relived the harsh grilling she received at the hands of the captain yesterday. A sudden worry today's encounter might prove equally uncomfortable twisted her stomach. With grave misgivings, she took a step forward. Then another. With a gulp of moist sea air to bolster her resolve, she rapped upon the door.

A gruff voice bade her enter.

Swallowing her unease, she turned the decorative

brass knob. When she stepped inside, Mulworthy's fork stopped short of his open mouth. "Salt of the dog!"

"Good morning, Captain." Despite her ragged nerves, she managed a light, happy tone. A dining table stood in the middle of the room, suspended on stout legs bolted to the floorboards. The detestable monster sat among three men she had yet to meet, breakfast dishes scattered before them, the smell of fresh coffee ripe in the air. Shock, followed quickly by delight, flitted over his companions' faces. Not so for Mulworthy, who glared at her with such contempt she dropped a hand to her chest, half expecting her heart to seize.

"I'm told this is where passengers take their meals."

"Faraday," he snarled. When there was no response, he shouted, "Faraday! What's this about?"

She heard a muffled grunt. Up from the corner of the room rose a pile of blankets. All at once, the bedding heaved and tumbled to the floor. Her heroic knight appeared and sent a shock wave through her body.

"What?" His hair spilled in a messy tangle over his shoulders. He blinked several times. When he noticed her, his jaw dropped. "What the—"

"Good morning." She threw as much good cheer into her voice as possible. So far, her perky performance had garnered universal attention.

Griffin flung the blankets off and scrabbled up in his stocking feet. His brows angled and creased his forehead. "What are you *doing*?"

In spite of his irritation, she felt sorry he'd spent the night on the floor without even a simple pallet to cushion his bones. *Poor man.*

Befuddled, he clawed a hand through the stubble on his chin, seeming to struggle with the woman before him. "Why are you dressed like *that*?"

She chose to ignore the gruff questions and graced him with a smile, grateful to have packed sensible garments that laced up the front. "I've decided to join you for breakfast. Since I missed supper last night, I'm famished."

Mulworthy's face quivered like a steam kettle about to blow.

"May I sit down, Captain?"

His beady eyes bulged with the possibility they might pop out and roll around on the floor. Before he could send her away, a young sailor, with hair as black as pitch, shot to his feet. "Permit me, madam." Bright with eagerness, he pulled a chair from the table and offered her a seat.

At least someone had manners.

"Thank you." She slid into place, thankful for a solid chair beneath her quaking knees.

"I'm Mr. Samuel Church," he gushed, all smiles and graciousness. "And this is Mr. Flint, the ship's steward."

A jolly fellow with a grin like a puppet jokester and a paunch as circular as his balding head nodded a welcome.

"Och, get on with it, Church," grumbled the ogre.
Beast.

Church gestured to the fellow next to him. "This is the ship's surgeon, Mr. Mead."

A thin man with straw-colored hair and spectacles nodded respectfully.

Griffin had donned his shoes and strolled toward the table. He settled next to her, smelling of sleep and muslin warmed in the sun. A carefree expression replaced his earlier air of annoyance and confusion. As if all was right with the world and only temperate days stretched before him, he poured a cup of coffee and filled one for her, too.

"Thank you."

As she sipped the tepid brew, Mulworthy jabbed a finger and sent fear up her spine. The sausage-sized digit wagged menacingly back and forth. "Dinna think ye can ignore me orders without some blowback."

Stomach curling, she wondered how Griffin managed to consume a biscuit as if Mulworthy didn't put him off his food.

"Ye won't get away with this."

At his veiled threat, the men looked everywhere but at her. Griffin, on the other hand, seemed unperturbed as he shook salt on his eggs.

Brow drawn in curiosity, Mr. Mead cleared his throat. "I daresay, Captain, I've missed something here." When Lily heard his cultured and schooled voice, she dared to hope he might inject some civility into the current tense proceedings, maybe even soften the ogre. "Permit me to welcome you aboard, Miss…"

"Miss Lily Fitzhugh." She smiled, but her taut face ached with the effort.

Lean, with long-boned arms and a pink flush to his cheeks, Mr. Mead wore his blond hair closely shorn to his head. "I didn't realize we were to travel with such a charming lady."

Mulworthy rolled his blood shot gaze heavenward and huffed in exasperation.

"I came aboard at the last minute."

"A stowaway she is," Mulworthy grumbled.

Anger raced up her spine. "I presume Tubbs gave you my fare, Captain."

Mulworthy grunted disagreeably.

"Eat," Griffin said and dolloped scrambled eggs on her plate.

She faced Mead, taking refuge in his interest. "I spent much of yesterday in my cabin."

The words *my cabin* caused Griffin to choke and cough. She glared at him, daring him to contradict.

"Ah. I see." Mead stared at the pillow and heaped blankets on the floor.

Conversation stalled. Lily picked at her eggs. Mulworthy hunched over his plate, his skin tone similar to raw liver. A muscle in his cheek pulsed with anger.

"Would you care for some ham, madam?" Mead lifted a platter in slender fingers well suited to play the violin or harpsichord. With his pleasant attitude and straight aristocratic nose, she found him likable.

"Thank you." Several thick slices, along with a biscuit, found a home on her plate. "You'll want the marmalade." Griffin shoved the jar closer with his pinky.

Fork grasped in his fist, Mulworthy speared a piece of meat from his plate and jammed it into his craw. His jaw ground the food, and she had an anxious notion he fantasized her as the morsel.

Never had she met such an unlikeable man and all because she dared to sneak aboard his ship. Yet the deed was done. *Let the anger go.* To her misfortune, he seemed unable to do so, and his intolerant attitude left an aftertaste in her mouth as bitter as the thick coffee.

Without doubt, her presence at his table, dressed in a gown rather than a servant's uniform, struck a blow to his authority—a blow she worried would cause serious repercussions.

Taking their cue from the captain, the men resumed eating. In spite of her jumpy stomach, Lily managed a few nibbles. Griffin, a man of surprising stamina and fully alert after a night upon the floor, devoured every morsel with a hearty appetite. No one spoke, and the slurp of coffee and the clink of silver on the plates drove her nerves to a higher pitch.

Mulworthy continued to scowl even as he downed the last dregs in his cup. With a screech of chairs legs against the floor, he shoved away from the table.

"All of ye. On deck at eight bells." His derisive gaze sliced into her. "Dinna be late."

The ominous message sent a ruffled chill over her shoulders. An urge to argue arose, but she knew the danger in challenging him. The man would cling to his resentment like a scar on skin. Doubtless, whatever waited for her on the deck would be unpleasant, perhaps even vile. For her disobedience, it was retribution at eight bells.

He marched from his quarters in a huffy flutter of righteous anger. Only when the door slammed behind him did she breathe again.

A silent message passed between Flint and Church. In unison, they stood.

"We must be off," stated Flint with forced cheeriness, but his darting, evasive gaze suggested trouble. "I wish to say, madam, how delighted we are to have such a lovely guest among us."

"Thank you both." She could scarcely form the

words in her anxiety.

When they were gone, she expected some rebuke from Griffin for her blatant disregard of the captain's orders. *I'm a civilian. I deserve respect,* she wanted to shout and steeled herself to his certain argument. However, his expression remained a blank mask as he sliced into his ham.

Lily fingered her coffee cup and wished she could will herself to New York as quick as a swallow of the dark brew. Mead offered her the platter of kippers. Nauseated by the smell, she declined.

"Since we are ship acquaintances, Miss Fitzhugh," the physician said as he set his fork and knife across his empty plate, "you must tell me about yourself."

At this, Griffin raised his head.

"There isn't much to tell. I'm on my way to see my father." She'd begun to tell her story when she heard the clang of bells.

Mead glanced warily at the door. "We are summoned. Our conversation will have to wait for another time." Without another word, he left the room.

In her head, Lily counted along with the bells. Her nerves ticked up with each toll.

"It's time." Griffin stood.

She tried to stand, but her legs wouldn't obey. Up to the challenge, Griffin hauled her to her feet. Hand at her back, he prodded her forward on feet heavy as iron anchors. Anne Boleyn, solemn and head bowed, trudging to the chopping block, figured in Lily's mind. "I wonder what awaits us."

Griffin replied with an unpleasant growl. "We'll soon find out."

There was something telling in his stoic

expression. She figured he knew, but for some reason, he declined to enlighten her.

When they stepped into the fresh air, the winds plucked at her hair. Mulworthy presided center stage, on the poop deck, elevated higher than the crew, a commander in supreme charge. Flint and Church flanked each side. Griffin touched her arm, and they joined them.

"Mr. Church, sound the whistle," the captain ordered.

The shrill whistle pealed three times. Within minutes, the entire crew had assembled on the quarterdeck. Dressed in a motley assortment of stripes, washed-out colors and ragged bandannas, they assembled in rows, like a haphazard army on parade. While they waited for the captain's address, they whispered among themselves and stared at her as though she were a freak of nature. It appeared they were due for a performance of sorts. With growing certainty, Lily anticipated it would not be a pleasant experience.

Suddenly, the crowd stirred. The men shifted. Their heads swiveled as they cast furtive glances over their shoulders. In the center, some shuffled aside, creating a path through their ranks. The man who'd taken her money and secreted her aboard, the man called Tubbs, stumbled up the makeshift aisle followed by two burly sailors. When the three reached the captain, they stopped. Tubbs lifted his gaze and spotting her, sneered.

Lily reared back. Her heart pummeled her ribs.

Mulworthy's voice boomed so all could hear over the flutter of the sails. "Mr. Church, read the charges."

A book propped open in his hands, Church sang out. "Sometime between the hours of…" He read the date and time along with the charges of theft and dereliction of duty. "Twenty lashes."

Racked with guilt, Lily clasped her fingers in a tight grip. She'd never considered the fallout of her sneaky action. Never imagined someone else might be hurt or punished. If only she hadn't listened to Cecil Jones. Yet there was no other choice when a father needed you.

"I'm sorry," she mouthed to Tubbs. With his gaze straight ahead and his spine rigid, he refused to grant her forgiveness.

"Captain! You mustn't do this."

Mulworthy wrinkled his nose. "Mr. Faraday. See to the *lady*."

Instantly, Uncle Percy's words, *you're no lady* came to mind.

Griffin inched closer, and the comfort and reassurance from his steadfast manner gave her a glimmer of hope. "Can't you make him understand?"

Her soft-spoken plea had no effect on her childhood friend. Face wooden, he remained silent. Anger burned a fast path up her throat and paralyzed her jaw. To do naught made him as much a monster as Mulworthy.

"Tie him to the grating," directed Mulworthy.

Horrified, she watched as a brawny sailor grabbed Tubbs by the scruff, thrust him face forward against a wooden trellis and bound his wrists above his head. Another sailor stripped the shirt from his back.

"Ye may begin."

From among the ranks, out stepped a swarthy man,

a coil of leather gripped in his hand. No one made a sound as the flogger drew his muscled arm back and unfurled the whip.

Crack!

Tubbs and Lily jerked in unison. The biting slash reverberated in her head.

Crack!

Sickened, she considered fleeing to the cabin but knew Mulworthy would drag her back.

Crack!

Tubbs grunted in pain. Three scarlet gashes glinted across his back.

Crack!

Repeatedly, taut leather lashed against muscle and skin. In its wake, it left a haphazard grid of gaping, ripped flesh. Her hands fisted as blood oozed from the wounds and mixed with the man's glistening sweat.

On and on, the relentless snap of the whip and the rasp of pain resounded in her head and echoed the length of her body. She cupped a hand over her mouth. Bile stung the back of her throat, bitter and vile. She turned to leave. Just as fast, Mulworthy gripped her forearm. "Stay."

"I won't."

"I insist."

Jaw clenched, she faced the tethered man. She hated Mulworthy with such intensity she feared it might consume her like a ball of fire. No doubt, he would have taken pleasure had it been *her* bare back cut to bloody ribbons. In defiance, and because she could no longer watch, she stared across the vast gray ocean, imagining she floated away. Yet the bite of leather and the pained groans juddered in her head, on and on until at last, it ended.

A guard cut Tubbs loose. Bloodied and wan, he sank to his knees. Mead went to him. Bending low, he spoke in his ear.

At Mulworthy's direction, Church declared the proceedings finished and ordered the men back to work.

"Consider it a lesson," Mulworthy snarled. "Now get below." He turned his back on her.

"Come, Lily." Griffin touched her elbow.

Furious, she wrenched away. "Don't touch me," she hissed. "You're all barbarians—the whole lot of you."

Her skirt clutched in a tight fist, she fled and sought peace in the cabin. The men, the relentless sway of the ship, the salty air, everything fell away as she raced into the quiet space and slammed the door. Stumbling the short distance to the bed, she fell across the madras cover and cried.

Moments later, someone knocked.

"Go away."

Griffin stuck his head inside. After a frank assessment, he came into the cabin and kicked the door closed with a foot. He held a bottle and two tankards.

"I'm not in the mood for visitors."

As if he were deaf, he crossed the room and set the items on his desk.

She stifled an offensive remark, appalled when he poured the liquid. He offered her one of the pewter cups. "It's beer. It'll make you feel better."

She sat up. *Get out* hovered on her tongue and she remembered it was his cabin. With some misgiving, she took the beer. The brew tasted warm and yeasty.

Further annoying her, he folded his long limbs into

the desk chair, clearly intending to stay. After taking a hearty swig, he said, "The first flogging I witnessed almost made me spill my supper on the foredeck."

A big manly man like you, she wanted to snort in derision.

"Twenty-five lashes." He grimaced as though it was his skin lacerated by the whip. "Not a pretty sight."

She sipped and studied him over the rim of her cup. His admission had a purpose. Implying she wasn't alone in her agony, he meant to soothe her hurt and anger.

His tone softened. "Flogging is not a sentence anyone likes to see."

"It was cruel and unnecessary. I shall hate him forever."

"Mulworthy?" He bared a lopsided grin. "He'll be heartbroken."

At the same instant her palm itched to slap him, a weight lifted in her chest.

"Don't waste your emotions on the man."

She fingered her cup, curious about Griffin's sudden kindness when he'd been stiff as granite during the flogging. "Couldn't you have stopped it?"

"A captain is master of his ship."

"You must have some influence over Mulworthy."

"It's not my decision to make." He propped an ankle over the opposite knee and hunkered loosely in the chair. "Besides, Tubbs deserves his punishment."

Outrage stole her breath.

"Tubbs flouted the rules when he allowed you to board."

"But the punishment is so extreme. Surely kindness…"

"It may seem harsh, but the consequences of ignoring one's duty could result in the death of the crew, the loss of cargo, or even conscription by an enemy vessel. England is at war. For all anyone realizes, you could be a spy."

"Spy?" A nervous giggle rippled from her lips. "I'm hardly a threat to the ship."

In his languid fashion, he studied her with a censorious glint and stirred a wave of discomfort. Surely, he had no reason to suspect her contract with Cecil Jones. When he glanced out the window, she relaxed.

"Rules are rules," he said. "Tubbs ignored rules when he allowed a stranger to board the ship. His greed did him in."

"Will Tubbs be all right, do you suppose?" She curled her legs beneath her on the bed.

"He's a hardy lad."

"And the other fellow? Twenty-five lashes, you say."

His smile was grim as he stood. "Mulworthy made you watch so you would appreciate the seriousness of Tubbs' actions."

"I won't deny it made a nasty impression. Still, it all seems so savage."

"It's not a world you're accustomed to. What happened today is not so unusual, given the hardships of a sailor's life."

"If what you describe is typical of a sailor's life, God help them."

"God help us all." He downed the last of his beer. "Remember, we aren't all barbarians."

"If it's all the same to you, I think I'll avoid

Mulworthy."

"Just as well. He's confined you to quarters."

Chapter Nine

"As fit as a fiddle," Sloane declared.

Griffin studied the bow-legged fellow who wore streaks of grime down the front of his apron. "And how, my good man, did you determine the fitness of Miss Fitzhugh?"

"I asked her, sir. When I arrived with coffee, she was at the desk writing. I inquired as to her health, and she smiled at me." A rhapsodic glow bloomed over the man's bony face, which nettled Griffin. "A pretty smile she has—"

Griffin waved a hand impatiently. "Go on about her health, man, not her physical attributes."

"Well, I set the tray down on the table and inquired as to her welfare. To which she replied, 'Prime, my good man, prime.'"

Griffin rolled his eyes.

"Her exact words, sir. Then she asked if I would bring her soup, bread and cheese. Don't reckon a person can eat so much if they be sick."

"Thank you, Sloane," Griffin grumbled, astounded he should be so unaccountably annoyed. No doubt the sour mood would soon pass. "You may go."

Sloane turned. Before he reached the door, Griffin added, "If she should refuse food or be in any way aggrieved, inform me immediately."

The man agreed and left Griffin to his thoughts and

coffee.

After pouring a cup, he eased once again onto the only comfortable chair Samuel Church owned. Out of necessity and privacy for Lily, Griffin had yielded her his cabin and agreed to Church's offer to share his tiny quarters. Three nights bedded down on a straw-filled pallet on the floor left him cranky while his achy hips and spine cried out for a more accommodating arrangement. Even worse, Church's love-struck comments about the *lovely Miss Fitzhugh* drove him barmy. Clearly the man was besotted, as he supposed was half the crew.

As to the ship's only temptress, he suspected Lily would choose the solitude of her room, confined or not, rather than risk a chance encounter with the captain. Each day, he checked on her. Though polite and sparse in her comments, it was clear she didn't want his company. A rap on the door swelled his hopes it might be her.

"Yes?"

Church stuck his head inside, a black slip of hair angled across his forehead. "French ship off the starboard."

Griffin's heart kicked a beat. "Thank you, Mr. Church. I'll join you topside in a moment." He spoke in an even, unrushed manner; his gut, nevertheless, churned with excitement. The news harkened the arrival of the pirate ship and the guns. He closed Shakespeare's *Henry IV*, shrugged into his jacket, and bounded from the cabin. Breathing faster, he stepped next door to his cabin and rapped.

No answer. Alarmed, he opened the door. "Lily?"

Dishes, an apple core, and several books decorated

the table. A nightgown lay on the bed, and something new graced his desk—a miniature oval portrait. But no Lily.

"Damn." Why today, of all days, did she venture out alone? If she saw the guns come aboard, it would raise unnecessary questions. He wanted her below, out of Mulworthy's sight. Where had she gone? Topside, most likely. He headed in its direction.

A bank of gray clouds hovered in the sky. On deck, brisk wind riffled Griffin's hair. He glanced beyond the complicated network of masts and riggings but didn't spot Lily.

Church flanked Mulworthy near the starboard rail. Spyglass plastered to his eyeball, the older man tittered with delight. Griffin joined them, astounded to see the rapid approach of a frigate, the fastest known vessel on the seas. The black painted craft slipped through the waves, its forward motion as sleek as a porpoise.

"Is it *Le Chien Noir*?' Griffin asked.

"Aye. The *Black Dog*. See for yourself." Mulworthy handed over the spyglass. Griffin adjusted the monocle. The picture clarified. Bold as ever, a flag of a black dog snapped in the stiff wind. A thrilling jolt shot through his body. "Are the conditions right?"

Mulworthy squinted at the horizon. "Aye, it'll be rocky, but we'll manage."

The vessel drew nearer. Griffin no longer needed the spyglass for he could plainly see the crew of the visitor ship loading a launch with cargo. An exhilarating charge surged the length of his arms and pulsed in his fingertips as he gripped the teak railing. The arrival of the military officer and the English guns would serve the Colonial army well. Once they'd transferred the property, his mission would be one step closer to completion.

"Mr. Church, raise the flag and sound the canon," Mulworthy directed. His pebble-sized eyes gleamed with intensity. "We're about to have guests."

The fellow hustled away, barking orders like a seal. The men scuttled to perform their duties with hasty efficiency. Within minutes, the big gun bellowed a message of welcome. Moments later the first launch set off from the *Black Dog* and cut across the choppy water to the *Providence*.

"Is something amiss?"

At the sound of the feminine voice, Griffin spun around, his heart in his throat. Lily stood just beyond the ladder of the poop deck, a paisley shawl around her shoulders, her expression curious. *So lovely.*

"Go below," he snapped.

Hurt flared in her face.

"You need to go below." He forced an even, insistent tone. This was not the place for her. Not here. Not now. "Please, Lily."

Mulworthy flapped a hand, seeming oddly unconcerned by her sudden appearance. "Let her stay. Saves me the trouble tae fetch her later."

"What do you mean?" Griffin asked wary at the man's unexpected calm.

"'Tis where she gets off."

"Off?" Lily repeated, coming closer.

"I'm unloading ye."

"You can't," she cried before Griffin had a chance to protest. As if he sported three heads, she gaped at Mulworthy, incredulous for an instant before fear and anger twisted her face. "I won't go. I won't be hoisted about like a sack of oats."

"Captain, consider—"

Cut off with an arm wave, Mulworthy cocked a coarse brow, his stony expression absolute. "I aim to see the back of ye today, girlie." The snorting, mirthless laugh raised the hackles on Griffin's neck.

What scarce color Lily possessed drained away. "My uncle will see you in jail."

Mulworthy hesitated, wetting his bottom lip with his tongue. "Perhaps. 'Tis more likely Lord Coventry will have my hide if I dinna send ye back."

In a clear dismissal, he rotated away from her. "Ah, gentlemen. Good of ye to join us."

Two men, off the first launch, picked their way across a deck congested with barrels, rope and animal pens. Griffin knew Jacques Dumelle, Captain of the *Black Dog* from when he'd arranged the theft of guns in London a week ago. The other man, Commander Moreau, he'd never met but knew from shared correspondence.

Dressed in a stylish embroidered topcoat and satin breeches, Moreau had agreed to play the part of Charles Laurent, a wealthy merchant, until his safe delivery into the hands of the Colonial Army. Well-experienced in the art of light infantry, Moreau's services would enhance the discipline and skilled marksmanship so dearly required of the young and disordered army.

Mulworthy's bunched cheeks beamed with good cheer as he made introductions, neither concerned nor aware Lily glowered at his back. If she'd had a knife in her fist, the captain chanced being nothing but tattered cloth and bloody strips of meat. Over his shoulder, he flicked a thumb at her. "This, gentlemen, is Miss

Fitzhugh."

Lily gawped at Dumelle as if he were a slavering dragon. His jagged tattoo held her attention. A snaky swirl branded both sides of the pirate's neck and climbed up his shaven head to circle with an artistic flourish around his ears.

"What better way to divert oneself from the boredom of travel than a beautiful companion." Laurent's heavy French accent laced his words.

"Don't get yer hairs up," Mulworthy groused. "She's leaving."

The Frenchman drew back in surprise while the captain added, "I'd be grateful for a bit of talk with ye, Black Jack."

Lily said, "Captain, I—"

"Take her below, Faraday. Get her out of me sight."

Griffin bit down hard. His pulse pounded with the certainty things were about to spiral out of control. He reached for her but she twisted away from any touch. Her scowl was murderous, yet in the depths of her anger, terror lurked. "Go below. I'll come to you soon."

As if rooted to the deck, she didn't budge.

"Lily. Please." The urgency to conceal her from the captain and the pirate drove into his chest like a sharp blade. A second clicked and then another. His stomach churned along with the roiling sea.

Off to the side, Mulworthy, Laurent and the pirate hovered close together, as they spoke in hushed voices. Dumelle's bald, tattooed head bobbed up and down, doubtless in agreement to some plan. When his black, greedy gaze slid over Lily, Griffin turned cold.

The pirate would take Lily and command a good

price for her, even when he ruined the goods before the sale.

Lily huffed and stomped off while a third launch, laden with more crates, sliced through the choppy water.

Griffin joined the men, wanting to curse at the cruel twist of fate that threatened to upend his life.

Mulworthy pried open a crate brought onboard. A quick survey confirmed the cache of sleek and deadly weaponry. From his coat pocket, Griffin extracted a leather pouch. The remainder of the money owed to the pirate. He handed it to Dumelle.

He thought of Lily. What price did a human life command? Would a hundred, a thousand, or a million pounds be enough to secure her safety? Though clever and resilient, she would never survive her ordeal with the *Black Dog* and come away unscarred.

"Captain. A word if you please."

The roughened, wind-blown man gave him a skeptical appraisal, as though anticipating some problem or perhaps a battle. Mulworthy spotted his assistant and snapped. "Mr. Church, take our guests to my stateroom. See to their comfort. I'll be along shortly."

Once the men were out of earshot, Griffin took a steadying breath, aware he was to embark on the most foolhardy mission of his less than noteworthy existence. "Captain..." He struggled to find the right words, to set the tone and make his announcement believable. In the end, he simply said, "I wish to marry the woman."

For a moment, the old goat was speechless. Then he barked a laugh. "Are ye daft?"

To marry her was absolute insanity. "Possibly.

Many a good man is brought to his knees by love, eh?"

"Love?" The feisty codger scoffed and unfurled a slug of saliva on the deck. "Ye can't mean it. Ye dinna love the little baggage."

"It's love as sure as I stand before you. We've known each other since we were children. I think, even then, I loved Lily." His impassioned plea almost made it sound believable.

"Children?"

As shrewd as the old man could be, Griffin doubted he would swallow the drivel. He'd never lied to him before, and it didn't go down easily. Still, against all logic and duty, he felt compelled to help the woman. "Being with her again, on this voyage, well, we can't deny our feelings for each other—honest, loving feelings." *What a load of cow shit.*

"Hmmm." Mulworthy tugged at his whiskered chin with thumb and forefinger, puzzling over the strange news. "I *have* seen ye moonin' over her...a regular sap, gawping and such."

Griffin startled. *Gawping?* He'd done no such thing, had he?

His brothers always joked that he fell too easily for a pretty face—as if one could control an emotion like love. After his last disastrous affair, he'd come to agree with them. Fortunate for him, love didn't figure into marriage with Lily.

The captain lobbed a doubtful gaze as though the odor of deceit lingered in Griffin's very words. "Do ye ken what ye're doing? She'll be the anchor around yer neck."

"I'll thank you not to speak ill of my future wife."

Mulworthy shook his head, pity plainly written on

his leathery face. "I never took ye for a skirt-chasin' hero. Do ye ken the damage she can bring ye?"

Only too well. "I'll keep her in line." He'd keep a close eye on her. What better way to discover if she was a spy?

"Aye, ye do it. Mayhap ye can turn her to yer side."

"Ever the optimist."

Their laughter rang with a bleak, ironic hollow.

"I *do* want to marry her." The lie unsettled him.

The other man made a crude noise. "I dinna trust her. The lass is trouble."

Griffin agreed but, too proud to admit the man was right, remained silent.

"I dinna like this. Still, a good Captain will no refuse his duties. Aye, I leave it tae ye tae work out the challenges."

****

"He can't do this!"

Lily stomped across the cabin and stopped abruptly when she reached the windows. Outside, the pirate ship bobbed in the choppy water like a hideous sea monster. The idea of placing even a foot upon its deck made the terror press against her chest, squeezing the very breath from her lungs.

She was so close to Papa. *So close.* Now Mulworthy meant to destroy her life. "Terrible, terrible man."

Her fingers itched to claw at his horrible little eyes. At the desk, she picked up a book. Spinning on her feet, she hurled it across the room. To her absolute surprise, Griffin stood in the doorway. The book slammed into the wall only an arm's length from his head. Horror-struck, she watched it plunge to the floor with a resounding bang.

"Take care to show more respect for my possessions, madam." The sight of him caused her heartbeat to leap.

"Oh, I...I..." Heat stung her cheeks. She stamped her foot. "Must you sneak up on me?" The words flowed harsher than she'd intended. Hot with shame, she marched over and snatched the tossed item from the floor.

He lingered in the doorway, all lanky beauty, observant and still. With a grace seldom seen in men, he stepped inside and closed the door quietly behind him.

"I'm sorry." She did her best to smooth a crinkled page before she replaced the book on the desk.

He glanced about, taking note of the shawl flung hastily over the back of a chair, her raggedy horse propped next to a stack of books, and her hairbrush and ribbons. "I see you've made yourself at home."

"I hope you don't mind." Fretful all at once, she worried she'd overstepped her bounds. Seeing the miniature portrait of her parents on the shelf filled her with such longing she wanted to cry.

"It's as much your cabin, Lily, as my own."

She flashed a brief and grateful smile. "Since Mulworthy is so intent to get rid of me..." Bitterness rasped in her words. "I suppose I should pack, but I can't seem to do it." If she could have chained her feet to the floor, she would have. "I won't go." Hands planted on her hips, she met his grim-lipped demeanor with a bold challenge. "Do you hear me?"

"Like a bell."

In a fit of anger, she seized her nightgown from the bed and crushed the fine cloth in her fist. "What am I to do?"

He crossed the room in three steps. "Lily, stop!" A hand settled over her wrist; the other uncurled her stiff fingers. Gently, he removed the garment and let it fall to the bed. He nudged her chin, holding her captive with his magnetic gaze.

"Marry me."

Her pulse quickened. Too stunned to speak, she simply blinked. Had he stripped her bare, she couldn't have been more shocked. Studying his face, she expected he would laugh at his joke. Oddly, his expression remained serious, even fierce.

He caught both of her hands and squeezed. She realized hers felt glacial.

"This sounds mad, but I convinced Mulworthy we're in love."

Cold skated up her arms, raced across her shoulders and coiled at the base of her neck. Frozen with fear, she couldn't utter a single word. He *was* mad.

"It's the only solution. Mulworthy means to see you off this ship. If you go with Dumelle, you'll never see New York."

Blood leached from her cheeks.

"Black Jack will sell you to the highest bidder. I daresay you'll garner great interest among the middle-eastern princes and sheiks."

"What?" Surely, she misheard. "He wouldn't. He couldn't."

"He can and he will." The pressure on her hands tightened until her bones ached.

"Is Black Jack a pirate?"

His gaze banked to the side, confirming her fear. She drew in a shaky breath.

"Marry me, Lily. It's the only way to keep you safe. Mulworthy won't deny us marriage."

No. No. Her head wagged back and forth. Unreality gripped her mind. *This isn't how a woman imagines a proposal.*

He tipped his face closer, his expression apologetic. "I realize how idiotic it sounds."

"Idiotic? This has the makings of a farce." *Perhaps a tragedy.*

"It will be a marriage in name only." His thumb skimmed the length of hers and despite the current craziness, sparked a pleasant reaction. "When we get to New York, we can seek an annulment or a divorce."

Annulment? Divorce? This was too much to absorb. "Why, Griffin? Why would you do this for me?"

His face reddened. Jaw set, he released her. "A million pounds wouldn't entice me to give Black Jack a flea-infested, howling cat, much less a woman."

"Protection? And no other reason?"

Only a fool would expect a heartfelt declaration of love. An act of chivalry and goodwill had prompted his offer of marriage. He didn't love her. Nor did she love him. Still, she ached with a clawing sense of disillusionment. Sadly, fanciful notions of pretty proposals and everlasting love were not today's order of business. Saving her life was.

"Mulworthy will marry us but we must hurry. What do you say?"

"A marriage in name only?"

His gaze slide quickly to the bed and back again. If

she was a puddle of emotion at the thought of marriage, the notion of coupling almost choked her airway.

"All right." The words rolled from her lips with so foreign a sound a stranger might have spoken them.

All the tightness in his face relaxed. When he smiled, it stirred a flutter in her chest.

Overcome with an array of powerful emotions, she ran a hand along a fold in her gown and patted nervously at her hair. Watching this, his face grew kind. "I'm sorry. These aren't the circumstances under which a woman expects to marry."

The tenderness in his voice warmed her chilled bones. For one brief moment, she almost believed everything would be all hope and light. As she searched his strong, handsome face, she recognized his earnest desire to help, and knew, at least in this regard, she could trust him.

He touched her elbow. "We must leave."

"Wait! Do I have time to change?"

He hesitated.

"What am I saying?" She felt ridiculous. "I don't have a gown suitable for a wedding." Disappointment swelled until she remembered. "I do have something." She swept toward her the washstand. As she fiddled with hair and ribbons, she watched Griffin, reflected in the wall mirror, unlock his trunk and sort through its contents. He slid something in his pocket before he relocked the chest and slipped the key into his coat. Finished tying the satin ribbon around her neck, she turned and faced him.

He stood quietly, his hands at his sides, seeming reflective. The discerning intensity of his gaze robbed her of breath. He moved closer and touched the tiny bow at her throat. It was a gentle gesture, nevertheless, it made her pulse jump.

"You are the most beautiful of brides."

She refused to cry, though hot tears threatened to spill. Unable to form a coherent word, she swallowed as a cacophony of emotions thrummed noisily inside.

Offering her his arm, he whispered, "Ready?"

Body a mass of trembling flesh and bone she simply nodded.

He opened the door and like a mama cat with her kitten, prodded her gently over the threshold.

Chapter Ten

Griffin paused outside the captain's door, his heart clicking much too fast. "Wait and see," he said to his affianced. "Things have a way of working out." *For the best*, he should have added, only his customary optimism seemed strangely absent.

Lily stared at the scrollwork above Mulworthy's door as if mesmerized with fear. Just when he considered he might have to carry her trembling body inside the captain's stateroom, she stunned him with the tiniest of hopeful smiles. The valiant effort unbolted a door into his heart and evoked an up swell of protectiveness.

"After you, madam." He offered a gallant arm sweep.

She fingered the bow at her neck, her throat working as she swallowed. Then she stepped across the threshold, seeming as prepared as one can be when faced with an impromptu wedding to a near stranger. A pleasant scent, a mixture of lavender and lemon, light and fresh, floated behind her.

Mulworthy, Church, Flint and Mead, enjoying refreshments at the table, hastened to their feet as the bride and groom entered.

Groom. The word sent a fluttering chill to his bones.

Even Laurent, a rich figure in ruffles, upturned coat

cuffs and satin breeches, stood with a pleasant yet curious expression on his broad-cheeked, Gallic face.

Dumelle, the last to lumber to his feet, offered a mocking sneer. In preparation for nightfall, several lanterns and tallow candles burned, reflecting a soulless glint in the man's jaded gaze. Lip curled, he made no secret of his annoyance at how the woman had slipped from his mercenary grasp. Griffin tucked away a satisfied grin, overjoyed to have snatched the prize from the pirate's greedy hands.

"Are ye still of a mind tae…" Mulworthy ticked his head in Lily's direction with a wince. When Griffin nodded without hesitation, the man, clearly resigned said, "Aye? Let's get started."

He flapped a thick hand, motioning them forward. The men gathered around and Mulworthy cracked open his Bible. Flipping pages, he found the select passage, raised his head and frowned. "Have ye someone to bear witness for ye?"

"Witness?" Griffin croaked. What an idiot to forget such an important detail. His gaze swept across the tiny audience, so erect and still. For obvious reasons he eliminated Laurent, Dumelle, Flint and finally, Church, whose choice would be cruel in the face of his lost opportunity to win the hand of the "lovely Miss Fitzhugh."

"Would you be so kind, Mr. Mead?"

The surgeon, his pince-nez halfway down his slender nose, dipped his sandy head in agreement. Formality thus settled, Mulworthy held the *Good Book* at arm's length and after licking his bottom lip, began to read. He stopped abruptly and frowned again. "Would ye join hands?"

"Oh, of course." More flustered than he'd been in years, he grasped Lily's hand and the shock of icy digits in his palm shook him.

Mulworthy exhaled a long-suffering sigh and started in again with the recitations. The words rasped on. They hummed in Griffin's brain. He'd considered marriage before and even proposed to Catherine Hawkins. In the end, she'd chosen Elliot. He didn't begrudge his brother's happy union. Nevertheless, the rejection hurt and left him wary of risking his heart. Yet even as he wooed Catherine, he never imagined how it might feel to stand before a clergyman and state vows melding one heart and life to another. The notion awed him and the enormity of it all left him almost breathless with anticipation and responsibility.

He regarded Lily, deathly pale at his side. If he didn't know better, he might believe she floated in the air like a specter with her wraithlike appearance. In the lamplight, her skin glowed with a shimmering luminosity. A beautiful bride, she possessed the kind of exquisiteness men stared at and wondered what it would be like to possess her. She was headstrong and proud, and so very vulnerable it made his heart ache.

Mulworthy carried on. "Do you, Griffin Alexander Faraday, take this woman to be…"

Given the sham of this marriage, the blessed words ought to mean nothing more than the lines of some theatrical drama, yet in the sanctity of the moment, Griffin was helpless to do anything but take them seriously. For the brief time they remained husband and wife, he would do everything in his power to protect her and give her some measure of comfort and happiness. But dear God, how would he make it through the next few weeks, sleeping in the same room with her, and not touch her tempting body?

"I do," he answered, both exhilarated and short on air.

"And do you..." Mulworthy paused and rolled a disgusting note in his throat before continuing. "Do you, Lily—"

"Amaryllis. My name is Amaryllis Charlotte Fitzhugh."

Laurent tittered, but his amusement died under the captain's disapproving glare. Mulworthy licked a thumb and started in again. "Do you, Amaryllis Charlotte Fitzhugh, take this man to be your lawful..."

She kept her gaze cast downward. As Griffin watched her breathing accelerate, one question circled in his head. *Are you out of your mind?* It was madness to marry, especially a British loyalist. Furthermore, the issue remained. Was Lily a spy sent to destroy him?

Mulworthy finished reading and glanced up, waiting for her answer. A moment, then two, elapsed.

"I do." Though spoken just above a whisper, the important words resonated as durable and real as a wall built of stone.

Mulworthy tapped his foot impatiently. "The ring, man. Have ye got a ring?"

Ring?

"Right." Amid a chorus of good-natured chuckles, he fumbled in his waistcoat pocket and produced a gold band.

Lily touched her throat. "I have nothing..."

"Hush," he whispered, grateful for the token in his hand.

"With this ring..." continued Mulworthy. Griffin

did his best to master his churning emotions as he slipped the ring on her slender finger. "I now pronounce ye man and wife." In the silent room, the words clamored in Griffin's head, louder than any church bell.

Man and wife.

For a second, he feared his lungs might burst. On a mighty exhalation, his chest cleared and he started to breathe again. Astoundingly, he managed to remain on his feet, even though at one point his knees grew wobbly. Shoulders drawn back, spine straight, he briefly glanced at the ceiling beams, and prayed life would go well for the short time he and Lily would share.

"Ye can kiss the bride," Mulworthy growled.

Kiss the bride?

"Give the lass a wee nip." A bushy brow cocked and his leering grin spoke of his enjoyment at Griffin's discomfort.

Heat flooded his body.

So rigid and still, Lily might've been a marble statue. Her gaze fixed on the dull brass buttons of Mulworthy's jacket. A rosy tint stippled her neck.

Look at me, Lily. Please.

At last, she turned to him—the sacrificial lamb.

With unsteady fingers, as though he had never touched much less kissed a woman, he cupped her chin, amazed to feel skin so unbelievably downy.

Scared and elated, he harnessed his emotions enough to dip his head and set to his task. Her warm lips were surprisingly pliant and shocked him when the kiss ignited his desire. Instead of doing the sensible thing and ending the formality with a chaste peck, he pressed harder. A hand dropped to her waist. He pulled her closer. Expectations he would act a part for the benefit of their audience fell away.

Everything except Lily dropped from his consciousness. He kissed her deeply, with feeling, wanting to give and receive. Her mouth moved against his, a tiny yielding, a push and pull of her lips. The scent of her filled his head. The slight weight of her hands on his shoulders grew heavier, holding him, and he wanted this moment to last forever.

In the background, somebody coughed. The spell broke. Reluctantly, he released her. Amid a hearty round of huzzahs and noisy clapping, two bright dots blazed on her cheeks.

****

At the boisterous cheer, Lily's face seared with embarrassment. No one had ever kissed her with such overt emotion. It was as though Griffin truly wanted to kiss her and enjoyed each second. In addition, to do so in front of ogling strangers added a bizarre twist. In spite of her initial reluctance, she couldn't deny the experience left her flushed and her breath unsteady. For a moment, she could almost believe in love, a place of peace, beauty, and contentment rather than this horrid ship.

She tried to step away, to put distance from these men, but Griffin held tight to her hand.

"A drink to the happy couple," Mulworthy announced, astonishing her with a sudden show of bonhomie and good cheer. A rare smiled exposed his stained teeth. He reached for a carafe from the china hutch, seemingly happy to play host. "There be just enough for drinks all around." Cackling like an old hen, he sent a sullen-faced Church for food while he poured wine into glass goblets he'd taken from a shelf.

Lily accepted the beverage, uncertain what to make of the ogre, who less than an hour ago didn't care if the thieving pirate ravaged her. While Dumelle no longer posed a threat, the glint and sneer of the tattooed man who skulked at the far end of the room jangled her nerves.

"Thank you, Captain." She took a sip, weak-kneed by the rapid turn in her fortunes. To think she possessed a husband, a man who vowed before God and witnesses to love and cherish her forever, left her reeling. Until they reached land and formally applied for dissolution, the marriage was legal.

Griffin also bore something of a stunned mien as he accepted wine and hearty back slaps. Color rode high in his cheeks and stained his throat visible above his cravat. Chin held high, his elegant stance was both authoritative and approachable. One would never suspect he had just married a woman he barely knew and didn't seem to like overly much.

As to his physical appeal, he was the most dignified and compelling of all the men present. Any woman would yearn for his acquaintance and friendship. He radiated grace and kindness, qualities far beyond his towering height that set him above Mead and Church, all men in their physical prime and attractive. She couldn't say if familiarity or comfort drew her to him, though he was the only one who made her heart stir.

Tenderly, he raised her hand to his lips, and with his gaze upon her, kissed her fingers. Her heart squeezed before it burst open with a sense of fullness. Tugged by an invisible thread, she leaned toward him, but stopped before she stroked his cheek. This wasn't love. It couldn't be. Despite his vast appeal, there remained the issue of him being a Colonial spy. As such, she couldn't trust him. In a few weeks, they would go their separate ways. Nevertheless, for his chivalrous offer of marriage, she would never forget him.

He kissed the center of her palm and in spite of all logic and sense, something bloomed inside.

Remember. A marriage in name only.

"Shall you sit?" He lugged a heavy ornate chair away from the table. A merry devilry flashed across his face. Alert to his sudden flirtatious mood, she slipped into place, resolved to keep her emotions under control and her attraction to him locked away. Yet his captivating presence wrapped around her, entangling her in a web she could not easily shed.

Bent at the waist, he brushed her neck with his lips, the pressure subtle yet explosive. She gave a start as a frisson of delight arched through her body. Her hand rose but stopped before she touched the spot where her skin burned.

What was he doing? He no longer needed to playact for these men. Under no circumstances would she allow him to ply these tricks when they were alone.

Across the table, Laurent watched every move and smirked. She returned a placid smile and questioned his sudden emergence on the ship. Why did he come by sea rather than board on land? Equally important, what was in those crates?

The men settled in around the table and drank heartily. They laughed and shared stories. Their voices strummed with a male vibrancy, all strength and deep tones, substantial as the earth, whereas she felt as rootless as a meteor flung across the night sky.

"May I say, madam, how happy we are to have a wedding on board the *Providence*." Mr. Flint's tonsure of curly hair stretched around his head, ear to ear, while the bald top glimmered with a patina of sweat.

Lily smiled politely. Given the captain's refusal to have women on board, it went without saying such a thing was unlikely to occur.

"Be careful of the man." Griffin leaned close as though they were co-conspirators—which in a way, they were. "It's rumored he can make a woman squeal with happiness."

"Oh, bosh." Flint colored, turning pink as a carnation.

"Gentlemen." Griffin stood and held aloft his wine glass. Somehow, he managed an air of resplendence even dressed in a sea blue frock coat with simple white linen tied at his throat. When the room fell silent, he caught and held her gaze. Candlelight flickered in his eyes along with something else…something sweet and tender. She pressed her curled fingers to her chest, aware of the heavy thump, thump. "A toast to my beautiful bride. May her days always be merry and—"

"And ze nights even merrier," joked Laurent who joined the men's jovial laughter. Even Dumelle, who lurked at the end of the table, grunted in a show of good humor.

Mortified and on fire, she snatched the glass she'd set aside earlier, hiding behind the goblet as the wine went down her throat.

Lit with amusement, Griffin took his seat and gave a reassuring pat to her fingers twisted together over her lap. Any comfort she might attain seemed lost to her.

Chortling, Mulworthy slapped the table, causing her to jerk. She watched in horror as he chugged back the last remnants in his glass. A scarlet rivulet slid down his chin. "Let's have another toast." Lips dewy and wet, he poured generous amounts of wine all around and hefted his cup in Griffin's direction. "Here's tae the groom, a gentleman who kept his head when he lost his heart."

An unfamiliar emotion, one she couldn't identify, flickered across Griffin's face. She wondered what he felt about all this and about her.

"Here, here!" The men drank with enthusiastic abandon. With an affable smile, Griffin joined them and appeared as if this debauched affair didn't disturb him in the least.

"Where is that confounded supper?" Mulworthy dragged the back of a paw across shiny lips.

As though miracles really did happen, Church materialized in the doorway, a tureen clasped in both hands. Sloane and the cook followed, laden with trays of steaming dishes. Mulworthy lifted a lid and noisily sniffed the contents with a rapturous gleam. "Simple but hearty fare. Compliments to the cook."

"Here, here!" Laughing, elbows bent, the raucous fellows tipped back more wine before they tucked into their dinner.

Lily sighed. How she wished for the peace and quiet of the cabin. Stomach soured by nerves, she picked at the beef, potatoes and pickled cabbage on her plate while pressure built in her head.

The men gossiped horribly. Griffin easily rebuffed their ribald teasing with clever rejoinders and humorous banter. In turn, the men guffawed even louder. Until tonight, she never knew how much she could blush. Clearly, the feast would end soon, probably when someone passed out. Just as she hoped the liquor would run dry and this debauchery would end, the captain clanked his empty glass upon the table. "Church. Ye best toddle off to the storeroom and bring us back some more of this fruity wine."

Her heart tugged in sympathy for Mulworthy's second in charge, treated like nothing more than an errand boy. Mouth clamped so tight his lips all but disappeared, Church ambled from the room.

The banging in Lily's head upped its tempo. No matter what calming words she fed herself, she couldn't relax. Whenever she longed for the tranquility of the cabin, images of the narrow bed bloomed in her mind and left her further rattled. *Remember, a marriage in name only.*

As if bedding down with Griffin wasn't scary enough, she had the nagging sense something wasn't solid about the delivery of goods and Laurent's presence. Any trade between a merchant vessel and a pirate ship was suspect. But a Frenchman delivered at sea?

"If you will allow my curiosity, Monsieur Laurent," she said. "The unusual means by which you arrived on board intrigues me."

For the first time since they entered the captain's quarters, the noise of cutlery and glass, and raucous conversation ceased. Everyone stared as if worms had fallen from the sky.

Griffin cocked his head. Disbelief colored his expression. Not until she'd spoken did she realize the irony of her statement. After all, she'd come aboard in the middle of the night posing as a servant.

Mulworthy's good cheer fell away. Once again, his nasty glower bore into her. Strengthened by wine, she didn't care. "One would think you might have boarded at Le Havre or some other French port."

Unhurried, Laurent set his fork to his plate and dabbed his mouth with a napkin. "It's not so uncommon to transfer ze passengers while at sea."

"It seems odd to me."

Griffin took this moment to press a bit of loose hair behind her ear. Ticklish, she drew up her shoulders. The fingers, which he rested on the back of her neck, were both pleasant and disrupting.

"I understand, Madam, your father is something of an inventor legend." Flint smiled encouragingly, waiting for a reply.

"Yes, he's designed..." Griffin gently kneaded her neck muscles. "Ah, he..." A shake of her head cleared her mind—for a second. "He's invented many things of practical use." How could she make him stop?

Mead said, "Your father also perfected a device for injecting medicine into the body."

Griffin flicked a finger lightly between her shoulder blades. As if stung by a bee, she shot forward. What was he doing?

"It's...it's been a challenge to make the needle point narrow enough for practical use," she managed to reply. Two of his fingers strolled down her spine, not in any hurry to reach the final destination—whatever that might be. Skittish, she almost wriggled away but pride stiffened her resolve.

"Yes, I should think so," the doctor murmured

seeming to reflect on the matter.

Griffin tucked one, two, and then all four fingers around the band at her waist and tugged at her skirt. She tried her best to remain calm. With a stern expression, she shot him a foul look with a clear warning to cease. When he smiled wickedly and patted her bum, her jaw dropped.

"Can't see why a man can't just swallow the medicine instead of being stabbed," Church complained.

Mulworthy rotated his wineglass, studying the swirl of the burgundy liquid. "Aye, *this* medicine works for me all the time." His leering wink so astonished her, she recoiled. The unexpected movement squashed Griffin's hand against the chair back and made the men howl.

With theatrical flair, he extracted his hand, stretching wide his long fingers, and grinned. "I shall be more careful next time."

There would be no *next time.*

In a flash, the men resumed their discussion of ships, the pros and cons, size and speed. As her shock burned off, she realized they'd cleverly overtaken the conversation. For the first time, they completely ignored her, which in itself was telling. What was it they all hoped to avoid?

Frustrated, tired, keyed up, she massaged the persistent throb in her temple and shoved away her plate. "Captain, is it customary to take on goods—"

"*Excusez-moi.*" Dumelle rose at the far end of the table. "I must take my leave."

Something like relief flashed across the faces of Flint and Church.

"I'll walk with ye," Mulworthy said.

Griffin leaned close, covered her hand and whispered, "I'll just be a minute." He was out of the chair in the next moment, a cocky grin on his face as he followed them.

At the door, Dumelle paused. He stared at her. Suddenly, she felt short of breath, as if he squeezed her throat. A laugh rumbled in his chest. "*Bon soir, Madame.*"

When he'd gone, the air in the stuffy room seemed to lift.

Out of sorts, Lily nevertheless managed to smile through another round of toasts. Before long Mulworthy returned and charged the air once again with his overbearing presence. Griffin followed, his smile directed only at her as he approached and reclaimed his seat.

She spoke softly at his ear. "I'd like to go to the cabin."

"I'll walk with you."

She dropped a hand upon his arm. "No. Stay."

"Nonsense. You're my wife." His lips came dangerously close to her face.

Her pulse raced aware of the recklessness of his seduction. It must stop. She rose from her seat and acted unaffected by his attention. The men stood in respect. She thanked them for their kind wishes.

"I expect ye'll be busy over the next days." Mulworthy smirked. Lily cursed the heat stinging her skin. "We'll no' bother ye. Take all the time ye need."

Flinch muffled a giggle.

Church raised his glass, seeming both wistful and hangdog. "To love."

"Hear, hear."

Chapter Eleven

A strange mix of excitement and caution rolled through Griffin as he followed his bride into their cabin. *Their cabin? Bride? Holy hell.*

The aftershock of stating vows and signing his name on the marriage document reverberated in his head. A quick shake did little to settle his mind. No doubt in time they'd figure out this temporary arrangement of husband and wife. Yet how could he act the gentleman when all he wanted was to touch her and take her to his bed?

A lit wall sconce near the bed and the candelabra on the table set the room in a subtle glow. Feeling like a stranger in his own cabin, he closed the door with a soft click. As if the sound tolled like a great clamor, Lily startled and swirled around. The action spurred a jolt of guilt for having alarmed her.

"No need to be scared." He hoped reassurance would lessen the fear she'd carried so visibly in her face and body since Mulworthy tried to fob her off on the pirate. "Upon my honor, I will see you safe."

Relief radiated in her tremulous smile. "Thank you, Griffin."

Enthralled by her spirit and beauty, he longed to sweep her into his arms and offer comfort and reassurance.

"Determination and a strong stomach..." He shot

her an encouraging grin. "It carried us through the wedding ceremony. And here we stand, hale and hearty."

"Just." Her lush mouth lifted in the briefest of smiles. "The marriage was quick witted on your part."

The compliment stirred a sense of satisfaction.

"I'll never forget your kindness."

He hadn't done it to win her praise. To ignore her need for aid would have been cowardly. Nor could he have lived with himself if she'd gone with Dumelle.

With his chin, he gestured toward the table. "I see the cook means to keep us fed and quenched on our most special night." Two bottles of wine, a pitcher of grog and a plate of cheese, biscuits, nuts and apples adorned the table. He uncorked a bottle, poured the burgundy, and after a quick sniff, offered her a glass.

"To us." He held his glass aloft for a toast. "May our time together be filled with laughter and joy."

As they sipped, she avoided looking at him and glanced at the trunks pushed against the wall. Finished with his drink, he pulled a chair for her to sit at the table. "Please. We're a married couple. Let's begin with a bit of togetherness." As he joined her, a laugh bubbled in his chest. The last time they sat across from each other, she'd been his servant. Now she was his wife!

In a serious vein, she skimmed a finger along a grain in the wood, absorbed in her thoughts. He wondered what was on her mind.

"Why did Captain Mulworthy allow a French frigate to come alongside?"

The persistence of her question on her wedding night, both here and in the Captain's quarters, left him stunned and suspicious. "You'll have to ask him."

"I tried."

He returned her direct gaze, admiring the play of candlelight in her pitch-black hair. Yet her bold questioning of the Frenchman had him worried. Naïveté coupled with an impulsive nature and a tenacity to probe spelled certain trouble. Spy or not.

"It's no secret to you," she said. "You know why the Frenchman came aboard and what was in those crates."

"Married several hours and already my wife reads my mind."

She was not amused. Rather, she studied him with grave intent, as if the answer might be writ upon his face. "You, as well as every man at our wedding, knew the real reason for Dumelle's visit. Why won't you tell me?"

If he told her the truth and she told the British authorities in New York, he could be arrested and hanged along with Mulworthy.

His sigh broke the festering tension. "This is a merchant vessel. It takes on goods. Neither Mulworthy nor I am about to forgo a profit simply because the goods are French, Spanish, German or from any other country—no matter what the popular political belief."

"You sound like a pirate yourself." Color rode hide in her cheeks.

At her poor opinion, he raised a brow. "I carry no marque of a privateer. There's a difference. I don't steal the goods. I pay for them."

Mistrust sobered her features. "And what sort of French goods did you buy today?"

"Lace."

She chortled. "I find that hard to believe."

"Ladies in the colonies are mad for the stuff."

Under her withering stare, he managed an implacable expression. "Let us abandon talk of commerce. This is our wedding night."

He caught her soft, indrawn breath. She gulped more wine. Was it fear or the excitement of a wedding night which so aroused her?

"This ring." She raised her left hand, inspecting the decorative gold band stamped with two interlacing vines. "Rather convenient of you to have one in your possession. I assume this was intended for a special lady?"

"At one time." He shrugged, feigning an indifference that had taken a year of frequent practice to master. The pain of Catherine Hawkins' rejection had been slow to dissipate. "The canny lady chose someone else."

"Oh, I am sorry."

"She and her husband are much better suited." His heart would forever bear the scar.

"When I saw the ring, I considered there must be a woman in New York. Someone you planned to marry upon your return home."

"No." It was pointless, even hurtful to state the truth. He kept the ring as a reminder never to marry. Fat lot of good the ring had done. Plans, even ones etched in metal, had a way of changing. He wanted no further talk of his personal life.

He tipped his head toward a hand-sized oval portrait newly stationed on his bookshelf. "You favor your mother."

She huffed a short laugh. "You don't think I resemble a cuddly bear?"

"If you refer to the old tutor, I'd have to say no." He smiled and held up his glass, signaling a toast. "To your father."

In silence, they both drank.

"Well, what shall we do to keep ourselves occupied for the next few days?" He tried very hard not to imagine the mischief two newlyweds, even pretend ones, might enjoy upon the bed.

As if a similar fantasy played in her mind, she drained her glass in one exhausting gulp and quickly set about refilling it to the rim.

An unfamiliar book lay upon the table. He flipped it open. "Logarithms?"

Staring at her lap, she brushed at her skirt as if to flush away dirt or wrinkles. "Papa will be happy I kept up with my mathematics in his absence."

"Is this what you do when you're alone?" he asked, incredulous. He knew so little of her.

"And reading. Mr. Church has been kind enough to visit me in the mornings."

Griffin rubbed his neck, prickling with annoyance. Already he acted the jealous husband. How pathetic. "Do you find Mr. Church good company?"

"He's excellent company."

The enthusiastic response further nettled him.

"He's an avid reader. We discuss literature."

"Somehow I would have suspected Mr. Church to whittle donkeys from whale bone in his spare time."

"Sarcasm, Mr. Faraday?" She cocked an inky brow grinning with such humorous abandon it pleased him beyond all reason.

"I will endeavor to be more generous in my comments...*dear*."

"How sweet of you...*darling*."

"However," he added, on the point of laughing. "As to amusing ourselves there are always essays on moral rectitude. And for the less serious, I've a good bottle of rum in my trunk and a passel of bawdy songs to sing."

"You jest."

"Not at all." Excited, he stood and circled once around the table, aware she watched his every step. At the desk, he paused and traced the spine of a book settled on a shelf. "Backgammon?"

"Yes, I'm partial to the game."

"And cards?"

She held open her hands. "What would life be like without a wicked game of cards?"

He grinned, feeling devilish. "And chess?"

"I adore it." She spoke in a breathy whisper the tone of which fueled his imagination. What he envisaged walloped him between the shoulder blades.

"And draughts?"

"I'm certain to make any man cry in shame when I defeat him."

Joy nudged at his heart. "Do you gamble?"

"Small coins." A mischievous gleam played across her face.

"Perhaps you'll allow me the opportunity to unload the change from your skirt pockets."

Her coy smile was all delectable innocence. "I'm available if you'd care to take a risk, though I hate to see a grown man thrash and wail when he loses."

"Wail? Never. So what is your pleasure?"

As she considered this with her brow drawn in concentration, her tongue skimmed along her upper lip.

A jolt of hot arousal slammed into him.

With a smug air, she leaned back in the chair, her confidence a sensual lure. She looked to him and said, "Chess."

****

"Will you do us the service of setting up the game?" Griffin placed a game board and a box of chess pieces on the table.

Happy for something to do, Lily began to lay out the carved wooden pieces. As he shrugged out of his coat, she found it near impossible not to steal looks at her tall partner. He loosened his cravat, slipped it from his neck, and let it fall over his coat draped on the desk chair. Dropping into the seat opposite her at the table, he focused on the arrangement of chess pieces while he undid the top of his shirt. The garment fell open to reveal a glimpse of a muscled chest sprinkled with the barest of hair.

Oh my. How beautiful.

Shifting in the chair, she forced her gaze to the rook in her hand, aware of the sudden warmth in the room. The tightness of her cotton stomacher pressed against her ribs and breasts. Griffin's apparent comfort in stripping off garments left her awed and fearful he might drop his breeches. In an effort to lessen her sudden shyness, she brought the wineglass once again to her lips, hoping the liquid might calm her nerves.

Married.

The fact unnerved her, even though the impromptu arrangement would end upon arrival in New York. Until she could obtain a legal dissolution, she remained chained to a captivating man who conducted business with a pirate along with those dubious snakes,

Mulworthy and Uncle Percy. Perhaps she might uncover evidence to prove him a spy. Then what? After his selfless act of kindness, could she expose him as a traitor?

Her brain pounded with a myriad of disjointed thoughts. To clear her mind, she gave a shake to her head, and dislodged the loose pins in her hair.

Griffin, resplendent and glorious, smiled. "Ready?"

Ready? No doubt he meant the game, yet she imagined his words held some greater importance. Was she ready for this sham union of husband and wife? In a matter of seconds, she had made a life-altering decision—a decision she hoped wouldn't torment her the rest of her days. Now, seated an arm's length away from a man who roused unfamiliar urges, her brain addled by wine, she feared she had made a terrible mistake. Yet what choice did she have?

Griffin studied the game pieces while he slipped the leather tie away from his hair. The chestnut brown hair fell to his shoulders, the curled ends so enticing she could scarcely draw her gaze away.

"You have the first move." He dipped a strong chin at the game board.

"Yes, of course." It required every ounce of concentration to ignore him in favor of her plan of attack. With an indrawn breath, she slid a pawn to a diagonal square. It took only a second for him to counter and set her off balance. Tilting up her glass, she sipped and the tangy liquid burned as it slid down her throat.

"Would you care for more wine?" she asked.

"Would you be trying to get me drunk?"

"Drunk? Never." She twittered nervously.

The man radiated more appeal than a roaring fire on a bitterly cold night. Her fingers itched to caress his face and trace the curved muscles in his shoulder. *Stop. Stop.*

A memory came to her. "We played once, when we were children."

"Who won?"

Disappointment stabbed at her when he had no recollection. "You won. I stewed about the loss for days and vowed there'd never be a repeat."

"Shall I start shaking in my shoes?" His saucy smile could decimate an army.

She slid forward a bishop. He countered with a clever play. In no time, they were in the thick of competition. Tongue loosened by spirits, she plied him with questions about his family and work. It surprised her to hear of his status as a published author. Not one to lose sight of her objectives and debt to Cecil Jones, she asked, "Do you write political commentary?"

"Fiction," he murmured distractedly. His long, blunt fingers traced the outer rim of his ear.

"Fiction?" The squawking tone should have been reason for embarrassment, yet the newness and unfamiliarity of her circumstances made her ill at ease and the alcohol clouded her head.

"Fiction only," he mused with his attention riveted to the board. "I use the time on these voyages to write." He sounded innocent of any ulterior motive. The daring transfer of his bishop brought forth a smirk. He lounged back in the chair, a picture of blissful satisfaction, and gave her his undivided attention just as he'd done to the game only moments ago.

Feeling much too warm, she widened the fichu

around her neck, exposing some skin. When his pupils flared at the sight, her breath hitched.

A moment later, his attention shifted back to the game board. As he concentrated on the game pieces, a finger skimmed absently over the cleft in his chin. It was sensual and suggestive, and she wondered if he was playing with her and creating a distraction? A silent voice cautioned, *look away*. Try as she might, she couldn't.

As she struggled to keep her wits intact, she laid her arm on the table. Her hand unexpectedly touched his. "Forgive me." Her voice cracked. Before she had a chance to pull away, he'd grasped her fingers. The heat of his hand bled into her bones.

"I am your husband. You may touch me."

Touch me echoed in her ears. How she yearned to touch and caress him, all of him. She tugged her hand away and severed the charged spell between them.

"A trifle more wine?" Her heart beat much too quickly. He declined. She topped off her glass.

"Does marriage to me frighten you?" he asked.

"No!" The word flew from her lips. "This is a marriage in name only." She cringed and couldn't understand why she'd brought it up.

"Is that what you want?"

She blinked in confusion. "Anything more would be foolhardy."

"I see." His face was unreadable. "Your restraint is commendable."

"Restraint?" She almost laughed at the absurdity because her self-control was melting faster than ice in a blazing sun.

Tired and dizzy, she closed her eyes but couldn't

escape the image of Griffin languidly stroking his chin.

A gentle hand upon her arm startled her awake. "You fell asleep," he said. "We can finish the game another time."

The light of the candelabra scampered like brilliant sprites in his hair. "Asleep? No, merely resting."

"Are you certain you wish to continue?"

A glance at the game fired her need to win. A practiced player, she'd set a skilled strategy. Spying her next opportunity, she made her move.

Griffin leaned forward. Face a mask of concentration, he studied the game.

The warm temperature in the room clung to her dewy skin. She fanned her damp face, short on air. When her head reeled, she grabbed the edge of the table to keep from toppling over.

"Are you all right?"

His concern, tinged with a honeyed tone, stoked her fevered state.

"Worry not." Blinking against the flickering light, she caught the gravity in his handsome features. She experienced the strangest desire to rest her head upon his chest.

The boat swayed with a constant rhythm back and forth and the effects of the wine sloshed in her head. Ladies did not get drunk. "I am no wady, I mean, lady." She'd said it more to herself than to him. Giggling, she waved for him to proceed.

For reasons she couldn't comprehend, his watchful pose stirred a desire to laugh all the harder. With a conscious effort, she managed to harness a minimum of composure. After suffering another minute of his scrutiny, he dropped his chin in his hand and set his focus on the game board. When she realized the most sensible choice for his next move, her stomach fluttered with excitement. She steeled her facial muscles to stone. On a sigh, as if he too recognized the inevitable trap, he took his turn.

It took all her control not to fly from her seat in glee as she slid the queen forward. "Checkmate."

He sat back, his face a blank mask.

"Well?" She smirked.

He exploded off the chair. Before she had a chance to react, he'd yanked her to her feet and thrust her against him. "Tomorrow? Backgammon?" His husky tone curled around her, exciting and dangerous. Tension rippled like a strong tide between them, rushing in and tearing away.

"Why not? I like a determined person."

Blood pounded in her ears when he dipped his head and kissed her. Bold hands traced the contours of her spine, ribs and waist. Had he not held her so tightly, her boneless legs would have collapsed. Tingling with pleasure, her hands grazed across a body composed of hard planes, smooth skin and silky hair. Hot and growing hotter, she heard a moan. Hers, she thought.

Scooped off her feet, head thrown back, she floated through the air as he carried her toward the bed. The mattress met her spine. She sank into the pillow. Shadowed by the candlelight, he loomed over her. His face wavered in and out.

"You, my dear, have had too much to drink." He backed away.

"No. Stay!" She reached out and grasped only air. The weight of the covers settled over her.

"Go to sleep," he whispered. His warm breath near

her cheek smelled of wine.

The sensation of his kiss to her forehead lingered long after he was gone.

Chapter Twelve

The jarring clang of a bell drove Lily from a heavy sleep. She sprang up with a cry of pain. Her head pounded. Then she saw him and fright spiked in her chest.

"Ohhh, no."

Griffin lay asleep next to her in bed. His naked shoulder, stunning for its beautifully contoured lines, stuck out from beneath a tangled sheet. The fingers of his left hand dangled over the edge of the bed. His rhythmic breathing sluiced, in and out.

Dear God? What had they done? A vague memory of a kiss last night excited a deep shudder. She'd been touched deeply by his chivalrous rescue from the pirate. Yet he stirred unsettling emotions she didn't want to confront. Sleeping together was very dangerous.

In spite of yesterday's trying circumstances, she was angry with herself for drinking too much wine. She tossed aside the few covers he'd left her, determined to crawl away. A stabbing pain in her skull put a quick stop to her plan. Moaning softly, she massaged her aching temple.

Griffin chose the moment to roll onto his back. Plop went a limp, heavy arm over her lap. She gasped and held still for fear of waking him. His bare chest expanded on a deep inhalation. A smattering of curled, fine hair feathered his curved pectoral muscles. Last night she'd been curious about what lay beneath his shirt. Now she knew.

The shocking novelty of a naked man in her bed flamed her cheeks. She licked her dry lips. However legitimate, the husband in her bed gave her scarce comfort.

His eyelids fluttered open and when he noticed her by his side, his head shot up from the pillow. "You're awake."

"Yes, I'm awake." It pleased her not to be the only one shocked by this new development.

"Good, good," he muttered, blinking as he took a moment to fully gain his bearings.

For the life of her, she saw little good to this arrangement. Mad perhaps? Definitely.

As he lowered his head to the pillow, his eyes smoldered with unmasked desire. It turned her insides to slush. Shy all of a sudden, she studied the sheet bunched in her clenched fingers. "May I ask what you're doing in my bed?"

"You mean *my bed*, don't you?" He grinned with that playful manner she'd come to adore.

She groaned and wondered how he found this predicament amusing.

"Headache?" he asked.

"Massive. A cudgel to the brain."

He grimaced in sympathy. "Stay in bed today. I'll see to breakfast."

"Remind me never to drink so much." Queasy, she settled a hand on her stomach and cringed at the wrinkled gown coiled about her hips. "Rather unseemly to sleep in the same dress in which you were married." A silk stocking bunched around an ankle. He must judge her so ill mannered.

He rolled onto his side and much too close for comfort in the narrow bed. Heat radiated from his body like a brazier. Head propped on an upraised palm, he watched her, appearing rested and relaxed. Perhaps waking next to a woman was commonplace and didn't shock him. The notion didn't please her.

"What do you remember about last night?" he asked.

"Last night?" A cold wind seemed to flitter across her shoulders and neck though it was warm next to him in the bed. "The wedding and celebratory supper." A drunken debauch she had feared might never end. "We came back here. Played chess."

"And me winning?"

"You didn't win," she shot back.

He laughed.

"You're teasing me." How easily she fell under his charm.

"And after chess?" Naughty innuendo infused his husky words. A quick flare of his pupils gave her an unexpected jolt.

"Must you make me spell it out?" Pride prevented her from admitting she remembered nothing except his kiss—a kiss she would never forget.

He nudged her leg playfully. "Come on, tell me." The languorous purr in his voice tickled like a feather drawn across her febrile skin. She closed her eyes in aroused agony.

The harder she tried to remember the more her brain ached. Quite frankly, she feared the truth. "I must have fallen asleep?"

"You did." He delivered the news in the same tone

used to speak of balmy weather. Her drunken behavior last night didn't seem to bother him. Abruptly, he sat up. His sudden energy joggled her already overtaxed system. She massaged her throbbing forehead and expected him to jump from the bed, eager to tear into the day. All she desired was an uninterrupted day, lost beneath the covers, oblivious in dreamland.

"I removed your shoes and tucked you under the covers." He produced a sheepish grin. "Sleeping on the floor near broke my back. Since you were dead to the world and I a practical man, I joined you in bed."

So they hadn't…He wouldn't, not while she slept. Relief gushed like a spring of water. She stifled an urge to chortle.

He brushed the covers aside and stood. Buff colored breeches clung tenuously to his slender hips. Yawning noisily, he stretched toned arms upward and touched the ceiling. The dreamy dance of sinuous muscles and tendons in his upper body made her body quicken. Barefooted, he padded to the washstand and checked for water in the ewer. "You can relax. Your virtue is intact."

Not knowing what to say to such a bizarre admission, she fell back on manners. "Thank you."

"I hope it gives you peace of mind."

"It does. Certainly." A convenient knock at the door saved her from further embarrassing discussion.

"Yes?" Griffin said.

"Sloane, sir. With hot water."

"One moment."

Griffin ambled to the door while she snatched the sheet and tucked it beneath her chin. Dismayed by her disarrayed hair and wrinkled dress, she imagined she resembled a strumpet who, for efficiency sake, merely hiked her skirts and got on with her business.

Griffin relieved the folded linen and water bucket from the kitchen assistant. The lad bobbed his head in a vain attempt to peek at her beyond Griffin's obscuring hulk in the doorway. "That'll be all, Sloane."

"I'll return with coffee and food, sir."

"Thank you." Griffin closed the door in his face.

"You do have your admirers," he remarked and set the items near the washstand. Without another word, he pulled on a shirt, tucked the ends into his breeches, stuffed his feet, sockless, into his black leather shoes and grabbed a coat from a hook alongside the door. Before stepping out, he turned and said, "I'll give you some privacy."

No, don't go, she wanted to say, but her lips wouldn't move.

****

Dressed in a fresh lavender and cream striped gown an hour later, Lily wiggled the hasp of Griffin's chest, frustrated to find it still locked after so many days out to sea. She wondered what could be so important and secretive he kept it under lock and key. Startled by a knock at the door, she snatched her hand away. "Come in."

Sloane stuck his strawberry blond head inside the gaping doorway, a grayed linen apron tied around his thin waist.

"More hot water, ma'am." A lad about sixteen or seventeen years of age toted a wooden bucket, the seams blackened with tar to prevent leaking. Steam from the liquid made his skin dewy.

She gestured to the washstand. "Thank you,

Sloane."

"It's Andrew. Andrew Sloane." His freckled face reddened.

"Perhaps you might answer a question for me, Mr. Sloane."

"I'll do my best, ma'am."

"Is it customary for a French frigate to come alongside?"

"It happens more often than you might think," he answered with a proud air.

"I had no idea ships did such a thing. What sort of cargo is exchanged at sea?"

"It can be anything. Wine, cloth, brandy, sometimes just passengers." He tossed water from the cleansing bowl out the window.

"And what did the French frigate transfer?"

He made to respond with a ready reply and paused as if the answer required great delicacy. "Ah, lace, madam."

And I'm Aphrodite. Even Sloane wouldn't tell the truth. Clearly, the entire crew saw her as an idiot easily pacified by evasive answers. They hadn't taken into account her status as the daughter of an eminent scientist. Empirical evidence mattered.

"And Monsieur Laurent? What of him?"

Sloane rubbed his hands down his apron and glanced aside. "What about him?"

She narrowed her lips, determined not to let the question alone.

"He's a lace merchant, ma'am."

"I see." Wondering if she'd ever hear the truth, she thanked him.

After he'd gone, she searched the desk again,

frustrated when she uncovered only the notes of a fanciful story about a boy lost in a magical kingdom. Did she honestly think a spy would be careless enough to leave incriminating evidence in his desk? There must be a better way to learn the facts.

She sank down at the table and dropped her chin in an upraised hand. Even if Cecil Jones didn't expect a confirmation about Griffin's secret activities, the suspicious events on ship and the men's caginess left her ill at ease. Something troublesome was going on, and to appease her ceaseless curiosity, she had to find the answer.

Another knock, this time a soft brush of knuckles, heightened her expectation. "Come in."

Griffin swept inside. His face brightened when he saw her. "All the men use one particular word to describe you—lovely. I have to agree with them."

A hand fluttered over the simple bodice of the gown. "A morning dress. Nothing fancy." The notion this selfless, generous man was a spy began to seem more and more ridiculous.

"Is that coffee?" He stepped toward the table.

"Yes. Breakfast, too. Mr. Sloane has been busy this morning seeing to our comfort. There's hot water in the ewer and bucket." She squeezed her hands together. "If you care to freshen up."

"Excellent." He shrugged out of his coat and tossed it across the bed she'd straightened earlier. "Don't wait for me. Go ahead and eat."

He grabbed his shirt by the back of the collar and effortlessly tugged it over his head. A slight undulation of muscle rippled his flat stomach. His upper body tapered to a narrow waist and the breeches hung low at his lean hips as if suspended by magic. She swallowed a flustered breath. "I'll step outside…to give you some privacy."

"Stay." He dropped his shirt alongside his coat on the bed. "Keep me company while I shave."

Her heart pushed against her ribs, urgent with a need to flee. She'd never witnessed such a private act. "All right," an unfamiliar voice replied, sounding much too calm.

At the washstand, he swung a towel over his bare shoulder and poured water into the basin. After stirring a sudsy lather in a cup, he brushed the foam over his chin and cheeks. He glanced in the mirror, catching her reflection. "You seem uncomfortable."

She cleared her throat, not certain how to explain what she didn't understand herself. "I've never watched a man shave."

The razor, grasped in his fingers, paused over his chin. "It's not such a strange phenomenon. Had you brothers, you would have seen a lot more than a man's soapy face." He flicked the blade expertly beneath his nose and wiped the suds on the towel.

She poured a cup of coffee, annoyed to see her hand quiver. "I would have loved brothers—one to chase away the bullies and a baby brother to fuss over."

"Have you experience with bullies?" Razor at his cheek, he watched her in the mirror.

She shrugged, unwilling to share stories of gossipy girls and the taunts of cruel boys.

"Brothers can be a trial, yet I wouldn't trade them for gold."

The notion of siblings and family settled heavily upon her shoulders. Envy for the family she never possessed always weighted her mood.

After giving a final wipe to the blade, he smiled into the mirror. "Good as new." Tapping his cheeks, he rinsed away the last of the soap. Face towel-dried, he selected a fresh shirt and dragged it over his head, his hands popping free at the cuffs. As he stuffed the fine linen into the front of his breeches, she dropped her gaze.

"Is there something fascinating on the floor?"

Her head snapped up.

Affable and fresh-faced, he shone with a sunny disposition irresistible as a dewy morn. "You might as well get used to me." He grinned with confidence. "We'll be seeing a lot of each other."

She cursed the heat creeping up her neck. The man recognized his appeal to women.

Pleased and easygoing, he slid into his seat at the table and peeked beneath the pewter covers. "Ah, eggs." Appearing delighted, he offered her a dish of fried ham. At her refusal, he doled food on his plate and tucked in—a veritable god at a feast.

"How strange to say you are my wife, and I am your beloved husband." White teeth sparkled as he grinned. "Once we go our separate ways, you're free to marry whomever you choose."

"For your considerate permission, I thank you," she mocked, stung with hurt. Why should she care when dissolution and separation from him was what she desired? "Since you're so eager to be rid of me, I'll compile a list of potential suitors as soon as breakfast is complete."

The man had the greatest of laughs, uninhibited and natural. Bright with amusement, he eased back into the chair and crossed one knee over the other. "No need to rush. The ink is barely dry on the document. We have weeks to go before we reach New York." He propped an elbow on the table. With his chin on his knuckles, he studied her with a singular focus. She shifted with discomfort. "For the time being, we are well and truly married."

The underlying message that she was his to love and to hold, at least for a while, conjured an agreeable feeling. It shot a glow in all the right places. Too often, as a lonely girl, living with Uncle Percy, and even living with a widowed Papa, she yearned for love. A simple show of affection was all she required. Even as a grown woman, she yearned for acceptance, which was why playacting at love was a dangerous game. If he knew what drove her to New York, if he knew how much she hungered for the reassurance of Papa's love, Griffin wouldn't be so cavalier about his teasing.

"We must play our parts," he added.

"Play at being loving newlyweds?" A vigorous shake of her head set off another jab of pain. "The *Black Dog* is long gone, and along with it, the threat. Since Mulworthy has yet to toss me in the ocean, I doubt he ever will."

Across the table, his strong jaw assumed a resolute set, reminding her again of the stubbornness of his character. "Mulworthy must never suspect I played him false when I told him of our love."

"What does it matter what he thinks?"

"It matters." He scrubbed a hand over the top of his head, pushing the loose strands away from his forehead. "The stage is set. It would be foolish not to act out our roles."

"What hold does Mulworthy have over you?"

"None except for my loyalty. In spite of his many faults, I won't break trust with him. I keep my word. You and I said our vows before witnesses. For better or worse, we are married."

He tossed a piece of crust on his plate and pushed it away with an affable smile. "What shall we lovebirds do today? Perhaps a walk around the deck?"

The rapid change in his mood threw her off balance. How was she to negotiate the next few hours, much less weeks, with this whirlwind?

A short while later, after they'd completed one complete loop of the ship, he asked, "What will you do when you reunite with your father?" A temperate breeze fluttered a loose strand of his hair. Unable to abide anything not in its proper place, she tucked it behind his ear and earned his smile.

"Assist Papa in his work." The notion made her smile.

"Like you did when you were younger?"

"More in the way of a full-fledged partner."

"You see yourself as an inventor?"

"I've studied mathematics and physics, disciplines which will further his work."

"Your uncle approved of such study?" He rested his elbows on the ship's railing and stared at the water glinting in the sunlight. "I'd imagined the art of threading a needle or the proper sequence in which to serve a fat goose—before or after the oysters—was his idea of a woman's education."

"Sssh." She held a finger to her lips. "He mustn't ever discover I bribed my tutor with a bit of coin so he might teach me. Uncle would have a fit."

"A unique gambit to secure a proper education."

"It was necessary."

"Do you always get what you want?"

She smirked. Blocking the sun with a hand to her brow, she caught his quizzical look. *Oh, blast.* He would persist until he had an explanation. "In truth, I seldom get what I want."

When his expression gentled, as though he understood, the brittle shell around her heart cracked. "I don't want your pity." The man had a sure way of breaking down her barriers. It left her exposed and vulnerable.

"Everyone has their share of disappointments and heartache. Why should I be exempt from misfortune?" She carried the deaths of Mama and Aunt Charlotte, and the absence of her father with her every day. "It's all in the past." She waved a dismissive hand. "It's too lovely a day to speak of gloomy things." How she wished the tree-lined shore of New York was on the visible horizon, anything to hasten their journey and lessen their time together.

"Lily."

The tenderness in his voice wrenched at her heart.

"Lily, anything you ask of me, I will try my best to see it complete."

A lump formed in her throat. Why was he so nice to her? People were seldom solicitous of her except when they wanted something. "You're too kind."

She cursed the sudden urge to cry along with the irritating confusion. After being selfish, rude and even calling him a prick, she didn't deserve his friendship. Yet, despite being a burden to him, he treated her with respect and kindness.

"When you marry," she asked. "Will it be for advantage or love?"

"Love, of course." The words sprang forth without the slightest hesitation.

"A romantic," she said and smiled.

He grunted.

"You don't wish to be a romantic?"

"My brothers and friends contend I fall in love too easily—a drooling puppy they call me where women are concerned."

She lifted a brow. "Do you fall in love easily?"

He cocked his head, his gaze steady, almost disarming in its boldness. "Not anymore."

Chapter Thirteen

"Aye, tha' does it for me," Mulworthy complained, and tossed his playing cards on the table.

Seated across from him, Griffin stretched back in his chair and worked the kinks from his stiff shoulders. Burning candles added heat to the stifling quarters. Whale oil in the lanterns spilled an unpleasant odor.

Laurent glanced up from the cards fanned in his hand. "Eet surprises me, *mon ami*, to see you when such a beautiful wife longs for your company, eh?"

Griffin rolled an unpleasant sound in his throat. The men didn't understand. Playing faro and whist in the captain's quarters gave him distance from Lily's allure. Despite the distraction of games and male comradery, she trampled his mind.

"My wife enjoys a few hours of quiet time...for prayer and reflection." His brows wiggled with humor.

Mulworthy grunted in disbelief.

In truth, it was anyone's guess what Lily did when she was alone. Each night and morning, he left the cabin, giving her private time for her personal needs. It would be madness to watch her in the act of undressing.

"Ah, much like my own mama." Laurent played a card. "Every day she prays the rosary."

Since the wedding, four days ago, his time with Lily had fallen into a predictable pattern. They acted out their roles as a married couple before the crew, they dined together, promenaded on the deck, laughed and flirted. To fill the hours, they discussed literature, science, history, and even ideas on child rearing. And each night his charming wife slept on the bed not five feet from him while he tossed and cursed quietly upon a pallet.

"Your wife is worried about the dark circles beneath your eyes and fears you are taking ill." Mead's stiff hair stood in tiny spikes on his head. "She asked my advice about restorative herbs to use in a broth."

Griffin smiled, recalling the hot mix she'd made for him under the cook's direction. Anxious to see him returned to good health, she'd fluttered around him like a mother hen, riffling his hair and setting a hand to his brow. At the same time, she glowed and appeared pleased at her culinary accomplishment. Her attentions contented him in ways too unwise for a man in his position. Little did she realize she was the cause of his poor sleep.

All too aware of her captivating magic, he knocked back the last of his brandy. Complex and contradictory, she acted brash and self-assured one moment and in the next, uncertain and short of confidence. Clearly life with Uncle Percy proved deficient in the most important elements—kindness and love. How achingly sad it was that she desired nothing more than the proof she mattered from a father too self-absorbed to care. Tough and sensitive in equal measure, she tugged at his heart in ways he never wanted and certainly didn't need.

"How long before we reach New York?" he asked.

Mulworthy tipped his head, thinking. "Two weeks, if the winds hold."

Griffin prayed Mulworthy was correct. The longer he spent in Lily's company, the greater the risk he would wake one morning a love-sick puppy licking her heels.

"Ah, you win again, mon ami." Laurent spread his cards on the table. "A better opponent could not be found." The Frenchman stood, withdrew a frilled hanky tucked in his sleeve and swiped it against his sweaty forehead. "Adieu, gentlemen." He bowed and yawned into his hand.

Mead gathered the cards and neatly stacked them. "I've reading to finish." He stood and nodded a polite farewell.

"I'll take my leave, as well." Griffin started for the door.

"A word, if you please, Mr. Faraday," said Mulworthy.

A cool undercurrent in his tone piqued Griffin's curiosity. Nevertheless, he paused, torn between a foolish desire to hurry back to Lily and Mulworthy's request. The Captain motioned him to join him at the table and poured another brandy.

"How goes it with yer wife?"

Griffin stiffened. He prayed the man didn't suspect his trickery about the marriage. "What, precisely, do you mean?"

"Dinna get yer knickers in a twist. Politics. Has she shifted to yer side?"

If she had, life would be so much simpler. "Her love for King and country remains unshaken. All my skill and willpower are necessary to act the Loyalist and not argue political points which would reveal my true beliefs."

Mulworthy pinched the bridge of his nose and shook his head. "'Tis a pity. She's been askin' questions about the shipment—an' about you."

A breath of cold air skittered across Griffin's neck. "To whom does she speak?"

"Sloane, Mead, Church. Anyone she has a mind to talk tae."

Griffin swore under his breath.

"She steps out alone."

"Damn."

"She's yer wife, man. Ye need tae keep an eye on her."

He'd tried, but exhausted from wretched nights on the floor, he'd surrendered to afternoon naps—an indulgence he would forgo in the future. His muscles tightened, affronted at the betrayal. She'd taken advantage of him when he'd been asleep and defenseless. Even worse, he'd foolishly lowered his guard and even thought his worst suspicions about her as a spy were unwarranted. Never again.

The Captain's beady gaze pounded into his face. "Disaster strikes if she talks to the wrong sailor. Ye ken a man can be bought."

Griffin snorted. "I should think there is little with which to bargain. You took her only money."

Mulworthy leaned forward, his gun-metal bristly eyebrows cocked in warning. "Payment for all the trouble she caused. Still, she has a few coins. Jewelry, too." He exhaled a foul breath. "A man canna ignore her obvious assets."

Griffin narrowed his gaze and dared him to continue.

"Och, man," he bellowed. "Ye ken what I mean.

She's flauntin' her looks."

"I don't believe it." If anything, she acted unimpressed, as if she didn't recognize or credit her beauty. She wouldn't exploit her attraction for personal gain.

"She hooked ye, dinna she? The men are dyin' for the feel of a comely lass, the smell of a woman, her taste…"

"Stop it."

Mulworthy's laugh was cruel. "Best keep the chit in line, eh. Find out what she's after."

On the table, Griffin's hands fisted. Lily made no secret of her curiosity about Laurent and the shipment. Now she was curious about him. What had he done to raise her suspicions? If she were, in fact, a spy sent to expose him, she didn't act alone. Someone more experienced in political intrigue, someone well placed in government or within the aristocracy must have put her up to this undercover work. Regardless of whom she worked for, she had tenacity and cunning. He would shore up his defenses against her sweet attentions. It wouldn't do to forget she'd managed to work her way onto the ship less than twelve hours after meeting him.

"Ye dinna want her tae ken about the guns, eh."

"She already suspects something is amiss."

Mulworthy sighed with weariness. "We'll hang if she can prove it."

"She won't betray me." The boast held a false note of confidence. He figured she'd go haring off to her father as soon as they got to New York. Perhaps even the British authorities. By then he and the guns would be long gone.

Griffin bid the captain goodnight and trudged toward his cabin. He considered how to question Lily without planting more doubt in her head. By the time he stood outside his cabin, a foul mood had him in a tight grip. No longer concerned about her privacy, he flung open the cabin door.

Lily?" The room stood empty. "Damn."

****

A soulful tune drawn on a fiddle drew Griffin toward the bow of the ship. The heaviness in the air suggested rain on the near horizon. Still, moonlight fell across the murky water. Lantern light spilled over four men hunkered around a compact brazier, their rough faces lit by the simmering coals. A lover of music, Lily stood at the rail, too close to the sailors for Griffin's comfort. He paused in the shadows, behind the main mast, keen to discover her objective.

The murmur of conversation floated over the constant creak and flutter of ship and sails and the repetitive slap of waves against the hull. Lily spoke to the men, but a sudden stiff breeze chased away her words. Then she laughed. Typically, he delighted in the sound. Tonight, it tore at him. She couldn't be so naïve as to think it safe to consort with these men. What drove her? Was she angling for more information about him? When Tubbs joined her, saying words he couldn't catch, Griffin felt a cold shiver up his spine.

"I don't wish to dance," she replied with a head shake.

"Sure you do." The hulking fellow held out his arms. "Just follow my steps."

Every muscle in Griffin's body tightened against the urge to rush ahead and bat away the man's hands.

143

Tubbs had every reason to despise Lily. A show of desire for her company meant one nasty thing.

"It's conversation I seek and not dance." Caution threaded Lily's voice.

Palms turned upward, Tubbs flashed a cheeky grin. "I'm all for obligin' *you*." The crude insinuation sickened Griffin. The sailor edged closer. "I'm good company," he boasted in a low rumble of improper intent. "The ladies all tell me so."

"I've no doubt," she replied, obliging his vanity. "It's only a bit of information I require."

The fiddler broke into a new tune. Tubbs gestured for her to step further away from the music. Lily foolishly complied. The two stood close enough for the man to grab her.

Griffin cursed silently.

"Are you healed since the flogging?" Lily asked.

A behemoth, Tubbs inched closer prompting her to step backwards. "Ah, don't be on about the past." He toyed with her and pretended she wielded the power when in one swipe of his massive arm, he could hurt her. Griffin's hands fisted, yet instinct suggested the sailor wouldn't act—not yet, not until he discovered what Lily wanted.

"How long have you worked on this ship, Mr. Tubbs?"

"Two years."

"Long enough to hold some position of authority."

Tubbs chortled with misplaced pride. "Not as much as some, but I manage."

"In your experience, is it customary while at sea to take on cargo and passengers from another vessel?"

The nerves prickled at the base of Griffin's neck.

144

Tubbs tilted his curly head, delaying his answer, as if reluctant. "The captain takes whatever business he can."

"What was in the cargo delivered by the pirate? Gold, brandy...guns?"

"Ssssh." Bug-eyed, Tubbs darted his head about and peered into the shadows. "I heard a noise."

Griffin suspected it might have been his gnashing teeth.

"I've a bit of money for your troubles, Mr. Tubbs."

The man's ugly scorn added more creases to his leathery face. "Took money from you once. You saw what happened."

"I'm sorry about the flogging. Truly. However, you needn't worry about speaking to me. I won't tell anyone."

"Oh?" Griffin materialized from the shadows. "You think to keep your spying a secret on a ship?"

Lily swirled around, her mouth a perfect oval.

Griffin kept his voice even, terse. "I've heard more than enough spoken between you two."

Tubbs glowered like a snarling dog.

It took only a moment for Lily to overcome her shock. "You...you..."

"Uh-ah," Griffin warned and forestalled any possibility of hearing a nasty epithet thrust at him. "Please leave us, Mr. Tubbs."

Anger rippled palpably through the man's taut body. "She owes me. For my troubles."

"Trouble you walked into with your eyes open and your pockets greedy. Now go before trouble comes again. Mulworthy won't hesitate to use the lash."

Tubbs bunched his ham-fisted hands into a

weapon. Griffin replied with legs braced apart, body primed to fight. He waited and willed his breath to slow while the man worked his lip, seeming to consider his options.

After a moment, Tubbs made a grating, dismissive noise directed at Lily. "Keep the money bi..." He caught himself before he made a serious error in judgment. To call a woman a bitch was so insulting, Griffin would have no choice but to crack his lumpy face.

"This is my wife." He spoke in a voice hard as iron. "You will speak to her with respect." He held the man's stony gaze. "Better yet, never talk to her again."

Unmasked fury flushed the sailor's skin. "Stay out of my way, woman." He jabbed a thick finger in her direction. When she flinched, pleasure lit his face. Before Griffin could throttle him, the ass stormed away, bypassing his speechless cohorts before descending below.

Griffin faced Lily. "You were saying, wife..." He managed to sound blasé in spite of the tension churning just below the surface. When she had the gall to spin away from him, he caught her elbow and snapped her about as if she were tethered to the end of a rope. His breath wafted out in angry waves.

Defiance stiffened her spine. She raised her chin. "I want to go below."

"Fine," he ground out between clenched teeth. What he had to say wasn't pretty. Best to deliver the words in private.

With an angry huff, she wrenched away and stomped off. He followed at a close distance, his body rigid as she swept down the ladder steps, pointedly ignoring him. The lantern light pitched the cabin in a subtle hue. Lily marched to the far side of the room, twirled around at the windows, and arms crossed beneath her breasts, glared at him.

Amazing.

Back to the door, he stood as far away from her as possible. Chest and gut tight, it took considerable effort for him to speak calmly. "Of all people, why Tubbs? You can't be so naïve to think he'd want to help you." Rape was more the sailor's style.

"I wanted to apologize about the flogging."

Unbelievable.

She'd sought information far more dangerous than the sailor's good graces. "You acted like the sweet lamb to a smiling jackal. Kind words of apology don't impress some men, no matter how innocent and appealing the apologizer."

She arched a dubious brow. "A matter familiar to you?"

He ignored her sarcasm. Rather than stomp about the room as he yearned to do, he advanced to the table. "Why is it so important to know what's stowed in the hold?"

When she didn't answer, he shouted, "Tell me."

Her nostrils flared. "Why should I tell you when it's you who's filled with secrets?"

His jaw fell, denial on his lips. "At the moment, only *your* actions concern me. You're a woman obsessed. What is it you hope to discover?"

Avoiding his gaze, she studied the planked floor then blew out a puff of air, rippling the wisps of hair at her forehead. "If I answer, will you answer a question for me?"

The girl intended to work him. A favor for a favor. *Incredible.*

"You aren't in any position to bargain."

She glanced away tapping her foot with a dogged stubbornness he couldn't bear. With a weary eye roll, he said, "You are so..." At his tone, she visibly stiffened. "Exasperating," he concluded drumming his fingers against the leg of his breeches.

"So I've been told often enough." Hurt rang in her words. She clasped her arms around her like a shield.

Sadly, the defensive stance would offer little protection. He felt churlish for caring. More astounding, he had an absurd notion to tuck her into his arms.

In fighting form, her nose lifted. "And you are—"

"Careful," he warned in a steady voice. "I don't want to fight. I simply want to understand your perplexing actions. If truth is so important to you then be truthful with me." It seemed ironic to expect her honesty when his work for the army disallowed him the same freedom. He snorted mirthlessly. "Do me the honor and trust me instead of some boor like Tubbs."

In silence, she skimmed her hands along the folds of her gown. With each breath, her chest rose and fell in a hypnotic rhythm, and he fought a desire to reach for her.

"Once," she announced and yanked him back to hard reality. "I told you of my persistence. It's a fault of mine, some would say. Yet, when a question sticks in my head, I need to find the answer—especially when those around me seem intent to hide the evidence. You see, I don't believe the story about the lace."

He threw up a hand. "You don't have to believe. It's not your concern. And what difference does it make whether it's lace, brandy, or bawdy trinkets?"

She sidled over to the desk, glided a finger around the edge of a book, seeming unaware of the effect she had over him. "Perhaps it makes no difference to you. Yet the truth matters."

His lips pinched. Damn the political circumstances that prevented his honesty. Yet it would be foolish to let down his guard again. Some truths came at a very dear price. Lives and the burden of freedom relied upon his discretion and secrecy.

"You solicit information about me. Why? Did Warwick put you up to this?"

"David?" Her brow creased with irritation. "Of course not."

Her surprise and offense appeared genuine. No, she didn't spy for her *beloved David,* he concluded and cursed the jealousy licking at his heart. "If not Warwick, who do you work for?"

Her lips parted in disbelief. "You don't understand me at all, do you?" Disappointment blazed across her face. "I'm inquisitive by nature. I like to probe and comprehend."

"A scientist," he muttered, skeptical of her explanation. "If you're so curious about me, why not ask me rather than query Mead, or Church, or God forbid, Tubbs?"

Color rose up her neck. Her gaze darted to the side where the desk sat. Seconds passed. "You're a closed book."

His molars ground together as he fought an urge to yank her into his arms. Intimacy was much more desirable between them than suspicion. *Do not touch her.* On purpose, he picked up an empty cup from the table, turned it in his hand, seeking distraction and a moment to refocus. "What would you like to know?"

Hands behind her back, she leaned against the wall, her bearing rigid as she probed and scrutinized him.

Jaw tight, he drummed the tabletop. "I work for my uncle in trade. I write. I've told you about my family. We've discussed all manner of topics. What more can I say?"

She sat upon the neatly ordered bed covers. "You tell me things you might tell any stranger."

The rebuke was a sharp prick in his side. Yet why be irritated when the comment was true? "So you judge my opinions and personal revelations as inadequate?"

"What a cruel thing to suggest. I am your wife. You can tell me everything."

Everything? She spoke with the certainty secrets did exist as though she believed he had things to hide. "A wife in name only," he countered, out-of-sorts and disliking the direction of the conversation.

"How can I forget when I hear constant reminders?"

"You set the terms of the agreement." What was he doing? To use one dangerous topic to avoid another was sheer stupidity. Recklessness drove him on. "Well?"

She tilted her head while a mix of unreadable emotions danced over her face. As if on the precipice of a major proclamation, she licked her lips. "Maybe I've changed my mind."

Something inside him jumped.

In the muted glow of lamplight, she gleamed with challenge, a coy allure that left him slack-jawed. Any reservations and doubts about her vanished in an instant. In answer to her invitation, he stepped toward her. When she flinched, he stopped abruptly. It was only the slightest gesture, yet significant in its meaning. "Ah," he murmured with a swell of frustration. "You don't mean it."

"Perhaps not." Her voice held a trace of defeat. She fiddled nervously with a strand of hair. "What can I say other than I am a stranger to myself these days—a constant wonder." Sighing, she picked at a pillow thread, her next words barely above a whisper. "My head is muddled when I'm near you."

Then stay away from me.

He considered winging it topside and leaving her to sort through her uncertain desires. Separation would serve them both well. He scrubbed a hand down his thigh. His restless muscles twitched with an impulse to touch her. He wanted her stretched out beneath him on the bed.

Hell and be damned.

He sauntered closer and the swift flare of her pupils, proof of her attraction to him, satisfied him immensely.

"Let's play a game, shall we?" Against her half-hearted protests, he tugged her to her feet. "It's called One Kiss."

One kiss was all he would ask of her. Ever.

Before she could utter another sound, he kissed her. She tasted of sweet wine and forbidden urges. Her lips were velvet in the sun. He teased her as a seasoned hunter toys with his prey. When her tongue circled his in a sensual dance, a pulsating charge tore through him. He drew her tighter against him, relishing the curves slipping beneath his hands. Fingers dipped inside her bodice and he knew a bounteous pleasure when she trembled at his caress.

A desire to lay her upon the bed and sink into her sweet body raged inside. Aware of his ebbing control, he tore his mouth away. Her mewl of frustration echoed his ragged breathing. Willful, beguiling, she gaped at him. Unable to stop, he came back for more. His mouth slid hungrily across the arch of her neck and nuzzled at the base of her throat, smelling and tasting.

"Lily." His voice rumbled against her hot skin.

"Hmmm?"

"One kiss and nothing more." When he released her, his hands were shaking.

Her lustrous hair curled at her frowning brow. "One kiss? What a silly game."

He skimmed his thumb across her rosy lips, tempted to taste her again. His body fought a battle to place hands on her in ways no other man on this ship would dare. It was wrong to tease and expect her surrender to passion when she was undecided and susceptible.

"Why did you kiss me, Griffin?"

Because I want you. He raked fingers through his hair and realized he'd lost its leather binding. "Because I'm weak."

"I don't believe it." She reached out a hand, paused and then dropped it at her side. "Is it weak to desire?"

He scoffed. "There's a right time and a wrong time. A man needs to respect the difference."

"Is now the wrong time?"

"It would be unwise to give in to passion. We are several weeks from New York and obligated to go our separate ways. It's what we agreed upon."

"Oh." She lowered her head. "I see."

A kick in the butt wouldn't be punishment enough for his behavior. Nor would it lessen his remorse when it came to a vulnerable and inexperienced woman. A man besotted with lust was the last thing she needed.

"Thank you for the reminder of our impending annulment."

The hostility in her words confused him. Surely, she understood and accepted the terms of their agreement. It was what she wanted, after all.

Face drawn, she picked up her nightgown from the corner of the bed. "I'm tired."

"It's late." He accepted the dismissal. "I'll leave you to prepare for sleep."

Still, he didn't leave.

There was an air of resignation as she lifted her hands above her head and removed what pins remained in her hair. Hypnotized by her sinuous movements, he stood paralyzed. His fingers twitched. He imagined what it would feel like to undress her. *No. No.* Opposing desires to stay or leave battled. Five lengthy, tortuous steps brought him to the door.

"Griffin." Entreaty and uncertainty flitted in her voice.

He paused, focused on the door, his hand gripped around the knob like a lifeline.

"Good-night, Lily."

Chapter Fourteen

Griffin scrambled up the stairs and burst onto the deck with a gulp of air. He grasped the railing and bent at the waist, exhaled a noisy, fractured breath.

One kiss? Was he harebrained enough to think one kiss would satisfy? He wagged his head in disbelief.

What right did he have to dally with her affections with asinine kissing games when committed to the military? Besides, her heart belonged to another.

A second headshake failed to purge her from his mind. The tilt of her mouth, the silky texture of her skin and the sound of her quickened breaths remained alive in his senses. He grunted with a pitiful laugh. When it came to women—he *was* a fool, especially where she was concerned.

How ironic. When he most wanted freedom from females, a captivating woman like Lily burst into his life. The very proximity of their close quarters commanded his time and attention. To ignore her was impossible.

He pinched the bony ridge above his nose. From the start, he knew the shared cabin arrangement would be a trying experience. Never did he expect bloody torture. A cat o' nine tails spun with sudden appeal. How much fortitude and resilience did she think he possessed?

Elbows planted on the teak rail, he dropped his

head into his hands and prayed for gusty winds to hasten a quick end to his journey and struggles. Yet the air seemed uncommonly still.

For his own safety and that of his mission, he would keep her in sight but at arm's length. Not an easy feat to accomplish when he was a man starved and she a tempting meal.

Nor could he overlook her spying. If she expected him to view reckless and blatant nosiness as simple, innocent curiosity, she was mistaken.

As to his evasiveness? War forced men to vile actions.

Breathing deeply, he hoped the briny smell would override her appealing scent. It didn't work. To repel her magic hold, he concentrated on his assignment for Washington. It took considerable effort. Time hobbled by like a creaky old man with a cane. Just as he deemed his efforts a success, the first cool drops of rain splattered his face.

Outside Mr. Church's door, he paused, swiped the moisture from his forehead and dried his hands on his breeches. Perhaps a night with the assistant rather than a temptress would aid his sleep. A cowardly notion, for certain, and the gesture would raise snickers and questions among the men he preferred not to answer. Impetuous and determined, she couldn't be trusted. Nor could the crew be trusted around her.

He walked on and entered his cabin. A single candle burned on the desk, half its stubby length melted. Quietly, he crossed the room and came to an abrupt stop. A picture of innocence, Lily lay asleep on the floor, covered by a blanket, her cheeks pink and pretty. Her hair fanned over the ivory linen of the pillow like an ink spill over parchment. Oh, Lily. After he'd so callously toyed with her affections, she'd sacrificed her comfort and slept upon the pallet so he might enjoy a decent night's sleep on the bed. If she meant to sway him by her goodness, this was the way.

A host of conflicting emotions tugged at him, guilt being the most prominent.

He crouched down, slid one arm beneath her knees, the other about her shoulders. As he scooped her from the lumpy mat, she whimpered and rubbed her cheek against his shirt. Once he'd settled her upon the bed, he drew the coverlet up to her shoulders. Behind closed lids, her eyes twitched. He wondered if she dreamt of Warwick. Was it vanity or foolishness to hope she might dream of him?

****

A drumming sound woke Lily from a heavy sleep. Groggy, she pushed up on an elbow and squinted at the window. The noise was not a woodpecker as she'd dreamt, but rain. It hammered against the ship and the glass of the port hole left open last night. Griffin must have closed it.

A shadowy memory emerged. Strong arms carried her to bed. The floor revealed a tangle of blankets heaped upon the empty pallet. A melon-sized depression in the pillow remained where Griffin had laid his head. How ironic. In doing him a kindness and taking the pallet, she found herself in bed. Though why she should have cared about his comfort when he trifled with her affection she couldn't say. He was a puzzle. A crafty man who reeled her in like a fish only to toss her away just as easily.

She shoved a couple of feather pillows behind her

back, aware of the many emotions he evoked. Lust. Joy. Happiness. Then again, was she merely obsessed, as he had accused? Whatever the answer, he roused emotions never before experienced and she yearned for more.

As much as she didn't understand him, she didn't understand herself. At times, when they laughed or shared a companionable silence, a fanciful wish they might remain husband and wife stole into her mind. However, when she found herself growing closer to him a wall appeared, and it was as much her construction as his. Adept at hoisting shields, she knew the safety offered by protective barriers. Yet Griffin was by far the greatest master at deflection. With his clever wit and easy conversation, he fooled people with his open friendliness. No one doubted his appeal, but behind the charming demeanor was a man skilled at holding folks at arm's length.

She twiddled a lock of hair around a finger, recalling the ridiculous kissing game. The daring sport risked the possibility of an aftermath neither of them wanted. She'd seen his hands tremble and heard his ragged breathing. The hardness of his desire had pressed against her, igniting heat. Yet in a show of strength and reason, he'd backed away.

"Bah!" How could a man exert such beastly control over his emotions? Perhaps he feared passion would bind them forever with a child. Maybe he found her lacking, much as Uncle Percy did. "Fool," she muttered irritably and vowed to see the situation in a more pragmatic light. Ever the gentleman, Griffin noticed her uncertainty and simply refused to take advantage. A good thing he had, too. Passion had no business in their impermanent arrangement.

From now on, she'd maintain a proper distance. Under no circumstances would he ever suspect how much his retreat hurt.

****

Griffin trudged back to his cabin, waterlogged from too much coffee and unable to offer any plausible reasons to linger further at the captain's table. All morning rain pelted the ship. The relentless storm showed no sign of abating. With nowhere else to go, he was stuck with Lily. Despite all sense, it was in his mind to take her to his bed and while away the remainder of the day.

Silently, he cursed.

Nitwit.

Hadn't he learned his lesson? He could no more touch her and come away unscathed than if he'd cradled hot coals in his hands.

Paused outside their cabin door, he steeled himself before he rapped lightly. When she responded, he stepped inside, his shield in place.

In position at the far side of the room, she stared out the port hole, her back to him. Dressed in a simple gown of periwinkle with ivory lace at the cuffs, she made a satisfying picture. He liked her even more for her simplicity.

"Good morning, wife." He couldn't understand why he insisted on using the term. It was pointless to address her as such. She would never, and could never, be his wife in the full meaning of the word.

As if reluctant, she faced him. She gave him a wary appraisal. "Griffin."

Consumed with an urge to caress her ivory skin, he strolled toward her, as if bound by an invisible force, each step purposeful yet unhurried. He set the apple beer he carried on the table. "Pray, do tell what fascinates you outside the window?" A nervous tremor vibrated in his voice. After numerous occasions spent with desirable women, it confused him why she, above all others, tested his confidence.

"Sea monsters." She turned and put her back to him, her focus once again the endless gray skyline. "I'm compelled to search for them."

"You do realize they're only myths?" He slid in behind her and stopped when the hem of her dress brushed against his ankle. "Besides, what can you possibly see in the rain?" Lavender and citrus clouded around her. He dipped his head, tracking the subtle odor to the hollow below her ear.

"I may never find one, but I won't stop the search." A wistful, almost aching tone lurked in her voice.

"Would you be disappointed if you never saw one?" He wondered if she would always search for things just beyond her grasp, even notions as fanciful as sea dragons.

He rested one hand on either side of the port hole, cocooning her in the center of his arms. She stiffened. Up came her shoulders before she spun around.

"May I ask what you're doing?" She nudged him away, hands firm against his chest.

He raised his palms in defense, laughing. "All right. If distance is what you seek, distance is what you shall have."

"Good. As to another matter…about last night with Tubbs." There was no mistaking her gravity. "I wish to apologize."

"It's finished. Consider it our first argument as a

married couple." A reassuring smile did not garner a return pleasantry. Instead, she tugged fretfully at her bottom lip with her teeth. He found it impossible to look away.

"There's more I need to say."

Her odd mix of regret and grit gave him pause.

"Any romantic notion, including kissing, seems unwise." She gave him a firm look as if she intended to hear an argument.

"What you say has merit." Part of him disliked her single-minded show of reasonableness.

"In view of last night," she added, "it's best we continue our roles in public. But when we are alone, we must remain uninvolved." Firm resolve tarnished her kind smile.

"I couldn't agree more," he replied pleasantly despite the petulance curling under his skin.

"Excellent." Fast as a rabbit, she slipped around him just as someone knocked.

He faced the door, irritated by her quickness to put distance between them. "Enter."

Sloane hefted a wooden tray loaded with dishes into the room. "Cook outdid himself with an early luncheon today." Bright with pride, he set the goods upon the table and off-loaded a tureen, bowls, cutlery and a hunk of bread.

"Thank you, Mr. Sloane. I'm sure it will be delicious." Lily smiled prettily, and the man's expression softened like melted butter. Griffin couldn't fault Sloane or Church, who acted like love-struck idiots when they gazed upon the lovely woman. On a tedious, lengthy voyage, even a foul-breath hawk-nosed hag would command the crew's febrile imagination.

Lily sparkled as incandescently as a star. Healthy and vibrant, she was a perfect flower with her graceful posture, fine bones and hardy laugh. She smelled wonderful, too.

"That'll be all," Griffin remarked harsher than necessary.

Sloane colored and slid the emptied tray under an arm. "Good day to you both."

When he'd gone, Griffin gestured for her to sit. "Please." He held a chair and she slid into it. Along with Church and Sloane, his desire for her remained as fundamental as a need for food and water. His standard of behavior would have to rise if he hoped to display more manners and control than the lust-crazed crew.

After she'd ladled the steaming concoction in each of their bowls, she sampled a bite. Her eyes closed, her face beamed in rapture. "Hmmm." Satisfaction purred in her throat like a petted cat and stirred his wish to stroke her hair and shoulders.

"I'm glad you enjoy it." His voice sounded raw and for both their sakes, he would not give in to his base urges. As she gleefully gobbled another bite, he joined her in the repast. "It *is* tasty." A flavorful burst of thyme and rosemary mingled with the tender meat.

Her light laugh conjured the sweet middle notes of a violin. "You must think I have no manners." The piece of bread she dipped into the stew disappeared into her mouth.

"No. No. A meal should be a..." He hesitated to state the obvious. "A sensual experience. Enjoy all you like."

Smiling agreeably, she broke off another crust of bread. "What I enjoyed is your *Mr. Picking's Guinea.*"

"Oh?" He'd given her the story to read yesterday morning. "I worried it would bore and put you to sleep."

"It's very humorous."

He cocked a dubious brow. "It's an essay on virtue."

"Now that you mention it…" Her eyes danced. "The young boy in the story is quite virtuous. No doubt he was modeled after you." She compressed her lips, trying not to laugh.

"The child's a troublemaker."

A light snort conveyed her disbelief. "Surely you weren't a bad boy. Who would dare punish you?"

"My father…" He shivered with exaggerated drama. "Brutal, he was."

"I don't believe it."

"And there was Cook. I couldn't keep my grabbers away from her ginger cookies or her apple pies."

"Apple pies? I shall make a point to remember." She hitched her brows, playful and light-hearted, filling him with joy.

"And who could forget the sadistic teachers." He ripped of a hunk of bread.

"Oh, pooh. You can't mean my father."

He took a moment to think on the matter. "You're right. By the time Henry Fitzhugh agreed to tutor me, I'd figured it was in my best interests to understand my studies."

"If I recall correctly, familiarity with the material was not always the case."

He sighed noisily for effect. "Leave it to the little tutor to remind me of my shortcomings."

"*Little* tutor?"

"Elliot and I called you Little Tutor. I lived in fear one day you would jump upon the desk and shriek like a rooster. I would have been mortified to cry in front of you."

"Bosh." She pouted in a playful manner and triggered another desire to kiss. "Surely I didn't terrify you?"

Griffin chuckled. "You were so earnest in your duties."

"I liked helping Papa."

"And thus earned his approval?"

"You make me sound so desperate and needy. My father is a good man. He loves me."

In a flash, her gay mood disappeared. Her expression went slack. Shoulders drooping, she stared into space and absently traced the handle of her spoon.

Damn the man who'd caused her such unhappiness. No longer hungry, he pushed away his half-eaten food. Maybe a story would help cheer her. "I remember a rainy day when Elliot and Rebecca were playing in the kitchen. Cook told them to stop but they disobeyed. Rebecca lobbed a rag ball to Elliot, who reached for it and missed. It landed in a golden, crusty pie Cook had just taken from the oven."

"Oh, no." She pressed her fingertips to her lips.

"In one moment of sheer anguish, the pie toppled to the floor. Apples, crumbs and juice mingled with the broken crockery. And who should walk in just then?"

She sat forward in her chair. "Your mother?"

Griffin smiled ruefully. "She could be fierce but it was the big man himself who marched in. 'Well,' my father barked. 'What have you to say?' Elliott went white, and Rebecca shook like a sapling in a stiff gale."

He smiled, pleased to have her complete attention. "I worried Rebecca would purge her breakfast and Elliot would faint. I couldn't stand to see it. Before I could stop myself, I'd confessed." Even after all these years, Griffin still found his action unbelievable.

"You protected them. Why?"

He shrugged. "It was for Rebecca's sake. She was so young. Elliott, almost five years older, should have realized the risk."

"What happened next?"

"For the next week, Elliott and I mucked out the stable. It was one of the hottest weeks of the summer. You can imagine the stench and flies." He made a sour face much to her amusement. "I hated Elliot for being such an idiot." He grinned. "So you see, even virtue has its pitfalls."

Her laughter spun notes of heaven. Suddenly his long-ago punishment seemed worthwhile.

"How precious," she said, all gaiety and light. "You do have the knack for amusing tales. I can see why you're a writer."

Any compliment from her was a gift.

She dropped her chin in her hand, suddenly serious. "Do you ever write about the conflict in the Colonies?"

Not this again. For sound reasons, he couldn't reveal his political commentaries written under the pseudonym of Fairley. "A person foolish enough to pen political opinions is likely to get tarred and feathered."

"Tarred and feathered," she scoffed. "What savages these radicals are to treat a man so. David and Uncle Percy often talked of the horrific crimes committed by the rebels—the destruction of property, the treasonous lies. Those so-called patriots have no regard for the law."

Griffin's fingers squeezed tighter around the pewter cup as he scrambled for a suitable response to maintain his cover.

"I've read pieces in the broadsheets," she said before he'd found his voice. "One writer wrote so eloquently about the rights of man, even suggesting all men should have equal rights under the law." She wiped at the glistening remnants of stew with a piece of bread. "I've never been treated as an equal. Imagine the day a man sees a woman his equal." She sighed wistfully. "Wouldn't it be a world to embrace?"

Her grace and sensitivity rendered him speechless. A lover of women, he cherished and respected them. He would do anything to see a woman cared for and protected. Why any woman would want the demanding trappings of a man simply puzzled him.

"There's a revolutionary slant to this author's writing." Her knowledge of political writers surprised him. "He even hinted that the King is a tyrant. Called him a silly popinjay." She pushed away her bowl and gave him a direct look. "G. A. Fairley is the writer's name."

Griffin's heart stopped. A moment later it kicked in with alarming speed. Could she have guessed he wrote under the name of Fairley? He did his best to assume a bland expression. "No doubt the man is intelligent and amusing."

"Oh, he is." A canny smile played at her lips. "Very amusing."

Her sudden intense scrutiny, as if she might see through his façade made him twitchy. The woman was too clever by half. He held her gaze, determined to have no further cloak and dagger intrigue between them today.

Chapter Fifteen

In the dead of night, Griffin woke with a start upon the pallet, senses instantly alert. Moonlight filtered through the windows. The snick of a door latch reverberated in his head. Perhaps it was a dream, and he'd imagined the sound. Instinct warned him the noise was all too real. His body tensed. Something was wrong.

He bolted to his feet and patted the bed mattress. Dread flared in his chest when, absent a body, he touched only the coarse weave of tangled sheets. "Lily?" he cried though he knew she'd gone.

At the desk, he reached for the lantern and found she'd taken it. Fumbling in the semi-darkness, he tossed a shirt over his head, jammed feet into shoes and unlocked the trunk. When his fingers grazed smooth metal, he grasped the revolver, stuffed it into his waistband and fled the room.

The deck bell clanged two times. What caused a woman to wander about a ship at this hour of the morning? Surely, she realized the danger.

Maybe she couldn't sleep and sought fresh air topside. He moved faster, worried she intended to meet someone, even after the debacle with Tubbs. As he planted one foot on the ladder rung to climb to the main deck, he noticed a light bobbing off to the side. A boy clad in a loose shirt and breeches carried a lantern. Not a boy. Lily.

About to call out, he held back choosing to follow her. The light hollowed her face in strange planes and shadows. Had he not recognized her, he might have considered her a skeleton or wraith that haunted the ship at night. Hungry, he concluded, when she disappeared into the galley. Seconds later, she reappeared in the doorway. When he saw a lethal butcher knife in her hand, the hair at the back of his neck rose. A moment later, he lost sight of her when she descended...

Dear Lord. No!

Pulse thudding, he crossed swiftly to the cargo entrance and paused at the opening. A light flared below some distance from the base of the steps then trailed into darkness. The hold held the mustiness, vermin and stink of the ship. During the day, the stench could make a man swoon. At night...when the rats hunted...

Soundlessly, he slipped down the ladder as agilely as a squirrel scampered across a tree trunk. At the vile smell of rotting garbage, damp wood, tar and the general reek of the bilge, his nose twitched.

Through a central walkway, Lily swung the lantern in a broad arc that illuminated the stored cargo of barrels and casks. Light bounced off the ceiling. A rat skittered across her path but didn't stop her. When she found the gun crates, she set the lantern on the tallest stack. Using the knife, she began to force a corner of one of the crates.

He swore but focused on her task, she didn't hear him. He raised his voice. "Don't move."

She whirled around. The knife pointed inches from

his gut. With savage fury, he snagged her wrist. "Give it to me."

They struggled. In the next instant, she stilled. Her fingers spread wide. The knife clattered to the floor.

Scowling, he released her, and kicked the knife aside. "Why, Lily? Why?"

She massaged her wrist while anger marred her face.

"After last night...I'd hoped you were quit of this obsession."

"Not quite."

"Explain yourself," he spat, snarly and livid.

Her mouth compressed.

He could almost see her mind as it tossed about explanations, perhaps selecting a misdirected snippet he might swallow in tasty bites. "Talk, for I'm in no mood for silly games." Legs wide spread, he jammed hands to hips. Somehow he resisted an urge to shake her by the arm and jiggle some sense into her. "I want the truth."

"Truth," she jeered. "No one on this ship cares about the truth except *me*."

Color rose up her neck. How pitiful that even in a fit of temper, she beguiled him. Clearly, obsession gripped them both. He was hooked on her, while she suffered from an inexhaustible search for evidence to prove them all liars, and worse, treasonous villains. He squeezed his hands tight. The nails bit into his palm.

"Talk or I'll have you fixed in the bilboes."

"Bilboes? You mean wrist and leg irons?" She made a rude, dismissive sound. "This isn't your ship. You have no authority."

Biting hard, he swallowed a harsh reply. Though foolhardy in her riled state, he laid a hand on her shoulder, near her neck. The pulse in her throat knocked a steady patter against his thumb. Touch me. Touch me he imaged it beckoned. He choked back a groan and silently cursed his body for wanting her.

"Why, Lily? Why won't you stop?" Her single-minded determination, one that might sadly be the death of her—or him—left him baffled. "You must realize the risk of coming here alone. What possessed you to do such a foolish act?"

She shoved ineffectively at his hand.

"Any sailor could have taken you."

She jerked away, damning him with her cold, flinty eyes. With the toe of her shoe, she nudged the knife. "This would scare away any man."

"Yes." His mocking tone tasted bitter on his tongue. "No doubt you've sliced a cake or two in your time. Don't delude yourself you're prepared to stab a man."

Her expression would have withered the stoutest of men.

Though aware of her objective, he felt compelled beyond all reason to ask. "What do you hope to find sneaking around in the middle of the night?"

She glanced at her clasped hands held so tight the knuckles gleamed with a sickly yellow.

Every muscle and fiber stretched taut. He wanted to throttle her. "Tell me!"

"All right." The blare of her voice echoed in the cavernous space. After she'd inhaled several deeps breaths, she spoke in a quieter voice. "Had I ventured here during the day, I would have been turned away."

After the men had taken their pleasure, he thought, sickened by the notion.

"I want to understand what is so hellfire important a pirate ship delivers goods at sea?"

"And you risked your neck to enter this hellhole to find it?" He wagged his head in both pity and disbelief. "Did you think the garments of a boy would garner you safety?"

She shrugged.

"Will nothing stop you when you have it in your mind to get your way?"

"It's said the truth shall set you free."

He stared at the hewn beams overhead and prayed for patience. "No Bible quotes. Please."

"I realize my behavior seems foolish and reckless." For once, she had the decency to act chagrined. "If you would be honest with me, there would be no need to skulk about."

"Oh? So *I'm* to blame for your irresponsible stroll in the hold?"

Her nostrils flared, and her chest rose and fell with rapid breaths, stirring his blood. He was besotted and hated it. "Tell me, wife. Is it my fault you won't accept the facts?" Unable to contain his agitation, his fingers tapped restlessly against his thigh.

"As I said before, *husband*." She ground the word like a spider beneath her shoe. "I don't believe these crates are filled with lace." A chin thrust dared him to disagree. "If you'll allow me to search, I can prove it."

An exasperated breath rushed out. "I'll say this again. It is no concern of yours if these crates are filled with watermelons or gold ingots."

"What can it hurt if I look?"

"Aye. What harm can there be if the lassie has a wee peek?"

Griffin spun around, heart in his throat. A cold sweat broke across his brow.

Mulworthy stood in half shadows, a candle stump in a pewter dish clutched in his fist. Gray hair unbound, it flowed about his head like a wind-tossed bush. "A wee stramish among love birds, eh?" As he approached, he stooped to pick up an iron bar from the floor. "I could hear the ruckus as far as Dundee."

Someone must have heard or seen them and notified the captain.

"Back tae playin' the boy, are ye?" He chuckled cruelly as he took her measure. "Ye'll have tae make up yer mind. Girl or boy."

He slapped a thick hand on a crate and handed Griffin the crow bar. "Do the honors, Mr. Faraday, and be quick about it. I don't aim to lose more sleep."

Griffin tipped his head at him, as if to say *are you certain?*

Mulworthy responded with a curt nod.

Baffled by Mulworthy's decision, Griffin seized the tool, resolved to deny knowledge of the guns. He pried open the crate, silently cursing what would soon be a disaster.

Lily stared at the contents with a rapturous gleam. "Why, it's beautiful," she whispered as her features softened.

Relief sluiced from his lungs. Griffin almost laughed at the bolts of lace nestled in rows in the crate.

"But..." She stroked the lace with her brow knitted in question. "I was certain there must be gold or..." As if hidden contraband lay beyond her grasp, she started to paw at the corner of the crate.

"Leave off," Mulworthy chided with a raised hand.

"Dinna go dirtyin' and messin' with the goods."

She snatched her hand away. "I'm sorry. I was so sure…"

"Let this be the end tae suspicions, lass. I'll tolerate no more of yer snoopin'."

She hung her head.

"If ye step foot in the hold again, I'll lock ye up. Do ye hear?"

Her head bobbed. Even in her humiliation, Griffin felt no sympathy. She deserved the reprimand, and for the life of him, he couldn't understand why the captain was so easy on her. Spy or not spy, she was trouble. Both he and Mulworthy would be wise not to forget it.

The captain flicked a wrist, indicating Griffin should close the lid. "Come away both of ye before I lose my temper. It's late. I want me sleep."

Before he'd uttered the last word, Lily grabbed the lantern and sprinted toward the stairs. They followed behind. Griffin retrieved the butcher knife from the floor to return to the galley. Near the base of the steps, he shot the old man a questioning glance. "Lace?" he said, his voice low with incredulity.

"Aye. I kent soon enough she'd go diggin' in the hold, desperate she was tae see. So I topped one of the crates with lace."

"So there really *is* lace."

"Aye. Lace and guns."

"Sly and rather risky to let her explore."

Mulworthy shrugged. "Risks all around. I set the one crate lower than the rest. As she's tiny, she'd go for the lower one."

"A bit of luck on your part."

The old buzzard tapped the side of his forehead and

grinned shrewdly. "'Tis all in the planning. Aye, and brains, too."

They both chuckled.

****

Griffin followed her back to their cabin and closed the door. In her volatile mood, even the light click of the key in the lock filled her with annoyance and foreboding. She spun around. The bed was at her left. The lantern sat on the table where she'd placed it moments ago. It filled the room with a dim light.

Arms crossed over his chest, he leaned against the door, his face composed, yet beneath the mask, she sensed a barely suppressed rage. "I won't apologize for following you."

She squirmed beneath his watchful gaze, and hated that she appeared like a youngster waiting for parental rebuke.

"My motives were as much for your safety as the safety of the ship," he said.

"You think I have it in my power to pose a threat to this ship?" She forced a skeptical laugh. "How absurd. What harm can *I* do?"

Grim-lipped, he dropped into a chair at the table. A vein throbbed in his temple. He sucked back a breath and released it with a noisy whoosh. "Consider the facts." His index finger shot in the air. "One. You bribed your way on board." He cocked his head to the side. The sinuous length of his smooth neck reminded her again of his male beauty. A second finger rose. "Two. You hid like a stowaway." The third finger joined the other two. "You sneak around in the middle of the night in a silly costume." All four fingers stood abreast like rigid soldiers. "And you break into property which doesn't belong to you."

"I didn't break into anything. You saw to that." Regrettably, she sounded like a petulant child. From his scornful expression, he thought so too.

"Tell me, *dear wife*. Does such behavior not sound odd and dubious to you?"

She chafed under the bluntness and candor of his words. Pride kept her from uttering any words of agreement. Still, she would have her say.

"Given the pirate ship and the secretiveness of the crew, I was certain illegal goods were stored in those crates." Her instincts seldom led her astray. Intuition accounted, in part, for why she continued to seek evidence. What a shock to find lace. Proven wrong, her silly quest and irresponsible actions left her humiliated and struggling with self-doubt. Perhaps one positive result emerged from her unfortunate persistence. All along, Griffin maintained the lace existed. And it did.

"Regardless of the four facts I mentioned, how could you even expect disclosure? Besides, it isn't your bloody business."

"Don't be angry, Griffin." Even to her ears, the comment sounded idiotic. He had every right to his anger. Never had she so despised her behavior.

"I'll sleep on the floor if you'd like." Offered as a peace gesture, she hoped it might soothe his ruffled mood. Yet given his penchant for chivalrous behavior, it was a token he would ultimately reject.

His chest expanded on a deep sigh. The tense lines in his face eased. "What am I to do with you, Lily?"

"Do with me? There is naught to do. I am as you see me, imperfections and all."

He offered no comment, no joke, nor a request for

some modification on her part and merely shook his head. Maybe he considered her too stubborn or unable to change. Regardless, he had no right to ask. More worrisome, she doubted whether she had it in her to make a transformation, even if he did ask her.

"I'm sorry if I disappoint or antagonize you." What was she saying? A moment ago, she never wanted to see him again.

The matter of his happiness and approval left her shocked.

Damn Cecil Jones. Damn her foolish promise to spy for the man. The voyage would have been so different if the attorney had not sullied Griffin's character with wild accusations. Without her bias, they might have remained friends. Their time together might have developed into something stronger, with trust and honesty a bridge between them.

Griffin a spy? It seemed unlikely. At the first opportunity, she would write and inform the man his information about Griffin was all wrong.

Thumbnail pressed to her mouth, she considered how to heat the distinct chill drifting between them in their tiny cabin refuge. Truth. She would tell the truth.

"Cecil Jones, Uncle Percy's solicitor…"

"I'm familiar with the man." Griffin's easy tone encouraged her to continue.

"He contends you are a spy."

Something shifted in his eyes, yet his facial expression remained placid. "Oh?" A weak smile could not hide his annoyance. "Pray tell what evidence does the man offer?"

Lily shared a few of Cecil's charges.

"So Jones is a suspicious man with no evidence?"

She nodded. "Don't be alarmed, Griffin. Jones has no reason to suspect you beyond the circumstances of your birthplace, family connections and frequent travel to England."

"Suppositions," he murmured. Forearm on the table, he skimmed the ring of a coffee mug, his gaze following the action in an abstracted way.

She considered whether to join him at the table or continue to stand. Decision made, she sank quietly onto the edge of the bed.

He stroked the slight indent in his chin, a telltale sign his brain churned with activity. "Is Jones your benefactor on this voyage?"

It hardly mattered if he knew, and she wearied of all the hidden meanings behind words. She wanted Cecil's fishing expedition ended and no further secrets to cause them grief. "Yes. I was desperate to get home to see Papa. He offered to help. It was his plan I should board as your servant."

"In exchange for…" No emotion showed on his face. His fingers drummed the table.

Shame pricked at her. Surely, her next admission would end their friendship. "He asked me to befriend you."

"To spy on me."

"Please don't be angry with me." It tore her to pieces when people she cared about were disapproving or hurt by her behavior.

The drumming stopped. His fingers curled into the palm of his hand. "What disturbs me most is Jones's use of you for his selfish, dangerous purposes. To send you alone to New York is unconscionable."

Her palms, gripped over her thighs, relaxed. How

sweet he cared so much about her welfare. "You did nothing to warrant the label of spy. You possess too much integrity to deceive in such a manner."

He grunted. "You're too kind-hearted. You see the good in others and are loyal to men who don't deserve such faithfulness—men like Warwick and Jones."

Chair legs scraped against the floor as he stood. She hoped he might come to her, take her hand in reassurance. Instead, he yanked the shirt over his head and dropped it on the back of a chair. The sight of his mussed hair and a healthy man utterly comfortable in his skin ignited an instant ripple of excitement.

He slipped out of his shoes and padded to the pallet. A vague smile played over his face, a complex tapestry of many colors she couldn't begin to separate and understand. "In the spirit of disclosure, I must tell you something."

She sat up straighter with a flutter of worry in her belly.

"Mulworthy is convinced you are a spy."

She spread her fingers against her breastbone and gaped. "Me?

He laughed as he lay down and draped the blanket over his prone form. "You don't need to fret. We figured you for a spy right from the start."

Chapter Sixteen

A tangy breeze slipped through the open window. Seated at his desk, Griffin paused in his writing, the pen poised above the paper when Lily entered the cabin. "You're back," he said, happy to see her though she'd been gone only a few hours.

His ill humor when he'd discovered her in the hold three nights ago had long since dissipated. Also absent these past few days was Lily's drive to prove him guilty of misdeeds and spying. It was as though she'd turned a corner and left behind all suspicion and doubt.

"Did you enjoy your stroll with Mr. Mead?" he teased. "Was he as fascinating as ever?"

She preened and tossed her wide brimmed bonnet on the bed. "You sound jealous."

"Me? Not the jealous type."

At his suggestion, Lily agreed to afternoon walks with Mead. The two shared a vast interest in science and could talk for hours. In her absence, Griffin wrote political essays and locked them away before her return.

"What have you there?" He jutted a chin at the covered dish in her hand.

She whipped off the checkered cloth.

He yelped in exaggerated astonishment. "An apple tart."

"Instead of exercise, I baked this for you." Aglow

with pride, she held out her delectable achievement. "Cook was brave enough to let me muck about in the galley—with Sloan's assistance, of course."

"No doubt the lad considers it one of the better afternoons of his illustrious sailing career." He couldn't help but smile. "And what of Mead?"

"When creativity calls, who is he to stand in the way?" She grinned. "His words. Not mine."

Smart man. "I'm touched." The delicious scent of cinnamon and apple wafted from the sweet goodness. Pleased beyond all measure, he accepted the gift. "Baking is another talent you can add to your list of accomplishments."

A shrugged shoulder minimized the praise. "Uncle Percy's cook labored to teach me the correct ways to knead dough and bake a decent pie."

He admired the golden crust almost as much as the satisfaction evident in her rosy cheeks. Seated at the desk, he leaned forward and placed the delicacy on the table with a long reach. "I shall enjoy it very much. Thank you."

As he eased back he gripped the chair arms, resisting the impulse to spring forward to embrace her. It hadn't been easy to keep his fingers from her silky skin these past few days. Fortunately, they'd settled once again into a cordial routine. Mulworthy hadn't questioned her behavior again. Still, circumstances required he maintain his guard.

Furthermore, he continued to sleep on the floor. In less than a week, when they reached land, they would go their separate ways. There were many facets of her he would miss—kindness, generosity, humor, and above all, her probing mind, the one trait to vex him the most.

"Would you join me for a slice?" Already an ache of loneliness stabbed his heart.

"Perhaps later. I've eaten too many apples. Please, go ahead and enjoy." Her lovely face reminded him of a rose with its perfection in every satiny petal.

"I'll wait until I can share it with you." He acted as if her very closeness didn't charge the atmosphere around them. "Until then, it's back to work for me."

"So dedicated." On a whiff of lavender, she floated closer and paused near the edge of the desk. His papers claimed her full attention.

"Curious, are you?" When she reached for the top sheet, he gripped her wrist, but his rash response hadn't been necessary. The writing was humorous fiction and not dangerous. Perhaps she hoped to discover treasonous words. "You're a nosy little thing."

She stared at his hand, watching as he released her. His heart sped. He licked his dry lips and tried not to think of kissing her silky throat.

"It's the latest chapter of my book." He caught the slight hitch in his voice. The air crackled with a sense of expectancy. An image came to him of two tigers circling over a bit of meat. Around and around they went, wary and attentive. Against her protesting yelp, he yanked her onto his lap. "Look at me, not my work," he growled.

Their gazes locked. In hers, he recognized surprise, excitement, and best of all, desire. The rousing emotions battered away his resolve. He cupped her head, intent on a sweet kiss, a light nibble to satisfy his hunger.

Her arms sidled over his shoulders. She hugged

him closer and further stirred his delight. As though she wanted this as much as him, she began to play. An explorer on a quest, she skimmed the planes of his face and the shape of his skull. All the while, she teased him with her lips. Against all logic and sensible restraint, the kiss deepened. Cinnamon and honey flavored her tongue. Her purring sounds intensified his need.

In less than a heartbeat, he was flying at the edge of his boundary. His breathing quickened. His body tightened. "I want you," he panted against the hot skin of her neck.

In a strong grip, she clasped the queue at the base of his head and anchored him, owning him before she took his mouth again.

He moaned with pleasure, aware he would give her all he had to give. Forever. Period.

Reluctant to stop, he slid a hand inside her bodice, excited with her cry of pleasure when he thumbed her taut nipple. She arched with her spine bowed. The other hand glided up her calf and slipped beneath her skirts. Her skin was incredibly smooth. He shifted her so both legs rested astride him.

"So much better to see and feel," he teased. A squeeze to her bottom elicited an eager yelp. "So much better for…"

Her kiss stopped his words.

"Hmmm." Lily moaned, shocked at the wanton sound that coiled from the depths of her throat. No man had ever touched her so intimately. At once, uncertainty set in. To cease seemed imperative. Pressing gently on his strong shoulder, she broke from his embrace, flushed and aroused with want and guilt. "This isn't…"

This isn't what?

"This isn't what I had in mind." Confusion jangled her thoughts. She wriggled in his lap, aware of his firm arousal. With a conscious effort, she slowed her rapid breathing.

He smiled lazily. Frank lust bristled in his naked gaze. "What *did* you have in mind?"

"Conversation and friendship."

With a delicious lopsided grin, he studied her through half-lowered lids. "What is it you play at? One minute it's *yes* and the next it's *no*."

She despised being so tentative and unsure. Yet if he continued kissing her, all would be lost. The heat of him against her skin and lips still simmered.

"You're all man," she said as if the fact weren't obvious. The very nature of their differences lured her. She tried in a vain hope to assert logical reason. "I adore your masculinity." She shook her head, thinking the comment idiotic. He was compelling, self-assured and displayed strength of character that comforted in the loneliest of times. But there was more to it.

The realization jolted her. She loved him.

They both acted in the same instant.

Forget reason and talk. Forget tentative touches. They kissed with a forceful urgency as though starved of oxygen. Her hands roved restlessly over his body and demanded to experience every fold and plane. He countered and stroked arms and legs until he scooped up her bottom and pressed her to the hard evidence of his longing. A shameless rumble vibrated in his throat.

"Lily." He sucked in a great, noisy breath. "I want you."

Every cell in her body quivered. "And I want you."

"Are you certain?"

She reached for him. Her kiss was possessive. A woman who took what she wanted.

He swept her into his arms and carried her to the bed. Too overcome to speak, she watched as Griffin fixed her with a gaze while his tapered fingers undid the ties of his shirt. Unlike their frenzied groping a few moments ago, he moved with a languid grace as he slipped the garment over his head and dropped it on the desk. In the same unrushed cadence, he removed his shoes and hose. She marveled at his self-control, for she was a restless tempest. She wanted, nay needed, to be doused in a passionate fit of lovemaking.

"I aim to be slow," he said as though he'd read her mind. "For your sake." He flashed an uneven grin. "I may not succeed, but I intend to try."

Devil.

"I don't care what you do. Just do it." Saucy words from a girl whose insides skittered in a rush of fearful anticipation.

Naked except for his blue breeches, he dropped a knee on the feather bed. "Don't be afraid."

Afraid? She was terrified yet nothing in the world could stop her from going forward. Swallowing her nerves, she placed a hand on his flat stomach—a smooth rock heated in the sun. *Beautiful* came to mind. His seductive gaze drove up her temperature.

She trembled as she skimmed the indentations of his broad chest, in awe when his nipple contracted. In an instant, he'd stretched out beside her, his body large and strong. She reveled in the sense of safety and protection within his arms.

At first his kiss was light, a promise of things to come. Impatient, she worked the leather thong in his hair away and tossed it aside.

He nibbled lightly at her earlobe. She melted beneath his warmth as he kissed her brow, her cheek, and worked his way to the soft spot beneath her chin. With a nimble touch, he loosened the laces of her gown. All the while, his hand roamed over the muslin, up and down arms and thighs, across stomach and hips, stimulating and surprising. The top of her dress fell away. He palmed her breast, his thumb circling and circling around the sensitive center, and she squirmed beneath him, alive with tingling sensations and agitated for reasons she couldn't understand.

"Ohhh." She moaned and thrashed against him, wanting more, wanting relief from the heat.

He tugged at her chemise. "Let's get this off," and like a puppet, she raised her arms and allowed him to glide the gossamer slip from her body.

"Lovely." His brazen stare fixed appreciatively on her breasts. "Come here," he rasped and applied himself with an earnest resolve. His tongue teased her nipple. It tightened in delectable agony and induced parallel upheavals in her muscles. Her head ground into the pillow, uncertain whether she could withstand the delicious agony—a pleasure so intense she feared she might go up in flames if he didn't stop.

"Please," she whimpered.

He sucked a nipple into his hot, hot mouth, tugging and tugging while a strange feline sound circled around her head. A cat in heat. She arched away from the mattress. He pressed her back, hand to her stomach. "Please," she cried, voice strangled.

Impatiently, he shoved aside the gown and petticoats twisted and bunched at her hips. His palm slid down her belly. One finger swept across the sensitive peak between her legs. The pressure intensified, the pleasure as exquisite as anything she'd ever experienced. She gripped his shoulder, solid and muscular, a counterpoint to her unraveling, jagged emotions. He switched to his thumb and strummed it back and forth. Desire gathered with a painful clenching, thrilling and unnerving.

"Please, I can't..." She feared she might burst into fire.

"You can," he urged. The certainty in his voice buoyed her spirit. "Trust me, Lily."

Trust me. Truth. It's what mattered.

Every muscle gripped taut. Her legs trembled. Her fingers bit into his skin. She was on fire and dying. A keening sound ripped from her throat. Her body exploded and rose from the bed. Suspended aloft, she splintered into tiny specks of brilliant light. As she floated back to the mattress, spineless and wispy as a feather, she grinned with utter joy.

Between hugs and kisses, he murmured endearments until her world came back to clear focus.

"Lily, my dearest."

She enjoyed the solid mass of muscle against the length of her body, the smell of his shaving soap, the glossy texture of his hair. He stroked her with lazy movements that soon became more determined and demanding. It amazed her how her body roused again to his thrilling touch. In no time, she was panting and writhing, an unashamed woman who needed as much to give pleasure to as to receive.

His breath turned ragged. Tension rippled through his body, and like her, he seemed on the edge of losing control. With one hand, he fumbled with the buttons of his breeches.

"I must have you," he breathed.

Her pulse thudded as he nudged her legs further apart. *This is it.* Scared witless and excited beyond all reason, she grabbed his hair and drew him to her.

He eased into her. A sharp pinch deep inside made her breath hitch. The pain eased away in seconds.

"Lily." He sounded frayed, at loose ends and not at all the contained man she'd come to know. "I...I'll be gentle."

She caressed his cheek appreciative of his intent. However he claimed his release, he wouldn't hurt her.

He moved inside her, slow at first, allowing her to experience the sublime pleasure he evoked. As if they were feathers, his fingers brushed against her breast while his breath was a hot mist against her neck. Their tongues melded in a twining dance. Instinctively, she flexed her hips to match his rhythm and curled her legs around his waist. Pressing her into the mattress, he thrust deeper and faster. The sheer delectable power of his body pounded into her and drove her wild. Her body tightened. Every muscle clenched. Her insides coiled until she cried out.

When his release came, he spilled across her belly with a tattered, wretched cry.

Clasped in his embrace, their chests rose on quick breaths while their hearts pounded together. Still breathing fast, he settled beside her, and she cuddled into his arms. Her head resting on his chest, she trailed a finger from his sternum to his navel, inhaling the unique smell of lust and sweat and marveled at the wonder of it all.

Though he couldn't see her face, he asked, "What are you smiling about?"

Her grin widened. "How can you tell I'm smiling?"

"I can *feel* you smile, deep in here." He touched his chest. "I can feel everything about you."

He shifted and stared into her face. "Let me make you smile again." Then he dipped his head and kissed her.

Chapter Seventeen

"Good morning," said a feminine voice.

Half asleep, Griffin reached for Lily. The effort seized him a bit of cool air and a lumpy pillow. Groaning, he opened his eyes to sunlight and beauty.

The object of his affection adorned a spot at the table holding a cup. Coffee, he suspected. Garbed in a lavender dressing gown tied about the waist, she looked luscious, even tastier than the apple tart devoured last evening after their ravenous exertions, licking the sweet juice from their fingers. "Sleep well?" She crossed her legs at the knees. The garment parted and revealed a glimpse of shapely calves and a length of creamy thigh. It stirred an immediate physical charge. A sigh of lusty contentment gushed forth. He recalled his exploration of those lovely legs, along with the rest of her appealing form, when he made love to her several times last evening. The knowledge she could rouse to his touch pleased him immensely.

"Would you believe, dear wife, I had the best night's sleep on this whole tiresome journey? Thank you." He stuffed a couple of pillows behind his shoulders and head and leaned against the wall. "Not one muscle aches."

"I'm glad to hear it." Her face beamed with humor. "I feared I might have bored you to sleep."

"Ha! You're many things, my sweet, but never

dull." In all the time he'd spent with her, boring did not apply. As to her disposition in bed... He smiled. "Come here." He reached for her. As she settled into his embrace upon the bed, he enjoyed a pleasant whiff of her feminine scent. He rested his chin on her head and wished the moment could last forever. Alas, he had a duty to perform. Where he needed to go, Lily couldn't join him.

"Lily." He paused to review his next statement. Above all, it required eloquence. "About last night..." The perfectionist writer had him quibbling over words.

"What is it, Griffin? You sound serious."

"Lily, last night..." He grasped her hands, surprised to find them so cold. "I was humbled and honored when you gave yourself to me."

Her breath tickled his clavicle when she laughed. "How gallant. For a moment, I feared you had..." The words fell away as her fingers trickled down his forearm.

"Had what? Had second thoughts?" A desire to express his eternal affection drummed in his chest. The words stuck in his throat. What right had he to proclaim his love? Nor could he expect hers in return when he hadn't been honest and forthright. His sworn duty to Washington tugged at him. Truth mattered. So did duty.

"I have no regrets making love to you."

Whether he should speak of his work for Washington, he was of two different minds. The proper time for disclosure would have been when she'd admitted spying for Jones. Yet, he'd kept quiet, perhaps foolishly so. Any revelation now, after the fact, would cause her pain. He didn't want to hurt her.

No matter what the future held for them, a part of

him would always belong to her. He loved her. Their night of passion couldn't be erased.

He caressed her slender arm. Such a delicate wrist bone and one to marvel at. Quiet hung in the air, weighty as wet leaves on a branch, waiting for a breeze to stir it to life. When they reached New York, he would state his political loyalties and reveal his association to General Washington. He owed her as much. Nevertheless, the truth would hurt and disappoint. If she rejected him outright, at least she had her father to offer comfort and support. Perhaps after some time, with the marriage dissolved, she might return to England and Warwick. The notion caused him immeasurable gloom. Having faced loneliness in his life, he hated to imagine the painful void of her absence.

"Sloane will be back with our breakfast," she said cheerily. "I told him not to rush as I wanted you to have your sleep."

"Sleep, is it?" He tugged at the knot in her sash, growing excited with her husky laugh. She batted away his hands. Undeterred, he threw a leg over hers and anchored her to the bed. He nuzzled her neck and relished her joyful squeaking noises.

"Griffin."

Somewhere deep in his brain her serious tone registered. "Yes?" He nipped gently at her earlobe. "Don't you want me? Am I not a great lover?"

"Ha," she laughed. "I see you're not without confidence and braggadocio." Slender fingers raked through his loose hair before she shifted away. "It's unfortunate I have no means to compare."

He chuckled at her teasing. "A man could drown,

quite happily, in the luminous depths of your midnight eyes."

"Such a poet." She sat up and tapped him once on the end of his nose. "As to your skills as a lover, you are as expressive as you are uninhibited. I was quite overcome." The tremor in her voice bore the depth of her truth and touched him deeply. "Had I been a fragile porcelain cup, prone to break easily, I don't think you could have treated me with more tenderness."

Satisfaction licked across his skin. Overcome with joy, he swallowed her in his arms. "I want to laze in our cocoon and make love to you all day."

A blasted knock upon the door interrupted his seduction. "Damn." Reluctantly, he released her, but not before giving one last squeeze to her rounded bottom in an assurance of enjoyable experiences to come. "No doubt it's Sloane. Don't move a muscle. I'll see to him."

Naked, he slipped out of bed. As he donned a pair of breeches, he flashed a suggestive grin. Instantly, her pupils flared. The tint of her skin deepened, and like his, he suspected her pulse raced at the notion of making love again.

He fastened the last of his buttons and padded bare foot over the wooden floor. "Who is it?"

"Church."

Griffin raised his brow at her as if to say, *what does he want?* With a sense of foreboding, he stepped into the corridor and closed the door behind him. "What is it, Mr. Church?"

A quick survey of Griffin's undressed state gave Church a puckered expression. "Captain wishes to see you without delay in his quarters."

"Inform Captain Mulworthy I'll join him in five minutes."

Burdened with curiosity and alarm, Griffin returned to the cabin and found Lily stretched like a languorous sea nymph beneath the sheet. It was all he could do not to pounce upon her inviting body.

"What is it?" she asked.

"Captain wishes to see me." With a good-natured wink, he sloughed off his concerns. "I suspect he'll wage a complaint about all the noise we made last night."

"Ha!" She tossed a pillow at his head.

He easily picked it out of the air before it hit its mark and grinned. "I won't be long."

****

Sunlight bounced off Mulworthy's ceiling. Griffin winced against the brilliant glare.

"Aye, tis the young buck, hisself," Mulworthy joked to Laurent. The two men sat at the captain's heavy rectangular table, the wooden landscape between them littered with dirty breakfast dishes and cutlery.

"Good morning, gentlemen."

In reply, the old geezer grunted while Laurent bobbed his wigged head in greeting. Griffin had gotten so used to merchant Laurent's false identity he'd almost forgotten the Frenchman's true name of Commander Moreau.

Mulworthy gestured to a chair. Griffin joined them, glad for the fresh air drifting through the open windows. As he helped himself to coffee, he noticed both men study him with an air of amusement. "What is it? Have I grown another head?"

Laurent leaned closer and pointed. "Do I believe

my eyes?"

"What?" Griffin patted his neck. He expected to find dirt or worse, hideous vermin nestled in the folds of his collar.

Mulworthy swatted aside his hand. "It won't do ye any good to search. It's a love bite, ye have."

Griffin swallowed his shock as the two men laughed at his expense.

Mulworthy clasped Griffin's shirt by the shoulder and tugged. The garment shifted, revealing more skin. "Another one," he cried and chuckled as Griffin batted away his hand like an annoying wasp.

"Busy night, *mon ami*?" Laurent dabbed his smirk with a napkin. "You look fatigued."

"But satisfied." Mulworthy beamed with smugness.

"Laugh all you want, gentlemen." Griffin tucked his enjoyment behind a scowl. Next time, before he left his cabin, he'd check the mirror.

"Och," Mulworthy snarled in his typical manner of business. "Ye best leave off the love-makin' and get some sleep. I need ye in good form tonight."

If Griffin harbored any fatigue, it vanished instantly. Excitement drove his blood. "We're close?"

Mulworthy nodded. "The end of the day should see us off the coast."

Griffin leaned forward as if the action might magically spur the ship to sail faster. At last, the time had arrived. The opportunity to complete his mission loomed hours away. How he'd planned and lied and longed for the moment when Commander Moreau and the guns rested safely in the hands of the Continental Army.

"Aye, there's a moon tonight. The transfer happens

at midnight as arranged."

Griffin set his cup down, his anticipation tight in the grip of his fingers around the cup's thick rim.

"Once the guns are gone we sail up Hudson Bay. Weather permittin', we arrive in a day or two.

Griffin wanted to jump with excitement.

"Will ye return with the launch?"

From the very outset, Griffin intended to accompany Moreau and the guns to General Washington. He'd planned for his trusted servant, Mr. Ludlow, to collect his possessions from the ship and carry them home. Now he had Lily to consider.

"Yes, I'll return to the ship."

"Does your wife know of your mission?" the Frenchman asked.

"No."

Laurent arched a questioning brow. "Her sentiments lie with the King?"

Griffin nodded, wishing it weren't so.

"How long do ye think ye can keep this a secret?" Mulworthy barked like a terrier, gruff and loud.

"I plan to tell her when I take her to her father. As to the two of you, she'll never hear of your involvement."

The French man nodded in acknowledgement. "Stay with your wife. The colonial soldiers will see me and the guns safely to Washington."

Over the past few days, Griffin had considered the matter. While the delivery of Laurent and the guns to Washington was a sign of a job well done, he couldn't abandon Lily. She deserved an explanation and his protection. He wouldn't leave her to arrive home alone.

"I'll slip out while she sleeps and be back before

she even wakes in the morning. Although she may be a British Loyalist, she'd never betray me." A woman couldn't make love with her whole heart and soul, only to shrug off her skin and deceive the man. The woman didn't have a mean bone in her body.

"'Tis not yer neck which concerns me but the welfare of the men. What if she wakes up while the guns are being unloaded?" Mulworthy dragged a palm across his grizzled chin. "Perhaps the good doctor has a sleep potion?"

Griffin gawked at him. "You want me to drug my wife?"

"Consider the war," the Captain snarled in frustration. "Should she squeal tae the Brits, I willna be in business much longer."

Mulworthy was a valuable tool for the Army. To lose his services would be a blow to Washington. Yet the idea of drugging Lily made his blood go cold. He stared long and hard at the man. "Consider the point taken. If we are quit of this matter, I'll see to my bride."

With a heavy heart, he trudged from the stateroom. He'd give her a drop or two, to make her sleep better. What could be the harm?

****

While Griffin was away, Lily washed and dressed, taking care to appear fresh and presentable in her much-worn gown. How she longed for a luxurious bath and clean clothes. As she inserted the last of the pins in her hair, she coasted on a wave of bliss and contentment.

Knuckles rapped against the door before it opened. It seemed impossible the mere sight of Griffin in the doorway, a tray laden with dishes in his hands, lifted her already heady mood. His gaze raked her with appreciation. "Lovely."

Warmed by his praise, she skimmed a hand over the waist of her blue gown. "What have you there?"

"I intercepted Sloane."

"Let me help you." In silence, they set the table laying out the bowls and cutlery and tucked into their porridge. The oats tasted nutty, topped with a few walnuts she'd carried away from Uncle Percy's home. Along with steaming coffee, Griffin finished off the bread and ham, unusually preoccupied since his visit with the captain.

"Is anything wrong?" she asked, uneasy with the absence of congenial conversation.

His quick denial and further silence incited a wave of insecurity. Maybe he did harbor some regrets for bedding her. Too afraid to have her fear confirmed, she didn't press him on the matter.

"How is Captain Mulworthy?" she asked.

"He softens like cheese in the sun. He has invited us to join him for supper tonight."

Lily raised a speculative brow.

"He's thankful the voyage is almost over. If the winds hold, we land in New York in one day. Two at the most."

"Two days!" A thrill touched off a wave of laughter. At last, the long wait and the promise of seeing her father was about to come true. "Oh, Griffin." She squeezed his hand. "I have you to thank for this."

"Me and Cecil Jones," he joked, but his pleasure was obvious.

Alive with excitement, she sat back in the chair and surveyed the possessions she would pack in her trunk. Once home, she could forget about Mulworthy, the pirate, the dreadful flogging, the awful smells and the constant heave and pitch of the ship. "At one time, I didn't think the time would ever pass quickly enough."

He set his coffee on the table. "Was it so bad?"

"To be fair, it wasn't all ghastly." One special person, who glowed like a shiny coin at the table, made the lengthy hours all worthwhile.

Griffin watched her in utter stillness. What would become of them? He'd not said a word about his desire to remain married. Too prideful, she couldn't ask.

As if he sensed her apprehension, he settled a light hand at her waist. "Don't worry. Nothing will prevent you from joining your father."

Not once had she mentioned Papa's imprisonment. Perhaps initially, fear of Griffin's reaction and her embarrassment prompted her silence. Now there seemed no point for him to know as they would go their separate ways once they reached New York.

To think she might never see Griffin again caused a hitch of despair in her chest.

"You didn't come all this way to lose your dream when it's so close to hand." He smiled with encouragement. For his hopeful words, she loved him even more. Yet he failed to speak of their shared future. No longer hungry, she shoved her bowl away. A world without Griffin sucked the very air from her lungs. No other man could ever rise high enough in her estimation to toss Griffin to the shadows.

"I shall be delighted to join the Captain's table."

Griffin stood and held out a hand. "The sun calls to me. Let's walk."

After three turns around the deck, they returned to the cabin. Griffin worked on his story while she finished *Gulliver's Travels*. They did not speak again of the previous night. Nor did they broach their strained silence. All the while, she tried not to worry about what the future had in store for them, much less the coming night. When the time came to join Mulworthy for dinner, Lily vowed to enjoy the evening.

Griffin donned a clean shirt, and the sight of him half-naked excited a familiar thrill.

"Allow me." As she worked his last button, he clasped and stilled her hand.

"Lily, I…"

"What is it?" She wanted to rub the grave expression from his face. "Am I to be eaten alive by the captain?" Her attempt to lighten the heaviness around them sank like a rock in mud. Neither of them laughed.

He pressed her hand to his heart, the strong beat steady against her palm. For a moment, she relaxed, but when he remained grim, worry again set in.

"In celebration of the journey's imminent end," he said. "The last hog has been slaughtered. Everyone, down to the lowest deck hand, will enjoy the succulent treat with their evening's ration. Let us enjoy the feast."

"How wonderful," she murmured baffled by his odd comment. Whatever bothered him had nothing to do with pork.

****

"As impossible as it seems," Lily said, walking through the doorway of their cabin. "The captain is almost agreeable when he puts his mind to it."

Griffin followed her inside, grateful to have completed a lengthy dinner without any trouble between Lily and Mulworthy.

The last trace of pink and gold sunlight filtered

through the windows. He closed the door and crossed the room while she sat on the bed and plucked ribbons and pins from her hair.

"I suppose *almost* is better than his customary querulous demeanor." He lit the candle on the desk. With trepidation, he snatched a bottle of brandy from a shelf and set it on the table with his back to her. "Can I interest you in a tot?"

"Just a small one."

From out of his coat pocket, he slipped out the tiny vial of laudanum Mead had given him earlier. He would dose her with the drug, a common enough medicine for aches and sleep and not because Mulworthy ordered it. He would do this to protect her from the truth—at least for a while longer. If she woke up and discovered what he—what they—were up to, she would be hurt and furious. Better she remain unaware of his activity until she had the support of home and father.

One drop instead of two, as Mead had instructed. A smaller dose would serve its purpose without any lasting ill effects. In a strange twist, the less he gave her, the less his guilt. He turned around and handed her the glass.

She sipped and her face soured. "Ooh, that's strong."

At her comical reaction, he smiled in earnest. "Lily, I do so enjoy you."

"You do?" She placed the unfinished drink in the built-in shelf above the bed.

It astounded him that such a remarkable woman could doubt her charm and likeability. "Of course. Surely you've noticed your charms."

She shrugged seeming shy or perhaps embarrassed.

"I'm glad to hear you speak of it. I thought…Well, you've been quiet today. Not quite yourself."

"A lot on my mind." *You mostly*, he'd almost revealed.

He yanked a chair from the table, set it close to the bed and took a seat. He grasped her hands knitted together over her lap. "Our time together has been very special."

"Has been?" She spoke in a near whisper.

"Yes, it is a joy to share your company again after all these years." All day he longed to caress her, to re-ignite the intimate bond they'd shared the previous night. Yet something held him back—duty perhaps, a commitment to a job she couldn't understand or could never partake of. Had he been a man bent on practicality above all else, he would deliver her to her father and never see her again. The notion left him morose.

Darkness threatened to claim him. A clear direction lay ahead. There was no question about what he should do. Another part of him dreamt about a wife and family. He sat forward, gripped her hands and fought against his desire. A force so compelling he couldn't control it shaped his words. "I regret the end of our arrangement."

All sound on the ship quieted. He held his breath, waiting, and searched for the right words.

"What are you saying, Griffin?"

His throat grew thick and his hands clammy. "If it pleases you, we can stay together—forever."

She touched the base of her throat as if confused.

"We don't have to dissolve our marriage when we reach New York."

She sat up straighter. Her gaze narrowed. "If you're teasing…"

"Good God, woman," he huffed, shocked at her intimation. He almost laughed though it was no laughing matter.

"Is this a proposal?"

He grinned at the absurdity and spread his upturned hands. "Since you are my wife, a proposal seems superfluous. However, if a proposal is what you desire, by all means, I would indulge you and see you happy." His knees landed on the floor with a thud. He squeezed her hands. "Please, Lily. Stay with me forever. Be mine and make me the happiest of men."

Her bottom lip trembled. When she didn't reply, something inside him froze. Fear niggled at his brain. Would her answer be a repeat of Katherine's rejection of his proposal?

"Of course," he hastened to add, assuming a confidence he didn't possess in the moment. "If you don't wish to stay married…"

A squeal peeled forth. She bounded off the bed and flung her arms about his neck. The momentum pitched him backwards. A hand to the floor kept him from collapsing like a house of cards. She knelt next to him. They clung to each other, laughing as they rocked back and forth.

"Do I hear a *yes*, my love?"

"Yes, yes, forever."

Happiness surged through him and warmed every bit of his skin. He surveyed the fine shape of her brow, the straight nose, her incandescent beauty.

She blinked rapidly, shuttering aside the surge of moisture.

He scooped her into another hug. It felt right, so perfect and wonderful to hold his wife in his arms. Not even the war or Washington could lessen his joy and enthusiasm.

"Come." He pushed to his feet before he helped her up. He kissed her thoroughly, tasting brandy on her tongue, and savored the possibility of countless times in the future when he would make love to her. For now... I want you."

Her pupils flared and drove his passion.

"First..." He reached for both their glasses. Guilt pricked him as she took her glass so trustingly from his hand.

He clicked his glass against hers. "To us."

Chapter Eighteen

Something thumped and scraped against the floorboards and woke Lily. Woozy, she grabbed her head. It felt thick as cotton. Somewhere outside the cabin, footsteps thudded. Brusque voices whispered. She strained to see in the shadows and half-expected a crazed marauder to barge through her doorway. A man swore and fright lodged in her throat. What in blazes was going on?

"Griffin." She swept a hand across his pillow. Cool and empty. "Griffin?"

Another unaccountable bump startled her.

We're under attack!

Panicked, she threw aside the covers and scrambled from the bed. Arms outstretched in the dark, she stumbled on rubbery legs to the desk, baffled by her unsteady gait. A quick headshake didn't dispel the drowsiness. Thickheaded and exhausted, she groped for the flint box, struck a flame and lit the wick. The pungent aroma of the spermaceti candle rose in the air. At once, she noted the absence of Griffin's clothes. He'd dropped them on a chair before they'd fallen into bed. The image of entwined arms and legs and hot kisses caused a pleasurable shiver. Enough time for memories later. She must find him.

After throwing on a dressing gown, she stuffed her feet into slippers. From the washstand, she grabbed

Griffin's straight razor to serve as a weapon. The pewter candleholder clutched in a clammy hand, she listened at the door but heard nothing beyond the noisy pulse in her head. She reached for the doorknob and hesitated. Perhaps it made more sense to remain inside the locked cabin. *Let them come to me* she reasoned boldly even as she quaked with fear.

Beyond the door, someone moaned with a sound so pitiful it echoed in her bones. Worried it was Griffin, she threw open the door. Without hesitation, she lumbered into the corridor, surprised at her clumsiness.

Light spilled from the surgeon's doorway. Though his back was to her, she recognized Samuel Church by his black hair and slender frame standing at the doctor's examination table. Mead, at the table's head, issued a command. Church shifted enough to reveal the bottom half of a man clothed in brown breeches stretched lengthwise on the slab.

Griffin. Her fear skyrocketed. Willing her leaden legs to respond, she shot across the corridor. At the door's threshold, a brawny arm blocked her path.

"Let me pass, Mr. Tubbs." The strength in her voice sounded more forceful than she felt.

The behemoth didn't budge. He eyed Mead, who after a moment's grave deliberation, nodded with a haggard, resigned expression. "Let her pass." Tubbs shrugged and dropped the thick tree-limb arm.

Lily drove past the giant into a room filled with hundreds of tiny colored bottles, brass bowls, and books shelved on the walls. Instantly, the rusty tang of blood, sweat and whale oil assaulted her.

Dour faced, Church looked none too happy at her intrusion. "It's best you not be here." Weariness bleached his typically sun-tanned skin. Eyeing the razor clutched in her stiff fingers, he dragged a hand across the black stubble on his chin. "You can put away the weapon. No one will hurt you."

"We're not under attack?"

"No."

Relieved to hear they weren't about to be murdered, she folded the razor and slipped it into the pocket of the dressing gown. She made to move around Church, but he grabbed her by the shoulders as if to protect her from a gruesome sight.

Fear gripped her belly. "What happened?"

"A bit of a scuffle."

"Scuffle? Let me see." She pushed against his arm. "He's my husband," she stated fiercely.

Church hesitated, seeming about to argue when Mead came to her defense.

"Let her be."

With a regretful shake to his head, Church released her and stepped aside.

Lily sucked in a cry of shock. Stretched out on his back, Griffin lay deathly still. A sickly pallor tinged his skin. "Dear Lord! Is he dead?" Blackish blood glistened in his matted hair. Blood saturated his torn shirt and speckled his breeches.

Church caught her by the arm, as if she might faint and took the candle from her clenched fingers.

"No, he's not dead," Mead said.

Her knees almost buckled. She reached out and touched Griffin's arm. He didn't react. The absence of all vigor and health strummed her worries. "What happened to him?"

No one answered. She looked to a sailor hunched

in a chair against the far wall who cradled an injured arm. She'd seen him before as he patched a torn sail with an enormous hooked needle. "Did you do this?" Accusation blared in her tone.

The man's greasy curls glimmered in the lantern light, and his face twisted in agony. "Not me, ma'am. I swear."

"Both are innocent," explained Mead, wiping his bloody hands on a cloth. Beads of sweat dotted his upper lip. "Griffin took a…" He faltered and glanced at a point somewhere beyond her shoulder. "Perhaps the captain would like to explain." Mead made a gracious half-bow to his superior, almost mocking in its formality.

Lily turned, distressed to see Mulworthy in the doorway. The old goat scowled and clomped inside, flicking a gaze between her and the body on the table.

"What are ye doin' here?" he barked. "Can no' a thing happen on the ship without ye stickin' yer nose in the shite?"

"I heard noises." She fisted the opening of her dressing gown as though the flimsy silk fabric offered a protective shield. "I heard someone cry out."

Mulworthy snorted and wrinkled his hawk-like nose. His leaden glower could make a strong man tremble. Lily steeled her spine and did her best to mask her discomfort.

"What happened?" Mulworthy said to Church.

"You're the captain!" Lily blurted. "Surely you—" A silent warning in Mead's expression cautioned her to cap her rising ire.

As supreme commander of this so-called floating empire, the man knew perfectly well. At least he ought to know the circumstances. If she were to ask him, she bet he'd deny any knowledge, just to be bad-tempered and uncooperative. She despised all the secretiveness.

Bits of gray hair escaped Mulworthy's queue and floated like feathers near his creased ear lobes. As he studied Griffin's bloodied face, his shoulders slumped. Worry burdened his features. A wave of sympathy arose in her for it seemed he truly cared about Griffin's welfare. How odd. Always at opposite poles, she and the loathsome man suddenly found a common concern.

Regardless of her compassion, she had a right to understand. "Pray, explain this calamity, Captain."

Pointedly ignored, Mulworthy addressed Mead. "Will the lad live?"

Mead felt Griffin's forehead. "It looks worse than it is."

Thank goodness. The tension eased in her shoulders.

"He bled like a…" Church snapped his gob closed when Mead shook his head.

"Rest and care are needed." The doctor dabbed at Griffin's dirty cheek. "A shot grazed him above the ear. He's unconscious." Mead spoke to the three of them all in line on one side of the examination table. "When he fell, he knocked his head on something rather hard."

"How long before he awakes?" Mulworthy's fatherly concern was so unexpected Lily could only stare.

"We must wait and see."

"Who shot him? Where did this happen?" Her shrill voice edged toward anger. "Not on the ship for I would have heard the ruckus."

Mulworthy gripped the lapel of his wrinkled coat

and displayed his typical scowl. "Come away, lass. Let the doctor do his work."

"No." With sheer force of will, she met his fierce glare. Samuel Church took a step closer, and she welcomed his supportive presence.

"At least let me help you," she pleaded to Mead. "I can clean his wound while you attend to the tailor."

The surgeon smiled wearily. "Thank you, but I'm almost finished. Go back to your cabin. We'll bring him to you."

"Aye, go along, lass." The captain appeared anxious to shoo her out the door.

"I still don't understand what's happened," she persisted.

Mulworthy's chest rose. It rattled as he expelled a breath so sour she winced. "Ye ask too many questions. Always have. I'll leave it up to him to tell ye." He curled a thumb at Griffin.

The sight of her husband so helpless on the surgeon's table, his skin stretched tight over his facial bones, clawed at her heart. She hesitated and debated whether to push the issue. Frustration blared in her voice. "I'm not so naïve to think you, as captain, aren't in some way behind this debacle." How she despised being treated like an idiot or a God forsaken curse. "Tell me."

Affronted, Mulworthy reared back. "Think what you will." He snapped a thick hand in the direction of the door. "Get out of me sight."

Her whole body shook, but she accepted the futility of arguing with a wall built of stone. Chin high, she took the candleholder from Church and marched from the surgery. In her cabin, she slammed the door. The sound reverberated in her head, like the bang of a gunshot. After setting the candleholder on the desk, she slumped down on the mussed bed and massaged the dull ache in her head. A mysterious, brutal event had occurred, and no one, not even Mead or Church, men she respected, would tell her how it happened.

Once again, she'd been ignored and left in the dark. *Damn their secrets.* She pounded the bed with her fist. For good measure, she gave it a second whack.

Mulworthy regarded her presence on his ship as a bad omen. It made sense that a cause beyond superstition and dislike of her influenced his silence. No doubt, she posed some threat to him. But what? He would never trust her, and because of it, hid things from her.

Gaze fixed on the two trunks against the far wall she racked her brain for some explanation. An idea bloomed in her mind so powerful it hurt. If crates of lace came aboard at sea, would it not be as likely they returned to shore in a similar sneaky fashion, all under the cover of darkness? She slapped a hand to her thigh. Yes, that must be it!

Mulworthy was a smuggler. The cheat unloaded crates while at sea to avoid duty taxes in the harbor.

And where did Griffin fit in the mix? The dubious answer left her chilled.

A notion to scamper into the fetid hold and confirm her suspicions played in her head. She'd bet her last coin the pirate crates were all gone. Before she could decide what to do, someone knocked. She shot off the bed, fought against dizziness, and threw open the cabin door. Brow drawn with worry, she watched as Church and Tubbs hefted Griffin on a canvas stretcher across the threshold. Mead took up the rear with Griffin's bloodied coat and shirt draped over a forearm.

"Let me prepare the bed." She rushed to smooth back the covers and plump up the pillows, still woozy, and wondered what was wrong with her.

Efficiently, as though the two men had practiced the maneuver, they settled Griffin on the bed. "Thank you," she said, grateful for their gentleness.

With a dismissal nod from Mead, the two men left, Church with a hopeful smile and his expressed goodnight.

"Let's get him out of these dirty breeches," Mead said and began undoing buttons. "Does he have a nightshirt?"

Lily swung toward Griffin's trunk. "It's locked." In search of the key, she reached for the dirty coat Mead had draped over the chair. She cringed when she touched the bloody garment, but in the next breath, she hugged it close to her chest and wondered about the odd smears on his sleeves. Inside a pocket, she found a tiny apothecary bottle. After extracting the cork, she sniffed the reddish-brown liquid and recognized the awful smell. *Laudanum.*

She'd seen the medicine often enough during Aunt Charlotte's illness and had even administered it to her for sleep and pain relief. Yet Griffin always slept sound as a baby. He didn't require medicine. Given the fog in her head, she might have concluded she had taken the drug.

"Mrs. Faraday, the nightshirt?"

"Yes, of course." Hurriedly she returned the bottle to the pocket, baffled by its presence. She searched until she found the key in the opposite pocket and unlocked the trunk. Even as she rifled through the trunk's contents, disturbing questions about who shot Griffin, and why, plagued her. Mead handed her the breeches, still warm from Griffin's body in exchange for the clean garment. Together they got the patient suited for bed.

After the surgeon had taken Griffin's pulse, he smiled. Over the glasses perched low on his nose, his pale blue eyes gentled, easing her worry. "I suspect he'll sleep peacefully. If he should grow hot or if there is any change, come and tell me."

"Thank you, Mr. Mead."

After he'd gone, Lily returned to Griffin. She stood at the side of the bed, hands together in prayer against her mouth and watched him slumber. The harsh white of the bandage wrapped about his head mirrored the paleness in his skin. How innocent he looked asleep. She wished she had such peace. Although she was still groggy, her emotions churned like water through a waterwheel. Unanswered questions shattered any hopes of serenity. "What have you been up to?" she whispered. "And just how, my dear man, did you manage to get grass stains on your coat sleeves?"

Chapter Nineteen

Lily shot up from the pallet. Confused, she squinted at the familiar surroundings as though she had never before seen the tiny cabin. Beyond the windows, gray clouds hovered low in the sky and cast a lackluster gloom to the morning. A pile of filthy, bloodstained clothes lay heaped on a chair in grim reminder of last night.

Oh, Griffin.

Guilt strummed in her chest. A capable nurse did not fall asleep when a patient needed her attention. Blame it on exhaustion—or laudanum.

The possibility Griffin drugged her was beyond unreal. Days ago, in the first rush of love, she would have discounted the horrific notion. Now, with the likelihood of Griffin's involvement in smuggling, she didn't know what to think. Her fingers tightened over the blanket. When he awoke, she would seek an explanation.

If he awoke.

Despite's Mead's positive prediction, Griffin could well die of a nasty infection and fever. The mere possibility knotted her gut.

Ashamed by her neglect, she lumbered to her feet amazed at the stiff achiness of her muscles. Respect emerged for Griffin's sacrifices these many nights asleep on the lumpy pallet.

She stepped to the bed. If he had tossed in his slumber, she couldn't tell. On his back, he slept with his lips slightly parted. A pink flush suffused his cheeks. Traces of fresh, bright blood stained the white linen bandage wrapped around his head. Dirty hair drooped about his face and pooled on the pillow. A sheen of sweat glistened on his forehead. She inched closer, eager for a sign of life. When his ribs expanded with an intake of air, she sagged with relief. A touch to his forehead singed her palm. *Fever.*

She hurried to the washbasin, filled the porcelain bowl halfway with water then sat in a chair near him. With a damp flannel cloth, she dabbed the sweat from his face and let the cool rag rest on his forehead. *Please, God. Let him recover.*

He didn't stir or acknowledge her presence. Just as well. She had yet to find the right words to ask about last night. For the time being, what mattered was that he lived. As to his activities on shore, for what else would explain the grass and soil stains on his coat sleeves, there would be time enough later to talk.

She sat back and gazed upon his still form. Why didn't he tell her about the smuggling? Was he afraid she would turn him in to the authorities? No longer love him? Love was not a window opened and closed at will. One couldn't stop caring as easily as tossing aside a holey pair of shoes. Nevertheless, the criminal activity tarnished his image and left the ground beneath her feet less solid.

She wanted to believe things weren't as bad as they appeared. Yet what good could come from merchandise taken from a pirate? Any distant hope his activities might be legal failed.

Slowly, she wrung the wet rag, unable to square the image of noble, kind Griffin with that of a contemptible criminal. If what she surmised was the truth, could she accept it? Would she continue to love him, as she once had?

Days ago, when she concluded Griffin was not a spy, the decision had left her pleased beyond relief. Now, as she dabbed away his sweat, she wondered if she had the strength to withstand any more surprises. For both their sakes, she would stave off judgment until she could hear his story. Pray God he would heal enough to explain.

As the minutes wore on, the questions and worry persisted. She was desperate to understand. Even as she lingered vigilant at his side, sensitive to his every breath, her mind tossed about possible answers. In all likelihood, the stored crates probably sat on some conveyance on land. As to Laurent, the merchant? Perhaps he was gone as well.

Oh, Griffin. What have you done?

How foolish to fall in love and give power to a fairy tale belief the future would be free of pain. Love hurt. Didn't she have the scars for proof? A mother dead. A father too stricken by grief to notice her. Why should Griffin be any different?

Stop it! Such pitiful thinking was pointless and beneath her. What she wanted, more than anything, was for Griffin to regain his health.

A rap sounded at the door. As she hurried to answer it, she raked fingers through her disordered hair, and tightened the sash of her dressing gown. "Sloane," she whispered, pleased to see him. "Come in."

A worried air strained the face of the slender youth.

He bore a tray with dishes and crossed the threshold. In his wake flowed a tasty aroma of something savory and delicious.

"This is perfect." She inspected the bowls beneath their lids.

"Beef broth for Mr. Faraday." He shot an uneasy glimpse at the lifeless form. "Porridge and tea, should you wish it."

"Thank you."

"Don't forget to pack, ma'am. Captain says we should see land sometime today."

"I'd almost forgotten," she said, comforted by images of home.

"It's been my pleasure to serve you, ma'am." He shifted and stared at his feet. "And God go with you." He jutted a chin at Griffin. "And him, too. I'll pray for him."

Lily swallowed the sudden lump in her throat. "Thank you, Mr. Sloane. I've said a few prayers myself."

When Sloane left, Lily perched on the side of the bed. She nudged Griffin gently. "Will you take broth?"

He moaned and turned his head away from the spoon she held at his lips. A deep sound rumbled in his chest.

"What did you say?" She cocked her ear closer.

"Water."

"Of course." Buoyed by the hope of his improvement, she poured liquid into a tumbler. "Drink this." Gently, she elevated his head and tipped the glass to his dry lips. His eyelids fluttered yet didn't open. A bead of water slipped down his chin and she caught it with a finger. When he motioned he had enough, she eased his head to the pillow.

"Will you drink broth?"

"Let me sleep."

Just those few words encouraged her. When he rolled to his side, giving her his back she didn't take offense. Since she could not force him to eat, she let him sleep.

At the table, she poured herself a cup of tea and dipped into her porridge, not caring that it had cooled. Sloane returned with hot water. Once he'd gone, she washed herself, dressed and despaired of wearing the blue muslin gown yet again. Even though they were close to land, it seemed the boat couldn't go fast enough to suit her.

The worry Griffin might die from infection left her frightened and unsettled. She paced about the small cabin. She watched for changes in his skin color and breathing. As morbid images of his dead body, shrouded in canvas, slipped into the shivery waters of the Atlantic, Mead appeared at the door. If it were possible, the lanky man looked even more haggard than early this morning when darkness blanketed the ship.

"How is he?" Half-moon spectacles rested low on his narrow, straight nose.

"He woke up only once to take water and slept all night." Too embarrassed to admit she also slept, she added, "He refused food and he's very warm."

Mead seemed to read her fear and examined Griffin with slow and steady hands. "The cabin is warm, as is the outside temperature. We'll wait and see and hope for the best." When he'd changed Griffin's bandage, he splashed alcohol across his hands and wiped them with a clean napkin. "The best thing is to continue with the cool compresses and encourage him to drink."

"I feel so utterly helpless." Arms clasped about her waist, she accompanied Mead into the corridor.

"He couldn't get better care than what you give to him." Mead smiled.

She doubted she deserved the praise. Nevertheless, she was touched by his kind words. It meant so much for her to do the best for Griffin.

"Why not get some rest yourself? Captain expects to sight New York late this afternoon."

"I'm too excited to rest. How is the tailor, the other injured man?"

"I trust he'll recover though the process is not without its trials."

"Will you tell me about last night?"

Chin dipped nearly to his chest, Mead eyed her over the silver rims of his spectacles.

"No need to keep secrets, Mr. Mead. I saw dirt stains on Griffin's coat. There's no doubt in my mind, he went ashore."

"Believe me when I say I'm sorry. I am not at liberty to speak."

Lily swallowed a caustic remark, frustrated by the thick wall that once again surrounded her against the truth. "I do believe you are sorry." She stepped into the cabin and closed the door.

As the morning lengthened, Griffin stirred restlessly. Every time he moaned, it felt like something ripped in her stomach. His shirt was damp with perspiration. It clung to his ribs. She tugged at the cloth and withdrew it from his torso. Bunched in her grasp, she used it to tamp the beads of moisture on his face and neck. She reveled at the flatness of his stomach and the dips and hollows of his chest. She blew a kiss across his sternum and with a whisper, ordered him to get better.

With a clean, dry shirt on her mind, she went to his trunk. She flipped up the lid left unlocked the previous evening. In her haste after Griffin's troubles, she'd failed to note any specific items. Today, with time on her hands, she noticed the assortment of books, the letters and papers tied in blue ribbon and the hand-sized double portrait of an older couple. His parents, she presumed, noting the strong resemblance though she couldn't recall ever meeting them. Griffin had his father's cleft chin and his mother's straight nose. Both handsome people much like Griffin.

Curious, she read the book titles, surprised to see in his possession authors such as Thomas Paine and Benjamin Franklin, both celebrated sympathizers of the Colonial cause. Griffin claimed scant interest in politics yet such questionable material contradicted his earlier comments. A new horror dawned as she dug through the rest of his trunk and extracted a ream of paper. She recognized Griffin's bold handwriting. The title of the piece read: *On a Nation Divided*. Her skin crawled as she read the first couple of paragraphs. "My God." She reared back with a fist pressed between her ribs. The seditious words damned him. As if hypnotized, she read on. With each sentence, her pulse beat harder. Her mind raced.

G. A. Fairley.

Griffin Alexander Faraday and G.A Fairley were the same person. She spun about and glared at the prone form on the bed, wanting to scream. "How could you?"

Afraid of what else she might discover, she forced herself to rake through the rest of his belongings. When she unearthed a notebook of secret code notations, her stomach turned. The discovery meant one damning thing.

She moaned and closed her eyes, sick to her stomach. He'd lied to her about everything. She clenched her fingers around the undeniable truth. The paper crackled. Griffin was a spy. Crushing the paper in her fist, she stomped once around the table, muttering in disbelief. How could he do this? He loved her.

She jerked to a stop. Her jaw dropped as a chilling realization danced across her shoulders. No, he'd never said anything about love, at least not directly. He said he wanted to remain married, which could be for any number of reasons and none to do with love. Would he use his status as a married man to hide his secret treasonous activity? Was it her uncle's position and connections in English society he hoped to exploit? Maybe he only wished to indulge in the physical aspects of marriage.

The room began to spin. Her knees hit the floor with a thunk. Pain radiated up her thighs. Grasping the edge of the trunk, she gulped back a rank taste in her mouth.

In her hands was evidence to prove Cecil Jones's claims—the very claims she believed untrue two days ago. Cecil's suspicions and need for proof made absolute sense. Against all hope to the contrary, Griffin was a firebrand seditionist and a spy. He insinuated himself into the highest circles of British society, the lawyer claimed, playing both sides of the fence. Regretfully, he'd played her too.

Dear Lord. She wished she'd never seen the condemning material. In spite of the irrefutable evidence, she struggled to connect the man she loved to a man who wrote inflammatory essays and passed secrets to the rebels. How could he? Slowly, she shook her head, aware of one fundamental and unavoidable fact. Even if she lived a hundred years, she could never accept his lies. His charm, his kindness, his humor, his humility; was it all a sham?

She pressed a hand to her raw, abraded heart. Tears pricked her eyes. She'd given him the best and trusted him with her body. In return, he betrayed her. Why didn't he have faith enough in her to share his political beliefs? Had he been only a smuggler, she might have accepted his folly, but his lack of confidence in her signaled a much greater grievance. His disloyalty to her and their country cleaved her in two. She was left with an aching gap even love couldn't mend.

The tears came, and she swept them away with both hands. After a while, when she gained control over her emotions, she straightened the items in the trunk and quietly closed the lid. With her soul in shreds, she set both the essays and the nightshirt on the table then went to the bed and watched him sleep.

Griffin moaned and shifted beneath the cotton sheet. The action brought on her sneer of contempt. She considered his discomfort just rewards for his deceit. It would satisfy her to see him tried and convicted for his crimes. An instant pang of guilt stabbed at her. Nevertheless...

Nostrils flared, she dropped into the desk chair resolved to do her duty, aware at some deeper level she sought retribution for the damage inflicted upon her

221

gullible heart. *You'll be sorry.* She dipped the quill into the inkpot and set nib to paper.

Dear Mr. Jones,

In my possession is the evidence you seek. Mr. Faraday is no Loyalist. He is, as you believed, a traitor and a spy.

He writes essays against the King under the pseudonym of G. A. Fairley. His dedication to the Colonial cause is fervent.

Any satisfaction she'd expected at the revelation eluded her.

Oh, why, she lamented, did Griffin have to be a rebel? Everyone she knew in London revered the King. With tight, quick movements, she folded the letter in half and stuffed it along with a page she ripped from his ciphering journal into an assigned envelope. For good measure, she included one of the more fiery essays.

Then, heavy on her feet, she crossed the room and dug her portmanteau from her trunk. In it, she packed a shawl, Papa's journal, a coin purse and what jewelry she possessed. Beneath all of this, she buried the envelope. Finished with her task, she sat down to wait. Time crawled on.

A great bellow jarred Lily awake. Her head snapped up with her stiff and sore neck evidence she'd fallen asleep.

Griffin sat up in bed, the covers rumpled, and clutched his left calf. "A cramp," he hissed. Teeth clenched, face flushed, he massaged his leg. "Sorry, I didn't mean to disturb you."

"Think nothing of it."

At her sarcasm, he stilled and lifted his head, possibly alert to a change in the atmosphere. The man knew how to survive.

"I'm almost finished with these." The words lashed with scorn. In illustration, she held up one of the essays along with the blue ribbon used to bind them all together.

"Ah," he muttered in recognition.

"Ah, indeed.*"*

He levered both legs off the bed and dangled his feet just above the floor. Face rigid with pain, he gripped the edge of the mattress, the skin over his knuckles stretched taut. "How long have I been asleep?"

How could he act so self-contained? Then again, she should have expected as much from a man who kept the most important secrets well hidden. After all, he was the *great manipulator*.

"Through breakfast and the noon meal," she answered.

He tried to stand and fell back to the bed.

"Careful!" She was out of the chair in a flash.

He thrust up a hand. "I'm fine. Just a bit dizzy."

She chided herself for caring. He didn't deserve her concern. Nevertheless, she handed him a glass of water.

He hesitated. Perhaps he felt a twinge of guilt. Then he took the glass and drank, the muscles in his throat moving as he swallowed.

An urge to feel his forehead like a worried mother came over her. She resisted. "How do you feel?"

Gingerly, he touched the bandaged wound over his ear. "Like I've been cracked on the head with the flat of an ax."

"Close." She took his empty glass and set it on the table. "A musket ball."

He shot her an uneasy look.

"Don't you remember?" Her jaw tightened with anger.

He patted the bandage with a light touch. "I have a vague recollection of a gun blast." Something like embarrassment or awkwardness scuttled his features, surprising in lieu of Griffin's typical grace and confidence.

"Gun or guns?" Tension rasped in her voice. "Was there one gun shot or many? Men on horses? A company of British soldiers dispatched to bring the smugglers to heel?"

He gazed up perhaps remembering the scene as well. "Your ability to see beyond the ship is extraordinary."

Shadowed circles pooled beneath his eyes. Dried blood on his bandage and dirty hair roughened his appearance. Still she cared, and the realization annoyed her.

He scrubbed a hand down his cheek, his brow furrowed as though tortured by a weighty decision. She wished his concerns didn't matter.

"Lily, I meant to tell you when we reached New York."

"Meant to tell me what?" Beneath the clipped pleasantness in her tone, her body quivered with pent-up emotion.

A hand skimmed across his chest and down his arm, as if in search of further wounds or maybe he meant to stall. She wondered if in this dire circumstance, when truth mattered as much as life, he considered dredging up more lies.

"It's only a minor head wound. Mr. Mead says

you'll live." Bitterness tolled loud and clear.

His mouth twitched, and she was appalled he found amusement in a near deadly disaster. "My mother will be happy to hear of it." He held her gaze. "I see you hold a different opinion."

She kept quiet.

"I don't remember anything after I got hit. Do you know what happened?" He arched a brow and winced.

"How ironic you should ask me. Everyone suggests *I* should ask *you* for an explanation. Once again, no one on this ship will speak—at least not to me. Am I a monster capable of destroying all and sundry? I can assure you it is a power I'd rather not possess." She wanted him off balance, as miserable as she felt.

"You're no monster. You're a loving—"

Unable to listen to his drivel, she cut him off. "I know what I am. And I know what you are, too."

He stiffened, still and taut as a hare sensed danger.

"Tell me. I deserve some truthful answers."

The muscles of his chest expanded when he drew in a big breath. She studied his strained expression. She could almost hear his brain whirring, coming up with lies.

"Please. Just listen."

It took considerable discipline not to shriek and howl her displeasure or stomp about the room like a mad woman. Grinding her teeth, she slid into the desk chair determined to steel her heart and spine to whatever he might dish her way.

Neither one spoke. He brushed a hand over his loose hair. The gesture dredged forth the memory of the first time she sat with him in this cabin—the first stirring attraction. "When you came aboard, dressed as a cabin boy, I thought you worked for the Crown or at least someone with ties close to the Crown.

She knew this and nodded, urging him on.

"When you revealed you worked for Cecil Jones, your behavior—the questions and snooping began to make sense."

"We've been through this," she said with testy impatience. "Just get to the point. What were you doing last night when you got shot?"

He lifted his chin and stared out the window. Clearly, he was in the midst of some internal struggle, and she despised him even more for the delay. Why couldn't he trust her?

After a few minutes, he faced her. "I pray you will not abuse the information I am about to reveal. Lives hang in the balance. What you do can mean life or death for Mulworthy and others."

There was no mistaking his serious intent or his plea for her cooperation. "You think I have no regard for the safety of the officers and the men on this ship?" Her hands shook at the insult. "How can you think so little of me?

"I'm sorry. I regret..." He paused. "War and duty..." He shrugged as if further explanation were unnecessary. "We delivered the crates and Laurent."

"The lace," she quipped.

"The guns," he added.

Her brows rose along with her shock. "So it was guns and not gold, as I suspected." Her mouth curled with derision. "And Laurent? Is he a wealthy merchant?"

"A skilled military officer."

"I see." Oh, how they must have laughed at her

naiveté as they sat around the Captain's table while they drank spirits and played cards. How Mulworthy must have sniggered at his ruse of the hidden guns beneath the lace.

"It's war, Lily."

"And you stand with the Colonists."

"I do."

Had he trusted her enough to share this information when she revealed her connection to Cecil Jones, she might have reached a place of understanding and acceptance. Confused, hurt, she couldn't deal with this pain, not now.

"Did you put laudanum in my brandy?"

He dropped his head and stared at the floor.

She rose from the chair, her hands fisted at her side. "I'll inform Mr. Mead you're awake and have Sloane bring you food."

"Lily, wait." Urgency strummed in his voice.

With an iron fist pressing against her breastbone, she left the cabin.

Chapter Twenty

Griffin fell back on the bed and groaned, his head juddering with pain when it smacked the pillow. She hated him. The clipped tone, the rigid stance and the march out the door—all signs of her fury. From her perspective, he'd betrayed her with his foul and unforgivable actions. The realization crushed him like a ton of ocean water over his chest. He gulped for air and squeezed his eyes shut against the pain.

He never wanted her to find out about the guns and certainly not this way. As for the use of laudanum, it disgusted him. One dose was all he'd added to her drink. He hoped the tiny amount would secure for her the sleep of a blessed child and obliterate the ruckus of crates and sailors going ashore.

Had a British scouting party not stumbled upon them at their delivery point, the mission would have gone off without a hitch. Once in New York, she would have left the *Providence*, Mulworthy, and the crew behind, happy in her ignorance, none the wiser for the charade. Unfortunately, he was neither God nor a miracle worker. He couldn't have foreseen what the British might do nor could he alter plans set in place a day before their departure from London. If only she had never come aboard. But he didn't mean that. He loved her and there was no regret in that.

Worried he'd lost her for good he pushed to his

feet and wobbled over to the nightstand. His head kicked and thumped like a fiddler marking time at a barn dance. A bleary face stared back at him from the mirror. He deliberated how to salvage his future with Lily. Optimism and confidence, his two strongest assets, seemed oddly lacking. He soaped his cheeks and shaved. With deft movements, he peeled the bandage from his head and swore when the wound began to bleed. A scrap of cloth staunched the flow.

Maybe once Lily left this stinking ship, resettled with her father and saw how things stood politically in New York, she'd see last night for what it was—a necessity of war. If he were lucky and Henry Fitzhugh sided with the Patriots, he might influence his daughter to their cause. He snorted. And he might grow another head. One with more common sense.

The side of his head burned, and though dizzy, he managed to don clean clothes. Sloane miraculously appeared with apple beer and beef stew. Mead followed the lad and Griffin offered himself up to inspection. He flinched when the doctor applied a dash of alcohol and something else equally stinging to his wound. "This will help to heal," his friend said. "I'll leave the bottle with you. Apply it four times a day."

Griffin nodded. "Were there any other casualties?"

"Just one. He'll live. Fortunate for you both, you'll be off the boat sometime today."

A picture of home and family flashed into Griffin's head offering a moment of joy.

"All things considered," Mead said wrapping a thin ribbon of cloth around Griffin's head to support the square bandage he'd replaced. "We've been lucky."

Griffin uttered a silent prayer of thanks no one had

been seriously hurt or killed on the voyage. The only victims, it seemed, were he and Lily.

"Well." Mead assessed his work with an ironic smile. "The patch adds panache and mystery to your customary debonair appeal."

Griffin cocked a dubious brow.

"Do go easy for a day or two," the good man advised.

When he was alone again, Griffin hurriedly ate the food and drank the beer. His physical being felt stronger for the sustenance, yet his mind remained uneasy. Without any further delay, he would find Lily and begin laying a road to peace. He rose from the table, and abruptly stopped. In her present furious state, she wouldn't listen. His efforts would be for naught. Later, after she'd had time to cool her ire, he would go to her.

From the desk, he gathered the political essays she'd left behind, saddened at the sight of his pseudonym *G.A. Fairley*. Based on her reaction, his written arguments had failed to sway her. Loyal to the Crown forever was no doubt her stand.

Riddled with regret, he began to pack. A neat and precise man by nature, he'd always kept his trunk in an orderly fashion with folded clothes on top, books and essays toward the bottom. At first glance, everything appeared in its proper place. Yet if she'd withdrawn the essays, what else might she have seen?

Beneath the books, he retrieved his ciphering journal and flipped through the pages. A jagged edge showed one page had been ripped from the binding. His breath hitched. *Oh, Lily.* Whatever she intended to do, it couldn't be good.

Griffin slammed the trunk lid and stomped from the cabin, mindful of the pounding in his head. He checked the galley and deck, all the obvious places a woman alone might go on a ship, even the bursar's office. Unease clawed like a cold hand against his skin when he didn't find her. Mulworthy and Church conferred on the poop deck, overseeing the preparations to land. Could she be bold or foolish enough to hide in the Captain's quarters? The rooms were empty. He asked around. In return, he received blank stares and ribbing for having lost a wife. No one had seen her. He considered the hold, but discounted the notion as a dozen sailors hauled kegs topside.

One last place to check, he went below. Lily's head shot up when he swung open the door to Church's cabin. Relief washed over him as he swept inside. She sat at Church's small desk with a book spread open over her lap.

"All packed and ready to leave." He angled his chin toward the leather portmanteau near her feet. "I believe you have something of mine."

Her gaze narrowed. He caught a glint of contained ferocity.

"I'd like it back."

Her dark brows cocked with an ironical slant. "You want the essay denouncing the King? Might I at least keep the page of ciphers?" Her cold smile was anything but kind. "You love to play games. Ciphering is just another game, isn't it?"

"With a lot more at stake." He could almost feel the woman's sharp claws on his neck, digging into his skin. "If it will help, I intended to tell you when we reached New York—about my role for the Colonial

Army."

"Instead, you drugged me."

"Protected you. It was meant to keep you out of this."

"Unaware you mean."

He held her glacial stare.

She gestured toward the end of Church's narrow bed. "Please, sit." Her mouth pinched in a visible struggle to control her emotions while patches of color stained her neck. "I hate it when you tower over me."

Resigned, he sank upon the narrow cot.

"You lied to me," she hissed. "Over and over. You're a traitor and a spy!" Her body visibly trembled. "How could you?"

"I never wanted to hurt you. When you sneaked onto this ship, I questioned whether you could be trusted. Every precaution had to be taken to ensure my mission's success…"

"That's what matters to you most—the outcome of this war, freedom from England."

"Yes, freedom. Yours. Mine. And for everybody else who is fearless enough to wrest it from the King." Conviction rang in his heated words.

"My freedom?" she mocked. "There'll be no freedom for me or any other woman. This is all about men. It always has been."

"Have more faith."

She could have sliced him with her cutting sneer.

"Give it to me." He held out his hand, palm up.

"Why should I? It would be a service to the Crown to expose you."

"Do you expect the British Army in New York to cheer and pin a medal on your chest?"

She didn't bother to reply. Her icy stare was answer enough.

"Are you so eager to see the noose around my neck?"

"It's what you deserve."

He couldn't believe it. She couldn't possibly be this cruel or narrow-minded. Unless he'd misjudged her. "What bothers you the most, Lily, my political beliefs or my lying to you?"

"You bastard."

On his feet in an instant, he wrenched her from the chair. He thrust her against him. His kiss was bruising, possessive, proof of his fierce need to have her, to make her understand. Struggling in his arms, she fought against his control. She sprang away from him, panting, her eyes wild, her cheeks flushed.

"I thought I meant something to you," she accused. The stays of the gown pressed against her heaving chest.

"My God, can you not see how much I love you?"

"Love me? How can you love me when you don't trust me? When you drug me to keep me in the dark?"

The use of laudanum was stupid of him, a regret he would hold forever. He reached for her. She jerked away and bumped against the desk.

"You're my wife. I'm your husband!"

"Not for long!"

"You can't mean it." His worst fear snagged him by the throat. It pressed against his vocal cords. "No, Lily," he rasped. He couldn't lose her. "You're angry, but please, don't give up on us." He reached for her.

"Don't touch me." Fear flickered in her face.

"I'm not a brute."

She snatched her bag. Her shoulders drawn and rigid. "I shall have my father's attorney dissolve our marital arrangement."

Uncertain what could change her mind, he sighed with regret and dragged a hand down his cheek. He'd never wanted to hurt her. If he could reverse time, he would do things differently. Although it would be the final nail to his coffin, he had to ask. "Before you leave…"

She hesitated and stared at his outstretched hand. "What makes you think I have it?"

Acid burned in his gut. She fully intended to make this difficult. Given her stubborn streak, he shouldn't have been surprised. "I searched the cabin—thoroughly."

"You broke into my chest?"

Though shamed by his action, he answered her question with his head held high. "This is no game I play. I will have my things."

She drew back, affronted as a rosy flush raced up her pale neck.

Tired of the fight, he expelled a slow breath. "I can prevent you from leaving the ship."

A light in her eyes flared and hardened. "You would hold me back; make me a prisoner?"

God, all he wanted was to smooth her ruffled feathers, pull her into his embrace and love her. "If you force me."

Her face pinched. She slammed the leather bag on the desk with a loud *thwap*. When she found the envelope with the page of ciphers and the essay, she thrust it into his hand.

His fingers curled about the rough paper.

Bag gripped in her hand, she stomped to the door and flung it wide. "And the *devil* take you."

****

Lily marched across the corridor, convinced she'd never care about him again. With no place else to go, she sailed into the surgery, shoulders heaving, and surprised Mead, who stood before a bank of shelves cluttered with an assortment of bottles and potted plants. Over the rim of his spectacles, he studied her. "Are you all right?"

She waved away his concern. "I'm, ah…" What could she say? Her knees weak, she sank into the nearest chair feeling as though a hand had plundered into her chest and plucked from it all her strength. "May I sit awhile?"

"Of course."

Unable to bear his gentle gaze, she stared at the floor. "Griffin and I have…" Fist jammed to her lips, she fought against the rise of hot tears.

"No need to explain," Mead offered in a kindly voice. Scuffed shoes and tapered calves encased in white stockings appeared in her lowered view as he stood before her. For such long, skinny fingers, the hand he settled at her shoulder was remarkably strong and soothing. "It's never pleasant to have a disagreement with someone you care about."

Care about? If only he knew how much she cared or had cared. It was all so confusing. Perhaps it was better to think in past tense, how much she *had* loved Griffin. After all the despicable things he'd done, the betrayal and lies, how could she in all good stead, a woman of pride and position, continue to love him? Yet she did. A tiny moan escaped her lips.

"Is there anything I can do for you?" Urgency colored his voice.

"Allow me to rest here, if you will, until the boat docks."

"Stay as long as you wish." Overhead, he extracted a bottle from one of the shelves. "Would you care for a spot of brandy?"

Brandy. Brandy and laudanum. She clenched the firm handles of her portmanteau sitting upon her lap. If only she could shut out the world and forget. "Yes, thank you."

In two tumblers, he poured a small amount and offered her one.

"To a most eventful voyage." He hefted his glass in a toast. "Thanks be to God it is at an end."

"Amen." She drank and coughed after she swallowed too much.

"May I help you pack?" She set her bag on the floor, feeling guilty for taking him away from his work.

"Already done." He inclined his sandy head to a leather satchel upon his worktable.

"You travel light."

"We, the crew, will be in New York a few days. Then we're off again."

"Where will you go?"

"Someplace where we can put into port and take the time needed for repairs."

"New York won't do?"

He smiled indulgently and she knew.

"The British soldiers." Could things really be so dangerous in New York? It dawned on her Mead might not trust her either. "I will never speak to anyone about what took place on this ship."

One blond brow shot up, creasing his forehead. "On behalf of the Captain, I wish to extend my appreciation for your generosity. It hasn't been an easy time for you, I suspect."

He pulled up a chair and sat. Kind, sensitive, and above all, good, Mead need never worry she would ever do anything to bring the wrath of the British down upon his head.

After another sip of brandy, she leaned her head back against the wall.

"What will you do when we dock?" he asked.

"Go to my father." Pray she would find him at home.

As if he guessed the reason for her heavy heart and mind, he didn't ask about Griffin and their future. They talked for a while, each partaking of more brandy. With good humor, he allowed her to ply him with questions about his research into plants. She would be forever grateful for his distraction. Still, when a prolonged silence crept into their conversation, she wept. Mead sat very still with an expression almost as sad as her heart-wrenching sorrow. He offered her a handkerchief to dab away the moisture from her cheeks.

"Shall we go above stairs?" he asked. "It may cheer you to see land."

Clutching the damp, wadded hanky, she followed him topside. The sun, past its zenith, had begun its afternoon descent. The morning cloud cover, long since blown away, left behind a stunning azure sky. The *Providence* passed through the narrows between Long and Staten Islands, and in the brisk breeze, steadily made its way to the city. Lily sorted through any memories of the time, years ago, when she sailed for

England. What stood out most was the shrinking image of Papa on the quay. Like then, tears clouded her vision.

"The waterways are so busy." Merchant vessels, frigates, sloops and a dozen man-of-war ships flying the Union Jack cluttered the dark blue waters.

"Too busy to get a dock," Mead replied as though he'd read her mind. "We'll weigh anchor in the East River, at Murray's Wharf for the night until a berth comes available tomorrow."

She rocked forward on her toes. "I can see buildings at the water's edge." She shifted for a better view. At the sight of Griffin, her excitement fell away and her stomach clenched. Inches taller than Mulworthy or Church, he stood with his back to her, in conversation with the two men.

Mulworthy spied her and cocked a bushy brow. He licked his lips and grinned, his color ruddy as ever as he waved her over. Mead must have sensed her hesitancy and ushered her forward. Griffin turned and watched her approach.

"Mrs. Faraday." Fists curled around his lapels, the captain appeared every inch a man pleased with himself. "'Tis time tae go ashore. Might I bid ye a fond farewell and good luck for the future."

No doubt, the old buzzard would rejoice at the sight of her receding skirts.

"You too, Captain." She tried very hard to ignore Griffin. Sadness rose again as she faced Samuel Church. "Thank you, Mr. Church, for all your attentive kindness. I shall miss our walks and spirited conversation." If she hoped to see some spark of jealousy in Griffin, she would remain disappointed at his blank expression.

"Give my regards to Mr. Flint and Sloane."

"It would be my pleasure," Church replied with a polite farewell nod.

Mead walked her toward the place she would disembark. At the forward section of the ship, sailors worked the capstan and lowered the iron anchor. Several launches slipped into the choppy water.

"Will you be going ashore, Mr. Mead?"

"Later." It was all she could do not to snuffle like a baby when she bid him goodbye.

Off to the side, she noticed Tubbs heave a barrel from the hold. She never believed it possible to think she would miss the burly giant, along with all the rest of them. What was wrong with her?

Emotions in a swirl, she wheeled toward the city, her throat thick. Good-byes always made her teary. Griffin was at her side in an instant. "Allow me to escort you."

As much as she yearned to lean against him, grateful for his steadying presence, she would not. "Your help won't be necessary."

"You're my responsibility." He leaned toward her. His warm breath skittered across her ear.

Responsibility. She almost choked. "Not for long."

At the railing, she passed her bag to a sailor who dropped it into the waiting hands of another man in the longboat.

"Hang on tight to the rope ladder," Griffin said and carefully directed her off the ship and down the ladder. Embarrassed by her lack of grace, she fell onto the launch seat. Griffin, nimble as a cat, settled across from her. She refused to acknowledge him and directed her attention to the shoreline.

The sailor barked a command. In unison, the oars dropped into the water. The boat rose and fell with the waves. It would take only a short while to reach the pier. A cold spray of water dampened her cheeks and she shivered. Only once did she glance back at the ship and kept her gaze riveted to the dock.

The thought of her future set butterflies winging in her stomach. Would home and Papa seem the same after years in London? She'd imagined it a million times; the sweep into his embrace, the furniture set just so in the parlor, and the big table in the kitchen. She leaned forward as though it might make the next anxious minutes move faster. Her mind jumped to Griffin. What would life be like without him? The question brought forth a hitch of pain.

The longboat neared the dock and floated into a pylon. The forward sailor in the launch welcomed a hand up and scrabbled to the pier. Thick rope in hand, he secured the bobbing boat to an iron cleat anchored to a wooden plank. Griffin and a sailor with bulging arm muscles assisted Lily off the boat.

"Thank you." Her gaze swept the busy pier, seeking out familiar faces. She saw none. Even though she stood on the solid boardwalk with the brackish smell of water assailing her head, she had the sensation of being on the boat, where she swayed with the waves.

"I'll get a carriage." Griffin set off. She clutched her satchel, and having rejected his earlier offer to carry it, skirted behind him as he threaded through the colorful horde of humanity.

Each step brought her closer to her final destination. The knowledge raised her anticipation until her gripped fingers dampened the bag's leather handle. She prayed Papa would be at home, ensconced in his work as Percy had suggested weeks ago. Would he still wear the same simple cutaway coat and hurry about with a preoccupied air? Worry clutched at her when she thought of him in jail. Was he even alive?

The wharf crawled with sailors, street hawkers, dogs and well-dressed aristocrats. No one would ever forget the British held the city. Scarlet-clad soldiers marched in formation across the square, their muskets slung over their shoulders. The noise of vendors, the clop of horses, and the creak of carts rang in her ears. A whiff of spicy gingerbread added to her nostalgia.

Griffin raised a hand in the air and whistled. Over the cacophony in the busy street, he caught the attention of a carriage for hire. Drawn by two chestnut sorrels, the carriage rolled forward and stopped before them. The driver hopped off his stoop. With a graceful flourish, he flung the door open, dropped the vehicle's steps and with a twinkle said, "Your ride, madam."

Lily hadn't expected such flair in a lowly hack driver in the Colonies. She thanked him and climbed inside after giving the driver the address. Griffin placed her bag next to her on the seat and made to join her.

"Wait." She thrust out a palm. "May I ask where you're going?"

Griffin paused, his brow knitted. "I'm taking you home."

"No, no." Adamant, shook her head. "This is where we part. I've waited long enough for the special moment when I'd see Papa again." Griffin's unwelcome presence would only sully the happy occasion.

"Please, Lily." His hand tightened around the door handle. Strained features spoke of his inner struggle, his desire to play the loving husband when the charade no longer mattered. At his wretchedness, an ache pressed against her breastbone, but she was determined to experience a glorious homecoming. She was determined to be quit of the man and his tricks. No painful baggage would linger and mar the pleasure and excitement of her reunion.

"From this point on, I'll finish my journey alone. I'm sure you can understand."

"I understand you're angry, but it needn't be this way."

Her hands tightened over her lap. "Please let go of the carriage. I've waited long enough to see Papa. I want no further delays." With a louder voice, she called out. "Driver!"

Griffin visibly stiffened. For a moment, she feared he might jump inside the cab. His face etched in pain, he quietly closed the door. The carriage shot ahead.

Griffin was no more.

Chapter Twenty-One

Lily perched at the edge of the carriage seat, nerves taut as any bowstring. Griffin would not ruin her homecoming. A buzz of activity churned outside the vehicle's windows. Talkative pedestrians conducted trade in the busy square and managed to avoid collisions with the carriages and carts that rattled noisily over cobblestones. Fruits, vegetables, fish, cloth and all manner of metal and porcelain gewgaws overflowed stalls and barrows. The aroma of coffee and fresh baked buns whetted her taste buds. Gulls squawked overhead to compete with laughter and conversation while ships, some with triple masts, received or unloaded their goods.

For all she could remember of New York, the crowded town might have been a marketplace in Venice or Istanbul, places about which she'd only read. None of the shop and tavern signs stirred a memory.

The raucous din and briny odor of the harbor fell away the farther she travelled from the pier. Soon the bark of vendors became gentle birdsong. Leafy elm and maple trees shaded the avenues. Block after block swept past. When the carriage veered right onto her street, she sat forward on the seat.

Her heart sped a little faster when she recognized her neighbor's houses. How insignificant the simple brick and clapboard structures looked compared to the spacious, stately architecture of London. Anxiously, she sought out one particular house in the middle of the block. Built of red brick with white trim, it looked charming and smaller than she remembered.

Ahead was the stoop where she'd sat on a hot summer day with her dolls, Abigail and Molly. They drank cool tea from a miniature china set of delicate saucers and cups that rested on a crocheted doily.

"Driver. Stop!" Unable to contain her excitement, she hopped out as soon as the carriage halted. Once she'd paid the fare and the carriage clattered away, she faced her home. Three slate steps led to the black painted front door. On each side of the landing, roses, perhaps the very ones planted by her mother years ago, drooped in the late afternoon heat. Weeds grew among the browning leaves. Saddened to see the neglect, she promised a little water and tender care would see the pink beauties rise to their former glory.

Taking a deep breath, she squared her shoulders then bounded up the steps. The clack of the brass knocker against the doorplate echoed loudly in the quiet street. When no one answered, she rapped harder. As Papa often ignored all intrusions when he worked, she didn't expect him to answer the summons. But where were the servants?

At last, the door inched opened. This is it, she thought with a tremor of expectation.

An elderly woman peeked out. Wisps of silvery white hair escaped her mobcap and curled over her forehead. "May I help you?"

"Agatha?" A bounty of wrinkles she couldn't remember bracketed the housekeeper's thin face and neck. "It's me. Lily Fitzhugh."

Agatha Duff's forehead creased as she studied Lily with eyes as round and gray as pebbles.

"Don't you remember me?" Her disappointment lifted as the woman brightened. A smile rearranged the myriad lines in her face.

"Little Lily?" Gnarled fingers swung the door all the way open. "Come in. Come in."

She started forward only to have the woman haul her across the threshold and swallow her in a hug.

"My Lily's come home," cried the woman.

Lily submitted to pats on the back much like a baby who required a good burp. Mindful not to squish the delicate woman, she hugged her back, inhaling her familiar scent of soap and roses.

"My, goodness. You're all grown up and such a lady." Agatha laughed and closed the door. "I can't believe you're here."

It thrilled her to hear the old dear cackle. After the death of her mother, the energetic housekeeper stepped in to offer comfort and guidance until Lily went to live with Aunt Charlotte. She fought against tears for she would always be appreciative of the attention shown to such a lonely child.

Lily set her bag off to the side of the foyer. While she untied the ribbons and removed her hat, she took a moment to absorb the place—the parlor to the left, the corridor that led to the back of the house and alongside it, the familiar polished banister on the staircase. On a wave of energy, she crossed the Turkish rug and came to an instant stop inside the parlor doorway. Across the room, above a fireplace mantel, hung an oil portrait. "Mama." She whispered past the knot in her throat.

Agatha came and stood next to her. "You resemble

her, what with your dark hair and the shape of your face."

"If I could be half so kind and gracious, I'll be more than satisfied." She swallowed hard. The ache of her mother's absence was a never-ending void. How she wished she were here, someone with whom to share her burdens and fears. *I love you, Mama.*

I love you, too, child, she imagined her reply.

Lily shivered as if the spirit of her mother brushed a hand across her skin. Through a haze of tears, she saw two upholstered chairs in blue stripe angled toward the fireplace, the favored spots where her parents sat in the evening. In the center, directly across from the hearth, stood a sofa where she used to curl up with her books. Sometimes Mama would let her stay up late. In between yawns, Lily listened to her parent's conversation and laughter, proud to be part of their adult world.

"Papa!" Against Agatha's cries to wait, she raced out the door. In the background, the caretaker's skirts rustled as she scuttled behind her toward the back of the long, narrow house. Like a fleet-footed girl, she charged into his study, excited with the possibility of finding a playful father perhaps hiding behind a chaise.

True to her memory, the room was a clutter of books and a big desk piled with papers. At its side stood the world globe she used to spin. Wherever her finger landed, she would fantasize about travelling to a strange and far off world. Worn but still plump leather chairs flanked the fireplace. Dust and tobacco scented the air.

"Where's Papa?" She turned and almost collided with Agatha, whose bleak expression triggered concern.

"You must be thirsty and hungry, child. Come along to the kitchen. I'll make you—"

"I'm fine," Lily snapped, regretful when Agatha blanched. "I'm sorry I sounded cross. It's just…" She twisted her fingers. "I've waited so long for this moment."

Agatha settled a kind hand upon Lily's arm. "Of course you have, dear."

With heavy steps, she followed Agatha through the dining room and down the stairs to the lower level kitchen. Despite the June day, a fire licked a blackened iron pot in the hearth. Lily's stomach growled at the aroma of chicken, thyme and onion.

"You better sit down. I'll get you some tea."

The housekeeper shuffled over the stone floor to claim a cup from a cupboard. Lily sank in a ladder-back chair and dropped her elbows on the well-scrubbed oak table, too tired and worried to care about posture and table manners.

A cup of steaming tea was set before her. "I've got soup." Agatha dashed around the table and snagged a soup plate from a wall rack. Moments later, she presented Lily a savory broth along with a loaf of bread.

Lily took a sip of soup then asked the dreaded question. "Is he dead?"

Agatha recoiled. "Dead? I should hope not, though anything can happen in those squalid places."

This couldn't be good. "What do you mean?"

"Oh, child. I hate to be the one to tell you."

Lily gripped the edge of the solid table.

"He's in prison."

"Still?" She wanted to cry. "I had hoped Fletcher would have gotten him released."

"You heard then."

247

Lily nodded as the woman collapsed into a chair and rested a palm against her cheek.

"A letter from Mr. Fletcher said Papa was too outspoken about the British officers housed here."

"He was and they're still here. A Sergeant Cook sleeps in your bed."

"In my bedchamber?" She tapped the spoon against the bowl, vexed at the thought of such trespass. As she considered how to reclaim what was rightfully hers, Agatha spoke again.

"There are those who think your father sides with the Sons of Liberty."

Lily reared back. Her shoulder blades smacked against the slats of the chair. "That's absurd. He's loyal to the—"

Her declaration was stopped by a raised hand riddled with brown spots. "Not according to some folks."

Any hope of his allegiance or that his incarceration was all a mistake slipped away.

"For all the goodness of the man, your father has his enemies. People have come forward and spoken against him."

The notion honest people endorsed such a ridiculous accusation made no sense. What insanity had taken hold of good New Yorkers?

"Who?"

A hot flame flared in the pit of her stomach as Agatha rattled off a few unfamiliar names and a few she recognized.

"They're jealous, jealous of what Papa has achieved. What else could account for their hostile behavior?" Neighbors turning against neighbors?

Soldiers billeted in a citizen's home? This was not the city she remembered. "When did you last see him?"

"Not since the British soldiers arrested him almost five months ago. The Redcoats came one snowy night. Won't ever forget it, neither."

Lily skimmed her hands over her chilled arms despite the fire in the hearth not six feet away. "Five months." She wrapped her fingers around the teacup. The warmth of the brew leached into her cold fingers. "Why didn't you write and tell me?"

"I did, dearie. When I saw you in the doorway, I thought you'd gotten my letter and hastened home."

Had a letter reached London? If so, what had become of it? Uncle Percy had no reason to withhold mail.

"Lost in transit, I suppose," Agatha said.

"Why hasn't Papa written?"

Agatha snorted. "Prisoners aren't allowed such a luxury."

Her body buzzed. Compelled to act, Lily jumped up, paced to the farthest wall. At the wooden hutch, she swirled about. "I must go to him at once." How often she'd uttered the same words over the past few months. "I've come so far…" Risked so much and endured such hardships. "I must see him."

"Sit," Agatha directed. "Rushing out on a cloud of desperation won't do any good unless you're a mermaid or an angel."

Brow puzzled, she did as ordered and dropped into the chair. "Mermaid?"

"He's on a prison ship in the harbor."

"A ship," she repeated dumbly.

"The British have rounded up so many troublemakers the jail couldn't hold them all. Some call the poor saps criminals, some calls 'em patriots. Take your pick."

Lily glanced around as if seeing the kitchen anew. "How did you manage here without Papa?"

"Your father granted Mr. Fletcher power to handle his affairs. The British officers billeted here pay for food and service, when they think of it." From her sour look, it was plain the old woman didn't think much of the arrangement. "I've two girls come in to clean and do laundry." She twirled a spoon in her teacup. "After Mr. Fitzhugh's arrest, Mr. Fletcher wrote letters." She shrugged as if it didn't matter. "It did no good. Though to his credit, he is reliable and remits a monthly bank note for necessities, and such." She picked at a thread in a quilted tea cozy. "Still, I had to let the gardener go. Since your father isn't around to supervise his assistant, he went as well."

"Oh, Agatha. It must be so difficult cooking for three men, which in itself is a day's work. Do these officers have any influence? Will they offer any help for Papa?"

"They've nothing to do with the prisons and prisoners. They're strictly to do with platoons. Two are off as we speak. I don't expect them back for a week." Agatha bent her head, hands clasped together over her lap. "Aye. I worry for your papa."

Lily swept forward and hugged the woman. "Thank you for your concern and loyalty to him."

Agatha patted Lily's hand. "'Tis fond of Mister Fitzhugh, I am. I pray every day to see him released."

Lily straightened. "I must go at once to speak with Mr. Fletcher."

"Aye, sit down and finish your tea and soup. It'll be dark soon. I'll take you to him tomorrow morning."

****

"It's up ahead." Agatha pointed a knobby finger at a narrow building situated between a bakery and a tavern. A white shellacked sign embellished with the name of Amos Fletcher, Attorney, draped from a dowel above a doorway and swayed in a morning breeze coming off the river.

Lily jabbed the point of her parasol on the carriage roof and called for the driver to stop.

"If it's all the same to you," Agatha proposed. "I'll come inside with you."

"As you wish." Lily welcomed her supportive presence, yet it curtailed any discussion with the attorney about her marital status. She supposed pride kept her secret intact about her marriage. The sooner she rid herself of a husband who drugged and lied to her, the sooner she could get on with her life. In her heart though, she would never forget him or the seven weeks in which they shared the tiny cabin—their haven from the world. A second visit with Fletcher would be necessary if she hoped to dissolve her arrangement with Griffin.

Lily hopped from the cab, helped Agatha out and asked the driver to wait. The homey smell of fresh baked bread fought with the stench of horse manure piled in the street. A barrel stood sentry near the tavern where unsavory refuse overflowed and spilled to the walkway. Her nose twitching at the odor, they entered the office, greeted by the jingle of a tiny brass bell attached to the door.

A sizeable, no-nonsense desk claimed the center of

the office. Off to the side sat a smaller desk befitting the duties of a legal assistant. An older, portly man appeared in a doorway at the back. He wore black breeches and a cut-away coat with cloth buttons on his silver waistcoat.

"Ladies." A gaze alive with intelligence flicked over them. "Ah, Mrs. Duff. I trust you are well. How may I be of service?" A dullish white periwig, and one to have seen better days, covered his natural hair. Spectacles perched at the end of his nose and wide nostrils conveniently stopped the frames from a downward pitch to the floor.

"Amos Fletcher?" Lily asked. Two thin lines, happy lines she liked to call them, flanked his mouth.

"In the flesh." With a perfunctory smile, he motioned them to armchairs near the big desk, and they all sat.

"My name, sir, is Lily Fitzhugh." She saw no reason to use Faraday. "I believe you are solicitor to my father, Henry Fitzhugh."

"I am." He settled elbows on the chair arms and his sudden serious expression filled her with unease. "I take it you received my missive," he said, his voice grave.

"Yes."

His brow knotted. "I worried it might not get through. Everything is so jumbled these days." Before she spoke a word, he asked, "Where do you reside, madam?" Alarm flared in his eyes. "Not in your father's house, not with the soldiers."

Clearly, he knew nothing of her stubborn nature. "No British soldier, or American for that matter, will keep me from my home." She recalled the awkward conversation with Sergeant Cook last evening at dinner. The occasion required every bit of charming persuasion she possessed to convince him he dined with a Loyalist and not a rebel. After a teeth-gritting discourse, she'd been asked not so subtly to affirm her allegiance in exchange for the return of her bedchamber. For the time being, he would bunk in one of the other officer's rooms.

Just thinking about Cook turned her prickly. Any lady would have expected a gentleman to offer up the space, regardless of political affiliations. It was her bedchamber, after all. Yet chivalry and courtesy, those fundamental social graces, seemed sadly lacking from the British soldier. Apparently, her familial association with a jailed Patriot offered her no favors or respect.

"However," Lily said, dismissing the bothersome Sergeant Cook, "what is being done to see my father freed from his captivity?"

The attorney shifted in his seat, as if he suffered an uncomfortable itch. "The evidence against him is his signature on a seized document where he claims full allegiance to the new Continental government."

"Surely this is a mistake. He's never been interested in political matters. I can't believe he'd act so recklessly."

Fletcher lifted both shoulders and brows as if to say *what could I do.* "People change. Your father has written any number of letters on his liberal position which were published in the broadsheets."

Like Griffin's essays. At least Griffin had the sense to use a pseudonym.

"Of course, he made quite a ruckus when his home was commandeered by the Army. Had his disloyalty to the King gone unnoticed, I believe I might have been able to intercede on his behalf, and he would be at home."

Fletcher tugged the high neckband of his shirt. "Your father is not alone in his beliefs yet more public than some."

Silently, Lily cursed the chaos brought on by war. If Papa had just kept his mouth shut, he'd be home with her at this very moment. Oh, why did politics have to interfere with their lives?

"Perhaps it's a misunderstanding," she offered. "If he had a chance to recant his position…"

A grave and serious Fletcher shook his head. "The same idea occurred to me. In fact, when I spoke of it to him, he rejected it outright. Oh, no, he won't countenance a retraction."

Lily gaped at him. "I can't believe it. It isn't what I would have expected of him."

Fletcher's expression puckered as though he too believed her father had lost his mind. "Henry Fitzhugh prefers to do his bit for progress and prove himself a hero in the end."

"A hero?" Papa had always been her hero. Such was the way of a daughter to a father, but a hero based on ideology? This was new territory.

"I struggle to accept the man would rather die for a political cause than continue his important scientific work." The astounding revelation swirled in her mind until it began to knock, much as a woodpecker hammered against a tree. As this was her skull under attack, she found it quite maddening. She thought she knew Papa better. "Maybe he has an enemy, someone who's jealous—"

The attorney cut her off with an airy wave. "Even though such a ruse might have worked in his favor, he wants no part of dishonesty. He publicized his opinions, even signed a document in support of the Patriots. And of course, there is the issue of his refusal to pay taxes."

Stunned, she shook her head, almost dizzy at his irresponsibility. "It's as though you speak of another man entirely. This isn't my father."

"These are difficult and dangerous times. Henry would stand up for his beliefs. Should he die because of them, he'd have the satisfaction of having sacrificed his life for a worthy cause."

Lily slumped forward and supported her head in her hand.

Fletcher continued. "The British arrest anyone they think a troublemaker, evidence or not. He's yet to stand trial and no one can say when to expect one."

"No!" She rubbed her temple, trying to fit this altered image with the one of years past, when Papa was a kindly if preoccupied scientist. The world had tipped and swerved in a direction she couldn't recognize. "He can't do this," she muttered in a puzzle to understand the confusing threads of a changed life. "What about me?" Even to her ears, the words sounded childish and selfish. Shame burned in her cheeks. "I've come all this way to offer help—to be the dutiful daughter." Without regard for her safety, reputation or future, she'd honored her obligation to Papa. For his part, he had spurned King and country, risked his life, and shirked his responsibility to her, his daughter.

"Is there but one thing you can do, Mr. Fletcher?"

Leaning forward, he pressed his palms upon the desk. "Perhaps I can arrange a visit. As to my influence…" He shrugged. "Trusting neighbors, even friends, is risky. The British hold the power in this town. We all live under the shadow of a possible arrest. Many of my contemporaries have already left the city. Loyalists flee their homes and return to England. My wife wishes to uproot to a safer city. I take her concern with great seriousness."

"I had no idea," Lily murmured and fanned her warm cheeks.

"Your father will be…" He paused, head tilted in thought. "He'll be overjoyed to see you, though it was his wish you remain in London for the duration of this conflict."

A melancholy gloom coiled inside like a vapor. It steamed into her arms and legs and threatened to drag her down and down. How could Papa have been so indifferent to their separation when for her it had been a constant ache? When all she'd thought about was coming home to him? It was as if he truly didn't care about her.

Struggling against despair, she forced out a question. "How long is this war expected to last?"

The man chuckled mirthlessly. "Only God can tell. The last I heard, He was mum on the topic. I suspect it could be two to three years or quite possibly more."

Lily gripped her hands, anything to give her a sense of solidity. Two years might certainly see Papa dead. Her vision clouded with unshed tears. She blinked them away when Agatha's scrawny fingers found her hand and gave it a squeeze.

"It's not as if he didn't want you with him," Fletcher added quickly, as if he'd sensed her downward spiral. "He doesn't want you to suffer for the choices he's made."

Suffer? Fletcher and Papa had no idea. Over the years, she'd faced hurt often. One might say they were best friends, but she refused to dwell in bitterness. "I suppose this means he'll never travel to England again." She imagined herself bigger than the character in *Gulliver's Travels*. So big she spanned the Atlantic, one foot placed in London and the other solid in New York.

Perhaps in kindness, Fletcher chose not to offer an opinion. Instead, he said, "As to financial matters, there is money set aside. Should you need anything..." He suggested a substantial amount. Clearly, Papa's endeavors and solid investments had fattened his pockets. They spent the next minutes on monetary details while he dipped a pen into the ink well and scratched a letter. He handed it to her with the particulars of the bank.

Lily thanked him and leaned forward. "How is Papa?"

He laced his fingers over his rounded stomach with a sigh. "I saw him a month ago. The prison officials discourage visitation. Since I'm legal counsel, I managed an interview." Lily was surprised to see a mischievous smile, as though he'd achieved a minor victory. "I suspect the army considers it too much trouble to ferry civilians to the ship. However, your father was in good spirits, all things considered."

She supposed the conditions were deplorable and sensed the man protected her by his omission of any detail. "I want to see him. Should I make arrangements with the prison officials?"

"Oh, no, no." He shook his head horrified as if a

dirty worm dangled before his face. "It will never do, madam. Allow me to pay Captain Babcock, the man in charge of prisoners, a call."

For the time being, Lily would show patience and trust Fletcher. She'd already waited seven years to see Papa. She supposed she could wait a while longer.

Chapter Twenty-Two

Griffin tugged on the reins, halting his horse on the narrow path. Immense oak and beech trees in the forested glen offered dappled shade from the late morning sun. On a deep breath, he inhaled the smell of campfire about a quarter mile off. Washington's camp, he guessed. With a jiggle to the reins, he angled west, anxious to speak with the man.

As he rode along, his thoughts turned once again to Lily. The image of her stony expression as she clattered away in the carriage two days ago remained fixed in his mind. Finished with him for good, she'd said. A part of him believed he deserved it.

Frustrated and angry after her departure, he'd gone straight to his home, only blocks from the river where he lived alone except for the caretakers, Mr. and Mrs. Ludlow. Ever faithful, their reliable attention to his home and property was a godsend.

"I'm afraid I won't be staying long," he'd said to Mrs. Ludlow minutes after he'd walked into his house, thankful for the tidiness of his parlor and the welcome scent of beeswax and old books. A wrinkle of disappointment clouded the plump face of the housekeeper who, only moments ago was flushed with happiness at his return.

"Are you off to see your parents, sir?" she said.

"Business comes first." Regrettably, the reunion

with his parents at their farm, some miles north of the city, would have to wait until he'd seen Washington. "I leave tomorrow at dawn and need provisions for a two-day ride."

In his comfortable study that smelled faintly of lemon and the rosemary plant near the window, he sat down at his desk. He flipped through a stack of unopened mail, happy in the familiarity and comfort of home, if only for a night.

Mrs. Ludlow followed him inside, saying, "No bad news, I hope,"

"Nothing so pressing it can't be postponed another week or two." Washington's assignment commanded his first priority. After completion of his duty, it was on to Lily. A solid plan, good luck and maybe even pleading would set things right between them.

The trip through the hardwood and pine forest had been a pleasant diversion even though he missed her horribly. The smell of campfires filled the air. Occasionally, when the breeze blew just right, he caught a whiff of fresh, hardy conifers. Met by a sentry, and after he'd showed his identification papers, Griffin followed the sweaty, sour-smelling soldier to Washington's tent while in his head he rehearsed his report.

"The General will see you." A tidy *aide de camp* held aside the tent flap, and Griffin slipped inside, his tricorn clutched to his chest. Washington, along with two other officers, assembled around a wooden table. A map of New York spread out before them.

Griffin saluted. Washington introduced a seated Lt. General Denning and Corporal McComb. After polite discussion about the trip, Washington asked him to sit and dispatched his aide for tea.

Washington, a commanding figure even as he settled into a spindly canvas chair, requested Griffin's full report.

When he'd finished telling about the guns and the skirmish, Corporal McComb said, "A mite risky to unload the guns so close to a British installation in New Jersey."

"All part of the strategy," Griffin explained amused by the irony. "The redcoats would never believe anyone would be foolish enough to take such a risk." After the laughter died down, Griffin added. "The Brits never would have appreciated lace."

"Very clever," said Denning.

Griffin experienced a moment of pride. "Captain Mulworthy is soon off to Boston and Commander Moreau is here, safe and sound."

"And not too soon either," Washington said. "He informs me there was an unexpected complication aboard the *Providence*."

Complication seemed an apt term to describe Lily. "Ah, yes, an informant set by Cecil Jones, a legal advisor to the King."

Washington shifted in his chair. "And what became of this person?"

To admit he married her didn't seem in his best interests. "She is with her father in New York."

"A woman?" McComb croaked with surprise.

"The daughter of the engineer and inventor, Henry Fitzhugh."

McComb whistled through his teeth.

"Let us pray she is not with her father," Denning added, "for the poor fellow was arrested and rots away in prison. I read it in the broadsheets."

"What?" Griffin couldn't believe it. "On what charge?"

"Crimes against the King," Denning continued. "He unwisely but nobly signed a document in which he swore support to the new government. The original sin was a ruckus he made when his house was sequestered for officers."

Griffin gave a start. *Lily among British soldiers?*

"Are you ill, Faraday?" McComb asked. "You've gone a bit peaked."

Griffin's fingers bit into the stiff felt of the hat upon his lap. Lily was not one to sit idle. Would she tell all she knew of him and Mulworthy? Dear Lily.

"What have you to say on the matter?" Washington probed.

Griffin quickly reordered his thoughts. "She was wholly convinced her father remained loyal to the King—insisted he had no interest in politics."

"Ha," Denning scoffed. "Such a state exists only for babies and the demented unfortunates."

"A spy cooped up with a spy," Washington mused, drawing fingers over his chin. "How many weeks was it?"

"About seven weeks, sir. I wouldn't call her a spy as much as an opportunist."

McComb cocked his head, interested to hear more.

In a spirit of being forthright on some points, he revealed how and why Lily came to be aboard the ship. "The woman was most determined. When her attempts to book passage failed, Cecil Jones offered his help to get her on board the *Providence* in exchange for evidence proving me a spy."

"Most intriguing," Washington replied. "Did she succeed?"

Heat climbed up Griffin's neck. "She suspected when we took possession of the guns from a pirate vessel but could never prove anything. As to me, I regret to say, sir, she did." Griffin wished for a hearty dose of brandy in his tea, anything to lessen his sense of failure in this regard. "The discovery of my political essays damned me in her view. The ciphering book belted the rope about my neck."

Demming whistled.

"She left the ship with nothing to show for her snooping."

"However, your secret identity is exposed," Washington concluded in a steady voice.

"I doubt she intends to use the knowledge." He wished he could be more certain.

"Explain."

"She has…" He paused, wondering how best to state her possible motivation and emotions. "I believe she has…" He tapped his fingers against his thigh. Despite her anger, he believed she had some allegiance to him. A glimmer of hope lingered. A thin thread.

McComb and Denning burst out laughing.

"You mean she fancies you," said McComb still chuckling.

Griffin demurred. "I don't wish to seem callous or indelicate."

"Do you fancy her?" McComb asked with a twinkle.

Griffin sat up straighter. "I'm a soldier and an agent, sir. My duty lies in my service to my country."

"George, I think we need to break out the brandy,"

said McComb, flushed and grinning.

"Will we be invited to the nuptials?" Denning asked.

Griffin gave a lopsided grin. "I'm afraid you're too late, gentlemen. I already married her."

"Well, I'll be tipped," McComb declared. "It's one way to keep your hide."

Griffin could only hope.

****

"Bad news?" Agatha set the tea tray on the parlor table.

Lily gripped the letter tighter. "Mr. Fletcher went to British headquarters. The request to visit Papa has been denied."

"Those nasty buggers."

Sunlight washed through the windows and brightened all the parlor furnishings until the wood shone like new. The pleasant view did little to lessen Lily's frustration. After three days in New York, she had so hoped to hear a positive word from the attorney. With no access to Papa, her patience was beginning to unravel.

"I'm sorry to hear it." The housekeeper poured a hot cup for Lily.

"Mr. Fletcher has discharged a letter to the Governor to intercede."

"We can only pray," Agatha muttered.

"I intend to do more than pray." Wound tight like a mechanical toy, she couldn't sit idle while Papa wasted away in a fetid prison waiting for some cock-eyed trial. After all the years of loneliness and the hungry ache for reunification, she had to see him, face to face, if only to give him a bear-sized hug. Only a few miles separated them, yet the distance seemed much greater, the risks more perilous than even the dangerous passage across the ocean. Aware he was so close yet out of reach was a cruel irony, indeed.

"On another sorry note…" Lily set the letter aside and picked up her teacup. "Mr. Fletcher has been called to Philadelphia on urgent business. He expects to be away three months."

"Hmmph! Urgent business indeed." The woman swiped a feather duster across two porcelain dogs seated on the fireplace mantel with more gusto than necessary. "Fleeing the redcoats, is more like it." Lily hoped Agatha's forceful swishing wouldn't crash the fragile items to the floor.

"He asks for my continued patience." Another irony. Time was of the essence. It disturbed her to think how long it might take to find a new attorney for Papa in Fletcher's absence.

The matter of her marriage and its dissolution also needed attention. Her fingers tightened about the cup. It saddened her to think of Griffin and the future they would never share. Each day his absence added to the hurt. Sometimes she feared he never loved her. Whether she wished it or not, his touch was imprinted on her flesh and his laughter embedded in her mind. His very essence permeated her soul.

No, don't dally in sorrow. It would do no good. Strong and clear-headed is what she needed.

"I miss him so much," she murmured seeing a vision of Griffin's lopsided grin.

"Of course you miss him, child."

Agatha had assumed she meant Papa. In truth, Lily held two men dear to her heart.

With the precision of a knife through butter, she cleaved Griffin from her mind.

"Time won't stand still." She resettled the delicate teacup on the saucer with firm resolve. "I shall speak to Captain Babcock. If that doesn't work, I'll go straight to the top." Where ever that might be.

"It's what your mama would have done."

It warmed Lily to hear her mama described as strong and decisive. Like a precious pearl, she savored the information then tucked it away for safekeeping.

The housekeeper's wizened face scrunched with satisfaction as she gave several final swipes to the gilded frame of Catherine Fitzhugh's portrait. "The apple doesn't fall far from the tree."

****

A breeze rippled the brim of Lily's hat and fluttered the Union Jack hanging from the front of the familiar brick house. She remembered visiting this stately home as a child with Papa and always admired its tall, white columns and double-hung sash windows.

"I can't recall the name of the family who used to live here," she said to Agatha. Together, they climbed the wide steps to the front door.

"Fled the British occupation, no doubt," Agatha replied. "Or they were afraid of the Patriots and high-tailed it to England."

"How sad. Like ours, this once happy family home is commandeered to serve the purposes of the army."

"It's happened all over the city." The old woman shrugged. "Last year, Washington's Army held the city and they booted out the Loyalists. This year, it's the British. Housing, as you see, is at a premium. The fire on the West Side ruined a good portion of the city.

People lost their homes, and the British soldiers crowded in. War upsets the natural order, it does."

"War. I hate it." Irritated but determined, Lily sailed through the door, Agatha at her heels.

"You needn't have come along," she said to her faithful chaperone.

"'Tis no place for a woman alone."

Lily dismissed the woman's concern. "There are British soldiers all over the place. I doubt any harm would come to me."

"When a man has mischief on his mind…"

The words trailed off, yet Lily caught the underlying meaning. She leaned closer and whispered, "They're *British* soldiers." As soon as the words hit the air, she realized her foolishness. Being British was no guarantee of law-abiding, moral character.

Agatha launched a withering look. "There are rotten apples in every basket. What color the uniform does not signify."

"Point taken." Griffin would never physically harm a woman, yet he'd broken her heart nonetheless. Part of her accepted it wasn't personal. It was a job, completed for the army and for ideological beliefs. Still…

She missed his touch, his humor and his… *Stop it!* This was not the time or place to dwell in the past.

Ignoring the confusion in her head along with the blatant stares of the soldiers in the grand foyer, she marched over to a soldier at the front desk. After receiving directions, they climbed above stairs. At the top of the wide landing, she recalled a time she'd played hide and seek in one of the many bedchambers that lead off the hallway. Same place but different times, and all the rooms converted to offices.

As they waited, seated on stiff wooden chairs set against the corridor wall, Lily wondered about the vacated family. She hoped they were happy and settled and that theirs lives didn't resemble her fractured and uncertain state.

A foot tapped impatiently, and she regretted the absence of a fan to stir the stuffy air. Moisture formed at her temples. She wiped it away with the back of her gloved hand. Just as she feared she would roast like a turkey in an oven, the young aide returned. He ushered them inside what was once the largest bedchamber in the house but now served as Captain Babcock's office. Noisily, the aide cleared his throat, calling attention to their presence.

A slender man at a desk, busy writing, snapped up his head. "Oh, my, yes." He shot to his feet, seeming quite put out to see guests in his office.

"Captain Babcock, sir. May I present Miss Fitzhugh," the aide announced. "And her companion, Miss Duff."

"Mrs. Duff, if you please," quipped Agatha with a proud tip of her pointed chin. The correction prompted a bilious eye roll from the soldier. Lily hoped she wouldn't poke him in the ribs and was grateful the woman left her parasol at home.

"You may leave us, Sergeant."

When they were alone, Captain Babcock gestured to the wingback chairs propped before his desk. "Please, sit."

As they took their places, Lily searched for some item she could attach to the previous owners. Sadly, only the tired, faded curtains remained.

"How may I be of service, Madam?"

The stuffy fellow didn't appear older than twenty-five or six at the most. Surely too young to administer the prisons, nevertheless, here he sat. She smiled with a desire to put them both at ease. With a strained effort, he returned her smile.

"Captain, I wondered if I might speak with you about my father, Henry Fitzhugh. He is, at this moment, aboard the prison ship, *Jersey*."

"Your father is a prisoner?" He skimmed a hand over his perfect, ordered black hair.

"An unfortunate circumstance and one I find impossible to believe." Tense fingers worked the grip of her cloth bag. She'd become such a liar. The new political side of her father, the defiant patriot, was troubling and not a wise fact to admit publicly. If spoken of here, it would surely hasten his ruin. "He is hardly a man to involve himself in politics. Mister Fitzhugh is a man of science and numbers. Through his discoveries, innumerable important contributions have been made and both King and country have benefitted from his many inventions."

Babcock shifted in his seat. His cornflower blue gaze sliced over to the window, seeming to only half-listen.

"Captain," she said to get his attention.

When he faced her, it was with hardened features. "I recall the circumstances which prompted your father's arrest. He vociferously claimed the officers quartered in his home disrupted his work."

"Wouldn't it pose a hardship were it you in similar circumstances?"

The man chose not to answer. Instead, he tapped the desk, his stare so brittle she feared he might crack.

"He then signed his name to a document which favored the illicit activities of the Patriots."

"There must be some misunderstanding." Against solid evidence, her claim sounded so feeble. Still, she had to try. "I'd like your permission to visit him and clear up this matter."

His black brows arched and crinkled his pale forehead. "Out of the question."

She drew back, astounded by his hasty denial when she'd expected his cooperation. In an attempt to appear calm, she pressed her hands together while her brain scrambled for another tactic.

"I've lived in London these past seven years. Seven long years in which I've not laid eyes on him. I'm his only family except for his brother by marriage, Lord Coventry." The mere mention of his name left her bothered. However, if the connection opened a door, so be it.

"Lord Coventry, you say?" Sweat broke out over his upper lip.

She forced a congenial smile, one meant to coax and flatter. "So you see it would be an extra kindness, one Englishman helping out another, if you were to allow me to see him." If she could gain his sympathy, he might see fit to help.

"A prison ship is not a fitting place for a woman."

Lily feared her ability to sweet talk might fall short. For an instant, she considered revealing her weeks aboard a ship filled with men and no chaperone. She imagined his shocked outrage. "I've just come from London where I resided for many years. May I ask, sir, where you call home?"

"Lambeth," he replied seeming baffled at her

inquiry.

"It makes you wonder why we never met before living so close to each other." The comment, intended to incite some regional loyalty, fell flat.

"Indeed."

Despite the firm set of his jaw, she plowed on. "I'm told the British Army is the most progressive army in the world and employs hygienic practices to see its inhabitants are well cared for." Nothing could be further from the truth from what she'd heard. "You need not worry I'll take ill."

"Illness is the least of my worries."

She arched a brow. Surely, he didn't fear she'd be molested by the prisoners. As a loyal servant of the Army, he probably didn't concern himself with the possibility of crude behavior perpetrated by a British soldier either. After all, integrity was the moral foundation of each good soldier, she thought with surprising cynicism. As Agatha said earlier, there were rotten apples in every bucket.

"As to humane practices, we do our best, madam. Nevertheless, conditions are crowded and quite unsuitable for a woman."

"Come, come," she chided with a feigned coyness. "There must be boats back and forth all the time, carrying supplies and what not."

"Yes, of course." He frowned, growing visibly annoyed.

"Well, there you have it. With your soldiers aboard, no harm will come to me."

A muscle twitched in his cheek. "No one would dare set a finger to you. Nevertheless, I have my orders." His lips flattened tight as any closed door. "I regret to disappoint you."

Anger followed on the heels of her disappointment. *Keep a clear head*, she urged. Tapping her bottom lip, she considered her next move. When she realized where Babcock's gaze lay, she dropped her hand.

"It would be a pity to lose Papa, a man of such stature. Not to mention the agony and grief I would feel after such an arduous journey from London and never once allowed to see him."

Babcock pressed his lips even tighter. A bead of sweat slipped down his cheek. "Miss Fitzhugh, I—"

"Lily. Please, call me Lily." She ignored the click of Agatha's disapproving tongue. "After all, we are country kin sharing the same ideals and in full support of the King." The deliberate words tripped out as easily as a happy child skips over grass. It was then she realized the sentiment no longer held any truth. If both Papa and Griffin, men she cared and respected, were willing to put their lives on the line, she must at least give credit to their beliefs. It was an odd and surprising reaction, and one she didn't have time to puzzle over at the present.

He swiped a folded handkerchief across his damp forehead. "Orders are orders, miss. I will not change my mind."

Her foot vibrated with an urge to stomp it to the floor in sheer frustration. What rotten luck to encounter another soldier who placed orders in front of human needs and... *Stop! Do not think of Griffin who was kind and charitable.*

"If you consider your hands tied, I have no choice but to speak with General Howe."

His nostrils flared. A deep swallow caused his

Adam's apple to bob like a cork in water. "I'm afraid he is… He is…" He glanced nervously at the door.

"The General and I are acquaintances—friends to be more precise." Desperation made her lie. "On occasion, he visited with my uncle, Lord Coventry, with whom I lived in London. I shouldn't think he would be pleased to hear of my dilemma."

Babcock tugged at his shirt opening like a man with a noose about his neck. "Madam, as you can imagine, the General is a very busy man. He would not favor involvement in the matter."

"Oh?" She arched her brows and waited for his capitulation.

Babcock exhaled a noisy breath and his shoulders dipped. "A packet leaves tomorrow morning at ten. You may visit him."

Chapter Twenty-Three

"This way, miss."

Having convinced Agatha to remain at home, Lily followed the soldier across the cluttered deck of the prison ship, determined to act unruffled by the filth and barefaced stares. What absolute squalor. A dozen emaciated wretches toiled in the scorching sun under the watchful gaze of armed sentries. The deplorable army couldn't see fit to adequately feed the half-starved prisoners. As she neared the passageway to the hold, an incredible stench rose, so overpowering it forced her to press a perfumed hanky to her nose.

The *Jersey,* one of a dozen obsolete and damaged ships, housed the overflow of captives. In comparison, the *Providence* appeared stellar and pristine. Wouldn't Mulworthy gloat? As despicable as the man was, even he would find the putrid conditions and malnourished men deplorable.

Sickened and helpless to provide any aid or comfort, she marched on past wounded men who bore open sores and ragged shirts stained with sweat and blood. On the heels of her guide, she descended to a lower level. The light was inadequate but enough to illuminate further decay and vermin. A rat with a hairless tail scuttled along the baseboard. Overpowered by the stink of rot and sickness, she pressed the linen tighter to her nostrils, unable to fathom how the British sanctioned this hellhole. Awash with queasiness and unease, she entered a windowless room pointed out by the soldier. A lantern blazed on the table. He motioned for her to sit in one of the two plain wooden chairs.

"I need to see the basket." Suspiciously, he ogled the goods she tucked protectively to her side.

"Of course."

To be treated like a common criminal who sneaked contraband in a gift of much needed rations raised her hackles. Once again, she realized the shift of her allegiance. A few days ago, King George held her complete support. The sacrifices of Papa and Griffin had muddied and strained her loyalty. The situation between England and the Colonies was more complex than she previously believed, and the right and wrong of a person's actions more difficult to judge. As a shocked witness to this travesty, she could understand why people called the King a tyrant.

"God forbid I should sneak a pistol or sword aboard."

The sour man glowered.

"Those poor, sick men might rise up in revolt and steal all the maggoty cheese from the larder." She placed the wicker parcel on the table and stripped away the towel. "You'll find fruit, nuts, bread and ham." For a better view, she angled the container. As though her effort lacked substance, he dragged the basket closer and jammed a hand inside.

"Apple brandy," she explained as he took the bottle.

He uncorked it and sniffed. "This isn't allowed."

What a lie.

"You have your orders." No doubt, the fellow

would consume the wine by nightfall.

"Five minutes," he grumbled. He stuffed the bottle inside his jacket and left her alone.

Five minutes to visit Papa. Such a short time when there was much to say and years to cover. How often she'd prayed for this moment, waited and waited. At last, the time had arrived, and it left her palms sweaty and her nerves jittery.

She sank into one of the chairs at the table. Tense fingers curled in her lap. What would he say? Would he be as thrilled to see her as she would him? For the hundredth time, she imagined the sheer joy of their reunion vivid on his face. Barely able to breathe for her excitement, she inhaled a nose full of rank air and winced.

When the door rattled, she startled.

A strange disheveled man with a scruffy beard stood in the doorway. Oily and haggard, his grimy, ill-fitting clothes sagged on his thin frame. Straggly gray hair brushed the top of his slumped shoulders. A beggar, she thought, one of those poor souls who lived every day on the edge of death. Uncertain what to say, she searched his eyes and caught a familiar, unmistakable twinkle.

"Papa!" She shot from the chair and seized him in a tight hug. His bones felt brittle as a twig and as precious as anything she'd ever held. A sharp odor of sickness and stale sweat rose from his body.

"My child. My baby." His voice cracked. With surprising strength, he held her at arm's length and studied her with a clear, steady gaze that hadn't changed over the years. A patchwork of wrinkles creased his forehead. Only a trace of the youthful, ebony hair remained in his brows. "You look so bonny. Just like your mama."

Tears arose, and she floated on a cloud of happiness. She kissed his cheek. The reek of his skin tasted bitter on her lips. Scratchy whiskers rasped her face.

"Come, sit down." Hands trembling, she led him to a chair, worried his spindly legs might collapse.

"I can't believe it." He cupped her chin, his fingers skeletal. "How did you get here? How did you find me?"

A high, quick laugh tumbled out, tinged with the pent-up anxiety of the last few days. "I knew, Papa. When your letters stopped, I knew something was wrong."

"Dear Lily. You remain as tenacious and loyal as ever, fiercer even than your mother. I should have realized you'd find a way to do battle on my behalf." As he'd done countless times in the past, he tweaked her nose, a playful gesture left over from her childhood.

"This place…" He glanced about. "I can't mail letters."

"I understand."

"If I had written, I would have begged you to stay in London."

Her smile fell away. "You don't want me?" All at once, she sounded like the frightened, unlovable child about to board the ship to England. Hurt and confused, she couldn't understand why he'd sent her away.

"Of course, I want you."

The earnest words boosted her spirit.

"With this bloody war, the civil unrest, I didn't want you to get hurt." He caressed her cheek and sighed.

Did he not understand that every day without him hurt? "I love you, Papa."

"And I love you."

Of course, he loved her. What a fool she'd been to doubt his sentiments. "You're my family, Papa. My home." She'd always known home wasn't London or Uncle Percy. It had taken the present to make things more certain. "If we aren't together now, when will we ever be?"

He dropped his gaze and wove his fingers together over the table. Dirt stained the skin folds in his knuckles. "I wasn't myself after your mother died."

The flat, monotone quality of his voice stirred her worry. Here it comes, she thought, the explanation for their years of separation. While in London, it remained a constant question, a persistent ache and fear, one in which she could never bring herself to seek clarification in a letter.

"When she died…"

The foul smell and the noise of the ship fell away. Only Papa remained and the need to hear and understand.

"I plunged into darkness, into a black well so deep I couldn't escape."

She clasped his hands and refused to let go. "You don't need to explain."

"I must, Lily. You need to understand, particularly under the circumstances. It's all I've thought about, being here and you so far away." His troubled gaze skirted over the stark surroundings, the mildewed walls, the rough plank flooring, his fear he might die in this dungeon etched in his lined face. "I felt only pain—my pain, irrespective of anyone or anything else. It was selfish."

"Papa, don't. You were sick."

"I thought if I could work, it would bring me to my senses…yet I couldn't think straight."

Day after day, Lily had gone to his study door, only to find it locked and Papa unavailable. "You tried, Papa."

"It wasn't right. I failed you." Slowly, as if weighted by an enormous burden, he hung his head and eased his hands from her grasp. "When this tiresome conflict with England arose, I had to do something, to make things better. I thought sending you to my sister Charlotte was the answer. Can you ever forgive me?"

"It's over, Papa." She swiped away the wetness on her cheek. "We're together. It's what matters. That and your return home."

The poor man was not the man of years ago. The former professor had withered away in mind and body. No longer did he possess full cheeks or a rounded belly but bony knobs on his collarbone grimed with dirt and sweat.

"Papa, please tell me you didn't sign your name to…"

He silenced her with a slight lift of a hand, and her spirit sank with foreboding. "Yes, I did sign the document."

"It's so foo—" She reddened.

"Foolish it might be, but necessary."

"Why? You aren't interested in politics."

He shrugged. "I never spoke politics in front of you. It doesn't mean I didn't read and form my own opinions."

Lily studied the new species sitting before her.

"Your mother and I discussed politics often."

She didn't remember any of this. Of course, she'd been a child. "You've always been so loyal to the King."

He cocked a brow. "Have I?"

"I just assumed." Somehow, those absolutes she believed of him no longer rang true.

He flicked a nervous glance at the door, and lowered his voice. "This is not the place to debate such matters. In the full analysis of ideas, being out from under the capricious whims of one single man makes sense."

Lily stared and tried to absorb this new man whose liberal attitudes would take time to appreciate. "You'll be hanged as a traitor."

"Do you think I'm a traitor?"

She nibbled her bottom lip, thinking. It was clear he no longer considered himself an English subject. America, his new country, held his allegiance. "No, you're not a traitor. You're a man who believes in a different political ideal."

Just like Griffin.

"The tides of change cannot be stopped," he said. "We'll win this war and with it a new country."

An overload of new information boggled her mind. Griffin and Papa subscribed to beliefs for which each would gladly die. Their convictions had the ring of truth and righteousness. Only a fool would turn against the truth. She must trust and believe.

"Enough about me. How are you, dear girl?" No sooner had he asked than he began to cough. His bony back rounded with his efforts. Helpless, she watched in fear as his thin shoulders heaved.

"You're sick," she cried and felt his clammy forehead. "Have you seen a doctor?"

After a bark of sarcastic laughter, he swiped his mouth with the back of his hand. "A little cough. It'll soon be gone."

"In a place like this?" Sickness and death could roll through a ship like a hurricane. "I won't lose you, Papa."

"Try not to worry about me."

How could she not? Nevertheless, she took a smidgen of relief from his reassuring smile.

"Are you happy?" he asked.

Her cheeks heated as Griffin wafted in her head. For a few weeks, she had been happy.

"My happiness isn't important. We have to get you off this ship." Her fretful gaze slid to the door monitored by the guard outside. Though she knew it wouldn't work, she considered throwing her thin cloak around him, a disguise to hustle him away from this hell.

"Why won't you declare it was all a mistake—suggest some enemy signed your name?"

"Lily." His rough voice scratched. "I won't be a coward to save my neck. Many people make greater sacrifices every day."

Again, the similarities to Griffin came to mind. "I need you," she whispered.

He skimmed a thumb over her cheek. "You'll always be my little girl."

"Oh, Papa." She threw herself at him while the tears washed once again over her cheeks. This heartbreak couldn't be real. As she clutched at his bony shoulders, afraid to let him go, she murmured words of hope.

Through her sobs, someone said, "Your time is up, Miss."

No. It couldn't end here.

Determined hands gently pushed her away. "It's time to go, Lily."

Through a hazy gaze, she memorized his face and form and the fragile bend in his spine—all so different from the vital man in his wedding portrait.

In the doorway, the guard exuded an air of impatience. "Come along, madam."

She glared at the soldier who seemed devoid of any sympathy. "I won't abandon you, Papa."

He kissed her forehead. "Don't worry. Once the war is over, we'll be together."

She gaped at his maddening confidence. He could be dead in a week, from starvation if disease didn't claim him first.

With an odd mix of bravado and gravity, he shrugged and smiled.

"There's food in the basket."

They hugged one last time.

A few labored steps took her across the small room. At the door, she hesitated. "I love you."

"And I, you."

Gulping back a sob, she whisked through the door, unable to bear his tears.

If he didn't get off this ship soon, he was as good as dead. They both knew it.

Chapter Twenty-Four

Seated in the front parlor, Lily nervously drummed her thigh. Ever since her visit to Papa yesterday, the urgency to rescue him had increased until she could barely sit still. One idea after another hurtled through her mind, scrambling about like frenzied ants under attack. Still, not one plan stood out better than any other. Nor was there any guarantee she wouldn't get them both shot or hanged if she attempted his liberation.

If only she knew someone with experience in whom to confide. Pride kept her from seeking Griffin's help. After several conversations with Sergeant Cook, it was clear he would offer no assistance. As to the other two officers billeted in her home, she'd yet to see their faces. Except for Agatha, she was utterly alone in this quandary. Meanwhile, Papa's health, his very life, in fact, hovered at her shoulder like a specter and set a chill to her bones.

On another note, Griffin's absence this past week meant one thing. He would not fight an annulment or divorce. Had he wanted to stay married, he would have visited and tried to change her mind. Surprised by her unexpected disappointment, she intended to remain philosophical. Why stay with a man when there was no trust and only betrayal?

No doubt he considered himself well rid of her.

Duty to the army and all that, she supposed bitterly. He'd made his priorities abundantly clear, and she wasn't one of them. Still, despite their troubles, she remained sentimental and filled with the hope he might change his mind. Regrettably, he hadn't. So be it.

As to neighbors and friends who might offer assistance to her and Papa, half had fled New York. The rest, suspicious and uncertain about the long-absent daughter of a traitor, kept their doors closed.

Throwing herself upon the mercy of General Howe or the Governor might be her only recourse. "I doubt you ever had to make such considerations," she muttered dispiritedly at her mother's portrait above the fireplace mantel.

"Excuse me, miss." Agatha stood in the parlor doorway, her ruffled mobcap low on her forehead, her expression serious.

"Yes?" The formality in the woman's voice strummed Lily's unease.

"Lord Warwick wishes to see you."

Lily grabbed the plump arm of the sofa. Her fingers dug into the horsehair padding. "Did you say Warwick?"

"You're as pale as a white dove. Shall I send him away?"

Good Lord. What was he doing in New York? "No. Send him in."

Lit with happiness, she rose from the sofa. In a state of nerves, she primped at her upturned hair, tweaking a ribbon then skimmed the overskirt of her gown, smoothing the fine silk material. David, here? She couldn't believe it.

"Lily!" He bounded into the parlor with

outstretched arms. Resplendent in cobalt blue, decorative buttons and a laced and ruffled shirt, he brought with him all the pomp and richness of Lord Percy's London.

"David." Her body rocked on her toes as he grabbed and hugged her close, his skin damp and hot on her cheek.

"Lily, my little fool."

Little fool?

His breath tickled her ear as he squeezed her again, tighter this time, and about crushed her. "I can scarce believe you're here," she said. "After a sea of strangers in New York, it's thrilling to see an old friend."

He stepped back and assessed her with a critical eye. "Lily." He spoke the name as if he couldn't believe she'd arrived in New York, whole and unmarred from whatever trials she endured these past two months without him.

"For such a long voyage, you appear remarkably fresh." His skin and hair glowed in a shaft of afternoon sunlight through the window.

"I went immediately to the *Dorchester*. I was told it's one of the finest lodging houses."

"And the crossing?"

He shuddered. "It was beastly, simply dreadful, though I must commend the crew. They tried their best to make the accommodations as much like home as possible."

She chortled lightly. "Given you can't live without a hundred servants it must have seemed a nightmare."

He wrinkled his nose. "You exaggerate." If it were possible, his discerning gaze sharpened. "Whatever possessed you to go haring off, in the middle of the night, no less?" His smile did not reach his eyes where anger radiated.

She sidled away, taking up residence near the fireplace and crossed her arms. "I left you a letter."

"A note," he amended with a crestfallen air. "Comprised of two short sentences. *'Sorry to leave but Papa needs me. I shall return. Love, Lily'.*"

The paltry words and her hasty departure stirred a degree of guilt. It had never been her intention to hurt him but clearly she had. What a lowly bug in the grass she was to cause him pain.

As if to signify it no longer mattered, he flapped a hand in dismissal. The lacy ruffle at his wrist swayed with the effort. "Your uncle was furious you'd gone." His lips pinched. "And you, leaving only a cryptic note."

At his censure, she stiffened. "I'm sorry." To be criticized and spoken to like a child put her on the defensive. "It was the only way, particularly as Uncle Percy left me no other choice. I daresay he recovered from the shock in quick order." She imagined Percy's ashen complexion flushed with anger at her bold disobedience and his failure to control her.

"Not so easily or quickly as you might think." He cocked his head like a bantam rooster, puffed and rigid with disapproval.

Over the years, she'd grown accustomed to David's tempers, his devilry and his generosity. Seldom did his moods bother her. Today, she struggled to be so easy-going. Something very essential between them had altered. She suspected Griffin was the cause.

"You must be tired after your trip. Please…" She indicated a comfortable chair with a view to the trees outside the window. "I want to hear all about London. How is everyone in England?"

With an elegant flip of the wrist, he separated the tails of his coat and plopped down on the sofa. "Oh, before I forget…"

Curious what he might reveal, she joined him there.

"The day before my departure, I chanced to see Cecil Jones. The conversation left a strange impression. When he heard I was to embark for New York, he asked me to pass along his regards. He anxiously awaits a letter from you. When I inquired as to the nature of this missive, he replied simply, he is curious of your view of the colonies." Brow wrinkled, he wagged his head. "I have the impression there is more to his interest."

"Mr. Jones is curious about many things." So consumed with worry about Papa, she'd forgotten all about the letter she'd written on the ship while in the throes of anger. From the end table, she picked up the tiny silver bell and gave it a shake. "I fear I've fallen behind in my correspondence. I shall assign him to the top of my list."

Agatha appeared so quickly Lily wondered if the housekeeper had been lurking outside the door. "Will you bring us tea and that delicious lemon cake?"

When the housekeeper left the room, Lily faced David with a twinge of regret that a disarmingly attractive secret agent was not the man seated next to her. "You must tell me all about your trip." She sank into the plush cushions, determined to focus on the present and not the past. "When did you arrive?"

His leg crossed at a knee, David settled his hands

in his lap, smug and assured. "Would you believe only several hours ago?"

She leaned toward him, encouraging conversation. "No deadly hurricanes, I hope." The twaddle would suffice while she waited to hear the real reason for his visit.

"Well…" He wavered when Agatha meandered in and set the tea tray on the low table near the sofa.

"I'll be in the kitchen if you require anything else." The woman ambled away muttering under her breath.

Disapproval again soured his features. "Rather familiar for a servant, wouldn't you say. If she were mine, I'd toss her out in a minute."

Lily bit down hard, cutting off her rebuke. Taut with sudden irritation, she poured them each a cup, her face bathed in the warm steam. "Agatha is more like family. She's been a part of this household since I was a toddler and used a bib at meals."

"Is she the only servant here?" David gingerly sipped the hot brew while she cut a slice of cake.

"It's a story left for later." The familiar duties of hostess calmed her. After licking sugar from her thumb, she slid cake on a plate and offered it to him. He declined.

"Did Uncle Percy send you?"

Ignoring the question, he set aside his cup before he rose and paced determinedly across the room. David didn't politely visit as much as insert himself into the parlor's very center. Once or twice, he paused to examine a statue or to test the weight of the curtain material between a thumb and index finger.

"Answer me." Impatience seeped into her words.

He stopped and faced her with a somber

expression. "I didn't come for Percy. I came of my own accord." His shoulders lifted on a huge breath. "On the day you left, I went to your Uncle and asked his permission for your hand in marriage." Color stained his cheeks as if the admission stirred deep emotions. "Before I had a chance to propose, you ran away."

"I...I'm sorry."

In a frown, he charged off again, circling once around the sofa. "Do you have any idea what it felt like to learn the woman I planned to marry had run away to the Colonies?"

Heat rose up her neck.

"I felt foolish and betrayed."

Guilt returned and churned in her gut. "As I mentioned, I had no other choice." Indeed, she hoped he'd understand her need for abrupt actions and forgive her.

His hand waved in the air, as if swatting an annoying bug. "At least I see you're unharmed. You had me quite worried."

"I'm touched by your concern." Years of friendship revealed he wasn't one to forgive hurtful offenses easily.

"You may be interested to learn another suitor professed his intentions to your uncle."

"*Who?*"

"Howard Chatham."

Lily reared back. "I'd no sooner marry Chatham than a loaf of bread. He's—"

"Doughy?" David laughed cruelly.

"He's barely spoken to me." Hands gripped to her knees, she struggled to harness her shock. "I'd have spent the rest of my life with someone who blushed and shriveled every time I looked at him."

"To his favor," David added, "he has more money than Croesus."

"It's of no consequence, at least not to me. Father will settle a fine dowry on me when the time comes."

"Your uncle mentioned as much."

"You discussed money with Percy?"

You ninny. Of course he had, when he'd asked Percy permission to marry her. The two men would speak of her dowry. Gaze narrowed with suspicion, she wondered if Percy had been correct when he suggested David wanted her only to reap the benefits of Papa's vast wealth. Never once while in England together, did David ever declare his love. Undoubtedly, he'd been her best friend, but he evoked none of the romantic sentiments engendered by Griffin.

Her suitor scanned the room. His shrewd gaze took note of the well-crafted, graceful furniture, the thick rugs and the oil paintings, as if the quality of the goods might give him a money amount. "Your uncle is most insistent to see you well placed."

For appearance sake, Percy would shine like the sun if his niece married into a titled family. And David would benefit from a sizeable cash dowry. It seemed cynical to think it, and it shamed her, but there it was.

"Dwellings are not so luxurious here as in London," she said. "My father is interested in his work and not lavish surroundings." It was a graceless point to make, and she could only think she did so to discourage him.

"Is your father at home? I should like to meet him."

"Ah." Aware David would be horrified to hear of Papa's treason, she would forgo telling him until later.

"Not at the moment."

"So you would deny your uncle the pleasure of seeing you married to that lump of flour, Chatham?" Smiling, he danced across the room and clasped her hand. "I can't tell you what this means to me."

Irritation flushed her face. "What right has Uncle Percy to plan the course of my future?"

"Indeed." His thumb skimmed over her clenched knuckles. "Besides, your father will give his approval for your hand."

"It is his right." She extricated her hand from his grasp, stricken with an image of Griffin on their wedding night. She would not discuss marriage to David when she was legally bound to another.

"You must wonder why I came such a great distance."

Say no more, she wanted to utter, but the words stuck in her throat.

He reclaimed her fingers curled in a tight knot over her lap. "The purpose is obvious to me. I suspect for you, as well."

Trained to be polite, she forced a pleasant smile in spite of her reluctance to hear more.

"Even though your note said you'd come back, I couldn't risk losing you. I came as soon as I could."

"How sweet and thoughtful." Though determined may have been a better choice of word.

"It's true. I *do* want to take you back to England. Not for your uncle but for me—as my wife."

Air rushed from her lungs. Two months ago, before she'd learned of Papa's troubles, such a declaration would have left her elated. Now it stirred confusion and a host of other emotions she needed time to sort.

As if Griffin needed to trounce any possibility of joy, he rose in her head, powerful and yet as insubstantial as a puff of air. The thought of him stirred a host of pleasurable memories which were quickly followed by disillusionment and confusion. How could she return to her former life in London, married to David, when the two people she loved the most, Griffin and Papa, lived right here in New York?

Before she could speak, David dropped next to her on the couch. "Marry me."

She shifted restlessly. A voice shrieked *no* from the deep recesses of her mind. A more sensible voice urged her to plan for a future without Griffin. If she were lucky, perhaps a marriage to David would eclipse all memory of the charming spy. Ha! And she would soon grow another head. What to do? What to do?

"There's no other woman more perfect for me. Say you'll return with me to London." He squeezed her hands, eager for her answer.

Around her, the air thinned. "I…I'm overwhelmed. Minutes ago, I feared I might faint from the shock of your visit. And now…".

"You will?" he said before she'd finished. Triumph radiated in his smile.

In the next instant, he'd swallowed her in his arms. Her head was crushed against his chest, her nose smashed against the satin of his elegant coat. She felt suffocated and ill. Under no circumstances did she want to cause him pain, but she never uttered *yes*. He'd assumed and misunderstood her silence. She must tell him of Griffin. "David, there's something…"

His ardent, demanding kiss ended her words. Shaken, she clung to him, distracted for a moment by the pressure of his mouth. No matter how pleasant the sensation, it paled in comparison to the feelings Griffin evoked. On track again, she pushed against his shoulder and broke away. "I must tell you…"

He dragged her back, squeezing what breath she had from her lungs. His moist lips skimmed from lips to ear. "Do tell, Lily. I want to hear every word." He laughed, giddy as a pupil with a prize. "When can I speak with your father?"

"It is what I wanted to talk about…"

Suddenly, the life went out of him. He eased his grip and stared at something beyond her shoulder. A hurried, backward glance revealed Agatha in the doorway, apron crunched in her fingers.

"Excuse me, miss. There's someone at the door to see you."

Lily discharged a grateful breath for the interruption. Pulling from his arms, she hoped the visitor brought encouraging news of Papa. "Please show the guest to Papa's study." Agatha left, while Lily, with a tremulous smile, stood. "This should only take a moment. Please, have more tea and cake. It's delicious."

With quick steps, she fled the parlor. Once in the hallway, she fell back against the closed door. "Sweet Jesus," she said on a fluttery breath.

"I've never been confused with him before," a pleasant voice responded.

At the familiar sound, her heart surged with one great leap against her ribs. Her head snapped up. Griffin stood in the front doorway, bathed in light, all wonderful flesh and substance, and fulfilled a reoccurring dream. He was here.

"Happy to see me?" he asked and tumbled her world.

Blood rushed to her toes. She tottered. He sprang to life, lurching across the entryway and caught her by the arms.

"Not here," she whispered, almost choking. Frantically, she gestured toward the far end of the house. Grabbing his coat sleeve, she tugged him down the hallway and into Papa's study. She closed the door, her legs shaking so much she sagged against it for support.

"People have been surprised to see me, but this is beyond rational." He looked anything but amused. "Are you all right? Shall I fetch water? Spirits?"

She flourished a hand, too overcome to speak and pained by the instant vulnerability and bewilderment in his face.

Griffin in her study. David in the parlor.

A moan escaped her tight throat. Why, today of all days, was he here? "I wasn't expecting you."

"Obviously," he countered sounding nettled. He stood ramrod straight next to Papa's desk. Dressed simply in a brown suit with black buttons, white shirt and hose, he looked so handsome she wanted to yelp for the glory of it.

Calm down. Calm down.

For days, she'd tried not to think of him. At night, thoughts of him kept her awake until sheer exhaustion claimed her. With a gulp of air, she pushed away from the door. Emotionally ragged at the appearance of both men, she could barely form a civil tone. "What are you doing here?"

"It's nice to see you too." His grim attempt at a

smile fell flat.

"Please, sit." Distraught at her ill-spoken words, she motioned to her father's favorite leather chair, well used and comfortable.

"After you." Ever polite, he indicated the armchair opposite from Papa's.

Lily sidled across the cluttered space, books on every shelf and table, and collapsed into the seat. A quick mental inventory of her appearance reminded her she wore her second-best day dress, a very fashionable number. Oh, what did it matter if the dress brought out the violet in her eyes? Annoyed with such frivolous concerns, she fell back on manners and said, "You're looking well." A jittery hand skimmed over the satiny folds of her gown. She couldn't take her gaze from his strong face, the dimple in his chin and those sensual lips that moved and formed words. "I'm sorry. What did you say?"

He raised a speculative brow. "I asked how you are."

Lord, where to begin?

"It's wonderful to be home." She feared her taut face might crack.

"Have you seen your father?" Concern caused a furrow in his brow.

"Yes, I can't tell you how happy..." Her cheeks flushed with embarrassment, and she hesitated to babble further. Unlike David, Griffin required no pretense or charade. He knew all the good and bad about her. More than anyone, he knew the risks she'd taken to reunite with Papa. She blinked once, slowly and wished she could block him, Papa and David from her mind.

"I'm sorry, Lily. I came as soon as I heard."

"What do you mean?"

"Surely someone told you?"

"That Papa's in prison? Yes, I know." She wanted to cry and laugh at the situation's absurdity. "The irony is he's imprisoned for being a Patriot. Can you believe it?"

Griffin had the grace to remain quiet.

"All those years, I assumed I knew him, his interests, his likes, and what made him happy. What a shock to return and find he's not what I believed. In some respects, he's like a stranger."

"And in other respects?" Griffin asked kindly.

"He's my father. I'll always love him." Head cocked, she appraised him head to foot, as if for the first time, she understood what made him tick. "Maybe no one is who we think they are. Perhaps we all live behind a façade."

Griffin didn't rise to the bait, just sat in the chair and watched her.

"It seems you two are cut from the same cloth."

"A good cloth, to be sure."

"Do you realize the funniest thing about this whole mess?"

He shook his head.

"I've come to realize the merit of those beliefs you and Papa hold so dear." Cecil Jones's fateful prediction blossomed in her mind. *Everyone must choose a side.*

Griffin's eyes lit up, a glorious bluish green. "So you've shed your Loyalist skin, have you?"

"As strange as it is to admit, yes. Fortunately, there are no British soldiers in my house at the moment to hear my admission, or I too could be tossed into jail."

The tension in her shoulders eased. All the pent-up confusion, ideas and positions harbored and fussed over, suddenly drained away like water from a broken cup.

"It is so sad. Tragic, really. It tears my heart to think Papa may never walk as a free man again." The words made her throat sting.

The chair squeaked when he stood and came to her, arms reaching. She stood and leaned into him. The familiar scent of his soap and skin, the solidness of his body, filled her with comfort. Cuddled and safe, she knew Griffin was home, even more so than the cluttered study or the familiar view of the garden outside these windows. Griffin. Her home.

"I'll help you, any way I can."

His even voice was the constancy she needed. Cocooned in his embrace, she nestled her cheek against his chest. His heart thumped, steady and reassuring. All worry disappeared. Only the present mattered, the feel of him beneath her fingertips. In that sweet, precious moment, David bellowed her name and jerked her back to harsh reality.

"Oh, no," she moaned.

"What is it?" Griffin tightened his hold. "Who's calling you?"

"Lily?" David's voice grew louder and more insistent.

The library door opened, and she pushed away from Griffin.

David surveyed their cozy tableau by the fireplace. His fingers gripped around the door handle turned white. In an instant, his gaze went from puzzled to icy slits of anger.

Lily's stomach dropped. Her brain scrambled for appropriate words.

David had no such difficulty and snarled, "I'll thank you to take your hands off my fiancée."

Griffin arched a brow. "Fiancée, is it?" He lowered his hand to her shoulder, his expression inscrutable. "Do the British tell a man when he can touch his wife?"

Chapter Twenty-Five

"What?" Color drained from Warwick's astounded face.

"Lily is my wife." Griffin took obstinate satisfaction from the fact.

The man began to sputter and gulp, and Griffin struggled not to laugh. The conceited ass blinked several times before his stricken gaze flicked between Lily and him. "I don't believe it." He drew himself up, his chest expanding then stomped into the room like a bulldog defending his territory.

"Did Lily fail to mention it?" Despite Griffin's glib tone and amused air, his back muscles tightened. "Isn't it funny how a matter as important as marriage can be overlooked?"

Lily reached out to the sorry fellow, who trembled and spluttered. "It's a long story, David, and a rather incredible one. I'm sure you'll find it quite humorous. Mr. Faraday is an old friend and he…"

Griffin flung up a hand. She would not minimize what they'd shared. "You don't need to explain."

"But I do," she insisted. She tipped her head issuing a silent, desperate plea for his tolerance or sympathy, but he was well past cooperation.

"We married seven weeks ago." Silently, he rejoiced when Warwick's jaw dropped.

"Seven weeks ago?" Horror swept across the broad

planes of the man's face as the realization sank in. "Gone from London a week when you married *him*?" The word dripped with contempt. "Of all people, Lily. Why him?"

Griffin felt himself go rigid. Although he was no Greek God, he exhibited more manners than this glaring prig. No one had ever mistaken Griffin Faraday for an ape or a boor.

"It's complicated," replied Lily.

Complicated was the least of it.

Griffin forced a smile and chose to view the present situation as silly playacting, a farce rather than a tragedy. Yet sadly, he didn't feel like laughing. An awful premonition chilled his bones, a fear Lily might slip from his grasp forever. Desperate to drive a wedge between the two, he said, "The ship was short on quarters. We became close—*very* quickly."

Warwick flushed. Fury worked its way into his pinked cheeks. Hardened eyes glinted like polished glass. Griffin didn't require sight to recognize a man on the point of shattering. More so, he'd welcome the explosion. It would please him to see Warwick go berserk and foam at the mouth.

"David." Palms outstretched, Lily beseeched him to understand. Whatever appeasement she hoped to achieve fell short when he continued to glower. "Calm down and I'll explain."

Explain? What a joke. In no way did she appear capable of such a feat. Pale and drawn, he expected her to buckle at any moment. Griffin wasn't certain she didn't deserve to.

A muscle twitched in Warwick's cheek as he kept Lily in his murderous stare. "I just proposed to you, and you didn't think to mention your marriage?"

Lily wrung her hands. "I haven't seen Griffin since we landed in New York. Imagine my surprise when both of you appeared today."

If she meant to imply he was an unwanted problem washed up at her door, he wouldn't stand for it. In coming here, he'd hoped to find her anger gone and, in its place, acceptance, or at least tolerance of his decisions on the ship. Perhaps he'd been foolish to dream she'd be blissfully happy to see him. He came expecting the best, but never ruled out a challenge. To win her, he'd been prepared to charm and cajole, if necessary. If his efforts failed to impress her, he intended a graceful acceptance of her wish to divorce, though it would slay him. Not in a million years did he expect Warwick to appear with a formal proposal of marriage.

Why had she not explained the situation to her suitor? The answer broke like a clap of thunder. On purpose, she'd withheld the truth. As a result, she could quietly shed him and marry Warwick with no one the wiser.

The cruel news raised the hurt of earlier rejections, Katherine Hawkins, in particular. As disappointing as it was at the time, life trudged on, altered by pain and doubt. This time, the wound cut deeper. The grave injury would make his recovery less certain. Perhaps impossible. His love for Lily was more complete and wonderful than he'd ever believed possible.

An impulse to drop to his knees before her arose. Pride stood in his way. He couldn't grovel. Not in front of Warwick. Furthermore, reasoning with her would do no good, not once she'd made up her mind. Instead, he did the one thing decency allowed. He gave a formal half bow. "Please accept my apologies for interrupting your happy reunion." Scorn riddled his voice. Body hard as stone, he started for the door. As he passed *his lordship*, the dolt swung an arm. Griffin ducked. The blow missed his head by a hair. Reflexively, he hurled a fist. Grim pleasure erupted when the man's head snapped back and blood exploded from his nose. Warwick stumbled and collapsed on a couch. Fists clenched, Griffin continued to the door.

"Griffin. Wait!"

Ignoring both her and the pain in his hand, Griffin marched stiffly from the old tutor's home, leaving the tutor's daughter, his wife, behind to comfort her fiancé. How absurd.

In the street, two lads juggled wooden discs in the air. When Griffin stormed across the walkway in their direction, the boys ceased their play and stared, open-mouthed. Unattended, the discs clattered against the wooden street pavers. One rolled into Griffin's path. A swift kick sent it flying. "Blasted toys," he mumbled and never once broke stride. "Keep the damn things off the street." Their astonished and curious gazes burned into him as he passed. No matter. He was beyond the point of caring.

Fiancé? After what they'd shared on ship, after her heartfelt declaration of love, he couldn't believe it. Had Lily succumbed to leprosy, he couldn't feel half so wretched. Affianced to Warwick, a mewling, pompous rodent…

At least Katherine had rejected him in favor of his brother, a man he respected. Warwick was an entirely different fish, and one that stunk.

Stomping along, Griffin swatted a nearby tree branch. For his effort, the spry limb rebounded and slapped his cheek. The sting felt good, deserved somehow, punishment for his weakness. He should have heeded his own counsel and never married. Still, he couldn't have let her go with the pirate. Yet did he have to fall in love? Experience taught him he lacked luck in those quarters. Why couldn't he have heeded the painful lessons of history? Some things never changed.

He grunted and trudged on. What an idiot. He could almost hear his brothers howl at his foolishness.

Mumbling, he kicked at the dusty street, disgusted with the lot of them, Warwick, Lily and most of all, himself. How could he have been so blind? They'd spent long hours together on the ship, laughing and sharing a tender friendship. He adored her and could have sworn their love was mutual in its intensity. The experience seemed pointless now. Sadly, his lies and betrayal had soured her affections.

He shook his head, aware he wasn't the only one to have played false. She'd strung him along as skillfully as any puppet master.

Another two blocks passed before he charged into the Leap Frog tavern. In the doorway, he paused to allow his vision to adjust to the dim surroundings. Half a dozen patrons, their trenchers of ale frozen in midair, stared quizzically at him. Griffin glowered and barreled to the bar. With a foot, he nudged aside a stool. The legs shrieked against the plank flooring. Not caring, he plopped down and grunted, "Give me an ale."

"Right away, sir." The alarmed barkeep set aside the pitcher he'd been wiping with a towel.

While he poured the drink, Griffin glared at the

two drinkers on his right. The men slowly rotated away from him, smart enough to avoid the trouble boiling at their side. He slapped a coin on the counter and mumbled his thanks when the barkeep carefully slid the ale toward him.

Griffin drank long and deep troubled by memories recent and old.

When he'd learned of Henry Fitzhugh's imprisonment from General Washington, he'd ridden directly to New York and Lily. And what did he find? That pumpernickel Warwick. Disgusted, he squeezed the tankard, his knuckles bruised and sore from Warwick's bones. At least he'd popped off a good one.

He hoisted the pewter cup and drank the frothy hops. Long past the age of fairy tales, he'd foolishly fallen for the damsel in distress. The worst part about all this was he still loved her.

****

Griffin slammed out of the house and turned Lily's world on its head. She stared into the empty space he'd occupied moments ago, her cold fingers pressed to her bloodless lips. Through the window, she watched him stomp across the walkway and into the street until she could no longer see him. His absence left her insides hollow.

David groaned and drew her attention. Head down, shoulders drawn up around his ears, he sat curled forward on the couch. Aware he needed comfort she reached out, but he snarled and wrenched away. She understood his distress. He'd been trounced by Griffin yet again and was doubtless humiliated. Any offer of aid would only add injury to his smarting pride. As to her in particular, the married woman to whom he'd proposed, well, her solace would be unbearable.

She signaled to Agatha, who hovered just beyond the door, for warm water and a towel.

"David, please." She cringed as he dabbed at his bloodied nose with a lace hankie he'd pulled from a pocket. "You'll just ruin it."

"This should be his blood I'm sopping. The filthy rogue." He stamped a foot then tried to stand. Swaying precariously, he gave up and collapsed on the sofa. "It would give me great pleasure to kill him."

She recoiled. "You don't mean it. Anger's got you in a vise."

His once attractive face twisted in anger. "Before I return to England, I'll see him arrested. A long visit in prison works wonders on a man."

The mention of prison, Papa's suffering, and Griffin—well, it was more than she could bear. Her legs no longer offered sufficient support, and she joined him on the couch.

"How could you marry him, Lily?" He tossed the soiled hankie into the unlit fireplace. Any errant strands of auburn hair were angrily shoved aside. "How could you do this to me?"

Hurt and pain contorted his features and roused her shame. She'd never meant for anyone to get hurt. "There was no other way."

Now seemed as good as any time to tell him about Mulworthy, the pirate and Griffin's rescue. Out of respect for David's bruised ego, she would forgo the term rescue. Maybe when he'd heard the whole tale, minus Griffin's work for the Colonial Army, he might understand and even accept her actions. Still, she wouldn't be surprised if he bolted out the door either.

After all, a man had his pride, too. He might want to forget her and this embarrassing situation.

On a sigh, she began her story. After she'd painted the broad details, she summed it up with, "Griffin and I agreed to a marriage in name only. Once we arrived in New York, we agreed to procure an annulment or divorce, whatever was quickest. I assure you, he didn't want to be married to me anymore than I desired him as a husband." Not about to rub salt in his wounds, she wouldn't mention the short period of bliss, the days she'd loved Griffin and wanted the marriage to last forever.

A muscle jumped in David's reddened cheek. She expected a harsh rebuke. Yet when he remained silent, the awkwardness of his quiet drove her to dip the flannel cloth in the water basin Agatha had placed on a table. "Let me wash away the blood."

It was then his winds lashed. "Do you think me so weak a mere blow can handicap me?"

Perhaps she deserved his wrath. Nevertheless, his barbed anger pricked her skin. Distraught and torn, she wrung the water from the towel and gently washed his face. After a few moments, his breathing slowed. The lines in his face relaxed. "I'm so sorry you came all this way only to find things in such a muddle."

"Don't fret, woman." The caress to her cheek was even more surprising than his gentle tone. "You do intend to get a divorce, don't you?"

He watched her intently, as if he might find the answer locked beneath the surface of her skin. She knew what he wanted to hear and what she ought to say, yet the words tangled and caught in her throat. Postponement of this conversation to another day would give her time to think and recoup. In the final analysis, what was there to review? Thus, she gave him the only answer she possessed. "It seems the wisest course."

"Good." Satisfaction lightened his expression.

It astounded her that in spite of his wounded pride, he still wished to marry her. If his arduous journey was any measure, he cared about her. Maybe he even loved her. But...

Like Uncle Percy, he cared about appearances, too. He was not the sort to accept the divorced cast-off of another man. Once the *ton* heard the scandalous news, they would snicker and gossip. They'd label him a fool. He had every reason to abandon her. So what motivated his commitment? He wasn't the romantic sort and had yet to proclaim his love. Perhaps his interest did lie more with Papa's money than with her. Self-reproach followed the unkind thought.

"Lily, my sweet." He slipped an arm around her waist.

A wish to keep her distance prompted her feeble push against his shoulders. "You've just been injured."

"I have energy enough for five men. You need never worry about my stamina."

If he meant this as a reference to sexual energy, she wanted no part of the conversation.

"Let's sit in the parlor." She scrambled to her feet, anxious to remove herself from the happy childhood memories engendered by Papa's study. Reminders of a young Griffin, under Papa's tutelage, would only cloud her judgment and serve no good to the present confusion.

At the door, he stopped her with a hand to her

elbow. "Tell me about you and Faraday."

Irritation pounded at her temples. If he intended to marry her, he had a right to hear an explanation, yet for some reason she balked. Head held high, she stepped light and fast toward the parlor at the front of the house.

"My intended spends weeks on a vessel with the filth and refuses to answer questions." Behind her, his footsteps stomped on the corridor's carpet. "Then the rogue shows up unannounced at her home. You can imagine my curiosity."

"I was a passenger on the ship. Same as him." Outside the parlor windows, a mass of heavy clouds gave the room a grayish tint and added to her peevish mood. "These questions are unnecessary."

Beliefs she held dear on the *Providence* clouded her mind in a gauzy web. A week ago, she loved Griffin and believed in their happy future. Because of lies and mistrust, the dream lay in shambles.

"I want to know." He stopped at the fireplace, hands clasped behind his back. "Anyone who travels by sea is aware of the lack of privacy."

"I won't speak of the voyage. Ever." She slashed a hand in the air. "It's over."

"I see."

"You don't see," she snapped. Only someone who'd experienced a similar circumstance could understand her fear and desperation stirred by Mulworthy's threats on the *Providence.* Only she could understand her relief and gratitude for Griffin's help and the ecstasy they'd shared. She would never admit she'd lost her heart to a man who lied and betrayed her. What was love without trust? Without it, there was nothing.

The tension in the parlor, as bad as in Papa's study, hung thick as molasses. She struggled to think of the right words to smooth the rift. A pot of tea and a filled teacup sat on the table. She tasted hers and made a face. "This is cold." She picked up the bell to summon Agatha. With a lifted hand and a headshake, he stopped her.

"Why did Faraday come here?"

Her thumb rubbed against the bell handle. She tried to pulverize every unpleasant emotion and failed miserably. Sighing, she set the bell aside. "He came to inquire after Papa."

David frowned. "Is your father ill?"

Given what transpired in the last minutes, she supposed it no longer mattered if he learned the truth. "Papa is in prison."

As if he couldn't understand, he blinked and blinked again. "Prison? For what crime?"

"For his outspoken support of the Colonial government." Suddenly weary, she sank into the sofa. "He publicly denounced the King."

"Treason?" He struggled not to laugh.

"It isn't funny."

Heeding her testy mood, he rearranged his amused features and became as placid and sober as a minister. When she scowled, he threw up his hands in defeat. "I'm not laughing."

"I should hope not. It's the most unfortunate of circumstances. Papa's never been political before. It seems everybody"—for emphasis, she flailed an arm—"everybody has taken a side. One is either a Patriot to be celebrated or a traitor to be vilified and ruined."

The sofa dipped when he sat next to her. "Surely

the situation can be rectified. A few words dropped in the right ear."

"I've already spoken to Captain Babcock, the army prison administrator. Sorry to say, he won't help."

"Babcock, you say." His voice lifted. "Lester Babcock?"

She nodded.

He broke into a laugh. "What a small world. I am acquainted with the man. He's a brother to Lord Chisholm, an old schoolmate. I can make inquiries. And money, well placed, often performs miracles."

Wasn't bribery a crime? She eyed him warily. "Do you think it could work?"

A snap of his fingers meant to dismiss her doubts. "For you, I would do anything."

In exchange for what and instantly regretted her skepticism. To see Papa released from jail, she might collaborate with the devil himself. "You'd help me?"

"I'll throw out the fishing net and let it drift, see if I catch anything." His gaze was nothing if not serious. "I trust you'll consider my proposal of marriage."

****

"Quite the excitement for one day, eh?" Agatha nudged the teapot aside on the tray to make room for the leftover cake and dirtied dishes.

"Hmmm," Lily replied, distracted.

David had left soon after Griffin's departure, his eyes ablaze with hope and seemingly pressured to renew his acquaintance with Captain Babcock. The unexpected visits of both men left her emotions a wind-tossed mess.

"Lord Warwick believes he can have Papa released from jail." She picked up a pillow from the parlor sofa and hugged it to her chest.

"That's big of him."

"You don't like Lord Warwick, do you?" No doubt, the ever-protective housekeeper heard more than she should when she'd hovered earlier in the hallway, ready to spring to Lily's defense, if necessary.

"I don't like to say…" Agatha pushed a crumb about the plate.

"I value your opinion."

The older woman hesitated appearing to stew over her answer before she spilled her thoughts. "He's puffed up. Just off the boat and a stranger in town, yet he thinks he can solve your troubles." She shrugged. "The man's a soufflé. He'll rise fast and fall just as quickly."

Lily snorted. "What would you say if I told you he wishes to marry me?"

"Then I say good luck."

"Agatha!"

"It's not my position to talk, but since you asked… He has a haughty air, thinking he's better than others."

So did much of the aristocracy. She tapped her bottom lip, aware of the allowances she'd made for David's arrogance and insecurity over the years. He, in turn, put up with her odd quirks and interests. Despite their shortcomings, they'd given each other the acceptance not found in their respective homes. Until today, she'd never questioned his innate goodness. "He's an old, dear friend, and is acquainted with Captain Babcock."

"You're a kind-hearted girl. Always did bring home the stray cat or dog, the injured bird. It's loyal you are." She smoothed her wrinkled hands down her apron. "If you don't mind me saying, loyalty isn't love."

Lily shrank back against her mama's needlepoint pillows. "What makes you think I don't love him?" In reply, she received a withering look. "All right," she conceded. "It seems you know me better than I know myself." So what if David didn't shake the air in the same manner as Griffin. "You've made your point."

"Besides," Agatha said. "I saw the way you looked at Mr. Faraday—like he walked on water. I take it he's one of the boys your papa used to tutor. Griffin, is it?"

"Yes, the entertaining one."

Agatha tugged at her chin, her brow creased in reflection. Whatever was on her mind and whatever she intended to say, Lily knew to appreciate its seriousness. "You might be better off marrying the Griffin bloke."

Lily hid her surprise behind a stern expression. For a second, she considered admitting they were married but couldn't see the point. How would it help?

"Griffin isn't interested in marriage." When he'd held her in his arms in Papa's study, it was to comfort. Not once did he express his love. Nor did he express a wish to remain married. Kindness and chivalry motivated his actions, just as he'd done when he rescued her from the pirate.

She released a sad, tired breath. For a few days on the voyage, their love seemed genuine and his sentiments authentic. Bah! Fairy tales never came true. Caught up in the forced intimacy of the ship's surroundings, they'd each played their part. At some point, they crossed the fine line of playacting. They came to believe what they shared would last forever. But it wasn't real. Once Griffin was home, his commitment to Washington became foremost in his mind. To dissolve their union made sense to him. Besides, he'd said he never wanted marriage, not as long as there was war.

"Marriage. What a fiddle faddle." She told herself her insides didn't bleed.

Had she not been reluctant to hurt David, or he so ready to hear what he wanted to hear, their situation might be clearer. Had she not been so desperate for his help, she might have spoken with more certainty. She might have told him she wouldn't marry him.

What to do? What to do? She rubbed at her forehead, confused by it all.

"Are you prepared to marry Lord Fine and Fancy in exchange for seeing your father out of prison?"

"Goodness, how much did you hear?" It wasn't her finest moment. If she had another choice, some other means to help Papa, she would grab at it and chortle thanks to the gods. As she lamented the scarcity of options, she realized the irony of her circumstances. She married Griffin to save herself from the pirate. Was she prepared to marry David to save her father?

The housekeeper scratched at an ear. "It's a painful state, your father in prison. Even so, he wouldn't want you to make such an important promise if you never intended to keep it." She shuffled closer and patted Lily's shoulder. "He never raised you to lie or mislead people."

Hot with shame, Lily glanced out the window to the yard shadowed by enormous elm trees. Griffin or David. Two very different men.

"David offered to help, but it comes with a condition. Griffin offered his service without any hint of gain whatsoever."

Agatha's craggy face lightened. "A man with integrity."

Lily chuckled mirthlessly. "I wouldn't have thought integrity and Griffin went hand in hand."

"Oh?" The woman's silvery brows rose. "What have you to say on the matter today?"

"I think I've been stupid."

Chapter Twenty-Six

Josiah Faraday hunkered at a cluttered desk stacked with papers and folders, studying an account ledger. In spite of the hour, ten o'clock in the morning, a lamp at the desk's edge illuminated his crumpled brow. As if he sensed a presence, he glanced up.

"Griffin," he exclaimed in a hearty welcome when he noticed him in the doorway. His uncle slid from his chair and crossed the room with outstretched arms, his angular face bathed in an infectious grin.

Griffin leaned into his uncle's hug. His head reeled from the simple movement, the result of a nasty hangover, compliments of last night's debauchery. Without resistance, he surrendered to the good-natured pat on the back before his uncle held him away for a quick study.

"Good God," he bellowed. "You look like death itself! Are you ill?" He sniffed, wrinkled his nose and jerked away. "Alcohol? Got yourself in quite a tosspot, eh?" Chuckling, he reached for a chair, dragged it close, and pressed a hand on Griffin's chest. He dropped like a sack of grain into the seat. Though he hadn't eaten in over twenty hours, his stomach sloshed side to side.

"I'd offer you some wine…"

Griffin begged off with a raised hand and a sharp ache behind his eyes.

His uncle plopped in his desk chair and studied him

quizzically. "It's good to see you. I regret I wasn't around when your ship arrived."

"You're here now." Griffin would be ever thankful for the man's interest and support. "Have you heard if the *Providence* got out of harbor without any trouble?" Despite the cloudy sky, the morning light blazed much too vividly and he squinted.

"None so far as I heard. Must be nigh on to Boston by this time. I happened to run into the good Captain before he sailed." Josiah smiled wickedly. "My, the ladies in New York do love their French lace."

They both chuckled, though the effort sparked a painful spasm in Griffin's head. Despite the tempest in his gut, the crew's safe passage from the harbor left him pleased. "How are things in New York?"

Josiah picked up a bottle of wine, uncorked it, poured the burgundy liquid in a glass, and sipped. "The British Army is a damned nuisance. I have my fingers crossed hoping the infantry will charge off across the river and not return. It seems the soldiers don't have enough to do so they march up and down the street and arrest good, hard-working citizens. Pompous martinets. They want to make New York into another London."

"It'll never happen."

"We can only pray." Josiah rotated the scarlet liquid in his glass. "What about you? Have you seen your parents?"

Griffin raised a finger, forestalling further talk, and crossed the office. After a quick glance into the warehouse, he shut the door. "One can never be too careful." He reclaimed his seat. "First thing, I went to see Washington. As soon as I'd given my report, I rushed back here."

His uncle frowned. "Does he send you on assignment so soon?"

He shook his head and wished he hadn't when he winced in pain. "I am suspected in London. I'm to wait for new orders."

"It won't be safe for you to remain in New York."

Griffin nodded, stoic about his need to temporarily forgo home and work for his uncle in lieu of his duty to his country.

Josiah sat back and his big hand curled about the arm of his chair. He grinned. "Tell me about this woman."

"What woman?" He shifted in his seat and considered denying her existence, but he couldn't fool his uncle. "How did you guess?"

"It's not like you to take the piss for no good reason. Doubtless a woman has driven you to the bottom of the beer barrel."

Griffin's transparency about women troubled and confused him. When it came to other matters, business, writing, his political beliefs, no one ever guessed what thoughts lurked in his head. But women? Uncertain where to begin he just sat there, an idiot in his prime.

"Did you meet her in London?"

He hesitated. "Yes. Then she showed up on the *Providence*."

Josiah gaped. "Mulworthy allowed it?"

"He didn't have a choice. By the time we found her we were too far out to sea."

"A stowaway."

"Unfortunately, yes." Griffin smiled at the image of Lily dressed in her ridiculous servant costume.

"Must be a special woman, eh, lad?"

Special wasn't the half of it, he concluded, massaging his temple.

"So what's the problem?"

Too embarrassed to admit Lily had chosen another man over him, he faltered. Yet he never could keep secrets from his uncle. "She's engaged to some—" The word *ass* stuck in his throat.

"I see." Josiah hooked his fingers together over his homespun waistcoat and shrugged as if it didn't really signify. "If she's the one you want—lay your claim. Wear her down."

Griffin produced a wry smile. "I never took you for the rough sort."

At Josiah's sudden faraway gleam, Griffin suspected his uncle remembered past times when he courted Aunt Maude, who died much too young.

"It's complicated." Griffin dared to use the same words Lily had used yesterday with Warwick. Suddenly averse to any pity or possible mockery, he declined to mention he'd married the woman.

Josiah shifted restlessly in the chair. "You're overthinking it, man."

"Maybe."

"But?"

"She's stubborn." Also sweet, spirited, and all sorts of other wonderful qualities. He realized he'd grown mushy.

"And you aren't?" Head tipped, Josiah's reddish hair caught the light and the strands glinted like bronze.

"She's competitive as any man."

"A woman to keep you on your toes." The older man rubbed his hands gleefully.

"She wants to marry a pompous cockatoo."

"A misguided woman. Do her a favor and show her a proper man—one with both heart and brains."

At the compliment, he rolled his eyes. Appreciative of his uncle's effort, he drummed fingers on his thigh, trying to block out the sound of Lily's musical laugh.

"She knows I'm a spy."

Josiah tugged at his lip. "Is she loyal to the King?"

"She claims little knowledge of politics. Cecil Jones set her up to spy on me."

"Ah." Any joy disappeared from the man's rugged face. "Jones is a poisonous snake. Ask your brother, Elliott. They've crossed paths."

Griffin nodded. He would discuss the matter when he saw his brother. "She may or may not inform on me to Jones. Her wings are in a mad flutter. No telling which way she might fly." Clearly, Warwick and London were on her map.

He hunched forward in the chair and hung his hands between his knees. "You may remember her. She's Lily Fitzhugh, the daughter of Henry Fitzhugh. Are your familiar with him?"

"Yes, but not well. He chains himself to home for months at a time working on his inventions. At present, he's in prison, rounded up along with a dozen others." He picked at his chin, lost in thought for a moment before he continued. "He doesn't strike me as the sort to make bold political statements. Still, the current state of affairs changes a man." He frowned. "I didn't recall Fitzhugh had a daughter."

"He does, and I intend to get him out of prison."

The older man reacted as one would when handed a monkey's head. His brows rose. "A noble way to win a lady's hand."

"I'm not doing it to win her favor. I made up my mind to help her days ago even before I heard about her engagement. He means the world to her." The gesture would be his final gift to Lily—a farewell present. The thought saddened him.

"You understand the risks, don't you? To help Henry Fitzhugh escape prison will put unwanted British attention on you. For all you can tell, she's already squawked your name to the authorities. You'd be arrested and hanged."

"I don't intend to get caught." He studied his uncle's face, a man he trusted as completely as he did his father. "Will you help me?"

****

"See that Schiller's Tavern gets ten of these cases." The man spoke with an easy authority, so much like Griffin who possessed a great surety and confidence.

The second man, presumably a clerk, scratched something on a slate with chalk. When he finished, he darted out a side door.

"Excuse me." Lily spoke from Josiah Faraday's office doorway.

Standing near a desk, the tall man turned and faced her. Through a window at his back, the late afternoon sun flashed over his head illuminating threads of silver in his auburn hair. A depression cleaved a space in his strong chin.

"May I help you, miss?"

She fisted her hand at her side, aware of the tension that rippled up her arm. She smiled politely. "I'm here to see Mr. Griffin Faraday. I understand he works here with his uncle."

"He does." Like Griffin's, his razor-sharp stare

disarmed her and it took conscious effort not to fidget with discomfort.

"I'm his uncle, Josiah Faraday." An attractive man in his forties or possibly fifty, he exuded an air of keen intelligence, and was not someone to be ignored. "You have me at a disadvantage, Miss…?"

"It's Fitzhugh. Lily Fitzhugh." She wondered if Griffin had spoken of her or mentioned their marriage.

By way of acknowledgment, he dipped his chin. The sudden lightness in his manner, as if amused, raised her curiosity.

"My nephew left some hours ago. I'm sorry to say he'll be in Philadelphia for the next week."

"Oh." Her shoulders slumped with disappointment.

"May I be of assistance, Miss Fitzhugh?"

In anticipation Washington might have dispatched Griffin to some far-off location, she'd come prepared. "When you see him, will you give him this?" Since he'd stormed from her house yesterday, she'd had plenty of time to reflect. When she arrived at a decision, she wrote several letters. From her purse, she retrieved the thick envelope and handed it to his uncle.

He glanced from it to her. "Wouldn't you prefer to keep it and give it to him yourself?"

"Things are rather unsettled." She wavered, questioning how much to reveal. "It would relieve me greatly if he saw this at the earliest convenience."

Brow drawn in thought, he tapped the sealed parchment upon his desk. "Rest assured I'll see he receives it."

It would have to do. "Thank you." She turned to go.

"A moment, if you please." She faced him,

surprised at his somber expression. "I'm sorry to hear about your father."

Had everyone in the city heard about Papa's imprisonment?

"It's a trying time for many families." His understanding tone tugged an inner ache.

"Yes, it is." She watched as he put her missive into a desk drawer.

"The British have jailed so many on these wretched ships. They would be well to accept people are not casks of wine to be stored in a crate at the bottom of a stinking boat."

She'd witnessed the deplorable conditions first hand and didn't need any reminders. "It's despicable."

Arms crossed, he set his feet wide apart. "It's a tragedy when a loved one is locked up for their political sentiments, wouldn't you agree?"

On the surface, his words registered as sympathetic to Papa's ordeal. Yet a subtle change had overcome the man. His sudden defensive stance and fierce gaze suggested a greater, underlying meaning to his words. An unspoken threat.

"It's the worst possible outcome," she answered.

"Were it a member of my family arrested, the occurrence would shake me to my very foundation."

Again, his intense demeanor and grave words clamored with warning. So he knew about her and Cecil Jones. Griffin must have told him. It made sense he also knew about Griffin's activities for the Colonial Army. "You're worried about Griffin, aren't you, Mr. Faraday?" And what she might do with the information.

"It would shatter me if my nephew came to harm." An unmistakable power vibrated in his words, as strong and forceful as his towering form. "I don't wish to see Griffin arrested for any reason, do you?"

She held his gaze, attuned to the heavy thump, thump in her head. "Not on my account." She forced a smile. "Good day, Mr. Faraday."

Chapter Twenty-Seven

Lily folded the last letter and sealed it with hot wax. Sighing, she leaned back in Papa's leather desk chair, satisfied with her efforts. She prayed the missives to the governor, Captain Babcock, and her uncle would garner support and bear fruit in regards to dear Papa. Although she accepted his right to take a political stance, she wouldn't let the stubborn man starve to death.

There was Griffin to consider as well. Would she ever see him again? Did he think of her? Did she matter to him at all?

Unwilling to sink in despair and uncertainty, she rose from the chair, braced with a new-found determination. Organizing Papa's study would occupy her mind and perhaps reap a sense of accomplishment to offset her gloomy mood.

After she sorted his messy desktop, she tackled the cluttered bookshelves. How did the man ever find anything? As she dusted, she removed a few books from a shelf and came upon a personal journal. Had it fallen behind the others and been forgotten, or had Papa meant to conceal it?

Baffled, she returned to the desk, where she flipped through the ink-stained pages, astonished at the drawings of firearms such as long muskets, both single and double-barreled. How odd, she thought, uneasy with her discovery. Yet on second thought, Papa's creative imagination ran the gamut of a vast assortment of devices, so why not guns?

One page contained a detailed chemical formula. "Gunpowder," she whispered realizing the significance of her find. If any of these ideas worked, it could outpace the current standard of weapons. Its application would have astounding results. The army with the best and most efficient weapons would have the greatest advantage.

She sank back in the chair. *Oh, Papa.* What did he plan to do with these drawings and formulas?

"Lord Warwick to see you, Miss."

Lily jumped and her gaze snapped toward the doorway. Wisely, Agatha had refrained from calling David *His Lord High and Mighty* though by the look of her thin-lipped grimace, the notion wasn't far from her mind. "I've put him in the parlor," she added.

"Thank you. I'll be with him in a moment." When Agatha had gone, Lily closed the journal and hid it again behind the other books. Under no circumstances could anyone, particularly the British Army, uncover its presence. Swallowing her trepidation, she brushed the dust from her hands, smoothed her hair and left the study.

Two days had passed since she'd last seen David. Hours of consideration had led her to an important decision. Though it would be difficult, she would tell him the hard truth. She could not marry him. Outside the front parlor, she paused and skimmed her damp palms down her skirt. Truth is always the best course, she reminded herself, a belief she learned early on from Papa, and one reinforced by her painful experience with

Griffin.

The tick of the grandfather clock in the entryway sounded menacing. She chalked up the ominous sensation to a simple case of jittery nerves. Smile in place, she floated into the formal room with the practiced charm of a stage performer.

"David, how nice to see you." Her taffeta underskirts swished as she crossed the thick, Turkish carpet toward the fireplace. David's blue hat, edged with fluffy ivory ostrich feathers, sat upon a side chair, no doubt carelessly tossed there when he'd come in earlier. "I take it you received my message left at the *Dorchester* yesterday afternoon."

"Yes. I would have been here sooner except for a pressing matter."

In an unexpected show of heightened emotion, he swept her into his arms and kissed her cheek. The gesture elicited a twinge. She nudged away and gestured to a Queen Anne chair covered in beige damask.

Not one to do as he was told, he sank onto the sofa and yanked her down with him. "Let's sit here."

Though annoyed by his rude penchant to control, she'd opted to ignore being jostled. "Tea?"

"No, thank you." His face glowed in the afternoon light with the sort of ebullient air often seen when one has achieved a great feat. He sobered and assessed her face with the seriousness of a curious physician. "You look pale today."

She fidgeted and clasped her hands over her lap. The emotional detachment she so desired eluded her. As she struggled with how to broach the subject, his thumb stroked her wrist. Marking her as his, she concluded with an irritated pang. "I…ah…"

"What is it?" He leaned closer.

This was harder than imagined, and her words stumbled out in a clumsy manner. "I'm honored by your proposal, but I can't marry you. I'm sorry."

"Why?" Two vertical lines creased his firm brow. "You said you'd obtain an annulment. It's too soon, isn't it? It's a shock with your father in prison."

"It is a shock." So too had been David's unexpected visit. Never did she think he'd follow her to America and propose. "Times are so troubled, both in my family and in this country."

"Don't worry. These ragtag ruffians will be defeated." He patted her hand. "England is certain to prevail and order will be restored once again. Life will return to normal. Have no fear."

She was neither naïve nor optimistic enough to believe the world as she knew it would ever be the same. Not in the Colonies or with her father who, by appearance and behavior, was almost a stranger. Yet by far the biggest change, and one she never imagined possible, had taken place within her. Under no circumstance could she return to London blind to what she'd seen in New York, blind to the British treatment of its citizens. Even more pressing, she couldn't marry David while she loved another, even though things with Griffin were…What?

Until she could speak with Griffin and sort the matter, she couldn't begin to understand much less predict her future. Yet one certainty remained. She didn't love David, not as a woman ought to love a man. "I will always count you as a good friend."

"It's the Colonial ruffian you want, isn't it?"

"This is between you and me. Let's not speak of him." She detested his uppity sneer, as though he believed himself the better man. She leaned away from his grasp, but tenacious, he held on. Even worse, he brought her hand to his mouth and kissed her tight, curled fingers. Stomach in a knot, she waited, aware of his wiliness and determination to have his way.

"You do realize, Lily, we are meant to be together."

"At one time perhaps." She wrested her hand away and earned a flash of his anger.

"Ever since we met, when you were a sad, pretty little girl, it's always been just the two of us."

"I admit, at one time we did need each other's friendship. Circumstances are vastly different at present. We're not children any longer." She expected him to scoff and criticize as she'd seen him do to others. Instead, the self-satisfaction on his face left her chilled.

"You can't deny we are well suited."

His easy smile suggested an unerring confidence he would win his argument. Casting him aside would not be easy.

"We enjoy the same interests—theatre, riding, parties, beautiful things—"

"Such diversions pale compared to…" Love and freedom. Her throat closed on a swell of raw emotion. "They don't matter here." In illustration, she pressed a fist to her heart. "Not any longer."

The words amused him, and he chuckled lightly. "I never considered you for a sentimentalist."

"You think love is sentimental?"

David represented the nobility who married for

position and wealth. If a couple experienced any romantic love, it happened by sheer luck. He didn't love her, not as she loved Griffin.

"Love is all well and good." He gave a halfhearted shrug as though it didn't signify. "If you need me to say it, I will. I love you. There, are you happy?"

"Oh, David." To hear his begrudging, perfunctory words filled her with sorrow. He cared for her as a friend, but a mature, passionate love seemed beyond his grasp.

"Be patient, Lily. Once we're in London, back to the parties and balls, to the world in which we belong, you'll feel different. I promise."

"You don't understand. I won't go back to England."

He jerked as if stung with a whip. "Not live in England? You can't be serious!" In disbelief, he looked about the parlor, to Mama's portrait, a lamp, a vase, the chairs with delicate curved legs. He made a face. "You propose to live *here*?" He spread his arms to encompass the whole room and stared with incredulity.

She brushed angrily at her ruffled skirt. "This is my home, with my father."

"But he's in prison, for God sake!"

"All the more reason to stay close. He needs me."

"And I don't?" he snapped. "I've pursued you. Don't forget I spent seven miserable weeks at sea. I endured the most primitive of conditions." He thumped his chest. "Don't my sacrifices mean anything to you?"

His selfishness sickened her. "It's regrettable such a colossal sacrifice was made on my account." Bitterness tinged her words.

"It's him you love, isn't it?" Angry splotches

mottled his cheeks.

"Mr. Faraday doesn't love me. He doesn't even trust me."

"I don't believe you."

She drew back in shock. "Am I to be mistrusted by you, as well?"

"I didn't come all this way to turn around and go back empty-handed. Why, I'd be the laughingstock of all London."

Could he think of no one but himself? "Let's speak no further on the subject." She rubbed the blossoming ache in her temple. "I won't return to London, married or unmarried."

Knowing David, she expected further argument. Instead, he smiled with such smug calculation she shivered, afraid to think what he might do next.

"What about your father?"

"What about my father?" she asked warily.

"You need my help."

Not at the expense of her happiness. Papa would never expect such a sacrifice. She'd find another way to free him from prison—somehow.

"I've already spoken to Lester Babcock." Oh, he looked arrogant. "The wheels are in motion."

"You'd still help Papa?" Such unexpected generosity astonished her.

He shrugged in an enigmatic manner as if to say *maybe—maybe not*.

With a narrowed gaze, she leaned closer. "Tell me. Will you or won't you?"

"These matters take time." The sudden flash of white teeth was chillingly diabolical. "It's a delicate balance."

"I see." She sat up straighter. All at once, she understood. For David, help would be quid pro quo. "Something for something, is it?"

"It is how problems are resolved in the *big* world."

"Your world, you mean."

"Our world." He brought his face closer. She feared he might kiss her, but he paused, his breath warm and intrusive on her cheek before he settled back against the cushions.

"I won't marry you, David. Not even for my father."

In an unexpected move, he exploded off the couch with a shout. "Give me a chance to change your mind." His vehemence frightened her. Color rode high on his cheeks. "At least consider my proposal." The shiny satin of his coat glimmered as his shoulders heaved. A muscle jumped in his strained jaw. "I'll go, but if you think I'll return to England alone, with my tail between my legs, you're sorely mistaken. This isn't over."

Chapter Twenty-Eight

The prison boat floated in the distant water, as massive and buoyant as a dead sperm whale. From the skiff, Griffin squinted through the mist at his target, just able to make out the bulky form.

A persistent charge of tension kept his mouth dry, the only thing to remain so in the wet morning. Driving rain had given way to a constant drizzle while low, bleak clouds hugged the horizon. Wisps of fog danced over the water.

Pinter and Munro, soldiers on loan from the Continental Army, rowed beneath a canvas tarp draped over their heads in a half-hearted effort to keep their "borrowed" British uniforms dry. They'd taken the uniforms just before dawn, leaving the swearing Captain Sprewell and his two subordinates trussed up like Christmas geese to cool their ill humors in a cellar some few blocks from the wharf.

"Miserable weather," snarled Pinter.

Griffin nodded. It had taken one complete day to draw the last details of his plan together. With help from the soldiers and two selfless patriots who believed cocking things up for the redcoats a special treat, the game was in play. Nervous anticipation fluttered in his chest as they cut through the gray waters toward the floating jail. Despite the best of plans, unexpected obstacles could, and usually did, occur. The slightest mishap, a recognition, a suspicion, any unforeseen factor could take them all down, even see them killed.

"How'd you ever talk Washington into this cockamamie plan?" Munro, a natural athlete, dipped the oar smoothly back into the water, showing no signs of strain from the repetitive effort.

"The General wants Fitzhugh for his engineering skills." When Griffin had mentioned his intention to free Lily's father during his visit earlier in the week, Washington accepted the opportunity without hesitation. Game to see the scientist's knowledge put to good use, the general spared no resources for the operation. Anything to the help the Army, he'd opined.

Nearing the prison ship, Griffin flinched at a horrid odor.

"Smells like rotting carcasses," muttered Munro with disgust.

"I hear the Redcoats toss the dead over the side," said Pinter.

Wincing, Griffin resisted the urge to scour the water's surface for bodies. "Let's do our business and not add to their numbers." He joined in their joyless chuckle.

For the rest of their ride, the only sounds heard were the clank of the oarlock and the splatter of drops on the boat's wooden surface. Griffin fingered the loaded pistol, kept dry inside his coat. The weight of another pistol dragged on the leather belt at his waist. With each man lost in his own anxious thoughts, no one spoke until a sentry shouted *ahoy* from the prison ship. Munro answered the call. Within minutes, they shored up alongside the former sixty-gun naval vessel.

Heart pumping faster than normal, Griffin swept

the rain cape off one shoulder and went first off the slender launch. Munro and Pinter, playing his trusted guards, followed.

A British soldier, musket slung over his shoulder by a strap, saluted Griffin as the senior officer so identified by the fine material and deep scarlet of his officer's coat. With this, he also wore pristine white breeches, damp now, and an ivory periwig bound with a black ribbon.

"I'm Sergeant Tuck." Another man bustled toward them where they stood on the main deck, his fingers working the buttons of his gaping vest.

"Captain Goodwill," Griffin replied, appreciating the sick humor in his false name. In hindsight, he hoped it wouldn't give Tuck a reason to question it.

"Haven't seen you lot before." Tuck didn't bother to hide his suspicious study of the three strangers who stood before him. "What happened to Sprewell?"

"New assignment." Thanks to a British informant, Griffin had precise information about prison dispatch, right down to the daily order agenda. If only Sprewell remained undiscovered until Fitzhugh and Lily were safe outside the city. From a pocket, he withdrew the fake orders drawn up the night before by one of Washington's best artists. He flashed the parchment before Tuck.

"Pardon me saying so, sir." Tuck clamped the note between greedy fingers. "We didn't expect you so early."

The pronouncement appeared obvious. A day-old beard sprouted across the man's chin and a bit of egg clung to his shirt.

Griffin harrumphed as though displeased. "A

soldier is prepared for any and all changes."

"So it seems," Tuck agreed, appearing none too certain. Rocking on his feet, he read the order and studied General Clinton's signature so long Griffin's anxiety rose at the anticipated trouble.

In a superior manner, Griffin thrust out his chin and purposely gazed the length of the man with a censorious air until the fellow squirmed.

"Right."

His cheeks reddened with embarrassment, Tuck returned the paper and Griffin folded it and tucked it inside his coat.

A flick of a wrist by the sergeant dispatched several guards below to retrieve the prisoner. "A spot of tea while you wait, sir?"

The notion of ingesting anything prepared on this slagheap almost made Griffin gag. He clasped his lapel with a tight fist, appearing stern and authoritative. "Fitzhugh is expected before the judge by nine. Another time, perhaps."

"Yes, another time. Well, if you'll come this way." Tuck stomped away.

Moments later, after the obligatory forms had been signed, Griffin left the sergeant's quarters, followed by Tuck. Munro and Pinter joined them near the main mast. A bedraggled man, unrecognizable behind the scraggly beard and hair, was shoved forward, hands tied before him with rope.

"Fitzhugh?" Griffin's shock gave way to anger at the pathetic state of the starving bag of bones shivering in front of him. An accused individual, particularly one not yet tried nor found guilty of a crime, deserved better treatment.

An oily head nodded.

"See the prisoner secured in the boat."

Munro and Pinter hustled the captive over the side.

"Keep up the good work, Tuck." Straight-faced, Griffin followed his men from the ship. Only when his feet hit the bottom boards of the launch did he expel a huge breath of relief.

"Take us away, men." He signaled to Munro and Pinter. The oars dipped into water. The path to freedom lay within their reach, and just when his mind began to rest easy, a desperate voice from above shouted, "Stop!"

Griffin's heart dropped to his knees. Munro and Pinter faltered and watched him with alarm while their tightly gripped oars paused over the choppy water. He motioned them to continue. The skiff swayed away from the ship's hull.

"Halt," Tuck shrieked. His head and upper body jutted over the railing. Deep lines etched his distressed features. "I say, Captain Goodwill. We've two dead men on board, fresh as clover. Would you take them to shore for burial?"

Griffin blanched. What rotten luck to transport the dead. Fresh as clover? In a pig's ass. Hidden behind his back, he fluttered his hand, urging the men to paddle faster. "Not today, Tuck. We're full up with bodies." *Live bodies.*

Tuck scrunched his face and frowned with unhappiness. If no other conveyance delivered him of the bodies, there was always the water.

Griffin allowed only a brief moment of satisfaction as they floated away. There was still much to do and danger ahead. To get safely past the guards on the pier posed a challenge. In addition, Lily and her father needed to be quietly hustled from the city. The risks were great.

Ashen and grizzled, their prize loot sat on the forward thwart, his shoulders hunched against the cool mist. Griffin could scarce recognize his old tutor. Nor did the man seem to recall him, either.

"What's going on here?" Fitzhugh asked. "What judge am I to see?"

"George Washington, if you're lucky." Griffin dug out a knife and sliced through the rope at the man's wrists.

"Where are you taking me?"

Griffin reached beneath the seat, tugged out a cape and flung it around the man's hunched shoulders. "A place ten miles outside the city. You'll be safe there."

"Why me? There are so many other suffering men, no doubt more deserving than I."

"Consider it a kindness for an old tutor."

Fitzhugh cocked his head, studying Griffin with great intensity. "Fairfax? No. Not Fairfax. It's Faraday."

"In the flesh." He smiled, pleased to be remembered.

Just like in the old days, the tutor wagged a finger of disapproval. "Because of you, I kept finding garter snakes in my study for a week."

Griffin raised his shoulders in a helpless shrug. "How was I to guess the snake was about to give birth?"

The man compressed his lips, as if angry, yet couldn't hide the humorous twinkle Griffin had often seen as a boy. "You'd be the younger one, the lanky lad who always got into trouble. I see you haven't changed much, though you're a good foot or two taller."

Henry stuck out his hand, grinning, and Griffin clasped the fellow's hardy thanks.

"You took quite a risk, young man. I never thought to leave the prison ship in such a manner. Thought I'd be taken out, feet first, and dead." His chuckle ended with a raspy cough. "What devilish trickery to ply such a ruse. Then again, you have the heart of a jokester. I knew your imagination would serve you well."

The praise released a gush of warmth through Griffin's icy bones. "All for a good cause. The Continental Army could use your skills."

Fitzhugh arched a brow. "I'm not military."

"The Army needs your expertise to reconfigure a rifle design."

"It's true I have an interest in all things mechanical, but so do other scientists." The man scrunched his filthy brow. "Is there more you're not telling me?"

"Simply this. I told Lily I would help you."

"What?" His worried gaze darted left and right. "Tell me she isn't involved in this risky affair?"

"She's in the dark about our escapade. It seemed safest to keep her uninformed. Later today, I'll bring her to you."

Fitzhugh's knobby fingers gripped the edges of his cape, pulling it tight across his shoulders. "Thank God." He sucked in a few breaths, not speaking, as he appeared to think. "Lily's been in England for years. How did you learn she arrived in New York?"

"It's a story best left for a night as you warm near the hearth."

"I see."

Griffin doubted the man could ever imagine what had transpired between him and his daughter.

"Until you're safe outside the city, say nothing."

Fitzhugh nodded. Griffin trusted he would cooperate without argument. The possibility of freedom was the best of motivators.

Fifty yards from the pier, the rain picked up. Despite the tightly woven cape, water saturated the wool of Griffin's military coat and trickled down his neck. His shirt clung to his skin. Drops of water dripped off the tapered end of his three-cornered hat. Sweat mixed with rain. As they approached land, he imagined Sprewell, escaped and furious, a gun cocked, waiting for them at the dock. Though an unlikely scenario, it filled him with dread.

He checked his pocket watch. Every action of his plan had been coordinated to the minute. "Slow it down, men."

In tandem, the rowers eased off the pace. Alert to any suspicious activity, nobody spoke as the boat slid into the pier.

The British Army supervised all activity at the wharf, so it was no surprise when several dock hands and a couple of armed lobsterbacks greeted their arrival. Pinter tossed a line and one of the dockworkers tied it around a pylon. Munro and Pinter climbed out first and assisted the bedraggled scientist.

Before Griffin could clamber from the launch, a cataclysmic explosion rocked the market square adjacent to the pier. Bricks, lumber, mortar shot high in the air. People screamed and scuttled, dodging the debris that rained down with a clatter on the wet cobblestones.

"Bloody hell!" The excited soldier waved his arm at a thick plume of smoke, black as charcoal. It spiraled upwards and stained the dreary horizon. "The blasted rebels blew up the Guard House."

Curious people, dazed and frightened, spilled out of nearby lodgings and businesses. Griffin smiled at the hordes and chaos. As he planned, the British soldiers raced to the burning building at the corner, too shocked and as yet, unaware of Fitzhugh's escape. The sound of gunshots popped somewhere down a nearby street and added to the pandemonium.

Griffin sprang from the boat, landing with sure, graceful feet upon the pier. His shoulders heaved. Blood raced through his veins. "Hurry, hurry," he urged under his breath though with all the cacophony, only those next to him could hear. "Act sharp."

Across the dock and past the market stalls they bounded, four men seemingly caught up in the excitement and fear of attack. At a side street, away from the clamor, they split up as arranged earlier. Pinter went one way. As Griffin, Munro and Fitzhugh took the opposite direction, another bomb detonated and spewed a mushroom-shaped column of smoke at the city's western edge.

"Is the city under siege?" Fitzhugh cried.

"In a manner of speaking." Griffin paused and cocked his ear. "There should be one more about..." Before he could say *now*, another boom, louder than thunder, rocked the heavens. "Ah, there it is." He flashed a brash smile. "Come along, men."

Off they sped, heads down, as though rushing to escape the persistent drizzle or the imminent invasion of the enemy. Another block to go. At this point, he might have relaxed as the mission was almost over. Instead, his instincts stirred. The hair at the back of his neck prickled. He hunched his shoulders in protection. An icy drop slipped beneath his shirt and he shivered.

"Halt!"

The sight of a British soldier, musket directed at him made his heart race. He considered making a run, but worried about the safety of the older man and Munro.

"Halt! I say."

The British soldier stepped farther from the building's doorway. Griffin nudged Fitzhugh behind him.

"I'm Captain Goodwill. What's the meaning of this?" On purpose, Griffin threw back his shoulders and lengthened his spine, creating more height. For good measure, he sneered.

The soldier licked his lips while his gaze darted side to side. "We're to stop everyone. If you'll come this way, sir." With the end of his rifle, he gestured toward the entrance of the building. "I'll need to see your papers."

"See here," Griffin complained with firm authority. "I'm a senior officer."

"I see, sir, but the orders come from the commanding officer himself." The poor fellow looked like he was going to be sick. "Something to do with a mishmash with Captain Sprewell this morning."

Griffin ground his teeth irritated by the quick discovery of the British captain. They would have to move faster if they hoped to squire Fitzhugh and Lily out of the city safely. He affected a noisy, tiresome sigh

341

and said with an edge to his voice, "Don't be an idiot. I have orders to take this man to the magistrate general."

"I'm sorry, sir. But orders…" The uncomfortable soldier glanced around as if he might sight a reinforcement or two, somebody to buck up his nerve.

With not a second to lose, Griffin angled his hand inside his coat. Seeing no other way, he aimed the pistol and squeezed the trigger. The blast rattled his eardrums and tore into the young soldier. The man recoiled. He staggered backwards, his face mottled with confusion, and dropped to his knees. As he slumped to the ground, the musket fell from his hand and clattered against the wooden pavers.

Munro already had the prisoner halfway down the block. Griffin caught up in seconds, breathing fast, sweating and unable to dwell upon the fallen soldier in the press to see Fitzhugh to safety. They made one last turn into a street empty of any life. Close on Munro's footsteps, he shoved Fitzhugh into a stable and closed the door quietly behind them.

Three horses, saddled and with provisions, stood hitched to a rail. "Quick." He thrust a bundle of clean, dry clothes at Fitzhugh.

Griffin threw off the hat and cape and stripped out of the uniform. Dressed in a minute, he wore the homespun clothes of a preacher and a broad-rimmed black hat pulled down over his face. Munro did the same. They stuffed the British uniforms under a bale of hay.

"The street's empty." Munro yanked his head back inside the barn and flung open the doors. "Hurry. I'll close up."

"This is where we part company," Griffin said to

Fitzhugh. "Munro will see to your safe passage. I'll bring Lily along before nightfall." He mounted his horse, about to leave, when Fitzhugh stopped him.

"One question, Mr. Faraday."

Griffin nodded tersely.

"Do you have feelings for her?"

His heart sputtered at the unexpected question. This was hardly the time or place. He blew out a breath, uncertain how to answer given all the complexities of his bizarre arrangement with the man's daughter. He dragged a hand over his damp face. "Last I heard she was betrothed to Lord Warwick."

Chapter Twenty-Nine

"Mister Warwick to see you."

Lily startled when she heard Agatha's voice in the doorway. At the nobleman's demotion to *Mister*, she felt compelled to correct the housekeeper. However, what did the snub matter, given the scope of difficulties in her beleaguered life?

"Shall I tell him you aren't home to visitors?"

Lily clutched her book to her chest with sudden unease. After yesterday's visit, she ought to send David away. They'd said all that needed to be said. God forbid he should attempt to overcome her rejection of his marriage proposal with stronger arguments. Still, he might have word about Papa.

"Send him in, please."

Agatha soured in a contraction of facial wrinkles. "Suit yourself. I'll be in the kitchen if you need me."

Lily slid the book on an end table, stood and faced the door, determined to meet whatever challenge David might impose. Seconds later, he rushed into the room, a glimmering blur of expensive gold brocade and creamy lace ruffles. In a courtly bow, he swept off his decorous ostrich plumed hat and waved it with a flourish. Once, she'd considered him handsome with his elegant clothes and his refined air that seemed to warm only for her. Today, a brilliant peacock came to mind. All show and no substance.

"Hello, David." Nervously, she tweaked a lavender ribbon attached to her bodice. "What brings you here today?"

"He's out."

The baffling announcement, along with his satisfied gloat, caused her to frown. "What do you mean?"

"He's out of prison."

"Papa?" His jubilant smile implied her guess was correct. A tingle shot the length of her legs. Knees shaky, she dropped to the sofa, a hand at her throat. "When?"

"This morning."

Papa. Free? Miracles did happen. "How?"

"I said I'd take care of it, didn't I?" Such a cocksure grin.

It was too incredible. If she could stop trembling, she would have danced on air. "I can't believe it."

After her sound rejection of his marriage proposal, she didn't expect his help. Perhaps she'd misjudged him, thinking him full of self-interest when he was far from selfish. She gripped the sofa arm to steady herself. "How did this wondrous thing come to pass?"

He shrugged, downplaying his triumph. "It's all to do with influence—a twist here, a shove there."

No false modesty for him.

"David, I..." Giddy with joy, she struggled to process the many questions tumbling at great speed in her head. She sprang from the sofa, light on her toes. "Where is he? When can I see him?"

He gripped her hands, subduing her impatience. "Soon. For safekeeping, he's hiding."

Worry set in. "Is he in danger?"

"No, but the venture is fraught with risk."

"Tell me what you heard. I want every last detail." He stroked her thumb, and she wanted to snatch her hand away.

"It's a convoluted story—one I'll share later."

As she made to speak, he threw his arms about her. She stiffened, but after a torturous week of relentless worry, she allowed him this celebratory gesture. "I can't thank you enough." He hugged her tighter. His mouth found hers and pressed too hard in a possessive kiss. "No, David." She shoved away.

His anger flared, but in a flash a sympathetic expression came over him. "Dear heart."

Troubled by his amorous words, she sidestepped away from his arms that again reached out to her. She took a position near the fireplace, wishing it were Griffin who'd delivered the news.

"I thought…" He faltered and glanced uncertainly at his hands. "I hoped you might see things differently for us since he's free."

Ah, the payback. A favor for a favor. Nothing short of accepting his proposal would give him satisfaction. Disappointment pricked at her. Was it too much to expect a selfless act simply because he valued her friendship?

David joined her at the fireplace. "You didn't really believe I'd leave New York without you?" He touched her cheek and she cringed. "You must think quite well of yourself if you believed you could fling me off so easily." As if he had the right, his hand slid about her waist.

Lily forced an icy smile. As she dug her fingernails into his wrist, she watched for any signs of discomfort.

He didn't flinch. "Don't do this, David. Please."

They shared a long history, one she didn't want sullied by his stubbornness or his need to control and get his way. If only he would abandon his quest and return alone to London. He could leave with pleasant memories of their shared past.

"You're so impetuous and unique." He swept a lock of hair from her forehead. "Do you have any idea how men covet you?"

"Nonsense." When he dared to draw a knuckle across her lips, she batted his hand away, causing him to chortle cruelly.

"Liar. How could you not have seen the lust writ upon their hungry faces?"

"I want you to leave."

"Lily, Lily." He crooned in a know-it-all tone she abhorred. "What a prize you are. So dazzling and feisty."

In the past, she'd seen his callous behavior towards others. For the first time, she was the recipient of his cruelty. The coldness in his smile frightened her. "You may not marry me, but what's to stop me from claiming the prize?"

"Stop it. We aren't children playing games."

He cocked a wry brow. "You *love* games. Does it not seem fitting as you win your father, I win you?"

"Have you gone mad?" She pushed away, but he grabbed her arm. His hold was surprisingly strong and she realized he meant to humiliate her for the pain she'd caused him. Jealousy, rejection, and desperation had driven him to this low point, yet her understanding of his behavior didn't lessen the offense.

"Kiss me, Lily. Kiss me like you kiss *him*."

That he dared to usurp Griffin's importance fueled her anger. How misguided to think his touch could replace the pleasure she received from Griffin. Touch was more than a tactile sensation. It had meaning and emotion. A wide gulf of differences existed between the two men. Griffin held her respect. While David...

Before she could protest, he shoved her to the couch and tumbled next to her. The urge to scream welled in her throat, but she choked it off, worried for Agatha. The old woman would come to her rescue. Lily wouldn't risk the chance Agatha might get hurt.

"Make love to me like you did to him." His wet lips seared her neck.

"Never!"

His head cocked back, his eyes alight with a sudden comprehension. "So you *have* made love to him. I knew it!"

"Stop it." She swung but before her palm connected with his cheek, he'd caught her wrist. He shoved her flat against the sofa and leaned over her. The odor of his wine-tinged breath turned her stomach. He pinned her hands alongside her head and his kiss aroused disgust.

She managed to drag her face away, her lips stinging. "Leave off!" She bucked against him and when she broke loose from his grip, she struck out wildly and clipped him on the ear. "Get off me!"

"You're lively." Flushed and wildly intent, he thrust a hand beneath her skirts.

It took a moment to recover from the shock. Every breath came in quick, shallow waves as she beat against his shoulders. As he squeezed and pawed, her anger soared.

Oh, David. Don't do this.

****

Griffin trotted his horse along Water Street, moving with subtle haste, but not enough to draw unnecessary attention. The rain had ceased. Puddles littered the street while the rich smell of damp earth clung in the heavy air. With his hat tugged low over his forehead, he scanned the familiar road. Beyond the heightened military presence of redcoats posted at every corner, trade flowed with its usual brisk rhythm. A casual observer would never guess the city had been under siege less than an hour ago by triple explosions.

Griffin couldn't claim the status of a casual observer. Staying alert and cautious had kept him out of the hands of the British forces. Luck played into his longevity as well. Senses sharp, he kept his head down. With a tug on the reins, he headed to an alley and tethered his horse to a hitching post around the back of his uncle's business.

A shipping clerk noticed Griffin as he stepped inside the large storehouse. The thin-haired man shoved his spectacles higher on his nose. "Good to see you back, sir." He pointed a bony finger at Josiah's door. "He's alone."

"Perfect." Griffin crossed the storeroom, stepped inside the office, and quietly closed the door. The soft click of the latch alerted Josiah, who looked up and brightened. "Taken up the ministry, have you." Chuckling, he leaned forward, his elbows down on the desktop.

Griffin glanced at his somber black and white costume of a Calvinist preacher with a sardonic grin. "Don't want to stand out in the crowd and risk recognition." He let his fingers play with the splayed stock at his throat, irreverently flipping it up and down.

"It's good to see you, boy." There was no mistaking Josiah's relief. "You've put the Reds in an uproar. They're chasing about like headless chickens."

"As intended." Griffin dropped down in a chair by his uncle's desk. "What have you heard?"

"One soldier was shot. He'll live."

Griffin knew a moment of reprieve from his worry as he suspected it was his bullet lodged in the young soldier.

"Although I'm sorry to say the soldier will return to harass the good citizens of New York," his uncle went on to say. "Some property destruction, but you probably already know as much. A few injuries. The British think the bombs were a ploy. They haven't pieced it all together yet."

"Your intelligence is impressive. What else did you hear?"

"Nobody recognized you, but circumstances could change at any moment." Josiah let out a breath and pressed his hands to his thighs. "It doesn't mean you're out of danger."

"Nobody is ever one hundred percent safe." What mattered most was Lily's protection.

"Unfortunately, Captain Sprewell was discovered shortly after he'd been bound and left in his smalls, early this morning." Josiah raised a speculative brow. "You wouldn't happen to know anything about this, would you?"

Griffin just smiled. "I figured somebody found Sprewell. It explained their quick mobilization. A launch must have been sent to investigate the prison ship, where it was learned Fitzhugh had been taken." With the Brits anxious to apprehend Fitzhugh, getting Lily out of the city preyed more heavily on his mind than ever. If she were in any way harmed, he would never forgive himself.

He jumped up. "I thank you for the news, but I must hurry."

"Be careful. The Redcoats are hopping mad. Nobody likes to be played for a fool."

"Perhaps they should go back to England if they hope to avoid more humiliation." He backed towards the door, keeping his uncle in his view. "You'll see the Fitzhugh housekeeper is safe?"

"Arrangements are already in place." Josiah stood tall, his manner grave. "You do a great service to this country, lad. I'm proud of you."

Happiness and pride rose inside. He bit back a smile.

"Speaking of good deeds..." The man snagged a thick envelope from a drawer and tossed it to him.

"What's this?"

"I couldn't say. She stopped in day before yesterday."

"Lily?" His heartbeat kicked up a notch.

"She seemed genuinely disappointed to find you'd gone. I told her you went to Philadelphia. A pity she's affianced to someone else."

Griffin only half-listened as he fought the urge to rip open the seal and read the missive. Worried it might be papers related to the dissolution of the marriage, he stuffed the packet in his coat pocket. Time enough for bad news later.

"The letter seemed important."

"Thanks for keeping it." His hand quivered as he patted his pocket.

"Another thing." Josiah sobered. "I sent two lads to keep surveillance on the Fitzhugh house. I'm sorry to tell you, it's already under watch."

Griffin cursed.

"If you hurry…"

Griffin stopped him with a raised palm. "I'll see it done."

Chapter Thirty

"Get off me," Lily shrieked. She kicked at David splayed across her on the couch. He was a stronger and weightier opponent than she would have guessed. It would take all her physical strength and then some to get out from under him.

"Stop!"

Lily couldn't place the unfamiliar voice. Footsteps thudded. She sensed a flurry of movement then heard a labored breath as someone ripped her assailant away and flung him aside.

She gaped in disbelief, scarcely able to catch her breath.

A red-faced Captain Babcock loomed over David who sprawled on the floor, legs and arms spread like a starfish. Revulsion contorted the soldier's features. Up and down went the epaulets of his scarlet jacket as his shoulders heaved.

"What's the meaning of this?" David bellowed in outrage. He sat up, huffing, his hair mussed and spilling over his forehead.

"Is this how you treat your fiancée, a woman who, not two days ago, you claimed to admire above all others?" Brow beetled, Babcock stroked the hilt of his sword, as if he considered carving his anger in David's skin.

"How dare you?" Up sprang David with a

murderous glare.

"Think before you act," Babcock growled. He raised his fists and braced his legs wide for an attack. Lily knew he would not hesitate to dismantle any threat posed by David. No doubt, the two other soldiers, primed like cocked guns ten feet away, would lend a hand.

David took a moment to assess the three men. With haughty aplomb, he snapped his jacket, yanked at his shirt, and shoved a lock of hair from his forehead. Stalling, Lily decided as he weighed different scenarios, judging the ploy that would gain him the upper hand.

"Sweet girl, are you hurt?" Agatha's tremulous voice crackled as she darted closer. Fingers curled like eagle talons scrunched her apron.

"I'm fine." Lily stood on unsteady legs and with trembling hands smoothed the skirts twisted about her limbs.

"I figured they'd help." The upset housekeeper jutted a chin at the soldiers.

"You did well, Agatha." Lily hadn't heard Babcock knock or the door answered, thanks to David and her shrieking. She forced a weak smile. Under no circumstances would she cry nor allow David the satisfaction of seeing her rattled. "Would you bring us some tea?"

The tiny woman hesitated while she judged the men for further threat. Satisfied no harm would befall Lily, she bobbed her head and left the charged atmosphere.

Lily took a deep breath and gathered her wits as she sat again.

She indicated the chairs near the fireplace. David

and Babcock glowered at each other and didn't budge. "Please." Civility was essential if she hoped to discover what brought the British Army to her door. Her fright and outrage would ebb in time but disappointment at David's reprehensible behavior would sting longer.

David discharged a huffy breath and sank into Papa's bigger chair.

"Wait outside," Babcock told his men. "And tell the housekeeper tea is unnecessary." When they'd left, he walked to the opposite end of the fireplace, but chose to stand. "Are you all right, Miss Fitzhugh?"

"Yes, thank you." Her voice sounded clipped and stiff, a vocal clue to the anger coursing through her limbs. "Let us not speak of this unfortunate instance again." It would please her immensely if David's boorish attack would vanish from everyone's mind. Yet she doubted anything she said or did would salvage what remained of her good reputation. "Please, captain."

Babcock shifted on his feet, his reluctance apparent. After a moment, he gave a terse nod and turned a stern expression on her aggressor. David met the man's critical appraisal with the elevated hauteur only someone born into nobility can muster, as though he could do no wrong. A show of humility would go a long way to cooling Babcock's ire. Sadly, David lacked such a quality.

"Assault, Warwick?" Babcock pounded the fireplace mantel with the butt of his palm. "I should have expected as much from you."

David scowled. "Don't think for one minute your smears perturb me. I'll have you put away."

"Save your conceit for another day. It doesn't

frighten me."

The tension hummed with such intensity it almost tingled in Lily's ears. After several unbearable moments, David blared, "What the devil do you want, Babcock? Why did you come here?"

Lily gave a slow shake to her head, appalled at David's absolute entitlement and rudeness. Why had she not seen his character sooner?

"Shut your gob," Babcock grumbled. "You always did talk too much. I'll ask the questions, *your grace*."

David elevated his chin, lengthened his spine and managed to look even haughtier than Uncle Percy. For once, he did as asked.

"What do you know about Henry Fitzhugh's escape from the *Jersey* early this morning?"

At the mention of her father, Lily's anxiety flared like an Oriental firecracker.

"Why ask me?" David sputtered. "How would I know?"

The inquisitor raised a black brow, clearly not fooled by David's innocent display. "You came to me two days ago and asked my help to have the man released. This morning three men dressed as British officers took Fitzhugh from the prison ship. Rather timely, don't you think? May I also state the men were *not* British soldiers? No one's seen Fitzhugh since."

Lily pressed a fist to her mouth and watched David blink with confusion. Then he frowned and seemed genuinely perplexed.

"Why interrogate me?" He'd regained his arrogant wind. "If you recall, you agreed to assist in freeing him."

A muscle jumped in Babcock's stern face. If a look

could cut, Lily figured his high and mighty would be in bloody tatters.

"If you recall"—Babcock did a perfect sneer using David's same words—"you asked me to risk my career and to act with dishonor. I never agreed to anything. You must think me a numbskull if you consider a lavish meal and copious wine a sufficient inducement to betray my duties."

David gawped, as if faced by a strange creature he couldn't comprehend. Within moments, he'd recovered his wits. "You intimated as much."

"You misjudged. While you prattled on and on, I kept silent. Perhaps you heard only what you wanted to hear, what you expected from a brother of one of your schoolmates. Grasp this, if you would. I scarcely tolerate my brother. I care even less for you."

David's fingers bit into the leather chair arms. Even seated ten feet away, his palpable vibrations washed across Lily's skin. At any moment, she expected him to leap in the air and attack the soldier.

The Captain raised a hand, as if the gesture would quell David's rage. To her surprise, it did the trick.

With a righteous air of self-importance, David tipped his nose in the air. "Your opinion of me doesn't matter. However, the implied accusation I caused Fitzhugh's escape is but a means for you to save face. Admit it. You seek a dupe to place the blame for your administrative incompetence." His lip curled. "I won't be your whipping boy."

A mottled stain worked its way into Babcock's ivory white neck. Fingers flexing, he visibly fought to curtail his emotions. "What I want," he said, breathing heavily, "is to find the men who helped Fitzhugh escape. You wanted him released. When I refused to aid you, you approached someone else to do your dirty work."

David shot out of the chair. "You're wrong. The man could have rotted in prison for all I cared."

"David!" She stared in disbelief.

"I came to you, Babcock, because of her." He pointed an accusing finger. "She wanted her father out. Not me. I was only thinking of her."

A hot flame engulfed Lily. Her hands fisted with an urge to claw at his face and pound on his chest. "How sweet of you," she simpered. "Always thinking of *my* benefit."

He overlooked her sarcasm and addressed Babcock. "Because you're commander of prisons, I believed you'd do me this simple favor and release Fitzhugh. How could she fail to regard me as next to God with her father freed?"

Babcock dropped a hand on his hilt. "Are you telling me you had nothing to do with this ruse?"

"I am." Perhaps shamed, he kept his gaze averted.

Oh, Lord, she thought. He ought to be ashamed.

Babcock's sword jiggled as he paced the length of the fireplace and returned. "Bribing an officer is not how things are done in the Army."

David shook his head pityingly, in clear disagreement. "You've been in the Colonies too long," he complained. "Your brother, Lord Chisholm, wouldn't have turned his back on a friend. We in the ruling class help and protect one another." In case Babcock or Lily had any doubt to whom he referred, David tapped his chest. "You've forgotten how it's done in England. If I didn't see you wearing a British uniform, I'd swear you were a bloody Patriot."

Babcock wisely chose to ignore this. "Tell me who you hired. It must have been you despite your pathetic attempt to make me think differently."

David blinked with astonishment. "No one."

"I won't hesitate to throw you in gaol. Maybe you'd like to warm the seat vacated by Fitzhugh."

"You can't be serious," David spluttered.

For the first time, fear shadowed his features. Lily could almost smell his mounting panic.

"You were my only resource. I spoke to no one else. I swear. Why, I'd be a fool to jeopardize my neck for some traitor."

"He's not a traitor," Lily shouted. "You're a pig. You only wanted to marry me for Papa's money."

Babcock flung up a hand, severing the argument. Lily snapped her teeth together, so furious she trembled.

"I swear to you," David implored, trying to regain favor despite Babcock's obvious revulsion. "As one British gentleman to another, I didn't aid Fitzhugh's escape. Why would I? I don't know the man. He's nothing to me. My appeal to you was a charade, a silly game to get what I wanted."

Over the years, Lily had witnessed David's lies. She knew the telltale signs, the shift of his crafty gaze, his detached air. She'd seen none of those behaviors today. David had spoken the truth. He didn't care what happened to Papa.

She bounded from the couch. "You lied to me. You…You wretch."

"Calm yourself, woman," Babcock ordered.

Shaking, Lily considered slapping away David's

smug expression. "Everything you told me was a lie, employed solely to manipulate me. How cruel. You know nothing of Papa's escape." If his sole intent was to hurt her, he'd done a fine job. "It's wicked to claim success for a feat accomplished by another. What did you think would happen when Papa didn't come home? Or if he did appear, what would you say then?"

"Frankly, I didn't care. Once you were convinced he was in hiding for his safety, I hoped you'd marry me."

"Do you really need Papa's money so desperately?"

He didn't answer and it was answer enough for her. Every positive belief she ever possessed about him disappeared.

With obvious disgust, the Captain shook his head. "As much as it would suit me to declare you guilty, Warwick, I see the insufficiency of your true character. You aren't chivalrous enough to risk your freedom for a woman. Furthermore, you lack the courage and skill to organize a caper such as the one executed this morning. As for intelligence, it remains to be seen."

David blanched. The soldier could not have spoken more insulting words. But if David proved unsuitable for the escapade, she wondered who else could have done the deed. She grasped the sofa to steady herself.

Griffin.

Griffin was selfless and brave. Moreover, he possessed the canny ability to perform such a clever stunt. As she tried to hide a smile, the soldier pivoted on his boot heel in her direction.

"What can you tell me about this, Miss Fitzhugh?"

She swallowed her fear. "The first I heard of

Papa's escape was when David told me just before you arrived."

"See here, man," David cried. "News of this escape is all over the city. I daresay there isn't a soul who hasn't heard of it."

Babcock let this comment pass and resumed his harsh appraisal. She sat deathly still. "As you believe your father wrongly imprisoned, perhaps *you* hired someone to take him from the *Jersey*."

"It's true I wanted his freedom. What daughter wouldn't? I hoped Papa's attorney would see him released. Forgive me, sir, but it's absurd to suspect me. I have no contacts, no family or friends in the city. I haven't lived here for years. Do you suppose I could arrange his escape from a boat in the harbor when I've been in New York only one week? Goodness, Captain, your opinion of me is too grand." She hadn't spoken this much since he'd arrived, and the effort left her depleted.

"What about your lover?" David asked.

She froze. Alternate responses darted in her head. With a show of calm grace, she met the triumph shining in his face. "I have no lover, you fool."

He wagged the digit again, the color rising in his cheeks as he gloated. "It's the Faraday cretin. He did this! He'd be fool enough to do it for you."

"Enough!" Babcock stomped a foot. "Not another word or I *will* throw you in gaol. Do you understand?"

David bristled, but after a moment, nodded with agreement.

Fear for Griffin coursed in her limbs. She clasped her hands, aware that they shook, and glowered at a man she once considered a friend. "This is all about jealousy. Shame on you! How dare you discredit an innocent man?" Her chest heaved as she sucked in air.

"I'll decide whether the man is innocent or not," Babcock countered. "Tell me about this Faraday, Miss Fitzhugh."

"The name is Griffin Faraday." She unfurled her clenched fingers. Care would be necessary to proceed safely across the prickly terrain.

"Ah, yes. I've heard of him."

Lily swallowed with difficulty and wondered whether the status was good or bad. "These allegations are false. It's pitiful Lord Warwick smears a man's reputation when Mr. Faraday is, at this moment, in Philadelphia and unable to defend his good name."

"You know this to be fact?" Something shifted in Babcock's tense face.

"He left a few days ago on business. Ask his uncle, Josiah Faraday."

"I will. In addition, my officers will search your house. Your father wouldn't be the first escapee to hide under his bed. Until capture of your father is complete, you are confined to your home under close watch."

"I understand."

"As for you…" Babcock scanned David with an unmistakable air of loathing. "You'll be confined to your rooms at the Dorchester until further notice. When the matter is resolved and your innocence proved, you will be escorted to the first available ship bound for England."

David roared his disapproval. "You have no right. I won't allow it."

Babcock drew back his shoulders and stared down his nose at the louse. All color drained from her old friend's face, though she realized she could no longer assign him the term friend.

"I have all the rights I need." Babcock boomed.

"David," Lily said with a smug smile. "Have a pleasant journey back to London."

Chapter Thirty-One

Griffin ambled along the walkway in his preacher's clothes, trying not to draw attention. Bound for Lily's home, he appeared in no particular rush despite his anxious nerves. Somehow, he would free her from the soldiers.

In the street, Josiah's boys, hired to watch Lily's house, batted a ball with a stick between them. A sentry stood guard on the Fitzhugh stoop. Perhaps bored, he watched the boys' energetic play. Minutes ago, Griffin had overtaken the soldier's compatriot at the back of the tall residence. The hapless fellow, now gagged and trussed, lay hidden away in Henry's Fitzhugh's stable.

Griffin unfurled his fingers, his knuckles scratched and sore from punching the man. One sentry subdued; another soon to follow.

As he neared the brick home, rehashing the details of his rescue plan, the black lacquered front door opened. Startled, he jumped behind a lilac hedge. Through a patch of separated branches, he saw the bright scarlet of a military jacket come through the door, a captain as evidenced by his insignia. The dark-haired soldier descended the front steps followed by…

Griffin's heart leapt.

Warwick came out the door followed by another soldier. It didn't take the vision of an eagle to recognize Warwick's stiff posture or the scowl on his crimped face. "Well," Griffin muttered buoyed with satisfaction. The cock robin was under military guard. What fortuitous event had occurred to cause such an unexpected turn of events?

The captain spoke and jumped into a waiting carriage. The guard signaled to Warwick and made the mistake of touching his arm. The dandy wrenched away and with a sneer, climbed aboard the carriage, followed by the soldier. The vehicle set off. The wheels clattered down the street. At the corner, it turned and left the lone sentry to resume his guard duties.

An agreeable sensation tickled up Griffin's arms. He smiled at the pleasant turn of fortune but sobered quickly. One very important task remained. Lily's freedom. Until he reunited father and daughter, he couldn't rest.

He located a pebble and lobbed it at the taller boy. When he had his attention, he gestured the boy closer, a finger to his lip to caution silence. The blond fellow gave a slight nod, said a few words to his friend and tossed the ball. Like a dog chasing a stick, his friend sprinted after it. So too, followed the sentry's gaze. Again Griffin smiled, certain the clever lad had a future as a spy for Washington.

Unnoticed, the boy slipped behind the lilac hedge.

"You're the lad Josiah Faraday hired?"

"I am."

Griffin handed him two coins even though Josiah would have already paid his service. "What do they call you?"

"Adam Beasley, sir."

"Are there any more soldiers besides the sentry?'

"No, sir."

"I've a job needs done. Are you willing to help?"

The boy nodded eagerly.

Minutes later, the plan in place, Griffin stood once again in the shaded back yard of the Fitzhugh house near the stable. A fence ran the length of both sides of the property. Trellised rose bushes, in full bloom, immersed the humid air in a heavy perfume. A staked vegetable garden grew in the south corner.

He hid behind the thick trunk of an oak tree and waited. As directed, Adam approached the front of the house and shouted, "Help! A soldier's been hurt." With the sentry's attention snagged, the lad sprinted toward the back yard, the sentry on his tail. Footsteps thudded on the stone pavers and grass. Adam flew past the oak tree. Griffin stuck out a leg. The soldier tripped and catapulted in the air with outstretched limbs. His musket spun out of his hands and landed in a clump of lettuce. As soon as he hit the ground, Griffin had him by the collar and drove a fist into his face. Off to the side, Adam brandished a plank of wood. He swung it fast. It struck the downed fellow, snapping his head aside. Knocked unconscious, the man went limp and slid into the grass.

"Did I ask you to hit him?" Griffin growled.

"No." Adam's voice wavered with the fear he'd erred.

"Well, much obliged for your help."

"Do you want me to tie him up?"

"If you insist." Griffin tried for a bland face befitting the seriousness of the occasion, despite his urge to laugh. He tugged several lengths of cord from a pocket and handed one to Adam. "Tie his legs." Griffin lashed the man's wrists and they dragged the lump inside the stable and propped him next to his partner. Assured the soldier would wake in time with a nasty headache, he closed the door behind them.

"Go fetch your friend and wait by the back steps. You'll escort the housekeeper to Josiah Faraday's warehouse."

The boy sprinted off.

"Walk," Griffin cautioned. "No need to act like a bucking horse."

When the lad trotted away, he glanced at the house excited to see Lily. The housekeeper, in a mobcap, stood in a window. Her face was blank. He raised a hand in greeting and strode across the yard. When he entered the kitchen, the woman had removed herself to a worktable cluttered with bowls, plates and a cutting board. She clutched a bread knife. The stuffy room smelled of vinegar and dill. He spied a jar of pickles.

"No need for silence," she said as if she'd read his mind. "It's only me and the mistress here not counting the two tethered guards. And you, of course."

"You saw the capture?"

"A grand spectacle it was and one to be cherished."

Her feisty, cynical nature amused Griffin, but there wasn't time to enjoy her company. "We haven't much time. Gather what you need. When you leave here, act as if you are on the way to the market. The two lads outside will take you to my uncle."

Before the woman could move, footsteps padded lightly in the corridor, quickening his pulse.

"Agatha, where's the sentry? He isn't..." Astonishing blue eyes opened wide. Lily stopped abruptly in the kitchen doorway and slapped a hand to her heart. "Griffin."

A jolt of pleasure drove through him. He thought he might melt with joy at the sight of her rapturous smile. In the next instant, she burst from the doorway and plowed into him with such force it rocked him back on his heels. He laughed and hugged her in his arms, absorbing the electrifying thrust of her energy. Lily. His Lily. The woman he wanted, forever.

"Thank you. Thank you so much." She stepped away with his hands in her tight grasp. Her face was lit with incandescent happiness. "I am forever indebted to you."

"For what?"

She tilted her head and frowned. "For getting Papa out of prison. What else did you think?"

"Yes, well..." He stammered like an idiot, disappointed it wasn't his lofty presence instead of her father's freedom that caused her excitement. "Who told you? The British Captain?" Alarm pulsed through his body.

"It was David. Captain Babcock suspected David freed Papa, but to save himself, he accused you of the deed." Her gaze clouded with regret. "I'm so sorry."

He squeezed her fingers. "It doesn't matter."

"I told Babcock you're in Philadelphia. He intends to verify this when he speaks to your uncle. All the Captain knows for certain is that Papa was removed from the ship by three men dressed as British soldiers."

Griffin's shoulders dipped with relief. He wished he might have spared Josiah's involvement in the dangerous affair, but his uncle would do anything for his nephew and his country. "Why do you suspect I freed your father?"

Her face brightened. "No one had to name you. I

simply knew."

Her joyous smile could have landed him on the moon.

"There isn't another man with your courage or who could have accomplished the feat with such panache and imagination."

Pride heated his skin. He was just about to wrap her in his arms and kiss her when a voice crackled at his side.

"I hate to interrupt."

He suddenly remembered the older woman.

"Shouldn't we go before more soldiers get here?

****

Lily nervously fingered the reins. The hazardous rendezvous with Papa would take some hours through city and countryside. Griffin knew the way and led them through the crooked, narrow streets, past the Old Dutch Church, the tannery, and new buildings under construction after the Big Fire. She prayed the passage would end without incident.

Earlier, at his bidding, she'd hurriedly packed a leather satchel and wrapped Papa's journal in a nightgown. She'd said farewell to Agatha and almost cried even though she trusted Griffin to see them reunited when the time was right.

It seemed her husband had planned for everything. And life was full of surprises.

Griffin traveled in black breeches and coat, much like a Calvinist minister. On his head, he wore a wide brimmed hat pulled low on his forehead. Riding slightly ahead of her, he cut a handsome, impressive figure on his horse. Clad as a man of the cloth and she a simply dressed woman, they appeared much like any other traveler. How noble of him to take such risks. So like him to be decent and helpful, despite the danger.

As they rode along in silence, she thought about the recent changes in her life. When Papa's freedom seemed beyond her reach, she'd almost given up hope she'd ever see him again. Because of Griffin, they'd soon be reunited. How she loved him for his bravery and nerve. He'd made an uncertain future more secure.

Griffin kept a steady pace in spite of the relentless heat. She sensed his tension and saw the quick shift of his gaze as they rode across the muddied roads.

The congested city fell away, replaced with farmsteads. Scattered structures built of brick and timber dotted the gently rolling landscape like currants in a muffin top. The sun had broken through the clouds. Light slanted through the damp leaves wetted by the early morning rain. Birds twittered. Under other circumstances, she would have enjoyed the tranquil surroundings. Today, a nervous energy gripped her.

Griffin reined his horse to an abrupt stop and hissed. "A sentry post."

Her pulse jumped. She halted her horse alongside his. Eyes shaded with a cupped hand, she peered into the distance. The unmistakable scarlet of the militia prickled her scalp. Six officers stood guard, armed and sizeable enough to cause trouble. An empty cart blocked the road and stopped all travelers. A queue of vehicles waited for permission to pass.

"What's happening?"

"Soldiers are questioning everyone."

Chilled despite the warmth of the sun, she drew the light cape tighter around her shoulders. Griffin glanced right and left to the thick wall of trees and bracken alongside the muddy path.

"Shall we turn back and cut through a field?" She eyed the dense foliage dubiously.

"The British have every major road blocked. Guards will be out, patrolling the nearby areas. They'll be suspicious of anyone skirting the road. We need to blend in, not stand out."

A risky venture either way, and while it made sense, it didn't smooth the anxious knot in her stomach.

"Try not to look frightened." Griffin smiled.

"How can you act so calm?"

"Think of your father. It may help to ease your spirits. So far, luck's been on my side."

With a cocksure grin, he cantered ahead, splashing through a puddle and kicking up damp earth. Reluctantly, she urged her horse forward, all too aware of the unreliable nature of luck. If ever there was a moment to trust him, it was now. Without fail, he would guard her with his life.

Together they rode into the line of fire. As they waited their turn for interrogation, she mimicked Griffin's nonchalant pose. The soldiers conducted a thorough search of a detained coach while several well-dressed gentlemen cooled their ire in the shade of a maple tree. Presumably satisfied no escapee hid inside any of their large trunks, the sentry sergeant waved the passengers and coach forward on their journey.

The sergeant turned his attention to the horse-drawn cart. After a brief inspection and tense interchange, the driver was also waved on.

When the sergeant gestured them to advance to the checkpoint, Lily did her best to mask her unease.

"Name, please." The hawk-nosed soldier stared

mercilessly at Griffin. Most people would have flinched or shown fear. Griffin met the man's stare as if unperturbed, his expression neutral, almost inviting.

"Reverend Faraday."

Fear skittered over her skin. Why hadn't he chosen an alias and lessened his risk?

The sergeant continued his sharp assessment. Would they be arrested? When the officer swung his attention her way, it took all her self-possession not to fall from the saddle.

"And the woman?" Though he ogled her, he meant for Griffin to answer.

"The woman, sir, is my wife."

The words, spoken with confidence and certainty, rang true. They *were* husband and wife. She rubbed the absence of her wedding ring through her gloved hand. Regrettably, she'd tossed it at him in a fury. How she missed it.

"I'm the most fortunate of women." She silently cursed the nerves that loosened her tongue.

Griffin broke into a grin. "Thank you dear. I, too, consider myself blessed."

The interchange seemed to nettle the officer who pursed his lips with impatience. She smiled hoping the friendly gesture might soften him. Seconds ticked away. The sergeant stared with bold authority and suspicion.

Breathe. Breathe. Breathe. Act natural.

"State your business."

Griffin leaned forward, hand curled loosely around the saddle pommel. He offered a steady, cooperative expression, as if they weren't in danger of arrest, or her of physical assault. "Off to see my ailing grandmother, some six miles up the road."

The soldier scrubbed a hand along his jaw, seeming to consider possibilities. Beads of sweat rolled down her spine. She pressed a hand to her stomach, short on oxygen. Just when she feared the worst, the sergeant nodded for them to proceed. Relief exploded like a geyser, but she managed a wooden expression.

"Good day, sir." Griffin tipped his hat and trotted ahead. Not a second was lost. In a whirl of exhilaration, she followed. Lips compressed, she hid her elation from the soldiers who watched along the roadside. Only when they were far enough away did she release a pent-up breath.

"We did it!" she whispered worried someone other than Griffin would hear.

Once they'd left the soldiers well behind, they urged their horses faster. In silence, they rode, putting as much distance as they could between them and the city. Lily prayed the rest of the journey would be safe. She was hot and thirsty, tired of heat and bugs, but the thought of Papa kept her going. At the top of a rise, Griffin angled from the main path. They stopped in the shade of a beech tree. Its leaves whispered in the breeze.

"How beautiful," she said. A broad vista lay before them, sloped and lush with foliage and tidy rows of verdant apples trees. Less than a half mile off stood a brick house with tall chimneys at each end. White shutters brightened its many windows. A barn and a collection of smaller structures sat at the back of the property.

"My grandparents' homestead." Griffin removed the minister's hat and swiped his damp forehead with his jacket sleeve. "My folks and younger brother and sister live there, too, since the British captured New York." He swung a leg over the horse and both feet landed on the ground. He helped her dismount and gazed toward the horizon. "Your father is with them."

"How can you be certain?"

"I had a note sent to my family. They were to hang a blue cloth from an upper window when he arrived. I knew you'd worry. I wanted to give you reassurance."

"I see it." She bounced on her toes, thrilled at the blue in the distance. "Papa's there." Happiness trilled in her excited voice. "You are so…" Overcome with gratitude, she paused to reflect on Griffin's many qualities. A dozen positive ones floated in her head. "You are so wonderful."

Her heart swelled when his face brightened. He smiled with that uneven grin she'd come to expect and adore. She loved him more than she could put into words. He was her hero, her friend, her lover, and if he would agree, her husband.

Griffin took a moment to stare at the hat in his hand as if uncertain. "I didn't think to inquire if you'd mind being a guest in my family's home until other lodgings can be arranged. I'm sorry, but you can't return to New York, not while the British occupy the city."

"Why would I mind?"

He shrugged. "You and Warwick have an agreement. I suppose you'll go to London with him."

She frowned. "Didn't you read my letters?"

"Letters?" His brow wrinkled. Hastily, he patted the pockets of his breeches and jacket and extracted the packet she'd given to his uncle. "In all my haste to see you from the city, I didn't have a moment to stop and read."

"Allow me." She flicked the envelope from his fingers, chuckling softly as she broke the seal. "This one is to Cecil Jones. Shall I read it?"

"The essence is all I require."

Touched by his fleeting uncertainty, she rose up on her toes and kissed his cheek.

"*Dear Mr. Jones*," she read. She skimmed down to the important part. "*In regards to our mutual matter, I have failed to discover any evidence, although I searched high and low, which lends credence to your theory regarding a certain gentleman. In my humble estimation, the man is who he claims to be—a loyal man in every sense of the word.*"

She looked at Griffin.

He stared at the letter as if it glittered like a precious jewel. "Thank you. You're support of me means..." Lips parted, he gave a slow, disbelieving shake of the head. "For once, I'm speechless."

He gathered her into his arms. His warmth, his solid, physical strength, and his every breath filled her with happiness.

"God love and keep you." He bent his head to kiss her.

"Wait!" She threw up a hand. "Don't you want to read the other one?"

****

All he wanted was to kiss her senseless. With great effort, he harnessed his emotions enough to release her and snatched the second missive from her hand.

"My dearest Griffin," he read aloud.

I had hoped to speak with you in person. In the

event I might not find you, I wrote a letter of the things I wished to say.

First, I enclosed a letter addressed to Cecil Jones. Please read it and send it off on the first ship to London. My obligation to Mr. Jones is complete.

As to your thrilling and desired presence at my father's home, it came as a shock and occurred only minutes after David proposed. I had yet to give him my answer before you appeared. The sight of you filled me with joy.

I don't need to remind you what happened next. You left and David stayed. Yet in your absence, your pledge to help remained. Even though you believed me engaged to David, you still offered to help Papa. Not many men would have been so generous or brave. The gesture spoke volumes and again revealed your selfless character. You are a man of great integrity. Please forgive me for doubting you.

David also offered aid but his support came with a price I wouldn't pay. More than ever, I understand the sort of man David has become. I could not marry him when I love you.

As to us, we've argued in the past, yet we laughed and loved more. I trust and respect you. Rest assured I will never hurt you.

I hope we shall meet again soon.

Love always, Lily

Solemnly, he lowered the letter, tongue-tied.

Lily stood quietly, her expectant gazed fixed on him.

"I…" Unable to form a coherent word, he dropped to one knee. He tried again to speak. "You mean everything to me. You are my life and breath." His heart beat in triple time. "I love you and promise to honor and protect you until my dying hour."

Tears glistened in her eyes. She tugged at his arm until he stood. She melted into his embrace. The kiss was perfect, timeless and conveyed the depth of his love.

"Will you honor me and be my wife?"

She laughed and brought music to his ears. "I am your wife, Griffin."

A word about the author...

Joyce grew up in Minnesota and attended college and grad school in Chicago. After working in mental health, she retired at a young age to write full-time. Her first book, *Eliza*, was published in 2012.

She is a Hearts through History winner for her hero in *Amaryllis*. When she isn't writing, she loves to swim, nature walk, and is a crossword puzzle fanatic.

Along with her husband, she winters in Florida and enjoys summers in Minnesota, in her very own little house on the prairie.

http://joyceproell.com

www.ingramcontent.com/pod-product-compliance
Lightning Source LLC
Chambersburg PA
CBHW070806030726
47504CB00003B/725